F
BUR

B&T
9/2013

PRAISE FOR

PLAYING TO WIN

"Burton knocks it out of the park. . . . With snappy back-and-forth dialogue as well as hot, sweaty, and utterly engaging bedroom play, readers will not be able to race through this book fast enough!"

—RT Book Reviews

"*Playing to Win* has all the characteristics that have put this series high on my must-read list—strong and independent women, emotional depth, personal transformation, and let's not forget smoking-hot athletes with rock-hard abs (this is definitely one time you can judge a book by its cover!)." *—Fresh Fiction*

"A great addition to Jaci Burton's popular Play-by-Play series. . . . It is a wonderful contemporary erotic romance that I recommend!"

—The Romance Dish

"What I love about *Playing to Win* and this series as a whole is that it's not just about the hot, steamy sex scenes (though it doesn't hurt), but also the likable and realistic characters. . . . It's the perfect combination of heat and romance that makes this series a must-read."

—Heroes and Heartbreakers

"A compulsively readable sexy story." *—Book Lovers Inc.*

TAKING A SHOT

"[Jaci Burton] delivers the passionate, inventive, sexually explicit love scenes that fans expect . . . However, *Taking a Shot* isn't just about hot sex. Burton offers plenty of emotion and conflict in a memorable, relationship-driven story." *—USA Today*

continued . . .

Wanaque Public Library
616 Ringwood Ave.
Wanaque, NJ 07465

"Ms. Burton has a way of writing intense scenes that are both sensual and raw . . . Plenty of romance, sexy men, hot steamy loving, and humor."
                                                —Smexy Books Romance Reviews

"For this third Play-by-Play entry, there's no shortage of volatile, steamy sex, but the story development is the key to this thoughtful tale. While the heroine figures her life out, the reader will enjoy the smokin'-hot sex that draws the protagonists together—over and over again."
                                                —RT Book Reviews

"Jenna and Ty's story far surpassed my expectations. This one is hot enough to melt the ice off the hockey rink on which its hero plays."
                                                —Romance Novel News

"A very spicy read. Jenna and Ty had great chemistry." *—Book Binge*

CHANGING THE GAME

"This book is wonderful from beginning to end, even for those who are not baseball fans."
                                                —RT Book Reviews

"*Changing the Game* is an extraordinary novel—a definite home run!"
                                                —Joyfully Reviewed

"A strong plot, complex characters, sexy athletes, and nonstop passion make this book a must-read."
                                                —Fresh Fiction

THE PERFECT PLAY

"The characters are incredible. They are human and complex and real and perfect."
                                                —Night Owl Reviews

"Holy smokes! I am pretty sure I saw steam rising from every page."
                                                —Fresh Fiction

Wanaque Public Library
616 Ringwood Ave.
Wanaque, NJ 07465

"This book delivers." —*Dear Author*

"A beautiful romance that is smooth as silk . . . [*The Perfect Play*] gives us all one hell of a good time, a romance to remember, and leaves us begging for more." —*Joyfully Reviewed*

"Hot, hot, hot! . . . Romance at its best! . . . Highly recommended! Very steamy." —*Coffee Table Reviews*

"The romance sparkles as the sex sizzles." —*RT Book Reviews*

FURTHER PRAISE FOR THE WORK OF

JACI BURTON

"Realistic dialogue, spicy bedroom scenes, and a spitfire heroine make this one to pick up and savor." —*Publishers Weekly*

"Jaci Burton delivers." —Cherry Adair, *New York Times* bestselling author

"Lively and funny . . . intense and loving." —*The Road to Romance*

"An invitation to every woman's wildest fantasies." —*Romance Junkies*

"As always, Jaci Burton delivers a hot read." —*Fresh Fiction*

"Burton is a master at sexual tension!" —*RT Book Reviews*

One
SWEET
Ride

JACI BURTON

B

BERKLEY SENSATION, NEW YORK

Wanaque Public Library
616 Ringwood Ave.
Wanaque, NJ 07465

THE BERKLEY PUBLISHING GROUP
Published by the Penguin Group
Penguin Group (USA) Inc.
375 Hudson Street, New York, New York 10014, USA

USA I Canada I UK I Ireland I Australia I New Zealand I India I South Africa I China

Penguin Books Ltd., Registered Offices: 80 Strand, London WC2R 0RL, England
For more information about the Penguin Group visit penguin.com

ONE SWEET RIDE

This book is an original publication of The Berkley Publishing Group.

Copyright © 2013 by Jaci Burton.
Excerpt from *Hope Flames* by Jaci Burton copyright © 2013 by Jaci Burton.
All rights reserved. No part of this book may be reproduced, scanned, or distributed in any
printed or electronic form without permission. Please do not participate in or encourage piracy
of copyrighted materials in violation of the author's rights. Purchase only authorized editions.

Berkley Sensation Books are published by The Berkley Publishing Group.
BERKLEY SENSATION® is a registered trademark of Penguin Group (USA) Inc.
The "B" design is a trademark of Penguin Group (USA) Inc.

Library of Congress Cataloging-in-Publication Data

Burton, Jaci.
One sweet ride / Jaci Burton.
pages cm
ISBN 978-0-425-25338-0
1. Presidential candidates—United States—Fiction.   2. Political campaigns—United States—Fiction.
3. Political fiction.   I. Title.
PS3602.U776O53   2013
813'.6—dc23   2013006290

PUBLISHING HISTORY
Berkley Sensation trade paperback edition / June 2013

PRINTED IN THE UNITED STATES OF AMERICA

10 9 8 7 6 5 4 3 2 1

Cover photo by Claudio Marinesco.
Cover design by Rita Frangie.
Interior text design by Kristin del Rosario.

This is a work of fiction. Names, characters, places, and incidents either are the product
of the author's imagination or are used fictitiously, and any resemblance to actual persons,
living or dead, business establishments, events, or locales is entirely coincidental.
The publisher does not have any control over and does not assume any responsibility for
author or third-party websites or their content.

ALWAYS LEARNING   PEARSON

To Charlie, for one sweet ride all these years.
I love you.

ACKNOWLEDGEMENTS

To the Berkley Art Department, for continually giving me, and my readers, covers to drool over. Thank you!

To my readers:

I've always loved stock car racing. There's nothing like hot men and fast cars to get one's motor running, is there? That being said, any changes to the stock car racing schedule or the way stock car racing is run is by my design and for purposes of story line.

I hope you enjoy!

Jaci

ONE

THERE WAS NOTHING THAT GOT GRAY PRESTON'S MOTOR revving more than a well-running engine, a fast car crossing the finish line in first place, and a hot, willing woman waiting for him at the end of a great day.

Too bad a blown engine had sent his car into the wall three laps shy of the finish line in Michigan. He'd been in second place and coming up alongside his competitor in a hurry, certain he'd be able to wrestle first place from Cal McClusky before the checkered flag.

That dream had gone up in smoke. So had the hot woman, one Sheila Tinsdale, a frequent visitor to his trailer and his bed over the past month. Smoking hot, platinum blonde, and stacked, Sheila put no strings on him and liked sex as much as he did. She was damn near the perfect woman.

Unfortunately, Sheila also had her eye on McClusky, and she bedded winners. So when McClusky crossed the finish line and

Gray hit the wall, Sheila hit McClusky's trailer faster than Gray's Chevy had spun out on turn three.

Not that he was surprised, and it hadn't hurt his feelings. Much. He wasn't emotionally invested in Sheila, and there were plenty more like her on the racing circuit.

So he had a big fat zero for today's events. No win, a smashed-up car, and no consolation sex. Plus, he'd dropped two spots in the points race and had a disappointed crew to deal with. As the owner of two cars for Preston Racing, and the driver of car number fifty-three, responsibility weighed heavily on him.

It was his goal to make something of himself, especially since he'd broken away from his former owner and gone out on his own two years ago. He had a lot to prove—to himself, to his team, to his fans, and . . .

It probably didn't do him any good to think about just how much he had to prove. And how much it would cost him, financially and otherwise, if he failed.

At least it was still early in the season. There was time to make up the ground he'd lost in today's race.

He made his way to the team garage where his crew was busy, their heads under the hood of his car.

His crew chief lifted his head. "That sucked today."

Gray nodded at Ian Smart. He and Ian had been together since Gray had first climbed into a race car, before he'd ever gone pro. "Understatement. Oil temp was screaming high toward the end. I pushed it too hard. But damn—I was so close."

As Gray leaned over and inspected the engine, Ian nudged him with his shoulder. "That's what you gotta do to win the race, buddy. Nothing you can do about it. We'll get 'em next time."

Yeah. Next time. He knew all about loss. His father was a senator, so he'd grown up around campaigns, around strategies for winning, and what you did to regroup when you didn't win.

Though his father rarely lost a race. He'd be disappointed in Gray's performance today. That was if he ever bothered to watch him race, which Gray knew damn well he didn't. Mitchell Preston wouldn't be caught dead lowering himself to watch auto racing. He considered it a redneck sport and beneath him. His father was involved in a big election this year and was more interested in his own race—which Gray had no doubt his father would win.

Gray lost a hell of a lot more races than his father ever had. Something his dad absolutely hated. Then again, his father disliked everything Gray did, as he had ever since Gray had turned down the Harvard scholarship and chosen the sports scholarship to Oklahoma. That had royally pissed off his dad, too.

At least that memory put Gray in a decidedly better frame of mind.

"Donny did pretty good, though. He rolled in twelfth."

Gray dragged his attention back to Ian. "Not bad, but I know he can do better. He needs to work on his focus more. I'll talk to him and his crew chief."

At least he could salvage something out of this shit day. Donny Duncan drove the new car Gray had brought into Preston Racing this season. At twenty-four, Donny was still a little green, having just made the switch to this level two years ago. But the kid had raw talent and great instincts. Gray was confident that if he continued to push Donny he'd see winning results.

Gray made the turn to head toward his trailer and saw someone waiting at his door.

Not just someone. A very attractive, way-overdressed-for-the-track female wearing a business suit and very high heels. He gave her an assessing look as he made his way toward her.

Media, maybe? Though he'd finished his interviews earlier.

She pulled down her sunglasses and gave him the once-over, too.

"Grayson Preston?"

Wow. She was a stunner, with her strawberry blonde hair expertly pulled up, her blue eyes assessing him, and her lips perfectly glossed. She sure as hell didn't belong here. Besides, nobody on the racing circuit called him Grayson. Hell, only his mom called him by that name. And his father.

"Yeah. And you are?"

She walked toward him, her steps sure and confident, then held out her hand. "Evelyn Hill. Do you have a moment?"

For her, he had a lot of moments. He shook her hand, noticing her manicured nails. Not those long, fake, clawlike nails some of the women around here wore. Evelyn's were short and unpainted. "Sure. Come on in."

He opened up the door to his trailer and waited while she climbed the stairs, which gave him an opportunity to ogle her very shapely legs and mighty fine ass. Too bad her skirt covered her knees. Normally the women around here wore their skirts a lot shorter. Then again, normally the women hitting on the racers didn't dress like they were going to have high tea somewhere.

She moved into the living area and he shut the door.

"What can I do for you, Evelyn?"

She turned to face him and gave him a smile. A practiced, professional, very businesslike smile. "I'm here representing your father, Senator Preston."

Just as he was focusing his radar on her, she had to go and ruin it by working for his father. Though at least he was sending better emissaries now. Gray went to his fridge and grabbed a beer. "Want one?"

"Oh. No, thank you."

He popped the top off the can and took a long swallow, his throat parched from all those laps and the interviews he'd had to do after the disastrous finish. "Did you see the race today?"

"As a matter of fact, I did. I'm sorry about your wreck, but I'm relieved you weren't hurt."

He shrugged. "It wasn't that hard a hit." He pointed to the small table. "Take a seat, Evelyn. You sure you don't want something to drink? I also have water and pop."

"No. I'm fine. But it was nice of you to offer."

Wasn't she polite? She slid into the booth and crossed one long leg over the other. He cleared his throat. "Okay, then, what did my father send you all the way to Michigan to talk to me about that one of you couldn't have called to say over the phone?"

She swept a curl behind her ear and folded her hands together on the table before focusing those gorgeous clear blue eyes directly at him. "As you are aware, or at least I hope you're aware, now that Senator Preston has dropped out of the presidential race, he has a good chance at being considered a viable candidate for vice president in the election this year."

He leaned back in the booth. "I knew he dropped out of the race, but didn't know he has a shot at the VP spot. Good for him. What does that have to do with me?"

"He'd be very grateful if you could assist him in his efforts."

Now this was a first. His father hadn't wanted anything to do with him for a long time now. "Is that right? And how am I supposed to help him?"

"You've done very well for yourself in this sport, Mr. Preston—"

"If you're going to keep talking to me, Evelyn, you'd better call me Gray."

She opened her mouth, paused, then nodded. "All right, Gray. As I was saying, you've become very successful in auto racing, which means you have a very dedicated fan base. A very dedicated nation-wide fan base."

Evelyn sure was pretty, and there was a light sprinkle of freckles across the bridge of her nose that spread to her cheeks, which did nothing to diminish how damn sexy she was, or how commanding her eyes were. Her beauty also didn't distract him from the very clear message she had just delivered on behalf of his father.

"I get it. A very dedicated nationwide fan base of registered voters who you think I could persuade to cast a few for my dad and the presidential candidate. And if I agree, that makes Mitchell Preston an even more attractive potential vice presidential candidate, what with all those critical southern votes I could help him garner."

She didn't avert her gaze. "Yes."

"Why didn't he come to me when he was running for president?"

"He would have, had his presidential bid continued."

"Huh. You do realize my father and I don't exactly see eye to eye on a lot of things, political issues included."

"I know a lot about you, including your likes and dislikes—politically, that is."

He wanted to laugh, but he could tell Evelyn was doing her best to perform the job she'd been assigned. It wasn't her fault she'd been assigned to Mitchell Preston's uncooperative sonofabitch of a son. "I'm surprised, given that I've never spoken publicly about my likes or dislikes—politically, that is."

She lifted her chin. "Your father has briefed me."

Now he did laugh, then took a long swallow of beer before answering. "Has he? My father doesn't know shit about me. We don't speak much at all. And since I inherited my trust fund from my grandfather when I turned twenty-five, he can't blackmail me into giving him what he wants by refusing to give me money, so we have no reason to communicate at all and I have no reason to give him my assistance."

He watched Evelyn squeeze her hands so tightly together that her knuckles turned white. "I see."

He started to get up. "So we're done?"

She didn't move. "Your mother wanted me to tell you that she would greatly appreciate your cooperation in this. She's sorry she didn't get a chance to talk to you herself, but she's been very busy on the campaign trail with your father, and of course, you're very difficult to get hold of now that you're racing every week."

Damn. "Cheap shot, Evelyn." He could tell his father to stick it. But he loved his mother and would do anything for her. Well, almost anything. His mother was well aware of his relationship with his dad and she skated that ice carefully, usually not interfering. But for some reason she adored the bastard and supported his political career.

Evelyn gave him a sympathetic look. "I'm sorry. I realize this is . . . difficult for you. But your support would help your father's campaign."

"My father is a misogynistic prick who treats women like servants. Why in hell are you working for him?"

Her lips curved. He liked her smile.

"Obviously you haven't spent much time around your father lately, have you?"

"Obviously the old man has you snowed, or you're utterly gullible."

She arched a brow. "I can assure you, Gray, I am never gullible."

He was sure Evelyn thought she knew all there was to know about Mitchell Preston. But Gray had grown up with the man and knew him better than anyone. And the one thing he'd witnessed time and again was how his father treated women. It was a wonder there were any women at all on the campaign given his father's condescending, dickhead behavior toward them, especially if they were young and vapid. And this was a man they were considering for the VP nomination? His father was an overbearing, unemotional douchebag. Gray didn't know how his mother had stood by his dad for thirty-three years without smothering him in his sleep or poisoning his coffee, but he'd never understood their marriage anyway.

"So, can we count on you for your cooperation?" Evelyn asked.

He couldn't help but laugh at her audacity to think he'd still be agreeable. "Not a chance. Let me walk you out."

She looked stunned. Obviously, she was used to people falling at the senator's feet. He wasn't one of them.

She stood. "Seriously?"

"Seriously. Sorry, Evelyn, but I don't kiss the senator's ass. You're going to have to find some other way to get votes for him."

"You do realize this could be beneficial for you. Think of the exposure you'd get, the new fans you could bring on board."

"I have plenty of fans already, but thanks." He handed her bag to her, rested his hand on her back, and directed her toward the door.

She stopped and turned to him. "This could be a way for you and your father to repair your relationship."

He could tell she was grasping at straws now. "My father knows my phone number. And my schedule. If he wanted to repair our relationship, he could have done that years ago."

That's when he saw the fight leave her eyes. "Then I'm sorry to have wasted your time."

"You didn't waste my time, Evelyn. You wasted yours." He held the door for her and walked her down the stairs.

She didn't even look back as she headed toward the parking lot.

Too bad she was here representing his father. Evelyn Hill was one hell of a beautiful woman, and he wouldn't have minded spending some time with her. But now that he knew she was associated with his father, he wanted nothing to do with her.

EVELYN THREW HER BAG DOWN ON THE BED IN THE hotel room, kicked off her shoes, and flung herself onto the chair, wincing as she curled her toes.

Stupid shoes. She grabbed the remote and turned on the television, which was set to the sports channel. Too tired to channel surf, she ordered room service, rolling her eyes as the replay of today's race events came on TV. Despite the childishness of the act, she stuck her tongue out at the screen when Gray Preston's handsome face appeared before her.

"Dickhead," she muttered, then grabbed her phone to check her email, grimacing when she saw one from the senator asking for a status update.

The most important task he'd ever given her, and she'd failed on the first try.

She lifted her gaze to see Gray's smiling face as he was interviewed by the media.

She'd been thwarted more than once in Washington, and she'd never given up. Where was her fight, her determination to win? That was how she'd gotten as far as she had. And she was so close to getting what she wanted, to being able to live her dream.

She knew exactly what she needed to do.

She scrolled through her phone and punched the number, grinning as it rang. If Gray thought he could say no and it was over, he'd soon realize she was more formidable than he thought. She'd never go down without a hard fight.

"Mrs. Preston? Hi, it's Evelyn . . . I'm fine, thank you, but we have a problem. It's your son, Gray."

TWO

A KNOCK ON HIS DOOR ROUSED GRAY FROM WHAT should have been his morning to sleep in. He blinked, growled, then rolled out of his bed, pulled on a pair of sweats, and ambled his way to the door as the knocking grew louder.

"Hang on one damn minute. I'm coming."

He jerked open the door, mentally swearing that if it was Donny or Ian he was going to kick their asses. His eyes widened when he saw his mother standing there.

"Mom. What are you doing here?"

"Don't you answer your damn phone?" She pushed past him and came inside.

He scratched his head. "Uh . . . my phone." He looked around, his head still fuzzy from sleep and now confusion. "I don't know where my phone is. And why are you here?"

Her brown eyes blazed fire at him. "I'm here because you're being uncooperative. Why did you say no to Evelyn?"

He was not awake enough for this conversation. Evelyn who? "I need coffee. Would you like coffee?"

"It's ten o'clock, Grayson. I've already had coffee and breakfast. Were you still asleep?"

"Yeah. Sorry. Let me make some coffee, then I promise to be coherent. Take a seat, Mom."

He got coffee brewing, then said, "I'm going to go put a shirt on. I'll be right back."

Shaking his head, he went back into the bedroom and grabbed a shirt, took a piss, and brushed his teeth, then found his phone and saw that he'd left his phone on vibrate, and that he'd missed four calls from his mother.

Shit.

By the time he got back, the coffee was ready. He poured a cup. "Would you like something to drink? Water, tea, pop?"

"I'm good, thank you. Sit down and drink your coffee."

Thank God. He downed the first cup as if it were the elixir of life, because he knew why his mother was here. So he went ahead and grabbed a second cup, and by then the caffeine was doing the job. He was at least awake.

"What did you do? Go on a bender after the race last weekend?" his mother asked.

He snorted. "No. It was a long, hot weekend. I'm tired and sleep helps me refuel."

His mother gave him the once-over. She looked beautiful as always in a summer dress with some kind of sweater thrown over it, her dark brown hair cut in some kind of short bob that grazed her chin.

"Hey, new haircut. You look nice, Mom. I'm glad to see you."

He bent over and kissed her cheek.

She didn't smile. "I wouldn't be here if you'd been cooperative."

"Oh, so this is my fault. Look, I appreciate that Dad has a new campaign, but that doesn't mean I have to participate."

She rolled her eyes. "It's not just a new campaign, Grayson. It's the potential to become the vice president of the United States."

He tried to muster up some kind of reply, but he came up blank.

"Didn't Evelyn tell you that I'd appreciate your cooperation on this?"

"She did. I still turned her down."

"I don't ask you for much, Grayson, and I typically don't interfere in your relationship with your father, but he's not the only one who has been in politics for over thirty years. So have I. I've stood by his side—through the bad as well as the good—I've fought with him through every campaign. And despite what you think, he's a very good man. If not for the current president endorsing Cameron, your father could very well have gotten the presidential nomination this year. I still believe he'll eventually end up there. In the meantime, there's the opportunity of a lifetime waiting for him. Something he's worked very hard to achieve."

Gray's mother spoke with passion, every one of her words punctuated with each day, each month, each year she'd given to his dad's political career. And yeah, he was listening. It was hard not to.

"It's also an opportunity for me, something I've worked for all my life. I have an agenda, Grayson, a chance to make a difference, to let my voice be heard. You know how much literacy and education means to me at the state level. If your father gets the vice presidency, it would mean so much more exposure for me and for my agenda. A chance to spread this message nationwide, to fight for more funding, to gain national attention for a cause that's so important for children everywhere. And if by the grace of God your father should someday get to the White House, this would be my platform, and who knows how much attention it would get."

She stopped and looked him directly in the eyes, and he saw the determination in hers. "If not for him, would you do this for me?"

Loretta Preston was a fire-breathing dragon when it came to the causes she wholeheartedly believed in. He hadn't once thought about her and what this would mean for her in terms of national exposure for her causes, because he'd been too busy holding on to the grudge against his father.

He was such a selfish asshole.

He reached across the table and held her hand. "I'm sorry, Mom. You know Dad and I don't see eye to eye and haven't for a long time. But you know how much I believe in you and in what you do. Hell, I wish *you* were the one running for president."

She sniffed, then laughed. "I don't think that's my cup of tea, son. And don't sell your father short. He's an amazing man and wants to do good things."

"Well, whatever. I'll do what I can to make sure your dreams come true."

She stood and hugged him. "Thank you for believing in me."

It felt good to feel his mother's arms wrapped around him. "I've always believed in you."

She pulled back. "You should try believing in your dad. Try talking to him, reconnecting with him. He's changed, Grayson."

"I don't know if I could ever believe that. But I'll help out the campaign. For you. And just for you."

She patted him on the cheek. "I'll take that. For now. But at some point, I think you'll see the light about your father."

He'd seen the light a long time ago. He'd rather stay in the dark.

She checked her watch. "Okay. I have to go. I need to be back in D.C. by tonight. I'll call Evelyn and let her know you'll meet with her at your next city—" She waved her hand and laughed. "Wherever that is. I can't keep up with you, son. But I always make sure to watch the races. I have one of the staff DVR them for me."

"Thanks. I appreciate that. And yeah, I'll work with Evelyn. She called and complained about me, didn't she?" he asked as he walked his mother to the private car that was waiting for her right outside the gate.

She held his hand and grinned. "Of course she did. She's a tiger, that one. I'm glad she's working for our side."

Gray shook his head. He'd underestimated Evelyn when he'd kicked her to the curb yesterday.

She kissed his cheek and hugged him again. "Be a good boy and behave. We'll talk soon. I love you, Grayson."

"Love you too, Mom."

He waved as the car pulled away. For some reason, his mother could always make him feel like he was a misbehaving eight-year-old again.

He headed back to the trailer with a mental list of a hundred things he'd have to do today before they pulled up and headed to Kentucky.

And then he'd have to deal with Evelyn.

But not until tomorrow. At least he could push her off his agenda until then.

Tomorrow, though, he and Evelyn were going to have a conversation and get a few ground rules straight.

THREE

EVELYN BLOW-DRIED HER HAIR, PULLED IT BACK IN A ponytail, then finished her makeup. She pulled on a pair of jeans and a tank top, then grabbed a long-sleeved white button-down shirt out of her suitcase, and finished off the outfit with a pair of ankle boots.

She'd been grossly overdressed for that first race. A misstep. She should have blended in with the crowd, made Gray feel more comfortable around her, instead of standing out like a bottle of expensive wine shoved in the soda section of the grocery store. Plus it had been damned uncomfortable, both physically and emotionally, dressed in her suit and wearing heels while sitting in the stands with the rowdy crowd. Everyone around her had stared at her, and rightly so. A designer suit did not go with beer and hot dogs. She wouldn't make the same mistake again.

Gray Preston was not at all what she'd imagined him to be. Yes, she'd fully read his bio and seen video of him doing pre- and post-race media interviews, and had gone over his family history with his mother, including all his childhood photos and academic and professional biography, but those didn't compare with meeting the man face-to-face.

He was stunning. Wet with sweat and smelling a lot like gasoline and motor oil, his hair clinging to his forehead and neck, and with his fire suit unzipped, he was the sexiest man she'd ever laid eyes on. And when he'd directed his warm, whiskey-colored eyes on her, something quivered between her legs.

Evelyn wasn't the type to go liquid over a good-looking man. Washington was filled with hot men, and if anyone was going to get her motor running, one would think it would be a political type. Business suit with a lock on a major office? Now that was her bailiwick. Not some scruffed-up, needed-a-shave grease monkey who craved a hot track over a hot political race. So her libido firing up over Gray Preston likely had more to do with him being the fastest way to get to the White House rather than his good looks and bedroom eyes. She wasn't the type to fall for a man simply because he was pretty.

Besides, he was stubborn and uncooperative and in her way, and she could already tell this assignment wasn't going to be easy. She'd rather be by Senator Preston's side, where she belonged, helping him onto the presidential ticket in November, rather than hand-hold his son and beg for his cooperation in order to get a few hundred thousand votes, even if those potential votes were important ones.

But she knew she'd do whatever it took, so when her phone rang and Gray told her where they could meet, she grabbed her bag, climbed into her rental car, and drove the short distance to the restaurant.

He was already waiting for her at the front door. And he didn't look happy about it, either.

Tough. She dealt with unpleasant people all the time. His attitude didn't faze her.

"Good morning," she said, pasting on her friendliest smile.

He nodded and held the door for her.

Okay, that's how it was going to be. She could deal. Eventually he'd have to talk to her.

The waitress, who obviously recognized Gray, grinned, pushed back her out-of-control, overprocessed hair, and hurried them to a booth at the back of the restaurant while giving Evelyn a look she wasn't certain was admiration or pure jealousy.

"Coffee?" the waitress asked. Her name was Aileen and she looked to be in her forties.

"Thank you, Aileen. With cream," Evelyn said.

"Same here," Gray said with a smile. At Aileen, of course.

At least she knew now that he wasn't suffering from laryngitis.

They looked over their menus, and by the time Aileen came with their coffees, they ordered breakfast. Since Evelyn hadn't had a chance to have a cup of coffee yet—usually her first task of the day, even before her shower— she took a couple quick sips, needing that caffeine surge. She added a couple more sips, sighed in contentment, then lifted her gaze to Gray, finding him staring at her.

"I can survive without it, but if you want to have an intelligent conversation with me, I'm better after coffee."

"Good to know." He lifted his cup, and she was struck again by his amazing eyes. He was very direct in staring at her, too, which she found decidedly . . . uncomfortable.

She laid her cup down. "Let's clear the air. You're obviously not happy with me."

"You called my mother."

She resisted the urge to smile at the accusatory tone in his voice. Evelyn loved Loretta Preston, one of the kindest, sweetest, most patient women she'd ever known. They'd had many conversations together, about both her husband and her son. She'd hoped Loretta had some influence on Gray and she'd obviously been right. The woman was fierce about her causes and didn't take no for an answer.

"Of course I did. You left me no choice."

"Sure I did. I said no. That was your cue to walk away."

Her lips lifted. "Clearly, you don't know me at all. I don't walk away when I'm given an assignment. Working with you is my assignment, and until I exhausted all avenues, I wasn't about to give up. And since your mother expressly asked me to convince you, I figured she'd be an asset in persuading you."

He didn't answer.

"You don't like your mother?"

His gaze shot to hers. "I love my mother."

"Then I don't see the problem."

"You went behind my back to serve your own purpose."

She rolled her eyes. "Do you have a fundamental disagreement with your mother's agenda?"

He frowned. "No."

"Then I don't see what the problem is."

"It's obvious we're not going to see eye to eye on this."

"That's okay with me. Did you have a chance to think about the plan?"

He gave her a blank stare. "I didn't know there was a plan."

"Oh. I thought maybe your mother talked to you about the campaign's objectives."

"My mother spoke to me about her objectives, and asked me to help. That was it."

Her lips curved.

"Obviously you know her."

"Very well. I've spent a lot of time with her over the past few years since I've been working with your father. She runs a tight ship and doesn't take no for an answer."

"Then you've come to know her well, and you know that while she has a soft voice, she has an iron will."

"Yes. She's a wonderful asset for your father, both personally and politically."

Gray stared down at his coffee. "My father doesn't deserve her."

She had no idea what Gray's relationship with his father was, nor was it her intention to pry. Her only job was to work with Gray on his father's campaign, not to get involved in family dynamics, unless it interfered in the political process. Then she was required to smooth things over, not intervene, and above all, never let things get messy. "So what's your conclusion?"

"I guess you and I will be working together."

She couldn't resist lifting her shoulders in excitement. "Wonderful. I'm thrilled about this, Gray, and I don't think you'll regret it."

"Oh, I already regret it. But this is important to my mother, so I'm doing it for her."

Evelyn didn't care who he did it for. She only cared that she was a success at her assignment. "Great. We'll hit the ground running. The first thing we'll need to do is work within your schedule. I know how busy you are."

They paused while the waitress brought their breakfast. Evelyn dug into her oatmeal and fruit while Gray pounded down some elaborate breakfast that consisted of eggs, bacon, pancakes, hash browns, and biscuits.

"Where do you put all those calories?" she asked.

"What?"

"That's a huge meal."

"Oh. I work out, and I also sweat it all out in the car. It's usually over a hundred degrees in there."

"My God. That can't be healthy."

He shrugged. "You get used to it."

No wonder he had a body like that, so tall and lean. But today he wore jeans and a tight T-shirt showing off some serious muscle. "So it's like a sauna."

"Yup."

"You have to stay in shape to drive a car."

He scooped up the last of his eggs with his fork, then finished off his orange juice. "You can't control a three-thousand-pound raging beast at a hundred and ninety miles an hour without some muscle, honey."

Her nerve endings tingled at the endearment. She pushed it aside. "I imagine that's true, though I freely admit my knowledge of the auto racing industry is somewhat sketchy."

"We'll have to change that, won't we?"

"I suppose we will. The more I know about what you do, the better equipped I'll be to integrate you into your father's campaign."

"And won't that be fun."

She pushed her bowl to the side and studied him. "I sense some hesitation."

"Not just some. A lot. You should know I'll be dragging my heels the entire way."

"I can work with that."

"Okay. I just wanted to be up front about it."

She liked him. "Thanks for that. So what's on your agenda for today?"

"Team meetings, then practice runs. I suppose you need to get back to D.C."

She gave him a blank look. "Uh, no. Perhaps I didn't outline the parameters clearly enough."

He frowned. "I don't understand."

"I'm assigned to you, Gray, and only you, from now until the election. I'll be with you the entire way."

FOUR

GRAY ALWAYS LIKED TO BE HANDS-ON WITH HIS TEAM, not leaving anything for them to handle without his involvement. Which meant setting up in the garage and checking out the cars they'd use for the races.

Now that they were in Kentucky, he was overseeing the team meeting for both race teams, and he had control. They went over the wreck last Sunday with the crew and mechanics, dissecting the engine failure. The engine team assured them it wouldn't happen again, that steps would be taken to ensure the engines for both cars would be in prime shape for the race this weekend.

Gray always kept a mental list of things to cover in team meetings, from tire inventory to which crew members would be on board for the next race. Everyone attended the meetings. It was mandatory. If you didn't show up, you were replaced on the crew or the mechanics team.

After the general meeting, Donny, his other driver, broke his crew out for their own meeting to discuss strategy for their car, while Gray did the same with his crew chief and team. The meeting went well and everyone was pumped for the upcoming race.

He had a good car and he knew he had a good chance for this season. So did Donny, but Donny was easily distracted. Which reminded Gray that he needed to have a chat with him. After Donny did his practice runs on the track today, he'd pull him aside and have a talk with him.

Donny had looked pale today in the meeting. Gray hoped he wasn't sick, because that was the last thing they needed. He wanted both his cars to do well this weekend.

He went up to the track where Donny was driving away to start up his practice run. After a warm-up lap, he got up to speed.

Huh. Maybe Gray was wrong about Donny being sick, because he was taking a fast lap. He had control of the wheel and had precision and confidence on the turns that Gray had never seen before from the young driver.

Impressive as hell. And one of the fastest runs Gray had ever seen the kid drive. Good. He needed to be great, because Gray had invested a lot of money into adding another car to Preston Racing, so Donny was going to have to do well. Gray didn't have a lot of time to spend on the kid.

"He's pretty good."

Alex Reed came up beside him to watch. Alex would be doing his practice run at the same time as Gray later. He and Alex had known each other a long time, had started on dirt tracks together back in Oklahoma. "Yeah. Has his head up his ass sometimes, but if he straightens out, he could be a great driver."

"Who hasn't had their head up their ass at that age?" Alex asked. "Remember when all we wanted to do was drive fast and party all night?"

Gray laughed. "Ah. The good old days when making money and worrying was someone else's problem."

Alex slapped him on the back. "I still drive for someone else's race team, buddy. It's still someone else's problem. You're the one who decided to go out on your own."

"Asshole."

Alex laughed and walked away. He knew better, too. Alex was as driven as they came, as focused on success as anyone he'd ever known. He put everything he had into racing, into winning, because it was all he had. Gray at least had the option of walking away from all this. He was lucky that he had money to back him up. Alex had grown up dirt-poor and had raced his way into success. Without racing, he had nothing. Gray couldn't imagine what that must be like.

He turned his attention back to Donny, watching his practice.

At least his focus was on racing and Donny this morning instead of on Evelyn, who had shocked the hell out of him when she'd told him she was going to become an extra appendage from now until the election.

Just what he didn't need. He'd only agreed to this because of his mother's urging. If he'd known that meant Evelyn would be following him from city to city, he might have rethought this whole deal.

He'd ignored her during his meetings this morning, but now, as he watched Donny race, he looked for her.

He scanned the track and found her sitting in the stands with some of the wives and girlfriends.

She'd changed that morning they had breakfast, and he'd been shocked by the transformation. In a suit, she looked like she belonged on his father's campaign. He could mentally compartmentalize her there. In a white button-down shirt and skintight jeans that showed off her body, she'd fit in at the track—in his world. And that made him just a little bit uncomfortable.

Maybe he didn't want her to fit in. Maybe he wanted her as uncomfortable as she made him. He was used to the women who frequented the track, women he knew, not this intelligent woman who regarded him like she knew all his secrets. Plus, she was part of his dad's world, and that made him even more uncomfortable.

When Donny pulled into the pit and climbed out, Gray started over to congratulate him on his practice run, determined to push Evelyn Hill out of his head for as long as possible.

Donny tossed his helmet into the driver's seat and graced him with a big smile. "That one felt good, boss."

"It was a good run." Gray looked over at Donny's crew chief, who nodded and brought over a digital notebook. As they walked away from the track, he looked at the numbers from Donny's run.

"Let's talk," Gray said, then led Donny to his trailer.

And there was Evelyn, just like he'd met her that first day. Only this time she was in jeans again. The heat was climbing, so she'd shed the long-sleeve shirt, leaving her in a white T-shirt that hugged tight to her full breasts.

He blew out a breath. So much for shoving her from his mind.

"Evelyn Hill, this is Donny Duncan."

"Ma'am," Donny said, shaking Evelyn's hand.

"It's very nice to meet you, Donny." She looked to Gray. "If you're busy, I can find something to do."

"If you're supposed to hang with me, then hang. Come on in. Donny and I are going to have a short chat, then we'll get started."

Donny gave Evelyn a once-over, and Gray was certain he was probably curious. He hadn't told anyone about Evelyn, wasn't sure what he was going to say, but he supposed he'd have to fill everyone in sooner rather than later.

"Take a seat," he said to her.

Evelyn found herself a seat in one of the far corners of the trailer, while he and Donny grabbed a spot at his table.

"Here are your numbers from your run this morning."

Donny grabbed the notebook from him, scanned it, then lifted his gaze to Gray and grinned. "Damn. I'm good."

"Don't get too full of yourself. It was a good practice run, but it wasn't a race. And you came in twelfth on Sunday with a car that was top five running shape."

Donny's smile died. He dragged his fingers through his dirty blond hair and nodded. "I know. I should have done better. The car was perfect, and you're right. I was top five the whole race. I just let them pass me the last ten laps. That one was on me. I lost my concentration. It won't happen again."

Hard to argue with that, and since Donny seemed to be aware of his failings, there was no point in Gray beating on him. "A good racer constantly evaluates what he could have done better. Since you've already done that, I guess you and I don't have anything to talk about. Unless it happens again."

"Understood, boss."

"I had a whole speech and everything, Donny," Gray said. "You kind of ruined it for me."

Donny laughed. "Sorry. Would you like me to fuck up again this Sunday?"

Gray cracked a smile. "I'd rather you didn't."

"Okay. My goal is to get a win."

"That's a good goal to have. Don't forget, you're not out there alone. You have an entire team behind you who'll help you get to the finish line, so listen to what they have to say. And pull your head out of your ass and start using your brain. Now get out of here."

Donny scrambled out of the seat, nodded at Evelyn, and left the trailer.

She stood and came over to him. Gray caught the subtle scent of something musky and very alluring. He tried not to lean in closer to figure out what it was since she was already distracting enough.

"Donny works for you?" she asked, placing her briefcase on his table.

"He drives the second car for Preston Racing. I added him this year. He's young, but has great skills."

"So you're developing him and he shows a lot of promise." She took a seat and pulled a laptop out of her bag, opened it, and started typing something.

He swung into the other side of the booth. "What are you doing?"

"Working on an amended bio for you."

"For?"

"I've already got some posts up about you."

Irritation made his jaw clench. "Uh . . . posts? What posts?"

"The senator's Facebook and Twitter accounts."

When he didn't say anything, she lifted her gaze to his over the top of her laptop. "Problem?"

"Big one. Let's get some rules down before we go any further. Rule number one: Don't write anything about me or connect me to the senator in any way without me seeing it first."

She leaned back in the booth. "I thought we'd already discussed this and it had been decided we'd work together. If I'm going to have to run everything by you, this is going to be difficult."

"Then it's going to be difficult. Show me what you've done and where you've posted it."

She continued to stare at him, and her gaze narrowed in irritation. Tough. He didn't like this already, and the fact that she'd put up some media bullshit about him pissed him off.

"All right. Give me a second here." She turned her attention to the laptop, then swiveled it to face him. "It's not much, just a general announcement that the senator is pleased to have his son working with him. It's very vague."

Gray read the post. It wasn't vague. It connected him and his racing team to his father and his father's political ambitions. It might as well say, "Gray Preston fully endorses his father."

"Goddammit, Evelyn. This isn't what I signed up for." He stood and paced for a few seconds, then turned to face her. "Pull that shit off. Now." He walked out of the trailer, fury boiling in his veins.

Without thinking, he headed toward the track, finding Ian waiting for him.

"You're early."

His teeth grinded against each other and he was ready to lash out, but his current state of mind wasn't Ian's fault. "I need to drive, now."

Ian took one look at him, then looked behind him. Gray turned to see Evelyn heading in his direction.

Oh, hell no. He turned back to Ian. "Now. I mean right fucking now."

"Sure." Ian got on the radio to one of the other teams. "Hey, can we slide into your spot? Gray has a time conflict."

In a few seconds, Ian nodded. "You sure?"

"Positive."

"Get into your suit. Your car is ready."

He got into his fire suit and climbed into his car, strapped in, and put on his helmet.

By the time he fired up the engine, he had an outlet for all this excess energy.

Getting behind the wheel and pulling out onto the track revved him up. Cranking up the speed made him forget everything but the feel of the track and testing the way the car handled.

He'd always been the most content when he was in his car. From the first time he'd climbed into one of his buddy's midget cars on a dirt track, he'd been hooked. Only sixteen years old at the time, the roar of the engine, the smell of oil and fuel and dirt flying into his face had been a lure he couldn't deny. He'd still been playing baseball at the time, with the promise of a sports scholarship and pressure from his father to pursue law and a future in politics. Under his

father's thumb and still tied to the Preston money, he'd toed the
family line, but found every opportunity he could to race cars and
learn about engines.

And still managed to piss off his father when he'd accepted the
baseball scholarship to Oklahoma.

As he cranked up his speed heading around the track, he cracked
a smile. Irritating his dad had always been one of his greatest plea-
sures. Maybe he could still find a way to do that. He might have
agreed to help him, but he didn't have to do it the Mitchell Preston
way. He could control Evelyn and her laptop and he'd make damn
sure nothing went onto the Internet that he didn't want on there,
worded exactly the way he wanted it.

This might be his father's race, but they were going to play by his
rules.

He downshifted around the curve, then laid on the throttle on
the straightaway and gave the car everything he had on the last lap.
By the time he began to slow down, the last of his adrenaline rush
had burned itself out.

Now he had a plan, and his car was in good shape. He felt good
about this race and the position of his race team. Of course this
was only the first practice run, but he had to keep a positive outlook.

He climbed out and Ian fell in step with him as the crew took
the car to the garage.

"Well?" he asked, his focus on the car and only on the car right
now.

"Decent time and the car looked good. You ran it a little tight
out there. You burning off some frustration?"

Ian knew him well, could always tell Gray's mood from the way
he drove. "Maybe a little."

"What's going on? And who's the hot blonde?"

He blew out a frustrated breath, ready to climb into his Chevy again and do more laps, the only thing that could ease his irritation. "She works for my father."

Ian stopped and stared at Evelyn, currently sitting in the front row of the stands, before turning his attention back to Gray. "No wonder you were so pissed off. What's she doing here?"

"It's complicated."

"I'm listening."

"I sort of agreed to help out my father's campaign."

Ian arched a brow. "No shit. Your dad dying or something? Because that's the only reason I can think of that you'd bend to the old man's will."

Gray snorted. "No. Not that I'm aware of, anyway. He's got a shot at the vice presidential nomination."

"Really."

"Yeah. And they think my fan base can make him look more attractive."

Ian laughed. "I'm sure they could. What I want to know is why you give a shit."

"My mom asked me to help."

"Oh. That's different."

"Yeah."

"And the hottie works for your dad?"

"Apparently she's my liaison to my dad, so she'll be with us for the time being."

"Sweet, man. You could have gotten some old fat bald guy. Instead you get a centerfold. Not really a hardship, is it?"

"I can already tell she's going to be a pain in my ass."

Ian slapped him on the back. "Oh. Gee. I feel really sorry for you. Having to put up with looking at her every day."

"Suck it, Ian."

He laughed. "I'll see you later. I think your centerfold looks like she wants to talk to you."

FIVE

GRAY LOOKED OVER TOWARD THE STANDS. EVELYN HAD gotten up and now leaned against one of the flagpoles.

He really wished Ian hadn't called her a centerfold. She had an arm casually wrapped around the flagpole, and his mind swam with visions of her naked and doing a slinky pole dance.

His cock tightened and he realized he liked her a lot better when he was raging and pissed off at her rather than thinking about her as beautiful or sexy or, God forbid, centerfold material. Which was completely inappropriate since he was working with her in a professional capacity and shouldn't be objectifying her by fantasizing about her and the flagpole.

Then again, when had his dick ever been appropriate? He probably got that from his father, which made him feel even worse.

She walked toward him. He met her halfway.

"I'm really sorry," she said before he could even open his mouth to apologize for acting like such an asshole and going off on her. "You're absolutely right. I got ahead of myself and posted something without your input. I've removed it and it won't happen again."

Well, hell. "You know, between you and Donny, you're both ruining my righteous speech-making abilities today."

Her lips curved. "You can go ahead and make your speech. I won't mind."

"I'll save it for another time when you piss me off."

"You're thinking there'll be another time."

"I'm sure of it. And apology accepted. I need a drink. Let's go to my trailer."

She walked in step beside him. "That's not really a trailer, Gray. It's more like a complete house on wheels."

He held the door for her and she stepped in. "It has to be. During the racing season we spend so much time on the road we rarely get home. This is comfortable and I hate hotels."

He opened the fridge and pulled out a bottled water, then turned to her. "You want one?"

"Yes, that would be nice. Thank you."

He grabbed another and handed it to her as he slid onto one of the sofas. "You don't always have to be so formal, Evelyn. If we're going to be spending a lot of time together over the next few months, you're going to have to chill a little."

She unscrewed the top and took a sip. "I don't really chill. Besides, this is work for me."

"Yeah, well, racing is work for me. Doesn't mean I can't enjoy it."

"I do enjoy my work. Very much. I just take it seriously."

She *was* serious. And too formal. He was going to have to lighten her up. Maybe when he went home, which couldn't be soon enough for him. "So tell me what the next steps are."

"Well, now that word is out—and again, I'm sorry about that—we need to do some rallying of your fans, make sure they get to know the senator and your connection to him. On your terms, of course."

"Okay. And how would you suggest doing that?"

She pulled open her laptop. "You could start mentioning him on your social media accounts. And of course, being seen in person with him would be very helpful."

He sighed. His mother had asked if he'd spend the Fourth of July with them. He preferred limiting the time spent with his father to as little as possible, usually at family events and only when his mother commanded. He never attended political functions.

This was going to be a nightmare.

"We'll do the Fourth of July thing my mom mentioned."

"The one at your family's home?" She smiled. "That's great. I'll make arrangements."

"I have a race that week so it'll have to be a fly in and out thing. And I want to spend one of those days at home, so I mean it when I say I want to spend as little time with my father as possible."

"No problem. I'll take care of everything. Let me pull up your schedule." Her fingers flew across the keyboard. "You have a race in Daytona the weekend after the fourth, is that correct?"

"Yeah. So we'll be running practices, but everyone will get a few days off."

"Okay."

Within ten minutes she'd made arrangements. "Okay, that's done. I'll alert your father's private secretary that you'll be at the family home. If you could give a speech—"

"No. Photographs with him will be enough, won't they?"

"You don't want to speak?"

He let out a short laugh. "No. I don't want to speak."

Evelyn let out a resigned sigh. "All right. Then photos will do.

Now, on to the social media aspect. We can promote this visit home. You can upload photos on Facebook and Twitter, talk about visiting with your parents—"

"Yeah, I don't really do that."

"I've noticed. For someone with your popularity, your social media accounts are rather threadbare. You could gain a lot more fans if you were more active. I can work with you on that. I'm part of your father's social media team. I'm very adept at that sort of integration."

That's what his sponsors had talked to him about, but hell, he was too busy running his business and racing cars to invest a lot of time in social media. "It's something I planned to work on. I just haven't had a lot of extra time."

"I can help you. Why don't you give me access to your social media accounts and I can take care of it for you. I promise not to upload anything without you approving it first. I know you'll be busy and you won't want to deal with the minutiae."

"That's fine." He gave her passwords to his accounts, then stood. "I've got work to do. You get started on that."

She looked up at him. "Where to now?"

"I've got meetings."

She grabbed her laptop. "Can I come along?"

"It's mostly boring car stuff."

"I don't find it boring at all. I have a lot to learn and I'd really enjoy sitting in, if you don't mind."

He shrugged. "Suit yourself."

BY THE END OF THE DAY, EVELYN HAD LEARNED ONE thing—there was a lot more to being a car owner and a driver than just writing the check and getting behind the wheel. There were meetings and phone calls with sponsors and talking to crew. After that came working with engineers and discussions about engines and body design followed by the selection of paint schemes and so many other things her head spun.

Her fingers and shoulders were sore from all the notes she'd made today. It was a good thing she had an above average intelligence and could absorb a lot of what she'd learned in a hurry. Which was what had made her an invaluable asset to Senator Preston's team, and would serve her well getting up to speed on Gray Preston, owner of and driver for Preston Racing.

She had made her way back to Gray's trailer while he went to yet another meeting with his crew to discuss some oil pressure problem with Donny's car. They had gotten deep into mechanical issues, so she decided to take this time to organize her notes and develop a social media plan for him.

She was fully into her outline when she heard a knock at the door. Since this wasn't her trailer, she debated whether or not to acknowledge the knock, but finally got up and went to the door.

A beautiful young woman was at the door. And she looked decidedly pissed off.

"Gray's not here. Are you looking for him?"

"Damn straight. Where the hell is he?"

"In a meeting."

The woman frowned. "Who are you?"

"I'm Evelyn Hill. And you are?"

"Stacie. I'm Donny's girlfriend."

"Oh. Would you like to come in?"

"I guess." She brushed past Evelyn, the scent of something strawberry filling the room as she turned and crossed her arms. "Do you know where Donny is?"

"I'm afraid not. Is there a problem?"

"Yeah, a big one." She looked around, and Evelyn could tell Stacie was highly upset. She sure was pretty, with long dark hair that spilled down to her waist and the most unusual gray eyes. She was slender, wearing short shorts and a belly-baring tight top that made Evelyn envious since it was very warm outside today.

"Why don't you have a seat? Would you like something to drink?"

"Is there any pop in the fridge?"

"I don't know, but I'll look." Evelyn went to the refrigerator. "Diet or regular."

"Regular is fine." When Evelyn brought a can along with a glass filled with ice, Stacie gave her a once-over. "You're nice. Not at all like the chicks Gray usually dates."

"Oh, we're not dating. I'm working for him." She wondered what kind of "chicks" Gray dated. Not that it mattered to her on a personal level, but image was everything in politics. She'd have to do some research into his social life.

"No wonder you're so nice. And you're pretty, too."

Evelyn arched a brow. "Thank you. I assume the women Gray dates are pretty, too."

Stacie shrugged and poured her soda into the glass. "If you like the trashy pit viper type."

"Trashy?"

"You know. He has a thing for blondes with huge tits."

"I see."

"He doesn't keep them very long. I think he picks them out just to get laid, and then they're on their way."

Well, wasn't she refreshingly honest. Either that or she liked to gossip. "So, Stacie, do you live around here?"

"I live with Donny, who's a giant pain in my ass right now. I should have known better than to agree to follow him on the circuit this season. I could have done another semester of school instead of putting up with his shit."

"School being college?"

Stacie laughed. "Of course. Why, do I look underage?"

"Kind of."

"That's funny. I get that a lot, I guess because I'm kind of short and skinny. I'm twenty-two, though. I'll be twenty-three in a few months."

"I'm relieved to know that."

"I like you—Evelyn, is it?"

"Yes."

"And how old are you, Evelyn?"

"Twenty-nine."

"Married?"

"Single."

Stacie took a couple drinks of her soda, then leaned back against the booth and glanced at Evelyn's laptop. "What kind of work are you doing for Gray?"

"Actually, I work for his father, Senator Mitchell Preston."

"Is that right? And you're working for Gray now, too? That's so . . . interesting. Is Gray getting involved in his dad's campaign? Because I know he's not leaving racing to run for congress or anything." Stacie leaned forward, a worried expression on her face. "He's not, is he?"

"That's really not for me to say."

"Good answer," Stacie said with a grin. "Makes me miss school and all the public relations courses I took. Which, if I hadn't agreed to accompany my moron of a boyfriend this year, I could still be taking."

"Is that your field of study?"

"Yes. Public relations and marketing. Which would be a perfect degree to assist Donny. If I don't dump him first."

"Trouble in paradise?"

"You could say that. He often has his head up his ass."

"That's pretty vague, Stacie. Would you like to talk about it in specifics, or would you like me to mind my own business?"

She shrugged, stared at her glass for a few minutes, then lifted her gaze to Evelyn. "He distracts easily, loses his focus. He can be such a great driver, but half the time I don't know where his head is during a race. And when he isn't racing, he's partying it up with the guys. I mean it's not like he's steppin' out on me. Believe me, if I thought he was cheating on me I'd bean him over the head with a crankshaft or carburetor or some other car thingy, and I'd be out of here faster than the track in Talladega. It's not that. It's just that he's so . . . unfocused and undecided about his direction.

"We've talked about it, but it's like he's keeping secrets. We've been together since we were in high school. I wanted to stay in college. He knows how important my education is, but he wanted me with him. Foolishly, I followed."

"Is that what you wanted, or are you with him this season because it's what he wanted?"

"A little of both, I think. He needs me. I help him stay focused. And I miss him when he's on the road. The season is so long and he doesn't come home all that much. So part of this is me and how much I want to be with him. Part of it is he can't concentrate without me. If I'm not here with him, then I'll spend that time worrying about him."

Evelyn had never had a long-term relationship, so she couldn't relate to this. But she knew one thing, and that was a woman should never give up everything for a man. "But shouldn't a relationship be able to thrive even during those times the two of you can't be together? Surely you can work something out so you can finish your education. It's important you be able to stand on your own and not sacrifice what you want in order for Donny to be happy."

"Believe me, I've thought long and hard about that. I've taken a few online courses in the spring and fall so I don't lose out on my status at my school."

"And what does Donny do to sacrifice for you?"

Stacie didn't have an answer for that.

"Shouldn't this be a two-way street? Shouldn't he be able to do without you for a little while, focus his attention on his racing so you don't have to worry about him? And then when you're finished, you can put that degree to good use by helping him out. Seems like a win/win for both of you, with a little sacrifice along the way."

She sighed. "You make it sound so simple. Love is never simple. When you love someone, you don't want to be separated from them."

"Well, I don't know about love, but I do know about giving up a part of yourself for someone else's happiness. I don't think that will make you happy in the long run. Do you?"

"You know, Evelyn, for someone who I just met about twenty minutes ago, I've sure shared a lot about my life. Why is that?"

Evelyn shrugged. "I have no idea. Maybe I'm a good listener."

"And maybe you give good advice. I like you."

She smiled. "I like you too, Stacie."

"I'm going to give this some thought. And try not to bash Donny's head in when I find him."

"Please don't bash his head in, Stacie. I need him to drive Sunday."

Gray had walked in and was standing near the door.

"Oh, hi, Gray," Stacie said, slipping out of the booth to toss her can in the trash and put her glass in the sink. "Thanks to Evelyn, here, I'm no longer pissed off at your driver. Well, still slightly pissed off, but I have a little perspective now." She turned to Evelyn. "Thanks for the chat."

Evelyn smiled. "Anytime."

"Ciao," Stacie said, and left.

Gray frowned after Stacie, then looked at Evelyn. "What was that about?"

"Relationships."

"Oh, God. I'm glad I wasn't here, then. Did you solve all her problems with Donny?"

"Not really. I think she just wanted someone to listen. And I might have told her she should go back to school."

He grabbed a beer from the refrigerator. "She probably should. She'll be a much more valuable asset to Donny after she gets her degree. And he needs to learn to suck it up and stand on his own without his girlfriend holding his hand."

Evelyn stared at him. "I'm kind of shocked."

He tipped the beer to his lips, then paused. "Yeah? Why?"

"I was prepared to have you yell at me again."

"Why would I yell at you?"

"I figured you'd tell me I should have minded my own business and stayed out of Stacie's relationship with Donny."

"Some parts of their relationship are none of my business. But I've been telling Donny he needs to stop mooning over that girl. She's smart and she needs to finish school. I think he's afraid if he isn't watching her every second, she'll run off with the first guy she sees."

"I don't think real love works that way."

"I don't think it does either, but I wouldn't know."

"Neither would I."

He took a seat across from her. "Never been in love, Evelyn?"

She looked down at her laptop. "Not really. Not that all-consuming kind of love Stacie was telling me about. The kind where you can't bear to be apart from the person you're crazy about."

"Yeah, me either. Half the time I think it's just a bunch of bullshit you see in the movies and read about in books and that love like that doesn't exist."

When he didn't say anything else, she met his gaze. "And the other half?"

He shrugged. "I guess I just haven't found the time to meet that person who makes me wish I could be with them all the time."

"Neither have I."

He took a long swallow of his beer. "Too busy with career to fall in love?"

"My career has been my number one priority ever since I graduated from Georgetown."

"On a career track, are you?"

"Yes. Very much so. I intend to end up at the White House."

His lips curved. "As president?"

"It's possible. Right now I'd be content working for someone in that position."

"If my father makes it to the vice presidency, you'll be close."

She took a deep breath and let it out, trying not to let the excitement at that thought make her wiggle in her seat. "Closer than I thought I'd get at this point in my career. When I first started working for your father, I knew he was a mover and a shaker with determined career aspirations. I told him then that wherever he was going, I not only wanted along for the ride, but I assured him I'd help him get there."

"I can only imagine how his ego ate that up."

"He's a very nice man, Gray, and dedicated to his constituents. I believe in his platform."

Gray rolled his eyes and took several swallows of beer, then laid the bottle on the table. "You've been poisoned by the Mitchell Preston Kool-Aid. I feel sorry for you."

She wanted to smack that smug look right off his face. "Do I look stupid?"

"Not particularly, but you're not the first woman to be taken in by the Preston charm."

She pinned him with a look. "I don't know about that. At this moment, I don't find you very charming."

"That's because I'm not turning my charm on you. You should see me when I do. You wouldn't be able to resist me."

Now she wanted to roll her eyes, but since he was technically a client, she didn't dare. "Oh, trust me. I'd be able to resist."

He stood and dumped the empty beer bottle in the recycle bin, then turned to her. "Get up. We're going out."

She slid out of the booth. "We are? Where? Do I need to change clothes?"

"Yeah. I'll take you to your hotel. Change into a dress."

She peeked at her calendar on her phone. "I don't see any event on your schedule."

"It's not an event, Evelyn. I'm taking you to dinner."

"Oh. And I need a dress."

"Yes. We're going to a party after. There might be dancing."

"Uh . . . if this isn't a scheduled event, I could just go to my hotel . . ."

"Oh, no. You're supposed to hang with me, right?"

"Well, yes, but . . ."

He slipped his hand in hers. "Then let's hang out."

SIX

OKAY, SO MAYBE GRAY DIDN'T NEED TO TAKE EVELYN TO dinner. He could have ended their night, she could have gone back to her hotel, and he could have gone over the stacks of paperwork and emails he knew were waiting for him.

Instead, all he'd thought about was her not finding him charming.

He could be fucking charming. He could charm the panties right off of her if he wanted to. He got a lot of women in his bed with very little effort. And if she thought for one second he couldn't turn the charm on full throttle and do the same to her without her even being aware of it, then she hadn't researched him as well as she thought.

Not that he had any intention of seducing her. She worked for his father and he wanted to keep things between them business only. The last thing he wanted was to get any closer to Evelyn Hill than was absolutely necessary.

But he could sure as hell show her that she couldn't resist his charms when he set his mind to it. No matter who she was.

He'd waited downstairs while she ran up to change clothes. He'd done that himself, switching from his jeans and T-shirt to a pair of black slacks and a white button-down shirt.

Evelyn came through the doors in a slinky red dress and high heels that nearly made his tongue fall out. Those legs—Christ, she had spectacular legs. His cock tightened and he was glad he'd left his shirt untucked because he was going to have a hard-on before she made it to the car.

He figured he deserved that for having nefarious plans where she was concerned. So his dick would just have to suffer the consequences tonight.

He got out and came around to the passenger side, making sure to lean in and whisper against her ear, "You look gorgeous."

She looked confused as she turned toward him. "Thank you."

Point one in his favor.

It was about an hour's drive, but well worth it, in his opinion, to eat at The Oak Room, one of his favorite restaurants in Louisville. And okay, he wanted to impress her. From her wide-eyed look at the menu, he'd succeeded.

"Wine or a bourbon tasting?" he asked. One of his favorite things about The Oak Room was their fine bourbon, though because of the long drive he wouldn't be able to indulge like he normally would if he was staying closer.

"By all means, please select however you'd like."

"You don't strike me as a bourbon drinker."

"You forget, I make my life around politicians. I adapt."

"Bourbon it is."

He ordered five different bourbons. Like a trouper, Evelyn sampled all of them and showed no signs of inebriation, though he made sure their waiter kept a steady supply of water at the table.

"You down the contents of those glasses like you know your way around a glass of bourbon."

She laid an empty glass aside. "These are excellent bourbons. And I told you, I work with politicians, some of whom are heavy drinkers and act insulted when you don't drink with them. I've learned to tolerate alcohol quite well."

"So what you're telling me is I won't be able to get you drunk tonight."

She laughed and took a couple sips of water. "I do have my limits, and I know what they are. But no. You won't get me drunk."

"Too bad. It must be a rough job having to deal with all those pain-in-the-ass politicians."

"They're not as bad as you paint them to be. And neither is your father."

He shrugged and downed the contents of a glass. It was a smooth bourbon with a sweet oak flavor that didn't burn on the way down, just the way he liked it.

After the tasting, they ordered their meal. Gray was happy to see Evelyn order both a salad appetizer and the duck for her main course. He had the beef tenderloins, which tasted just as good as he'd remembered from the last time he was there.

He was mostly interested to see Evelyn eat. Sometimes the women he took out barely touched their food, then bragged that they were watching their figures like he should hand them some kind of trophy for starvation. Evelyn was slender, but she obviously worked out or she had a great metabolism, because she clearly enjoyed her food and ate almost everything on her plate.

She caught him watching, because at one point, she paused with her fork midway to her mouth. "Do I have food on my face or something?"

"No. I just like watching a woman eat. And where do you put it?"

"I have an amazing metabolism. I'm very lucky. It's a good thing, too, because I really like food, and this meal is incredible. Thank you for bringing me here."

"You're welcome. I'm glad you like it."

"You should come to D.C. There are some fantastic restaurants there."

"I try to avoid the capitol."

"Because your father's there."

He polished off the last of his steak and set his plate to the side. "Mainly, yes."

"Do you want to tell me what your problem is with your father?"

"Not particularly."

"All right." She finished her duck and took a drink of water.

He liked that she didn't push for more details about his relationship with his dad, because he sure as hell didn't like talking about it. But he did like talking to her. Liked being with her, too, even if she did represent his dad. And she sure was pretty to look at, especially tonight, with her hair swept up. And that dress. Damn that dress. It was cut tight across her breasts and had thin straps, and he could already imagine sliding it off her creamy shoulders while he kissed her neck.

Shit. He'd promised he wasn't going to think about her that way, and he was doing it anyway.

"What are you thinking about?"

He lifted his gaze to hers. "Huh?"

"You were lost in thought and staring somewhere in the vicinity of my breasts."

"Probably because of your dress. Sorry, I was staring. It was rude."

Her lips curved. "Complimentary. I'm sorry if the dress disturbs you."

"Oh, the dress definitely disturbs me, Evelyn. But not in a bad way."

He paid the bill and came around to pull her chair out, taking a moment to lean in and inhale her scent. So subtle. She didn't load herself down in perfume, making him nearly choke. Evelyn's scent was definitely all Evelyn.

His dick took notice. Hell, his dick took notice of everything having to do with her.

Wasn't he the one who was supposed to pour on the charm tonight? It seemed like their roles were being reversed. He was ready to fall at her feet, and she wasn't even trying.

Time to change that.

"Tell me about this party we're going to," Evelyn said as they left the restaurant.

"Craig and I went to college together. We played baseball together, too. Craig got drafted by Cincinnati after college and played three seasons for them before an injury ended his career."

"Oh, I'm sorry to hear that."

"Don't feel too sorry for him. He's doing just fine," Gray said, taking an exit and heading toward a residential area.

"Obviously. This seems like a very nice neighborhood."

"It is. Like me, Craig comes from old family money, so after he left baseball he had a fallback position in his father's company."

She looked at him. "I like that you don't apologize for that."

"For what?"

"For having family money."

He shrugged. "Why should I? It's no fault of mine. The trust my grandfather left me gave me the stake I needed to separate myself from my father and to help build Preston Racing. I've also worked my ass off to make more money. I've set up several charities, because my grandfather taught me it's important to share the wealth when you have money. And it's not like I spend my life sailing or traveling or pissing the money away sitting on my butt doing nothing, so I don't see any reason to apologize for having money."

"It's a good outlook to have. As someone who doesn't come from money, I don't begrudge you. I imagine others do."

"Frankly, I don't give a shit what others think. I have a lot of close friends who haven't grown up rich. None of them have ever judged me for it."

"I imagine that's why they're your close friends."

He smiled. "You're right."

"So tell me more about Craig."

"His family is from around here, so he settled here and went to work for his father's company after he left baseball. He married one hell of a stunning woman. But Miranda isn't a gold digger. She, like a lot of my friends, didn't grow up with money. He met her at one of the charity fund-raisers he was participating in. She was running it, along with about ten others she's involved in. Philanthropy is what she does best. She believes in giving back, too, and she's brought out the best in Craig. They've been married three years and have a baby on the way."

"How nice for them."

"Yeah, I think you'll like them."

"Maybe I'll hit them up for a campaign contribution."

Gray shot her a horrified look.

Evelyn laughed. "I'm joking."

"You scare me, Evelyn."

"And you need to get to know me."

"Obviously, I do."

Gray pulled up to the gate and gave his name to the guard there, who punched a button and let them through. Evelyn didn't comment. He imagined since she dealt with some of the high rollers in D.C., Craig's five-thousand-square-foot home wouldn't impress her.

"Oh, would you look at the size of those trees in their front yard. Can you imagine a tire swing in one of those?"

That wasn't at all what he expected her to say. "A tire swing?"

He pulled behind one of the cars and got out, then walked over to her side and let her out.

"Of course. You said they're having a baby, right?"

"Yeah."

"I can picture this huge yard, a bunch of kids, and a tire swing. I always wanted one of those."

"You did, huh?"

She let out a soft laugh. "I did. My parents never owned property and we never had a big yard. We lived in apartments. Of course there were playgrounds, but I always coveted a yard that belonged to just me, with a lot of big trees and a tire swing. It's something I vowed I'd give my own children someday."

Now that was a revelation. He suddenly wanted to know more about Evelyn. A lot more. Unfortunately, they now stood at the threshold to Craig's front door, and this wasn't the time to ask probing questions, so he tabled that thought for later.

Craig opened the door and grinned. "Gray! I didn't think you'd come. I know you're busy with race stuff."

Gray hugged him and they slapped each other on the back. "We never get to see each other. When I got your call saying you were having a birthday party, how could I not be here for it?"

"I'm glad."

"Thirty, huh? Man, you're old."

Craig laughed. "And so are you. And where are my manners?" He turned to Evelyn and shook her hand. "Craig Reynolds. Welcome."

"Evelyn Hill."

Craig gave a look to Gray. "You've moved up in the world of women. Evelyn, you're gorgeous. Come on inside and meet my wife."

Used to large crowds of people she didn't know, Evelyn wasn't the slightest bit intimidated. Craig was tall and lean, with sandy brown hair cut short. He wore dark glasses that did nothing to mar his incredible good looks. Instead, they gave him a Clark Kent mystique that made him utterly good-looking.

There were quite a few people in attendance, and obviously some that Gray knew, because he stopped to shake hands or smile and wave as they walked by. When they made their way to a gorgeous woman with chin-length brown hair who looked to be about six months pregnant, she turned and presented them with a glowing smile.

She leaned into Gray and hugged him, then kissed his cheek. "Gray. It's been too long."

"Not since my last race here, I'm afraid. And I'm sorry about that, because you look even more beautiful now than you looked last year."

She wrinkled her nose. "My ankles are swelling and I'm enjoying M&M's far too much." She turned to Evelyn. "And who is this gorgeous woman you've brought with you?"

"I'm Evelyn Hill. It's very nice to meet you."

Miranda gave her a hug. "I'm Miranda Reynolds. It's nice to meet you, too, Evelyn. Thank you for being here tonight."

Miranda had one of those soft, welcoming voices that made you feel you were her very best friend from the moment you met her. She had warm brown eyes and the most perfect smile that you just knew was genuine. And considering the line of work Evelyn was in, she could spot a phony from an entire room away. Both Miranda and Craig were the real deal. She had never felt instantly comfortable with people before, but with this couple, she was. They offered her and Gray a drink, and they settled out on the patio, which was breathtaking, with an Olympic-sized pool, a hot tub, and a magnificent garden area beyond that Evelyn would love to see in the daylight.

"Your home is lovely, Miranda," Evelyn said while Gray and Craig talked racing and caught up on each other's lives.

"Thank you so much. I'm so very fortunate to be living the life I have." She rubbed her belly. "I hope this child and any others we're blessed with realize how lucky they are, when so many others don't have half the advantages we do."

"I have a feeling you're going to do your best to enlighten them?"

She smiled. "Yes. As soon as the children are old enough we'll involve them in our charitable works. It's a huge passion of mine."

"Gray told me about some of that on our way over, but not in detail. I'd love to know more."

Miranda explained how she sat on the foundation of several charities, locally, nationally, and globally, and was an ambassador for a fund-raising effort to bring clean water to impoverished nations. As soon as she was able, she would continue her efforts to bring needed medicines to Africa.

"I work for Gray's father, Senator Mitchell Preston. He sits on several committees I think could be beneficial to some of your causes. If you'd like, I'd be happy to speak to him to see what he could do to assist you with your efforts."

Miranda's eyes widened. "Oh, would you mind? That would be so helpful. We try hard to enlist the aid of as many politicians as we can. It's so hard to gain an audience, as you can imagine."

"I'll make a call first thing in the morning. If you give me your number, I'll have someone from the senator's office contact you directly."

Miranda grabbed Evelyn's hand and squeezed it. "I can't tell you how much that would mean to me. To the foundation."

"I'm happy to help. And I know the senator would be, too."

Not wanting to monopolize too much of Miranda's time, she excused herself and wound her way into the gardens. Well lit, it wasn't as magnificent a view as it would be in the daytime, but it was, nevertheless, stunning, with fountains, butterfly and hummingbird gardens, and a lighted statuary amidst the foliage. She followed the statues, stopping at each one to marvel at their construction. These weren't replicas of other famous statues. They appeared to have been sculpted just for Craig and Miranda. In fact, there was one of a couple entwined, staring at each other, that were mirror images of them. How romantic.

She wondered if Craig and Miranda would notice if she hid out here all night until sunrise.

"I suppose you want to have a big-ass garden in your huge backyard in your fantasy home someday, too?"

She turned to see Gray behind her. "I don't need some fantastically large house. Just a big tree for a tire swing. And okay, a nice-sized backyard for my currently nonexistent children that I hope to have someday."

He stepped up to her. "Going to be hard to have all that and your epic career in the White House, too."

She lifted her chin. "Why can't I have both? Why do I have to choose?"

He looked taken aback and she realized she was letting her passion for this topic get the best of her. "Sorry. It's a subject I've had some rather heated debates about."

They had been walking through the garden and Gray led her to a bench overlooking a rather impressive fountain. She took a seat and he sat next to her.

"Hey, I was joking. But obviously someone told you that you couldn't have a career and your fantasy husband, children, and house with the tire swing?"

"I was once told that I could choose my career track to the White House or a family, but I'd have to sacrifice one in order to have the other, and I'd have to choose."

"Probably my father."

"No. It wasn't your father. It was someone else. A mentor whom I admired very much. And a woman. She told me I'd be great in political office, but I'd never be successful at it if I also wanted to have a family. It would stretch me too thin."

He laid his arm over the back of the bench and stared at the dolphins spouting water out their mouths. "Frankly, I think that's a crock of shit and seems like a very old-school way of thinking."

She turned toward him. "Are you just feeding me a line?"

"No. There are plenty of congresswomen and senators with husbands and children, aren't there?"

"Yes."

"Then why couldn't you have both?"

She looked down at her lap. "Honestly? Despite it being what I'd like, it really is a fantasy. I don't see myself ever having a career in public office. I don't have the background for it."

"Bullshit, Evelyn. Where was that fire from a minute ago, when you said you wouldn't settle for less than everything you wanted?"

She always did this, always vacillated between what she wanted and what she knew she'd likely never have. A poor girl with no roots, no established background, and no means didn't—shouldn't ever—have aspirations like she had.

But she did have those aspirations, wanted those things, and she couldn't help herself.

"Tell me where you're from," he said, his voice soft as the darkness.

His tone eased some of her anxiety. She leaned back, the solid feel of his arm a comfort instead of a distraction.

"I'm from everywhere. My father did construction jobs, so we moved around a lot when I was a kid."

"How much is a lot?"

She thought back. "Probably once a year at least. Sometimes more, depending on the work. It was important to him to always have a job so he could provide for the family, so we went wherever the work was."

"Which was why you never had a house."

She turned to face him. "Yes. There was no sense in putting

down roots when we knew we'd have to pull them up and move on at a moment's notice."

He rubbed her back, his fingers trailing down her spine. She shivered.

"It must have been hard for you to do that."

She shrugged. "It was an adventure, at least when I was younger. Seeing new cities and towns was fun. My teen years were more difficult. It's harder to fit in and make friends when you get to high school and you're in and out like that."

"But you settled in at college?"

She smiled at the memory. "You have no idea what it was like to be able to spend that many years in one place. It gave me such a sense of peace and belonging. I formed friendships there that I'll have for a lifetime."

"See, that's the kind of human interest stories that voters love. I can't imagine you as anything other than a viable candidate, especially since you've put down roots in D.C., which I assume you have."

"It's where I've lived ever since I graduated college. I got my master's degree at Georgetown, too."

"Look at you. Already a lock for political office."

She laughed. "I don't know about that, but I have goals. Pretty lofty ones."

"So what do you want to do when you grow up?" he asked with a teasing smile.

"Seriously? I'd like to run for office. Start locally, then work my way up to a statewide office. Then . . . we'll see. I don't want there to be limitations."

"Those are good goals to have. And you're plenty young enough to see them through. Are you even thirty yet?"

"Not quite yet."

"Lots of time to have everything you want, Evelyn. The career, the husband, the kids, and that house with the tire swing."

She sighed and stared at the fountain. Gray was right. She could have it all. She had to continue to believe in herself. "Thank you."

"For what?"

"For believing in the things you think I can do. You don't even know me." No one knew her. She did her job and did it well and efficiently. That's how she ended up working for someone as high up the political ladder as Senator Preston. She had a social circle of friends who knew her, at least knew the Evelyn Hill she wanted them to know. But no one knew the child she had been, knew her dreams about the tire swing.

Now Gray knew. He was the last person she would have thought to tell that story to. She figured him to be the silent, brooding, good-looking type, more about himself and his cars than interested in hearing about her life.

Yet here they sat in this garden while she had done all the talking. He asked all the right questions, made it easy for her to open up, something she so rarely did. Usually she was the one asking all the questions.

What a twist.

"Hey, are you two hiding and making out here? We're about to set fire to my cake. A lot of candles, you know."

Gray stood and laughed at Craig, then he held out his hand for her.

"Wouldn't miss that for the world," Gray said, and he led her down the path toward the house.

SEVEN

THE CAKE WAS THREE TIERED, AND CRAIG WAS RIGHT, IT had been filled with candles—definitely more than thirty. It took him three tries to blow them all out. After everyone ate, they were led out a side door where a band had set up on the deck. People took seats around the deck and pool area where the band had started to play.

Gray led Evelyn to a cushioned love seat near the pool. They still had a great view of the band and the dance floor that had been created in front of the deck.

"In college, Craig always aspired to be a deejay," Gray said. "And a singer. I wouldn't be surprised if he got up and sang with the band tonight."

One of the singers got up to jam a seriously cool hip-hop tune, one of her favorites.

She half turned to face him. "I can't quite picture him belting out a song like that."

"Oh, you might be surprised. He's the Vanilla Ice of our generation."

"Not Eminem?"

"Not even close."

She laughed.

A slow R&B song came up, sung by a female member of the band with a voice as smooth as melted butter.

Gray stood and held out his hand. "Dance?"

She shouldn't, but she loved the song and couldn't resist. "I'd love to."

He led her down the path from the pool toward the dance floor. When he pulled her against him, she couldn't resist the thrill as her body met his.

It was innocent, just a dance and nothing more, and the only reason he was holding her in his arms. The patio was crowded with people and they weren't alone. Other couples merged in very close to them, trying to find their own spots to dance. There was nothing intimate about this, and yet as Gray looked down at her, his fingers grazed up and down the bare skin of her back. Electricity sizzled between them, and as she met his gaze, and it suddenly occurred to her that it didn't matter how many people surrounded them—the chemistry between them was as intimate as it could get. There could be a thousand people dancing nearby and it would seem as if it were only the two of them. The music was slow and sinful, her pulse had kicked up, and Gray only looked at her.

She was grateful for the public venue, because the intent in his eyes was clear. And if he leaned in for a kiss, she wasn't sure she'd be able to say no.

Fortunately, she was fairly certain he wouldn't do that in this crowd of people. But suddenly he moved them through the crowd, maneuvering her away from the others to a side patio shielded from everyone else. It was a walkway leading from the backyard to the front, only no one was here.

No one but Gray and her.

He took a step forward, pressing her against the side of the house, the brick still retaining the day's heat. Not that she needed it. Her body was already in flames, and as he bent and put his mouth on hers, she couldn't muster up a single thing to say or do in resistance, because kissing Gray seemed as natural to her as breathing.

He brushed his lips across hers—a tease, maybe, or a test to see if she'd push him away. She had no intention of doing that. Her breasts swelled and her nipples tightened, and with his body flush against hers, the only thing she wanted to do now was deepen the kiss and explore. So when he did, pressing his mouth more firmly against hers, she sighed in contentment.

Evelyn lost herself in the sensations bombarding her. Gray's mouth was pure heaven, his slow, drugging kisses slowing down time. She felt dizzy, swamped with a heavy fog of desire that enveloped her in a hazy cloud. Gray swept an arm around her back to tug her against him, his fingers dipping toward her butt. They were just resting there—he was being such a gentleman, when all she wanted was for him to grab her ass and draw her closer.

And what kind of sex-starved woman did that make her? Granted, it had been a long dry spell, but she worked for his father, and now they were making out in the dark at his friend's house and she was mentally complaining that it wasn't going fast enough?

If this kiss had been happening in her hotel room—or in his trailer—right now she'd be figuring out a way to get him out of his clothes. With her hands on his arms, she felt the flexing of his biceps. She knew he had a body and she longed to see it, to feel it, on top of her, inside her.

She shuddered and his fingers dipped lower, his tongue delving into her mouth at the same time he grabbed a handful of her ass and drew her against his erection.

Oh, yes.

He slid his lips from hers and pressed a kiss to the column of her throat, using his teeth to nip at her flesh. Goose bumps pricked her skin and she could imagine his mouth—his teeth—on other parts of her.

Oh, most definitely yes. She would have to get him naked, and her, too. She wondered if Craig and Miranda had an extra bedroom they wouldn't mind them using.

"I don't know, but I sure as hell could ask them."

She pulled back to look at him. "Did I say that out loud?"

"Yes. Hell yes. Let's go."

She grabbed his arms as the cold slap of reality hit her. They were an hour away from her hotel. At his friends' home. And she wasn't behaving at all like the woman who worked for his father. What must he think of her?

"Yes. Let's go. Back to my hotel."

His lips curved. "You sure you want to wait that long?"

His bottom lip was full. Sexy. She wanted to lift up and take a bite out of it.

Good lord, what was wrong with her?

The need for him warred with that damn logic and common sense that told her this was the wrong thing to do.

"No. I mean. No. We're not doing this."

Now he frowned. "*This* being sex."

"Yes. I mean no. Definitely not having sex."

He took a deep breath and let it out. She expected him to lead her out of the walkway. Instead, he leaned his hand against the wall and stared down at the ground.

Concerned, she asked, "Gray. Are you all right?"

"I'm going to need a minute here, Evelyn."

She rubbed up and down his arm. "Is something wrong?"

He lifted his gaze to hers and gave her a wry smile. "It would help if you didn't touch me like that."

It took her a few seconds, then her gaze drifted to his very obvious erection. She took a quick step back. "I'm sorry."

He laughed. "Don't be sorry about that. I'm sure as hell not. Though I'm sorry we're not seeing things through, but that's your call to make."

She blew out a very frustrated breath. "Believe me, if we were anywhere but here, your . . . problem, wouldn't be a problem for long."

He dropped his head and gave her a look that scorched her. "Not helping the issue here, Evelyn."

"Sorry." She turned around, thinking that might help.

"Neither is that great view of the skin of your back, your very fine ass, and those legs of yours."

She couldn't help but smile as she turned back to face him. "I think I'll go seek out the restroom to . . . repair the damage."

"You do that. I'll find you in a minute or two."

Despite the frustration, she smiled the entire way there.

True to his word, Gray was waiting for her as she exited the bathroom a few minutes later. She couldn't resist glancing down where his shirt covered his slacks.

"All better now?"

"Not if you keep staring."

She grinned. "I'm not going to apologize again."

He laughed and took her hand. "Let's go find Craig and Miranda. This is going to be a long drive back."

They found Craig, who was singing with the band, just as Gray said he would be.

And like Gray said, Craig was definitely no expert rapper, but his exuberance was infectious and the crowd bobbed up and down, clapping and singing along. Craig appeared to be having a blast. They waited until he finished, then made their way over to tell him they were leaving.

"Thank you. I had a wonderful time," Evelyn said.

Craig hugged her. "You keep watch over this one. Make sure he doesn't drive too fast."

She laughed. "I'm not sure I can do anything about that, at least when he's on the track."

After she gave Gray a hug, Miranda clasped both her hands. "Thank you for coming. And for your offer."

Gray slanted a curious gaze her way. "What offer?"

Miranda answered. "She's going to enlist your father's aid with some of my charities. I'm so grateful. You know how hard it is to get anyone in the political sphere to even take your calls when you're trying to cut through red tape. She's going to help me leap a few steps."

Gray looked over at her, and he didn't look happy, but he smiled at Miranda. "Isn't that just great."

They said good night and made their way back to the car. Gray was silent for at least ten minutes. She could tell from the tight set to his jaw that he wasn't happy, but since he hadn't said anything directly to her, she had no idea what had upset him.

"Is something wrong?"

"So you couldn't resist the opportunity to play politics with my friends?"

She blinked. "Excuse me?"

"Miranda. Her charities."

"Oh, that. She told me about the issues she'd been having getting funding and access for some of her causes. I know your father could assist with some of that, so I offered. Is that a problem?"

"You also know that Craig and Miranda have a lot of money. My father helps them out, then they help him out. That'll work out well for the senator's campaign, won't it?"

She was momentarily stunned and without a comeback to that, something that rarely happened to her. She was well trained to handle insults. Politics was all about firing insults and innuendo, and she could deal with anything thrown her way. She just hadn't expected it to be thrown by Gray.

"You're kidding, right? I didn't even know where we were going tonight. Do you think I hid in the bathroom and pulled up Craig and Miranda's bio and financials, then decided to feel her out to see if I could finagle a way to do her a favor so they'd be in the senator's debt and toss some money his way?"

His hands tightened on the steering wheel. "I don't know. Did you?"

She rolled her eyes. "No. Of course not. And I'm offended you'd even think so."

"Well, I don't really know you, do I?"

"No, you don't. Which is why we will not be sleeping together tonight."

He pulled onto the highway. "No, we won't."

She fumed silently on her side of the car, and he did the same.

"But if we had ended up in bed together tonight, I can guarantee you there wouldn't have been any sleeping, Evelyn."

Asshole. He just had to throw that out there, didn't he? Not that she cared anyway. He'd pissed her off and she no longer found him appealing in the least.

And she wouldn't even think about having sex with him ever again.

EIGHT

IT WAS A DAMN GOOD THING GRAY HAD HIS HEAD screwed on straight, and that he was back on the track where he belonged.

He'd almost done something stupid last night, had almost taken Evelyn to bed. He'd listened to her background story and had actually felt sorry for her, when the whole time she'd been manipulating him behind his back.

What a sucker he'd been. It was just like all the times his dad had shown up at his sporting events at school. Those were such rare occasions, and Gray had gotten his hopes up, so excited to see his father there. And during the opportunities he'd had to glance up and see his father in the stands, it would turn out his dad hadn't been watching the game at all. Instead, he'd been off wandering the bleachers, glad-handing all the parents and stumping for votes.

God forbid he actually show up for his own kid. No, that wouldn't be self-serving, and if there was one thing Mitchell Preston did and did well, it was serve himself.

Obviously his father had been teaching Evelyn the finer points of that game, a game Gray wanted no part of.

She'd suckered him in well enough with her sad story of how she wanted a family and a tree swing, how she wanted to be able to balance that with a career. He'd been impressed, and he wasn't often impressed, especially by anyone in politics. He'd even been dumb enough to believe her, too, which was his own damn fault. He'd started to think she was genuine and honest, that her rockin' killer body also accompanied a true heart, something so rare in the political world, and even rarer in his father's circle.

He'd been wrong.

That wouldn't happen again.

He pulled out onto the track, pushing Evelyn and anything about her to the back of his mind. Now it was time to concentrate on his car and his practice run. He wanted the pole for this weekend's race. That was the only thing he needed to focus on, because there was nothing better than starting the race in front of the pack.

He hit top speed and his mind went blank, like it always did when he surrounded himself with a great track and an awesome car. Ian and the crew had done their jobs this week. The number fifty-three was running in optimum condition, and by the time he finished his laps he was sure he had a good shot at grabbing the pole in this weekend's race.

"That was a good run," Ian said after Gray climbed out. "Keep running like that and you should kick everyone's butts in qualifying."

"That's what I'm hoping for. The car's running good. The only thing I felt was a shimmy in the left front when I hit top speed."

Ian nodded and plugged that into his notebook as they walked along. "We'll take a look at it. Probably nothing."

Gray hoped not. He was ready to race.

He hung around to watch Donny during his practice run. The kid did decently, seemed to have a little more focus than he'd had the previous week, and his speed was where it needed to be.

He also noticed Evelyn hanging out in the stands with Stacie, the two of their heads bowed together during Donny's run. He hadn't spoken to her since last night, figured she wouldn't even show up at the track today. Instead, she'd been there as soon as the track opened, sitting in the stands. Stacie had joined her there early, too, both of them hanging with the other women watching all the drivers.

Whatever. He didn't care what she did as long as she stayed the hell out of his way. She'd shown what she was after last night and he wanted no part of it.

"So what's the deal with the new chick?" Donny asked as they made their way to the garage to go over their cars' performances.

He shrugged. "Nothing."

"Stacie seems to like her. She came back to our trailer the other day busting my balls about 'Evelyn said this and Evelyn said that.' Kept me up half the night wanting to talk. Man, I hate talking."

"Yeah, well, Evelyn doesn't know everything."

"So you think I'm right."

He paused in the walkway, his head filled with track speed and not focused on what Donny was talking about. "Right about what?"

"On wanting Stacie to stay with me this season. She said Evelyn was filling her head with going back to school."

"Look, Donny. Whatever your relationship is with Stacie is none of my business. That's up to the two of you to figure out." He started walking toward the garage.

When they got there, Donny said, "That's what I told Stacie. But no, she has to talk to all her girlfriends about what's best for her. For us. Things are working fine."

"Are they?"

Donny frowned. "Huh?"

"Are they fine? Because it seems to me your woman isn't happy."

Donny looked down at his shoes. "Okay, maybe she isn't."

"Then figure out a way to make it work so that you're both happy. It isn't always just about you and what you need. Sometimes you have to meet your lady halfway."

"She wants to finish school. I want her with me. She can do school during the times I'm not racing."

"Which is what? Two months out of the year? Not very practical for her, is it?"

Donny stared at the ground.

"Do you want her with you because you'll miss her, or because you're afraid if she's not with you all the time she'll find someone else?"

Gray caught the worried expression on Donny's face.

"I'm not the sharpest tool in the shed, you know," Donny said. "I barely got out of high school. And Stacie—God, that girl is smart. Sometimes I don't know what she's doing with someone like me."

"She's here, isn't she?"

"Yeah."

"Maybe she loves you, though God only knows why. You're a dick sometimes, you drink and party too much, and your head is up your ass more often than not. But she does care about you and she sacrifices a lot for you. Maybe you should consider doing the same thing for her. If you love her."

He lifted his chin, clearly pissed off. "I do."

"Then trust her. That's what love is built on, Donny. Without it, you're toast and so is your relationship."

Donny clamped his lips together as they walked, then finally nodded. "You know what? You're right. If I don't start trusting in her—in us—I'm gonna lose her. I can already feel her slipping through my fingers."

"Then do something about it. You worrying about your girl makes you lose focus on racing, and that's where I need your attention to be. Understood?"

Donny gave him a quick nod. "Got it, boss."

Gray slapped Donny on the arm. "Good talk. Now let's figure out what's going on with your engine. I heard something I didn't like during your practice run today."

EVELYN HOVERED NEAR THE ENTRANCE TO THE GArage, having overheard Gray's conversation with Donny.

Stacie had taken off for her trailer, claiming she had some laundry to do, followed by studying. Since Evelyn didn't have access to Gray's trailer, and since she needed access to Gray, she figured the only thing she could do was suck it up and talk to him, much as she didn't want to.

But then she overheard him giving Donny advice on his relationship with Stacie, and good advice at that, which surprised her.

It seemed like he was always surprising her, either in good ways or bad. The man was utterly unpredictable, which wasn't a good thing at all. She liked the people she worked with to be dependable in their actions and responses. Gray seemed like a wild card to her, and she couldn't trust what he'd do or say.

At least in politics she knew all the players. This was Gray Preston, an unknown, who lived in a world she had been thrust into and was utterly unfamiliar with. It was already clear he was nothing like his father, who was a known quantity. Mitchell Preston had played the political game for years. He knew the score, and so did Evelyn.

Gray wasn't going to play the game her way. He was already angry with her for trying to help out his friend. Favors were done all the time in Washington. Sometimes they came with a price tag. The one she'd offered to do for Miranda last night had been offered without strings. Because Gray didn't know her, he just assumed she'd want something in return. Or that his father would.

If he'd bothered to ask her, she could have told him that. But no, he'd decided to act like an arrogant douchebag and make assumptions without knowledge, so she'd be damned if she was going to be nice to him.

Unfortunately, she did still have to do her job. Which right now consisted of leaning against the wall of the garage and watching his very fine ass as he bent over the hood of his race car, deep in conversation with his crew chief and several members of his team. Whether he knew she was there or not, she had no idea, nor did she care. She pulled her phone out of her pocket and answered a few emails. After a while, someone on the team must have noticed her, because they brought her a folding chair. She smiled her thanks and took a seat inside the garage, where it was shady and much cooler than it was outside.

Admittedly, watching hot guys work on even hotter cars wasn't a bad way to pass the time. And since it was clear Gray wasn't going to talk to her right now, it wasn't a bad gig. Better than running around after senators and representatives and fetching coffee and sending emails and composing letters. She was so used to the fast pace of life in D.C., this was like watching grass grow, especially since she knew absolutely zip about automobiles and racing. It would help her to gain an understanding of what the fans found so exhilarating about this sport so she'd be able to integrate Gray's passion for the sport with the upcoming election. Again, it would be fruitless to ask Gray. He hadn't once looked her way or acknowledged her at all.

She supposed she could try, though. She'd never been a coward and she wasn't going to be one now. She stood and headed over to the car, inching ever closer, wincing a bit as the sound of some tool she was unfamiliar with howled in a piercing, staccato beat from underneath the vehicle.

She hovered close and eavesdropped on their conversation, all of which went right over her head. Manifolds and oil pressure and gauges and gear boxes. They might as well be speaking a foreign language—one that she didn't speak, anyway.

Gray finally lifted his head, a streak of dark grease across his jaw, which only enhanced his rugged good looks. His crew chief, Ian, stepped away, allowing her to draw closer.

"What are you working on?" she asked.

He frowned. "The car, obviously."

Oh, he was still in a mood. "Obviously. I was wondering if you'd teach me a bit about it."

"Not now, Evelyn. Kind of busy here."

"Can I just hang out and watch, then?"

"You're in the way."

His tone was sharp. Rude. And she grabbed a clue in a hurry.

"Certainly. Of course. Some other time, then. I'm sorry to have disturbed you." With a nod to Ian, she moved away, clearly dismissed.

He'd irritated the hell out of her last night, making untrue accusations about her. She could brush that aside so they could work together. Gray, on the other hand, held a grudge.

Fine. She left the garage and wandered, debating whether or not to call it a day and head to her hotel since she was getting nowhere by hovering. He'd talk to her when he was ready, and he evidently wasn't ready today. And she refused to bother Stacie when she needed to be studying.

So when she saw one of the drivers, still in his fire suit, leaving the track area, she decided maybe she could gain her auto racing education in another way.

She smiled and approached him. "Excuse me."

He stopped and his lips curled in a genuine smile. "Hi there. You're with Gray Preston, aren't you?"

She was about to explain, but if it got her an audience with the guy, why bother? "Yes, I am. I'm Evelyn Hill."

He shook her hand. "Calvin McClusky. I drive the number twelve Ford."

"Nice to meet you, Mr. McClusky."

"You can call me Cal. All my close friends do."

He was totally hitting on her. Great-looking guy. Tall, looked well built under that fire suit, and with serious blue eyes, spiky dark blond hair, and the kind of killer smile that she was certain divested many a woman of her panties.

"Okay, Cal. Are you busy right now?"

"Just drove my practice run and now I'm heading to my garage."

"Perfect. Would you mind if I tagged along?"

"Not at all, darlin'. Come on."

Cal had a very southern accent that Evelyn found quite appealing. No wonder these guys had so many groupies. All that charm.

Except, Gray, of course, who she didn't find charming in the least, especially not today.

Cal introduced her to his crew, who were all as friendly as he was.

"So, you're Gray's new girl?" Cal asked as he climbed out of his fire suit, revealing a body that should be declared illegal. Wide shoulders, lean waist, and thighs that had obviously spent some time in the gym.

"I'm nobody's girl. But yes, Gray and I have been spending some time together."

Cal arched a brow. "Oh, a smart woman. Just my type. Can I get you something to drink?" he asked as he headed over to a refrigerator in the garage.

"A water would be great, if you have one."

He pulled out a water for her and an energy drink for himself, then came back to stand in front of her.

"Thank you. So what do you do with your car after your practice run?" she asked, unscrewing the top of the water to take a couple sips.

"We go over it, make sure the laps didn't do any damage, and make sure it's still running prime. We download the data we gathered from the laps we ran and check the car over. Next step tomorrow is qualifying. That's when you want the car at its best, so this is our last chance to fix anything."

"So if there are any mechanical problems or engine problems, you can still fix them."

"Right."

He let her lean over the quarter panel and look inside the car as he pointed out various parts of the engine and explained their function. Since Evelyn had a near eidetic memory, this was proving to be so useful. Plus, Cal was easy, and not just on the eyes. There was a definite plus in that she didn't work for his father. There was no end goal in sight other than to enjoy his company. And he was definitely enjoyable.

After a while, he led her away from the car. "So, are you and Gray in some kind of relationship?"

"No, we're not."

"Which means you'd be free to go out with me."

Now that was a sticky situation. "Actually, I'm here to work."

"For Gray."

"Sort of."

"So you're still free to go out with me." He gave her the kind of easygoing smile that would be nearly impossible to resist, if she were looking for a hot guy to spend an evening with. Which she wasn't.

"I'm sorry, I really can't." She laid her hand on his arm. "But if I was going to go out with someone, Cal, it would definitely be you."

He smiled at her, so he took the rejection well. "I guess I'll take that as a decent enough consolation."

She laughed. "I hope so. And I do appreciate the offer. Believe me, today was the perfect day to receive it."

"Rough one?"

"Yes. So thank you."

"What the hell are you doing, Evelyn?"

She spun around to see Gray barreling down on them. As was his typical demeanor since last night, he looked angry. She'd had just about enough of him being angry for no reason, so she gave him a laid-back stare and didn't move. There was no reason for her to feel guilty for spending time with Cal. She might work for his father, but she didn't work for him. He didn't own her.

"As a matter of fact, I was spending time with Cal."

Gray gave Cal what could only be described as a death glare, the kind she'd seen many times when two political opponents faced off. "What are you doing with Evelyn?"

"I was giving her some car lessons."

"Why?"

Evelyn decided she could handle this. "Because I asked him and he was gracious enough to give me some of his time, something you couldn't be bothered with today."

Cal crossed his arms and smirked at Gray.

"I was goddamn busy today."

"Only takes a few minutes to explain the physical and mechanical aspects of your race car, Gray," Cal said. "Especially to a smart woman like Evelyn. What bug crawled up your ass today?"

"None of your fucking business, McClusky. Let's go, Evelyn."

He was treating her like she was his property, and she didn't like it. Instead, she turned her back to Gray and faced Cal. "I've changed my mind. I'd love to go out with you tonight, Cal."

Cal grinned. "Great. Are you staying nearby?"

"Yes." She gave him her hotel information and her cell phone number, feeling Gray's gaze burn into her the entire time.

"I'll pick you up at seven?" Cal asked.

"Sounds perfect. Thank you again for the tour today. I really appreciate it."

"Anytime. See you tonight, darlin'."

With a wink to Gray, Cal walked off, leaving her alone with Gray.

"You can't really mean to go out with him."

"Last time I checked, I'm over the age of twenty-one and you are not related to me. In fact, this is the first time today you've even spoken to me. Besides, you made it pretty clear last night you want nothing to do with me, so butt out of my personal life." She pivoted and headed toward the parking lot, knowing she was acting like a hurt girlfriend, but these were her emotions and she was going with it.

Gray followed, his long strides easily staying in step with her short, angry ones. "Don't trust him. He may seem like a nice guy, but he's got issues."

And Gray didn't? She waved her hand in dismissal at him. "I think I can handle myself just fine."

When she got to her car, she unlocked her door and started to open it. Gray shut it and leaned against it, commandeering her attention. "I'm serious about Cal McClusky, Evelyn. His only goal is to win, and he knows there's something going on between you and me. That's the only reason he wants to go out with you."

Could he be more insulting? "So you're saying I have nothing to offer a man?"

He rolled his eyes. "That's not what I said at all."

"Get out of my way, Gray. And stay out of my personal life."

Anger flared in his eyes. "Why? You're in mine. Shouldn't that give me the same right to be in yours?"

"No. Now move."

He hesitated, then took a step back. She slid in her seat, started the car, and drove off, a vision of Gray standing in the parking lot firmly planted in her rearview mirror.

NINE

THIS HAD BEEN SUCH A STUPID IDEA. SHE WAS ABOUT as interested in going out with Cal McClusky tonight as she was in switching political affiliations. But she'd had to be stubborn and show Gray that he couldn't boss her around.

Since when did she get so reactive? She'd always been so calm and unruffled, the perfect demeanor for a career in politics. A few days around Gray Preston and she was acting like a fourteen-year-old.

And now she was going out on a date with a guy she wasn't even attracted to. A nice enough guy, but still, a man she normally would have given a polite no to. In fact, she had said no, until Gray had gone all caveman on her and started issuing commands, as if she were some stuffing-brained Barbie Doll. That had set her off, and now here she stood, in front of her closet, wondering what the hell she was going to wear, when instead she could be curled up in bed reading her favorite Maya Banks romance, or unwinding by watching reality TV, her guiltiest pleasure. Or she could go over her boss's agenda for the next month. You know, performing the functions of her damn job like she should be doing.

Ugh.

She chose a basic black dress with a covered neckline and short sleeves, finishing off the outfit with a bland pair of black pumps. Conservative, not sexy, and would in no way lead Cal to believe she was giving him any signals. In fact, it was the perfect outfit for attending a funeral, or an appearance on the congressional floor.

What a boring outfit. She wouldn't be caught dead wearing this thing on a date—not typically, anyway.

The poor guy. He'd been so nice to her, too.

When he knocked on her hotel room door, she grabbed her purse and her phone, noting the time.

He was punctual, too. She pasted on a smile. "Cal."

"Evelyn."

He wore jeans, a button-down shirt, boots, and a cowboy hat. Even in her funeral dress, she was overdressed.

"Am I overdressed?"

"No. You look gorgeous."

He had to be lying. She looked like a freakin' pilgrim.

He held out his arm for her. She shut the door and he led her toward his car, which was a pickup truck, so he had to help her climb into that, too.

"Sorry. I trailer it and bring it everywhere we go. It's my favorite ride."

"It's no problem," she said as she buckled up her seat belt, then held on when he fired up the engine, which sounded as loud and rumbly as a race car.

"Sweet, huh?" he asked with a grin.

She offered another benign smile. "You bet."

Dinner was at some swanky steakhouse, dark and private. He seemed to know the people there, because they led him to a private, dark corner booth. The waitress set him up with a beer and whiskey as soon as they were seated.

Evelyn felt the beginnings of a headache in her temples, so she ordered an iced tea.

"Sure you don't want anything stronger, honey?"

"No, the tea is fine for me."

"Maybe after dinner, then. I thought we'd hit a club."

Oh. Joy. "So, tell me about your race career."

He leaned back and puffed up his chest. "Won the championship three years ago. Third in the standings right now, so it's only a matter of time before I win it again this year."

"That's great. I'm sure a lot of that is having a good race car and a great team behind you."

The waitress came over with menus, which Cal pushed to the side. "You might as well bring me another round, honey. It's been a long day. And keep 'em comin', too." The waitress nodded and Cal downed his beer in about four quick swallows, then focused his attention back on Evelyn.

"A good team is great and all that, but a lot of my success comes from having a damn good driver behind the wheel. I didn't get where I am by not knowing what the hell I'm doing. I've worked my ass off the past five years, ever since I got to drive in the big series. Winning the championship three years ago has given me a taste of what that's like. I want it again."

She heard this over and over again in politics. Winning was everything. The competitive spirit fired the blood of so many politicians, so this wasn't new to her. "Drive and ambition will take you a long way."

The waitress sat Cal's second beer down in front of him, along with the shot. He downed the shot first, then took two quick gulps of beer. "Like I said honey, keep 'em comin'. It was hot out there today." He gave the waitress a wink and she scurried off.

Evelyn arched a brow and made a point of opening her menu. "Would you like to order dinner?"

"Not just yet, darlin'." He tipped his beer to his lips and took a couple more long swallows, emptying it.

Uh, wow. She took a sip of tea.

"So where was I?"

Talking about himself, mostly. Who *was* this guy? He'd been so nice to her that afternoon, so charming and such a gentleman. All that evaporated as he spent the next hour not only drinking heavily, but regaling her with stories of his superb driving ability, and his entire life story, not once asking her anything about herself. For all he cared, she could have been a stranger he'd picked up on the side of the road and brought along to dinner. Not that there was any dinner on the horizon for that matter, either. She was starving and about to fling herself on the table closest to them just to steal a slice of their bread.

After about two and a half hours, Cal was three sheets to the wind, Evelyn was starving, and it was clear there was going to be no dinner. He was slurring every other word and she was certain if she asked him her name, he'd have no clue who she was.

The waitress seemed familiar with him, because she patiently came back to see if Cal wanted a refill.

Hunkered back in the booth and barely able to keep himself upright, he nodded yes.

"I think he's had enough," Evelyn said. "I'll take a steak salad to go, with a lot of bread on the side. And please bring the check."

The waitress gave her a knowing smile. "Yes, ma'am."

"Hey, the party's just gettin' shtarted, honey," Cal said, his eyelids drooping as he slunk back against the booth. "Let's go danshing."

"Honey," she said, exaggerating the endearment. "Your party is over for the night."

"Are you sure? I could show you shuch a good time." He made a valiant try at winking, though he used both of his eyes.

She'd wager a month's salary he couldn't get it up right now if she stripped naked and danced on the table.

She paid the bill and a couple of the waiters helped her hoist Cal into the passenger side of his truck. She fired up the vibrating tank and drove it back to the track, grateful she'd paid attention to where they were going when they made their way to the restaurant.

Getting him into the truck had been easy, since she'd had help. Getting him out might be more difficult. Though she wasn't at all adverse to leaving him in his truck to sleep it off tonight. Dickhead.

She parked the truck and looked over at him. "Cal."

He was slumped over in the seat and snoring. She shoved at him. "Cal."

He snorted once, then fell over against the window and continued snoring.

Rolling her eyes, she gave up, slid out of the truck, and shut the door, figuring someone must be out and about who could help her get the moron out of the truck and into his trailer.

She walked to the end of the parking lot and saw a dark shape coming toward her. Her stomach twisted in knots when she realized who it was.

Gray.

Shit.

GRAY'S BROWS KNIT WHEN HE SAW EVELYN WALKING alone from Cal's truck. He'd hated that she was going out with that asshole tonight, knowing Cal's reputation. He quickened his step until he met her halfway.

"Are you all right?"

"I'm fine. Cal's not, though. Can you help me?"

He looked over his shoulder at the truck. "What's wrong with Cal?"

"Drunk and passed out."

That didn't surprise him. Cal's drinking problem wasn't a big secret. "What happened?"

She told him about dinner—or their lack of dinner.

"Leave him," Gray said.

"I can't just leave him in there."

"Sure you can. I'll call his crew chief and he and the guys can pull him out of the truck and shove him in his trailer. I'm sure as hell not doing it."

"Well, hang on. I have food in there. I sat through almost three hours of his droning on and drinking. I'm starving."

"I'll walk with you."

She gave a quick nod and he walked with her to Cal's truck.

"Give me his keys. I'll toss them in the truck and grab your food." He opened the door and took a look at Cal, wishing he could give the douchebag a swift kick in the nuts for treating Evelyn this way, but since she was right there, he figured that wouldn't be a good idea. Instead, he grabbed her bag of food and shut the door.

Then he pulled out his phone and called Fred, Cal's crew chief, explaining Cal's current predicament. After a few well-deserved expletives, Fred said they'd be out in a few to retrieve Cal and put him to bed.

He turned to Evelyn. "They'll come get him."

"Thank you." She looked around. "I guess I need a ride back to my hotel."

"I'll take you." He looked at her bag. "What have you got in there?"

"Steak salad."

"Come on back to my trailer and eat first. You must be hungry."

"Beyond hungry."

He motioned with his head. "Come on. I've got pop in the trailer."

She hesitated for a second, then nodded. "Okay. Thank you."

He didn't know why he invited her to come back with him, other than he felt bad for the way Cal had behaved with her, and for the way he had acted today. He'd been angry about last night, but that didn't give him the right to treat a woman the way he'd treated her today. He'd shut her out, and given Cal the opening to pounce. He took responsibility for that. There were nice guys in his sport, and the opportunistic type. Cal was the latter, and it irritated him that Evelyn had to spend the evening with a drunken piece of shit like Cal.

Of course, it had been Evelyn's choice to go out with Cal, but he knew she'd done it just to piss him off.

It *had* pissed him off. He didn't like admitting that, because it meant she mattered to him. And she didn't matter to him. He hardly knew her, and it wasn't like they were dating. He might have kissed her once, but other than that they were nothing to each other. She worked for his father and they were supposed to spend time together. He was still trying to figure out how they were supposed to handle that.

In the meantime, maybe he'd have to learn to temper his anger over stuff about his dad and not jump all over her.

They entered his trailer and he got her a drink. She slid into the booth and opened her bag, dragging out a salad and some bread.

"Did you eat?" she asked. "I have plenty here."

"I ate earlier. Go ahead."

She dove into her food and he could tell she was hungry, which only served to make him angrier with Cal. He refilled his drink and took a seat across from her.

"Cal has a drinking problem."

She took a few bites of salad and then a sip of her drink. "No kidding. That was obvious after his eighth beer and fourth shot of whiskey."

"The bad thing is, he's an awesome driver. When he's sober, he's one of the best out there. He just can't lay off the alcohol. It's been a problem for a while now. The year after he won the championship, it went to his head. Big time. He thought he was hot shit, really bought into all the hype and the media bullshit. Women flocking to him, fans all over him, it messed him up. He ended up losing a really great wife who couldn't handle his cheating."

Evelyn paused and looked at him. "I'm sorry to hear that. He was so nice to me earlier today."

"Like I said, when he's sober, he can be a really nice guy, but then it's like there's this switch inside him, and when it gets flipped, he turns into someone completely different."

She bit into a slice of bread. "Yeah. An asshole."

"Exactly."

After she finished her food, she took a long swallow of soda. "I'm sorry about Cal. I see a lot of parallels to that in Washington. Nice people get elected, their heads filled with all the great things they think they can do. Then all that changes when they come to Washington. All that power corrupting and all."

He shrugged. "Some people are weak. They can't handle fame and fortune and being handed things. You go from nothing one day to having a staff of people asking what they can do for you the next. They don't know what to do with it and it affects them negatively. Their egos explode."

"I agree."

He wanted to throw his father into that mix, but they were having a good conversation right now and he didn't want to fuck it up.

"Has anyone talked to Cal about rehab?" Evelyn asked.

He let out a laugh. "Yeah. Tons of people, from his ex-wife to his crew chief to the head of the racing division. He won't listen. And he never drinks when he's racing, he's never late for a practice or a qualifying or a race. He's never had a DUI, so they can't sanction him. When he goes out drinking, he tips the places well. And he does a lot of his famous partying in his trailer, surrounded by people he trusts. His fans don't know about it because he keeps it on the down low."

It wasn't very down low tonight. She wondered how many of his fans were at the restaurant. It was dark and private and there weren't very many people there. Maybe that's why he brought her there, because he liked the anonymity of the place.

She nodded. "He has to want to help himself anyway. Until he does, there's really nothing you can do."

"The other drivers worry, though. Everybody's afraid that someday he's going to show up drunk for a race and hurt himself—or one of us. Then all hell is going to break loose."

"God, I hope that doesn't happen."

"Me, too. It'll end his career. Or one of ours."

They both went silent then, and Gray knew this was the moment he needed to man up and say something about last night.

"I'm sorry."

She lifted her gaze to his. "About what?"

"Last night. About jumping all over you about helping out Miranda. I shouldn't have done that."

"You're sensitive about anything having to do with your father. I understand that. Instead of talking it out with you, I reacted negatively. I'm sorry, too."

She'd let him off the hook a lot easier than he deserved.

"I'm sorry about today, too. You wanted to learn about the cars and I was a dick about it."

"Yes, you were. But the whole thing with Cal was my doing."

"To make me mad, I know. You obviously aren't attracted to him."

She crossed her arms. "And how do you know that?"

He nodded toward her outfit. "Look at what you're wearing."

"Hey. What's wrong with my dress?"

"You look like you just stepped off the *Mayflower*. No woman who wants to impress a guy would wear a dress like that."

She laughed, obviously not insulted. "Okay, fine. You've got me there. So, we'll start over?"

He smiled at her. "Yeah. We'll start over."

Her lips lifted too, making his gaze gravitate to them and stay there. He remembered last night and what it felt like to kiss her. He wanted to kiss her again, to take up where they left off. She'd felt good against him, her body molded to his, pliant and welcoming. He wondered what would have happened if they'd been someplace more private.

Like here.

He lifted his gaze to her eyes, saw the desire and wariness mixed there. Maybe Evelyn was remembering the same thing.

She should be wary. The two of them together wasn't a good thing.

He took that back. Getting her in his bed would be a great thing, followed by the morning after, which would mean he'd still have to see her, work with her, and be reminded that she worked for his father. It would be a hell of a mess, which was why, despite her killer body and sexy mouth, he wasn't going to take her to bed.

"I should go." She stood, and despite that ugly-as-hell dress and the even worse shoes she wore, she looked as sexy tonight as she had last night. He didn't think it had anything to do with the attire. Had to be the woman.

His dick totally agreed, because it twitched, still obviously thinking of kissing her and touching her last night. And his dick had a mind of its own. "You could stay for a while."

She cocked a brow. "And do what? I left my laptop in my hotel room. We can't work."

Good. He liked the idea of not working, of not thinking of her as being part of his father's life. He wanted to think of her as a desirable woman he could take to bed.

He took a step closer, inhaling her scent. Something clean and sweet. Not perfume, though. "There are other things to do besides work, Evelyn."

"I'm pretty sure you made it clear last night you wanted nothing to do with me on a personal level."

She'd worn her hair pulled back. He reached behind her and easily unclipped it, then spread her hair over her shoulders. "I was mad last night."

She tilted her head back, meeting his gaze. Her breathing was hard and fast. "So was I."

"You mad now?"

"No."

"Good." He slid his hand around the nape of her neck, closed what little distance there was between them, and did what he'd been dying to do—angry or not—all goddamn day long.

He kissed her.

TEN

EVELYN'S BREATH CAUGHT AT THE FIRST TOUCH OF Gray's lips to hers.

A thousand reasons why this was a colossally bad idea ran through her mind, but then she leaned against a wall of hard male muscle, and all those reasons flitted right out of her head. All she could think about was the fullness of his lips, the way he brushed them back and forth against hers, and then his tongue invaded her mouth, sliding against hers. Her belly tumbled, her legs trembled, and she was lost.

She laid a hand on his well-toned abs, wound one into his hair and clenched a handful. He groaned against her mouth, and she let out a moan. When he cupped her butt to draw her closer, she knew she was a goner. Whatever objection she thought she might make wasn't going to happen. She was in this to the finish line tonight. Her clit tingled with need, her breasts felt swollen and heavy, and all she needed to know was how fast they were going to get to the bedroom, because she wanted to be naked and have Gray inside her as soon as humanly possible.

She slipped her hand between them and reached for the very hard part of him nestling against her hip, stopping short when Gray grabbed her wrist.

He looked down at her. "Whoa. In a hurry?"

"Actually, yes. Shall we move this to the bedroom?"

His gaze burned hot, but he shook his head. "I've got a better idea. Let's slow this down a little."

Oh, God. He was going to tell her he changed his mind. How embarrassing. He was right. This was a really bad idea. Where had her common sense gone? She knew where it had gone—somewhere between her legs.

Except Gray slid his hands down her sides, a slow trek that ended at her hips. And when he gathered her dress in his hands and began to raise it, her hem rising over her thighs, she looked down, then up at him, confusion reigning.

He held the material of her dress bunched in his hands, his breathing heavy, that hot, panty-melting look doing nothing to cool her libido.

She thought he was stopping things. This most definitely didn't appear to be a thudding halt. And when he grabbed her butt and lifted her, he said, "Wrap your legs around me."

Maybe they were heading to the bedroom after all. She laid her hands on his shoulders and wrapped her legs around his hips as he carried her toward the bedroom.

But he stopped in the kitchen and placed her on his countertop. *Oh, my.*

She'd always been a strictly bedroom type of woman. But as Gray pulled her shoes off, then pushed her dress over her hips, she was beginning to see the benefits of out-of-bed experiences. This was decadent, air from the vent of the air conditioner pouring down over them as he reached for her panties. And thank God she'd worn something other than random white ones.

"These black lacy things are sexy," he said as he drew them down her legs. "You wear them for Cal?"

"There wasn't a chance in hell that Cal McClusky was going to see my underwear tonight."

He gave her a wicked, half smile as he looked up at her. "Good to know. Is that why you wore this hideous dress?"

"Hey. It's not that bad."

"Yeah, it is. It's like a dress a nun would wear. You wore it to be sexless, didn't you?"

She shrugged. "Maybe."

"You couldn't be sexless if you wore a dress made out of porcupine quills, Evelyn." He smoothed his hands up her legs, then circled her inner thighs with his thumbs. "Because you are one hot woman, and no matter what you wear, you outshine it."

Oh, he was smooth, and said all the right things. She melted under his questing fingers.

He tipped his gaze up to meet hers. "But underneath? This underwear is sexy as hell. Does the bra match?"

She was finding it hard to breathe with him touching her like that. "Yes."

"Let's have a look."

As if he undressed women every day—and for all she knew, maybe he did—he reached behind her and deftly drew her zipper down, then raised her dress over her head. He tossed it on the chair by the table, then took a step back.

"Wow. Yeah, I like that bra. Let's take it off."

The clasp was on the front. Gray, apparently being a master of all things women wore, seemed to instinctively know that. With two fingers he flicked it and it came apart for him. Evelyn tried not to think about how many women he'd undressed before in this very trailer, because tonight he was only undressing her.

He drew the cups aside and she wriggled out of the bra, handing it to him so he could add it to her pile of clothing.

She swallowed, her throat going dry as he stared at her. She had a decent body—nice-sized breasts and she worked out—but whenever she had sex, they usually just got right to it. She wasn't used to being looked at for as long as Gray looked at her. When he laid his hands on her thighs, she trembled.

"Cold? Nervous?"

"Maybe a little nervous."

He raised a brow. "Why?"

"Well, first, you're still dressed and I'm naked. And second, you're staring at me."

He drew his sleeveless shirt off, baring his chest. And wow, what a chest, exactly as she imagined. Well sculpted, with an amazing set of abs. She'd really like to map his stomach with her tongue.

He reached for the button of his jeans. "I'm staring at you because you have a beautiful body, Evelyn."

She took a deep breath, not knowing what to say in response to that. And then she lost all thought because he dropped his jeans to the floor.

He'd gone commando, and oh, now that he was naked? Those fire suits didn't do him justice. And with a very thick erection to add to that amazing body?

Perfection.

"You're hot," she blurted, then realized she'd said it out loud.

He laughed. "Well, thank you," he said, moving from between her legs to cup her neck between his hands. "I think you're hot, too."

Her pulse beat wildly against his hand as he took her mouth in a kiss that wasn't at all as gentle as his first kiss had been. This one was filled with need and passion, fueling the fire that had begun the first moment she'd laid eyes on him.

He kissed her jaw, then dragged his tongue across her throat. Her eyes closed, Evelyn held on to his shoulders, her pussy damp with desire as he grabbed her earlobe with his teeth and tugged before circling it with his tongue.

"I'd like to know what else you can do with that magical tongue of yours."

He lifted his head and looked at her. "I can lick your pussy until you scream."

She raised her chin. "I do not scream."

He arched a brow. "Wanna bet?"

She let out a resigned sigh. "I hate to disappoint you, but I tend to be a little on the . . . reserved side."

"Is that right? You, the one who just asked me what I can do with my tongue? That doesn't sound reserved."

"Not that way. I mean I'm quiet. It's become a necessity because of the condo I live in. Very thin walls."

"So, you get a lot of sex in this condo."

"No. Not at all. Very little sex, in fact. I have very old neighbors and they . . . complained once."

"About how loud you were?"

She felt the blush heat her cheeks. "Yes."

"I like loud."

"I've just about trained it out of me."

"We're isolated here. There's nobody nearby. You can scream your fucking head off and trust me, no one will hear you."

"That sounds like an ad for a serial killer movie."

He laughed. "Can you die from a really great orgasm?"

"I don't know. Why don't you give it a shot?"

He gave her a look that made her toes curl, then spread her legs.

"I can guarantee you I can't come sitting on your kitchen counter."

He laid a palm on said counter. "Really. And why is that?"

She owed it to him to be honest. Might as well not have him waste his time. "I do enjoy sex. It's just that . . . I have trouble coming unless I'm in certain positions."

"Really. Who told you that?"

"No one. It's my body. I'm difficult. So I don't want you to work so hard when if you just lay me on the bed in a certain position, it'll happen much easier for me."

He shook his head. "All these *don'ts* and *can'ts*. I think you should just relax and enjoy it, no matter where it takes place."

"I didn't say I wouldn't enjoy it, Gray. Just that I wouldn't be able to come."

He bent, kissed her, framing her face with his hands, his tongue diving in so deeply, his hand wrapping around her and pulling her close against him and kissing her so long she forgot all about where she was. He palmed her breast, his thumb lazily grazing a nipple until she thought she'd die from the sheer pleasure of it. And when he released her, he bent her backward and put his mouth on her nipple, taking it between his lips to nibble and suck until her pussy throbbed.

He laid her down on the counter and teased her other nipple. She gave up being uncomfortable or worrying about heading to the bedroom. They'd get there in time, and then maybe she could instruct him on the proper technique to make her—

Oh. He palmed her sex and sucked her nipple, and now he swept his hand back and forth over the most sensitive part of her. And when he lifted one of her legs and laid it over his shoulder, she knew then it wouldn't happen for her. Not in this position.

Except he kissed his way down her ribs, taking his damn sweet time about mapping her body with his tongue. She lifted onto her elbows, watching as he made his way south, dipping his tongue into her belly button. He rubbed his face across the hairs at the top of her sex, delving ever lower, his hand gliding across her the whole time, teasing her, making her wet, making her throb with need.

He slid his hand under her butt and raised her. And then he put his mouth on her, and oh, it was so good, his tongue warm and wet and so damned masterful. He knew where to lick her, and when he added a finger inside her, she quivered, tensing with need and anticipation.

He lifted his head. "Lie down, Evelyn. You don't have to control this. Relax and enjoy it."

She realized she was tense. All over. She rested her head on the counter and he put his mouth on her again, lazily lapping at her pussy like he'd go at it all night. She finally let go, realizing she had nothing to prove. She'd already told him she couldn't, but the odd thing was, she could. She might. And as he worked her over with his magnificent tongue, she realized, oh, God, she was going to.

"Gray," she murmured, gripping his forearm with her hand.

Of course, he didn't answer her. He was too busy working magic on her sex, turning her world upside down, and dragging her right to the edge of reason.

This couldn't be happening, not on his kitchen counter. Not in this position. But he knew just where, and just how, and he took his time, finding the spots that gave her the greatest pleasure. And when he hit them, tuned in to her cries and moans, he stayed there, driving his tongue and his fingers right to that spot until she arched, wrapping her leg around his head to hold him there while she hovered so close. So damn close she shook from the sheer pleasure of it.

He lifted his head, replacing his mouth with stroking fingers. "Let go, Evelyn. Let me hear you."

She closed her eyes and when she felt the warm wetness of his tongue again, she flew.

And she cried out, remembering that she wasn't in her condo, that she was free to scream out in release.

Her orgasm was a shock of intense pleasure, so surprising she could only buck against him while wave after wave blasted through her until she was so spent she lay there, unable to move.

Gray finally hovered above her, kissing her with soft brushes of his lips over hers. She cupped her hand over the nape of his neck, feeling languid and satiated for the first time in so long.

She smiled up at him. "Okay, so about all that stuff I said? I might have been wrong. You're very good at what you do."

"You have an amazingly responsive body, Evelyn. You just need to relax."

"Apparently."

"Also, you taste really good."

She shuddered, and he scooped her off the counter into his arms and carried her into his bedroom.

When he placed her onto his bed, she kneeled. "Now it's my turn to touch you." She reached for his cock, anxious to get her hands on him. "To taste you."

GRAY HAD TO HOLD HIMSELF IN CHECK AS HE LOOKED at Evelyn, naked and disheveled on his bed. The way she had moved under his mouth with such wild joy had nearly undone him.

He laid his hand over hers. "Much as I'd like that, it's been a while for me. You put your mouth on me and this is going to be over with in a hurry."

She brushed his hand aside. "I don't mind that. Then we'll wait a bit and go for round two."

Evelyn pushed him down on the bed. Granted, he only went because he wanted to, but he'd let her have her way, this time. And frankly, all he'd been thinking about lately was her mouth. He wanted it on his cock.

Clothed, she was beautiful. Naked, she was a knockout, with full breasts, slim hips, and the longest damn legs he couldn't wait to have wrapped around him when he was inside her.

But right now, she was on top of him, kissing him, and he didn't mind that part at all, because her breasts brushed against his chest. He reached for her breasts, cupping them to tease her nipples, listening to her breath rush in as he played with the hardened buds.

She had sensitive nipples, and despite what she thought, she could definitely come, and pretty damned easily, too. He didn't know what kind of notions she had about sex, but he'd bet it had a lot to do with her provincial neighbors and some assholes in her past who hadn't known how to take their time in pleasuring her. Or maybe she didn't have a lot of practice in pleasuring herself. Maybe they could work on that together.

The thought of watching her touch herself made his balls tighten.

When she pulled back and kissed her way down his stomach, he filed that thought away for some other time.

Because there'd definitely be another time. Once wouldn't be enough with Evelyn. He should send a thank-you note to Cal Mc-Clusky for being such a fuckhead tonight. Without that, she wouldn't be here with him right now, skimming her hand over his abs, making his stomach tighten as she got within an inch of his dick.

And when she wrapped her hand around his length, he arched into her.

She looked at him and smiled, then began to stroke him.

"I like that," he said, lifting his hips to help her as she wound her hands around him. "I'll like it even more when you suck me."

She wound her hair around, pulling it over her shoulder out of the way. "And I like you telling me what turns you on."

She got up on her knees, her lips bobbing over his cock. She licked her lips and his cock lurched upward.

"You know what turns me on, Evelyn?"

She paused, turned to look at him. "What?"

"You. Naked you. Clothed you. Your mouth. Your legs. The way you talk. Arguing with you. Your smile. Every fucking thing about you turns me on."

Her lips curved, then she turned and took his cock in her mouth. He shuddered as her wet, warm lips surrounded him.

"Fuck. Yes, that's good. Take it deep."

She grabbed the base of his cock and fed it into her mouth, taking him inch by inch until it disappeared, then released him, his dick wet with her saliva. Then she took him again. And again. She snaked her tongue around him, using suction to draw him deep into her hot, sweet mouth until he was ready to explode. When she reached down and gave a gentle squeeze of his balls, he felt the impending release.

He reached for her hair and let it fall over his thighs like a silken waterfall. "I'm going to come, Evelyn. You ready for it?"

She only hummed against his cock, then drew him deep again, this time only letting go partway before clenching his shaft between her tongue and the roof of her mouth. He pumped into her, letting go with a loud groan as he released into her waiting mouth.

Evelyn held on to him as he bucked and shuddered through his release until he was spent. Only then did she let go and crawl up his body to lay her head on his shoulder.

It took Gray a while to catch his breath.

"I felt that one all the way through my spine," he said.

"You're welcome." She splayed her hand on his chest. "Your heart is beating fast."

"It was a damn good orgasm." He tipped her chin back and kissed her, then rolled her onto her back and deepened the kiss.

He wouldn't get enough of her tonight. He already knew that.

It was going to be a long night.

ELEVEN

EVELYN HAD EXPECTED GRAY WOULD NEED SOME RE-
covery time. But five minutes of some very heavy kissing and his
erection was back.

The man was a machine.

No, she took that back. No machine could kiss her like this,
could make her wet like this, could make her crave the kind of intimacy she craved when she was with Gray.

She'd had some pretty darn good sexual encounters in her past,
but she'd never had a night of marathon sex.

Not that they'd actually had sex yet. She had a feeling she wasn't
going to get much sleep tonight. And she wouldn't complain a bit
about it in the morning either, because as Gray used his hands to
bring her right to the edge of orgasm again, she was delirious with
desire and the feeling that this man instinctively knew her body better than even she did. And then he expertly made her fly, using the

heel of his hand against her clit, his fingers inside her, creating the kind of orgasm that made her scream.

Oh, and could she ever scream. Apparently all that condo repression was being released tonight.

And when he finally reached into his bedside drawer for a condom, she could have wept. Because he hadn't stopped after she'd come again. He'd given her a few minutes to recover, then he'd kissed her again, and touched her again, getting her so wound up and so close to orgasm, she thought maybe after they were done fucking he could get her there yet again.

He put the condom on and hovered over her.

"I should inform you that I can't come this way. But maybe after, you could . . ."

He cocked his head to the side. "Again with this *can't* thing, Evelyn?"

"I've already had two orgasms, Gray. Even when I'm really turned on, without having had a release first, I can't come during traditional intercourse."

He spread her legs and nestled his body on top of hers, holding his weight off her with his arms. "I'll tell you what. Just relax and enjoy it as much as you can."

"Oh. I love sex. I can't wait to feel you inside me. This is the most intimate act and I've been waiting for this. Gray, I don't want you to think—"

"Evelyn."

"Yes."

"Shut up and let's fuck, okay?"

"Okay."

He slid inside her, so slowly she thought she might die from the pleasure, especially since he held himself above her and looked into her eyes at the same time he entered her. And when he seated himself fully inside her, she quivered, so turned on and so filled with him that it took her a moment to fully register that what she felt was much more than simply physical pleasure—though that was immensely profound. It was also emotional impact.

She shuddered and brushed the emotion aside to concentrate on the amazing physical part of being joined with him. He filled her and her body cried for joy, tightening around him. She lifted and he groaned, rolling his hips over her and causing sparks to fly out of her hair. She could have sworn it was her hair, because she'd never felt anything like the feeling she had when he rolled his body over her. The contact was electrifying.

"Do that again," she said.

He did it again.

"Oh, you're touching my clit while you're fucking me."

He brushed her hair away from her face. "Imagine that." He lifted, and rolled, over and over again, giving her the friction she needed. Her body was so languid after the orgasms, yet so sensitized, so tuned into pleasure, that she felt the tight coils of need swirling around her.

She gripped his arms, her gaze locked with his in shock as she realized what was happening. She couldn't breathe, could only marvel that this was possible. She was afraid to move at all because she didn't want these incredible sensations to disappear. "Gray."

"Yeah, I feel it, too. Breathe, Evelyn. And let's make you come."

"Oh, God, yes." She let down her guard, relaxed, and dragged her nails down his arms. And when he began to move in earnest, deepening his thrusts, she cried out, wrapping her legs around him and lifting her hips to meet him.

And that's when she came, a burst of orgasm that blinded her to everything but the surprising, exquisite pleasure that exploded throughout her.

"Fuck. Yes," Gray said, and pumped inside her hard and fast, which only increased the surge of her climax. He gripped her hips while she was still in the throes of her mind-blowing orgasm and emptied himself inside her with a shuddering groan, the two of them finishing together, spent and sweating.

Uh. Wow. That had been intense. Unexpected. And kind of earth-shattering.

It was several moments before Evelyn could speak. Or breathe. Or comprehend what had happened to her tonight.

Maybe Gray had some kind of super sex powers, which was why she had suddenly been able to have those intense orgasms.

She laughed at the thought.

"What are you laughing about?" he asked.

"I had this thought that you must have superhuman sex powers, and that's why I came so many times."

Now he laughed. "Well, I appreciate the compliment, but I'm just a normal guy."

She rested her hand on his chest. "I beg to differ. I'm wrecked. And thank you."

"For what?" Gray asked, rolling them to the side so they faced each other.

"For this. Three orgasms? Or was it four? I think I lost count. And in all new positions? And during sex? Do you do this with all your women?"

"Uh . . . I don't know how to answer that."

"Don't. I'm sorry. I just mean this was amazing for me. As you can imagine."

"Well, I'm happy it was good for you. The male ego and all that. And I have to tell you, it's possible you've taken screaming to a whole new level."

She gave him a satisfied grin. "I'm not even going to be embarrassed about that."

"You shouldn't be. In fact, the louder you scream when you come, the harder it makes me."

"Then I guess you were rock hard tonight."

"Damn straight."

He swept his hand over her hair, then kissed her, this time an easy, gentle kiss that made her feel all soft and squishy inside.

"I'm glad you're here," he said.

And that made her stomach tumble even more. Which made her guard go up, because the last thing she needed in her life right now was a man. Especially a man like Gray Preston. He made her feel way too good. It would be so easy to wrap herself around him and spend the night.

But there'd still be tomorrow to deal with, and she needed to remain emotionally detached. She wasn't going to do that sleeping with him.

"I'm glad, too. But I should probably get out of here."

He frowned. "You're not going to stay tonight?"

She slid out of bed. "Not a good idea. The media will be here tomorrow, and all I have with me is my dress. I don't need that walk of shame in front of the media. Too obvious. If they spot me, that would bring a lot of questions."

He got up, too, following her into the kitchen where she grabbed her underwear. Though he stayed naked, which was quite a distraction since she'd like nothing better than to spend all night touching him. And sleeping next to him. Or not sleeping. Yes, definitely not sleeping.

"I can get you out of here early enough. Before the media arrives."

She hooked up her bra and slid into her panties. "I don't think it's a good idea to take a chance like that. Especially with me being tied to your father's campaign."

"Right." Gray raked his fingers through his hair. "Because it's all about what's best for my dad's reputation."

She pulled her dress over her head. "Gray. Please. That's not what I meant. I had such an incredible night with you. Let's not end it on a sour note."

He gave her a short nod. "You're right. I need some sleep tonight anyway. Tomorrow's qualifying and media interviews. It's a long day."

Somehow she didn't believe that he agreed with her, but she had to do what was best for her career, even if it wasn't what she wanted tonight, either.

He went into the bedroom and pulled on a pair of shorts and slid into a pair of canvas tennis shoes. He grabbed his keys and drove her to her hotel.

He parked in front and got out.

She gave him a quizzical look. "I can make it upstairs just fine."

"I'll walk you up to your room."

"It's not that far."

He gave her a look. "I'll walk you up. No way in hell am I letting you go up in the elevator or down the hall to your room at this late an hour."

She nodded. "Okay. Thank you."

They took the elevator ride and the walk down the hall to her room, neither of them saying anything.

When she got to her room, he took her key card and opened the door for her. She suddenly wanted to fling herself into his arms and beg him to come in and spend the night with her.

But that wouldn't be a wise career move, and she'd spent her entire adult life making the right career choices. This wouldn't be the time to screw that up.

He flipped on the lights and gave her room the once-over, which she found very sweet.

"Okay, I guess I'll head out."

She nodded and he pulled her into his arms and kissed her so thoroughly it took everything in her not to drag him into her bed. She took a deep breath. "Good night, Gray."

"Night, Evelyn."

She waited until he disappeared around the corner of the hallway before she closed the door.

Despite having one of the absolute best nights of her life, she felt like shit as she undressed and climbed into bed.

And she knew why.

Because she was sleeping alone tonight. And that was her choice.

The wrong choice.

TWELVE

SO MUCH FOR EVELYN'S RESOLVE. SHE'D SPENT ALL this time warring against her attraction to Gray, only to succumb and have sex with him. She knew it had been a bad idea, that it would muddy the waters of their professional relationship.

Interns and staffers did it with their bosses all the time in Washington. It was a way to climb the ladder faster. She vowed she would never do that, and she hadn't. She'd earned her way up based on her skills alone. She was a professional and was determined to always act like one.

Yeah, about that determination. She'd survived six years in the hotbed of sex and scandal of politics in D.C., only to crumble in an auto racer's bed in Kentucky during the first week. She should be ashamed.

Surprisingly, she felt no shame whatsoever. She'd been a little sore in spots since she hadn't had sex in a long time. But for some reason, she couldn't seem to wipe the smile off her face.

She supposed several rounds of awesome sex could do that to a person.

Maybe sometime soon the guilt would rear its ugly head. Until then, she'd continue to fondly remember the awesome sex she'd had.

It was race day, and Evelyn had been granted a pass to be in the pits. She'd stayed in the background during qualifying, watching Gray do his thing.

He was very good with the media during interviews. He was smooth on camera, was nice to reporters, and handled the media very well. She'd watched a lot of video on him and that was one of the reasons she'd convinced the senator he'd be a viable resource to use in the campaign, despite the senator's objections.

She wondered what Gray would say if he knew this had been her idea. She knew he probably figured this had been his father's doing, when it was the complete opposite. Mitchell Preston thought Gray would turn her down. She told him she could convince Gray to help, and she'd take full responsibility for making it happen. He'd told her he hated losing her during such an important time, because they'd worked so closely together for many years now and he needed her.

Evelyn knew he relied on her expertise, especially during the most critical election year of his life. But having Gray's legions of fans could be such a boon, especially the younger voters and those in the South. If they could secure those votes, and if Mitchell did, indeed, get the VP nomination, they could ride this wave all the way to the White House.

Or at least the vice president's house. Which would be as high as Evelyn had ever gotten up the political ladder.

The thought of it surged in her blood, as exciting as listening to the cars start their engines at the beginning of the race. Her earplugs firmly intact, she watched the cars pull onto the track to begin their warm-up laps.

"You'll want to climb up into the pit box, ma'am."

She turned as—oh, what was his name? Steve, maybe? He was one of the crew, and he pointed up the ladder to a booth where the crew chief sat.

"I don't think I'm supposed to go up there."

Steve, a young guy with dark brown eyes and a sweet smile, pointed to his ears. "Actually, Ian just communicated to me that's where you're supposed to be. We'll be running back and forth around here all day. Tires will be tossed and other shi—things. Don't want you to get hurt. You'll be safer up in the communications booth. Plus, it's a great view of the race."

"Oh. Okay."

She found the stairs and made her way up into the booth. Ian barely paid attention to her, his gaze fixed on Gray's car and the screens in front of him. He pointed to the empty seat and she took it, then searched the track for Gray's car.

He'd qualified in the sixth position, and as the cars lined up in tight formation for the start, her chest tightened.

She wasn't normally a race fan, but she had watched videos of racing and had been to one live race—the first one where she'd met Gray. And she'd done a lot of research on racing, so she'd be educated. She knew what was at stake for Gray.

As they waved the checkered flag and the crowd roared, the cars jammed together and accelerated. Evelyn's heart flew into her throat as the speeds climbed higher. With every lap the drivers took, her stomach tightened.

A crash on lap three had her leaping out of her seat, leaning forward to check Gray's position. He'd barely missed it, had accelerated down to the—what was the bottom of the track called? The apron. That was it.

"You might as well relax, Evelyn," Ian said, "or you're never going to make it to the end of the race."

She sat down and watched as the safety crews and trucks came to clean up the mess. "Relax? How am I supposed to relax? Did you see how close Gray was to that wreck?"

Ian, on the other hand, leaned back in his chair, his gaze firmly fixed on the monitors. "You get used to it. If you think you're nervous now, wait 'til the end of the race."

"God. I'll need a Valium by the end of the race."

The first one she'd watched hadn't been like this. She hadn't been . . . invested. Today, she'd expected to be bored. She'd figured she'd get caught up on her email and look up periodically to check Gray's progress.

Ha. Her gaze was glued to the number fifty-three the entire time. The race was intense. By the hundredth lap there had been four wrecks, and each time Gray had come through unscathed, though he'd dropped back in position to eighteenth due to what Ian had called pit road miscues. Ian wasn't happy with his crew at all, though he remained calm when he talked to Gray and said they'd make up the positions, that there was still a lot of time left.

She listened to Ian giving Gray feedback through his headset, wondering what Gray was telling him.

Car stuff, no doubt. She wanted to ask, but she didn't want to do anything to direct Ian's attention away from whatever he was doing to help Gray drive the hell out of his car. So instead, she leaned over and watched the screens.

"Fuel mileage. Lap speed. Tire wear," Ian said without looking at her. "Some of that gets communicated to Gray, most of it's just for me and the crew so we're aware of how his car's performing. About the only thing he'll need to stay aware of is fuel mileage. Can't have him running out of gas on the last lap. Plus, he needs to know when to pit."

"Because there's no gas gauge in the cars."

"No. And even if there was, it wouldn't help. A lap's worth of gas can make all the difference, and there's no way a gauge could tell you how much that is."

"So you go by mileage."

"Exactly."

"Thank you. It's helpful to have that education. So he tells you stuff, and you tell him stuff."

"Yeah. Sometimes he'll bitch a blue streak about the car being loose, or tight, some vibration or the car just not running right. That's when I know we need to make adjustments during the next pit stop. Other times he'll be quiet for a lot of laps and just drive. That's when I know the car's running good."

"And has he been quiet so far today?"

Ian laughed. "No. He's been complaining about the car. Everything about the car. Nonstop."

"Damn." She laid her hands in her lap.

Ian laughed. "The good news is, sometimes a driver will think there's something wrong with the car, when in fact it's just the track. He's been steadily moving up since the jackman had trouble on his last pit road stop. There's nothing wrong with his car."

She tore her gaze away from Gray's car only long enough to look at Ian.

"Really?"

Ian didn't bother to look at her, because his attention was focused like a laser on his screens. "Really. So relax. I have a good feeling about today's race. The car is strong, and Gray's a damn good driver."

Evelyn tried to relax, but the race was a nail-biter. As Ian said, there was a lot of time left, and Gray had steadily made his way back to the front. Gray and Cal McClusky ended up racing off pit road nearly tied for first with thirty laps to go. Cal gained an edge by . . . she had no idea, since she couldn't see, but from what she could see it must have been as close as the hairs on a gnat's butt. Either way, before their next restart after a caution, Cal chose the outside lane. To her, it seemed like they'd restart tied, but Ian explained that the outside lane was faster.

Whatever. She needed an antacid, because at the restart they were neck and neck, then Gray pulled ahead and took first. She screamed and yelled for Gray to go faster, and didn't sit down until he took the checkered flag, barely a bumper ahead of Cal.

Okay, she still didn't sit down. Like Ian, she tore off her earplugs and raced down the ladder, as enthusiastic as Gray's pit crew over the win. And when Gray did a spectacular burnout to the wild applause of the fans, smoke spilling over the track and into the stands, she screamed even louder and clapped along with everyone there.

When he pulled into the victory circle and climbed out of his car, God, he looked delicious. His hair was a wild mess, sweat soaked, curling against the nape of his neck. He wore a day's growth of stubble on his jaw and he looked dangerously fierce and sexy, like he'd just conquered the tallest mountain.

She wanted to run to him, to throw her arms around him, kiss him and congratulate him, then lick that sweat beading against his neck and crawl all over his body. Lord, who knew racing could be so intense, could fire her blood in this way?

As he was surrounded by media, Evelyn stayed in the background while he poured soda over his crew, hugged Ian, did his interviews to thank his sponsors, and stayed after for what seemed like a thousand photographs and even more interviews. She waited, patience her middle name since she often had to wait for the senator while he either voted or debated or had to do a myriad of interviews himself. Sometimes she waited for hours, like she did now.

When Gray finally finished for the day, when the track had quieted down and everyone left, he met her at his trailer, obviously in a good mood since he was smiling as wide as she'd ever seen.

"I thought you'd have left for your hotel a long time ago."

"Are you serious? I wanted to congratulate you in person. It was an amazing race today. You dominated."

He was still grinning as he opened the door, waiting for her to go in. When she did, he shut the door behind them. "I sucked the first half of the race. I just couldn't get a feel for the track. And then we had that fuckup in the pits and I thought I was dead in the water, because there were at least six cars as good as or better than me today."

"Obviously not, because you fought your way back. And you won."

"It was close. I got a few lucky breaks, and made up for the ugly pit stop by having the final one go like clockwork. The crew saved my ass."

"You saved your own ass. It seemed like really good driving to me."

"It's always a team effort."

"Hey, it's just us in here, now. I think you can take a little credit for that win today."

He laughed. "Well. Thanks. I need a shower. And something to eat. Will you wait for me?"

"Of course. I'm hungry, too. Would you like me to fix us something while you're showering?"

"You don't have to. We can go out somewhere."

She rolled her eyes. "Do you really want to be mobbed by fans out there?"

He gazed at the door and grimaced. "Not particularly."

"I'll see what you have in here." She shooed him with her hands. "Go. Shower."

"All right."

After he left, she rummaged through his fridge and found bacon and eggs and, surprisingly, tomatoes, mushrooms, and a green pepper. She grabbed a skillet, fried up the bacon, and started mixing up the eggs while chopping the vegetables. When the bacon was finished she pulled it out, wiped out the grease, and threw the vegetables in, sautéing them until they were tender.

"That smells good," Gray said as he came out of the bathroom smelling even better than the food.

He wore a pair of shorts and a sleeveless shirt, making her mouth water.

She threw the eggs in with the vegetables. "Feel better?"

"Starting to. What can I do to help?"

"How about some juice with this? I saw some in your fridge."

"Sure."

He pulled out plates and glasses while she fixed the oversized omelet in the skillet. When it was done, she cut it in half and slid the two pieces onto two plates, along with the bacon. They grabbed seats in the booth.

"Omelets and bacon? You're my savior. I'd have probably eaten toast."

She sliced into her omelet with a fork, so hungry she had to take a couple bites before she replied. "Come on. You have food in your refrigerator. You have to know how to cook."

"I do. But I was really hungry. These interviews take hours. Toast is quick. And I have peanut butter."

She shook her head. "You need a wife." At his quizzical look, she added, "Or a live-in cook."

"Maybe if she's hot. And French, or something."

Evelyn laughed. *"La cuisine française est très bonne."*

He lifted his gaze to hers and laid his fork down. "Fuck. You speak French?"

She blushed. *"Un peu."*

"That's hot, Evelyn. Do it some more."

Her lips curved. She could tell him how he smelled. So good. Like the crisp, clear mountains. *"Tu sens bon. Comme les montagnes."*

He arched a brow, his lids dropping partway closed. *"Tu es sexy. Je tiens à vous lécher partout."*

Oh, God. He understood. "You speak French, too." He'd told her she was sexy and he wanted to lick her . . . everywhere. She shuddered at the mental images, the way his gaze bore into hers, melting her to the booth.

He broke the spell when he grabbed a piece of bacon and took a bite, then grinned at her. "Four years in college. It was an easy course because I'd had a French nanny for years. She taught me to speak it fluently."

She laid her napkin on the table. "You suck."

He laughed. "Sorry. It was an easy tease. But you sound so goddamn sexy when you speak French."

So did he, which she wasn't about to tell him. "I took it in college, too. Along with Spanish and German."

"Aren't you an overachiever?"

She shrugged. "I like languages."

"I liked the easy grade for a language I already knew."

"I'm sure you did. And what else did you study in college?"

"Girls, mainly."

"Seriously, Gray."

"I am being serious. School just wasn't my thing. I was focused on baseball, and then racing. I was so burnt out on school by the time I got to college, and so damn glad to be out from under my father's thumb that I played as much as I could, and didn't focus on my studies. I coasted."

"You didn't."

"I did."

"But you graduated with a degree in prelaw."

"Yeah, well, that was to make my dad think I might entertain the concept of going to Harvard someday, when really I had no intention."

"Still, I've seen your transcripts. You graduated with the highest honors, so you hardly coasted."

He got up and grabbed the dishes. "I didn't give it my all, that's for sure."

She watched him as he loaded the dishwasher, wondering why he spent so much time trying to downplay his education while playing up the sports side.

She carried their juice glasses to the sink.

"Do you regret not following through on law school?"

He frowned, turned his head to look at her. "No. I'm doing exactly what I want to do with my life, what I love to do. I've got plenty of money to continue to do it for a long time."

She leaned against the counter and crossed her arms. "I sense a *but* in there somewhere."

He finished loading the glasses and utensils, then shut the dishwasher and dried his hands. "No *but* in there at all. I was meant to race. Otherwise, I'd have played baseball."

"And what about after?"

"After what?"

"After racing is over?"

He stared at her, then pushed off the counter. "Want something to drink? A beer? I feel like celebrating."

And avoiding her question. "Sure. A beer sounds great. It was hot out there today. How hot does it get in the car?"

"A lot hotter than outside." He grabbed two beers, then motioned for her to join him in the living area. He pressed a button on the remote and a TV screen popped up. He switched to the racing channel, where they were replaying the events of the day.

"That's handy."

"Yeah." He handed her one of the beers. "So you enjoyed the race today?"

She took a sip of the beer and nodded. "If heart-in-your-throat, nonstop panic and anxiety could be considered enjoying the race."

He tucked her hair behind her ear. "Awww. You were worried about me."

She had been. But she didn't want him knowing how much. "Well, we can't have you losing your fan base. If you end up in the back of the pack, your fans will think you suck and then you'll start losing them. Then what good would you be to me?"

She could tell from the smirk on his face that he wasn't buying it.

"Oh, right. All those registered voters. So important to my father and all."

"Exactly. I need you to keep on winning for purely selfish reasons. My job is on the line."

He turned to face her, setting his beer on top of the sill. "Tell me about your job."

"Really?"

"Yeah."

He hadn't wanted to hear anything about her work with his father before. This was progress. "What would you like to know?"

"What do you do for the senator when you aren't charged with getting me to help you secure votes for him?"

"I started out as an aide. Which basically meant a glorified flunky. I did anything and everything, including making phone calls, having copies made, running errands. You name it, I did it."

He looked at her and didn't say anything. She knew the question that wasn't being asked.

"He never hit on me. Not once. Nor did I ever see him behaving inappropriately with any female on his staff. He was always a gentleman. So busy with the duties of office."

"An appropriately worded statement coming from one of his staffers."

She rolled her eyes. "You're hardly the press. You're his son. You know him better than anyone."

He raked his fingers through his hair. "Sometimes I think I don't know him at all."

"Maybe it's time you get to know him."

"Not all that interested. He had a lifetime to get to know me. He didn't take the time."

She laid her hand on his arm. "I'm sorry for that. I can tell it bothers you that he didn't make time for you when you were younger. Obviously he let his job take precedence over raising you."

Gray shrugged. "My mom was good at taking care of the things that needed taking care of."

"But a boy needs his father."

"I managed all right without him. But this isn't about me. Tell me what you do for him."

"Right now I'm working very closely with him on building his constituent base, specifically at the national level. When he was running his presidential campaign, my job was to increase his exposure in all states, blitzing media campaigns, working with his local campaigns in every state and checking with the polls daily to determine which states needed the most attention."

"So why did he fail?"

Her lips lifted. "I don't know that he failed in his bid for the presidential nomination. I think the American people—and our party—feel that John Cameron has more to offer as a presidential candidate at this time. Plus Cameron has the backing of our current president."

"Hard to beat that."

"Indeed. Which isn't to say that your father wouldn't be a viable candidate in eight years, once Cameron is elected and serves his two terms."

He laughed. "Thinking positively, aren't you?"

"It's my job to think that way. If I thought the other candidate would win, or that Senator Preston wouldn't end up getting the vice presidential nomination, I shouldn't be in this position."

"Good point. So, you have a very important job."

"Thank you. I'd like to think so."

"Why did my father pull you off your current job to come babysit me?"

She laughed. "I'm hardly babysitting you. But in answer to your question, because we feel you're a critical component to his potential to become the vice presidential nominee. You can assist him, and Governor Cameron, in garnering critical votes. I'm right where I need to be."

He played with her hair, causing goose bumps to pop out on her skin. "Do you know when you talk about politics your eyes flash with excitement?"

"Do they?"

"Yeah."

She ran a fingertip down his arm. "Do you know when you talk about racing your eyes do the same thing?"

He smiled. "I'm not surprised. I love it."

"I should hope so, since you're circling around that track at death-defying speeds."

"It's fun. You should try it sometime."

"Oh. No thanks. I'm content to just watch."

"It's exhilarating."

"Again, no thanks."

"Surely you dated some boy when you were young who wanted to impress you by drag racing down a deserted street at a hundred miles an hour."

"Uh . . . no."

He grinned. "Wait 'til we get to Florida for the next race. I'm taking you on the track for a drive."

She sat straighter. "What? I can't get on the track."

"Sure you can. You can even drive one of the cars yourself."

He was out of his mind. Just the thought of getting behind the wheel of one of those demonic, potentially-out-of-control speeding death traps was enough to make the hairs on the back of her neck stand on end. "Oh, I don't think so."

"Oh, I *do* think so. You seem so fearless, Evelyn. Surely the thought of driving a race car excites you."

"Not in the least."

"Scared, huh?"

"Not really. Just not something I'd ever thought about doing."

"That's okay. I'll just take you in one of the cars on a slower ride around the track. Wouldn't you want a tour of the track in Daytona?"

She calmed somewhat. The thought of getting a view of what he saw from the track would be educational. "Okay. Sure. That might be fun."

She didn't trust the gleam in his eyes, though.

They settled in and watched the racing channel on television for a while so Gray could get caught up on the news of his win.

"So you never had a hot boyfriend who treated you to a thrilling high-speed ride in a fast car, huh?"

She tore her gaze away from the TV. "No. Why? Is that some teen girl right of passage I missed out on?"

"Yes. You were deprived."

She rolled her eyes. "And to think I made it to adulthood without breaking land/speed records in some guy's Camaro."

He patted her leg. "Don't worry. I'm going to fix that for you."

"That's exactly what worries me."

He'd left his hand on her leg, and while they watched television, she became conscious of him squeezing her thigh, running his hand up and down her leg to her knee. It was disconcerting. It felt good, made her feminine parts squeal with joy and beg for more.

She wasn't going to get more. She'd resolved that one time was the only time. They—no, *she*—had to keep the professional line drawn between them.

It was time to put a stop to the places her thoughts were going, the way her body yearned for him—before she got herself in all kinds of trouble.

She stood and grabbed her purse and keys.

THIRTEEN

GRAY LOOKED UP AT HER. "WHERE ARE YOU GOING?"

"It's getting late. I should go."

"Really? It's still early."

"I have . . . things to do."

"What kinds of things?"

He wasn't going to make this easy for her, was he? "Paperwork. I need to file my report with the senator."

He arched a brow. "A report? What type of report?"

Evelyn had given him a bullshit answer, and now she had to lie. "I do have to justify my job, Gray. I'm not following you around the country like some track groupie, you know."

"You aren't? Now I'm disappointed."

She rolled her eyes. "You'll have to live with it."

He stood and followed her as she made her way to the door.

She wished she didn't like him so much. But things between them had been great. She had thought this job assignment was going to be difficult, that he'd be angry and defensive because of his father. They'd gotten off to a rough start, but after that he'd made it easy for her—much easier than she'd anticipated. Plus, he was smoking-hot sexy, the sport intrigued her, and she learned about new facets of Gray every day.

And the way he touched her brought out responses in her body she didn't know she could have.

She inhaled, let it out, more reluctant to leave with every step she took toward the door. She paused at the steps and turned to him.

She could tell from the way he looked at her that he read her hesitation. In Washington, your face and body language could give away all your secrets. She'd always kept herself guarded. With Gray it was impossible, because he relaxed her and those walls came crashing down.

Which made him dangerous. "Thank you for letting me stay for dinner."

He cracked an easy smile. "I should be the one thanking you. You cooked for me and saved me from having to go out to eat."

"Anytime. I enjoyed it."

She started to turn away, but he slid his hand into hers. "Are you sure you want to leave?"

No. She didn't want to go. Just the touch of his hand in hers sent her body spiraling off-kilter. Someone should bottle the kind of sparks his touch set off. It could power an entire city.

"I don't know how to answer that question."

"It's an easy enough question, Evelyn. You either want to go, or you don't."

"I should go."

He cocked his head to the side. "Why *should* you go?"

"Because it would be inappropriate for us to have a relationship."

He laughed. "We're not having a relationship. We're just having sex. I don't think either of us wants to get involved. I know I don't. I have way too much going on in my life to think about settling down with a woman. And you're going to be President of the United States someday, so you don't want some auto racer for a boyfriend."

She couldn't help the laugh that spilled out. "Well, thanks for thinking so highly of me. But you're right. I'm not looking for a relationship."

"Great. Now that we've settled on what we both *don't* want, why don't you relax and stay? I want to fuck you. I've been thinking about it all day."

"I think you thought about racing all day."

"I can handle driving my car and thinking about being inside you at the same time."

There were no artful discussions with Gray, no beating around the bush as far as his intentions went. His blunt honesty caused heat to settle low in her belly, and all her reservations about him—about them—disappeared. "Okay. Why don't I stay?"

He grabbed her purse and her keys and threw them on the counter, then backed her up against the wall and slid his fingers in her hair.

"Always give in to your instincts, Evelyn. They'll never steer you wrong."

She wasn't sure she agreed with him on that, but then he put his mouth on hers and kissed her—deeply—and she lost all logical thought as passion took over.

That was the one thing Gray gave her that so many men before him hadn't—a deep, natural passion that never failed to stoke the fires of her hunger. He grabbed her ass and drew her against the hard ridge of his erection. She loved how fast he got hard, the fact he wanted her with such a desperate need that he groaned against her lips as he rocked against her, deepening the kiss until her limbs felt heavy and she fought for breath. And when he angled her head to the side to press his lips to her throat, her nipples tightened, her pussy damp with arousal and pulsing with anticipation.

She'd always been normally sexual, had always enjoyed the act, but it hadn't been all-consuming to her. She could do fine with it, and equally fine going long periods without it. After all, that's what vibrators were for.

Since meeting Gray, she'd thought about sex a lot, possibly because he was so damn good at it. His hands were masterful, and when he popped the button on her jeans, drew the zipper down, and slid his hand inside to cup her sex, she let out a soft cry.

"You're wet."

"Yes. What are you going to do about that?"

"I'm going to make you come, but goddamn, these pants are tight. You need to start wearing dresses," he whispered against her ear. "So I can lift them up and fuck you when I'm in a hurry."

She turned to meet his gaze. "Are you in a hurry?"

He rocked his hard-on against her hip. "When I'm around you, all I think about is being inside you. So yes, I'm in a fucking hurry, and you're wearing pants that are cutting off the circulation in my hand. You're killing me here, Evelyn."

It was nice knowing he was as tormented as she was. She kicked off her sandals and he kneeled, cussing while he struggled to get her jeans down her legs.

She stifled a laugh. "Sorry. I'll try not to wear tight jeans next time."

"They do make your ass look great," he said. "But they're gone. And these are next."

He hooked her panties with a finger and pulled those off. Still on his knees, he drew her legs apart, then pressed a kiss to her thighs.

She barely had time to hitch a breath before his mouth was on her sex. She let out a low moan as sweet pleasure flooded her and she arched forward, reaching for him, needing to touch him while he touched her. The silken strands of his hair slid across her fingers and she latched on as he licked the length of her, driving her instantly crazy and so near the brink she was shocked.

She looked down at him, watching him as he swiped his tongue over her clit and drove her to dizzying heights. He lifted one of her legs over his shoulder, spreading her further, then speared a finger inside her, followed by another, spreading her while using his tongue in devilish, masterful ways.

She shuddered, so close to orgasm. It was the sweetest sensation, the way he pleasured her with his tongue and his lips. She didn't want it to end, but oh, she craved the climax that hovered so close. And when he paused, lifted his gaze to hers, and smiled, she knew he owned her, that he could take her there with one swipe of his tongue, one suck of her clit between his lips.

This shocked her, because she'd been so used to using the bedroom, to being in one position to come. How quickly he'd changed her, turned her into a woman who had lost all her inhibitions. She was so tuned in to him, to his mouth, his touch, that he made her relax and let go.

And he knew it, too, from the smile he gave her. She didn't care, because her body tightened with the need to let go.

"Yes," she whispered. "Make me come."

He captured her clit and flicked his tongue over it. She tightened, the first tremors building until he covered her clit with his mouth and rolled his tongue flat. She rocked against him as he fucked her with his fingers. She drove toward the sensation, the orgasm hovering so close she trembled with the need to let go. And when it hit, she let loose a wailing cry, feeling so free to let go with him that it doubled her pleasure.

When the tremors subsided, he rose and took her mouth in a blinding kiss. She wrapped her hand around the nape of his neck and slid her tongue in his mouth, needing to hold that connection that had left her breathless.

He lifted her and she wrapped her legs around him while he carried her back into the living room, depositing her on the sofa.

He undressed in a hurry. Glad to get her hands on him, she slid to the floor and wrapped her hand around the thick, hard part of him that bobbed in front of her. She stroked the length of him, loving the way he hissed as she squeezed his cock.

He swept his fingers over her jaw. "I like your hands on me."

She licked her lips. "How about my mouth? Do you want that?"

His chest rose. "You know I do. Suck my cock, Evelyn."

The way his voice went deep made her shudder, made her pussy clench in anticipation of what would come. She leaned forward and wrapped her lips around his cockhead.

"Ah, Christ, that's good," he said, sweeping his hand over the back of her head. "Suck it in deep."

She loved the way he talked to her as she drew his shaft deeper into her mouth.

"This is what I thought about today," he said as she bobbed her head forward, taking him fully between her lips. "Your mouth on me. So hot and wet, making my balls tighten."

She took his cockhead to the back of her throat and swallowed, squeezing him. He let out a groan.

Something about having a man so hard and strong and powerful brought to his knees by having his cock in her mouth made her wet, made her nipples tighten and her pussy throb. She wanted him to fuck her, but first, she wanted him to come and come hard, to shatter in the same way she had. She pressed the roof of her mouth down onto his shaft, rolling her tongue over him.

"That's going to make me come." He thrust into her mouth and she grabbed the base of his cock, squeezing him, tunneling more of it into her mouth.

With a loud groan, he erupted, grabbing a handful of her hair as he emptied himself. She let go of his cock so he could shove into her, knowing going deep would give him pleasure.

When he settled, his legs were shaking. She let go and looked up at him, licked her lips, and smiled.

"Fuck, Evelyn, I think I lost some brain cells."

She laughed. He bent and lifted her up against him to kiss her, tunneling his fingers through her hair. The kiss was so deep, so thorough, that it left her languid, her limbs so relaxed she was glad he held her.

"I want you here. From behind, so I can fuck you deep."

She slid to her knees and draped herself against the sofa, giving him a look over her shoulder. "Let's get you inside me."

His swift intake of breath told her he was more than ready. He left only long enough to grab a condom. He sheathed his cock, then swept her hair away from the back of her neck to kiss her there. When his teeth scraped her neck, she shivered and dug her nails into the couch cushions.

"I like that," she said.

"I'll remember that." He trailed his fingers down her back, following it up by pressing his lips over her spine, moving his mouth all the way down to her butt. When he gave her a love bite on one cheek, she yelped.

He laughed, then gave her a smack on the butt. She turned. "I like that, too."

His eyes blazed hot. "I'll definitely remember that."

She'd never played like this before, had never been with a man she'd felt free enough with to express her desires to. With Gray, it was like she could trust him, could tell him anything. She didn't know why. Feminine instinct, maybe. A woman could just tell the difference between being with the right guy and the wrong guy.

And when he curved his hand over her butt, then spread her legs and positioned himself behind her, she knew it felt right.

At least for sex. She trusted him wholly there. And when he slid his cock home, he fit her—perfectly. She quivered, tightened around him, and he pulled out, taking his time to ease inside her again, taking care with her until her body adjusted to him.

She bent over the sofa cushion and spread her legs wider, giving him access to power in deeper. He smoothed his hands over her hips, then grasped them and thrust. She cried out as pleasure speared her.

"Okay?" he asked, leaning over to press a kiss to her back.

"Better than okay. Keep doing that."

"This?" He rubbed her butt, using soft, circular motions.

"That's . . . nice."

He laughed. "Yeah, you don't want nice though, do you?"

Not particularly. So when he gave her butt cheek a light tap, her pussy clenched hard on his cock.

"I didn't think so. You like it a little harder." He smacked her again, this time on the other cheek, and a little harder.

The sting made her wet, made her buck back against him.

"Yes," she said, grinding against him. She reached between her legs to rub her clit, and he spanked her again, then reared back and began to thrust deeper.

She liked it—more than she thought she would. Her butt cheeks tingled, which only made her pussy quiver and clench around his cock. And as she thrummed her clit, she careened closer and closer to orgasm.

Gray leaned over and kissed the back of her neck, then teased her with his teeth, making her quiver and teeter on the very edge of reason. And when he sank his teeth into her flesh, she went over, crying out and rocking back against his cock.

"Fuck," he said, roaring out his release as he went with her. He gripped her hips and shoved his cock in, shuddering as he came.

He wrapped an arm around her and held her, gentling his kisses over her neck and shoulders as they both came down from that incredible high.

He finally withdrew, lifting her with him. They went into the bathroom and cleaned up, then climbed into his bed. He pulled her against his chest and stroked her hair and her back.

"I should head back to my hotel," she said.

"Why would you want to do that?" He still moved his hands over her. All over her. It was quite distracting, but in a good way.

"Well, you'll be packing up and leaving tomorrow, right?"

"Yeah."

"I need to pack, too."

"You can do that in the morning."

"I suppose." She was running out of excuses not to spend the night with him. Except spending the night—at least to her—meant a relationship, and she was trying her best to keep this sex only.

"Evelyn." He tipped her chin so she was looking up at him, their faces so close their lips would touch if he moved a little.

"Yes?"

"It's okay to have sex and stay overnight. I promise not to ask you to marry me in the morning."

She laughed, and some of her tension dissolved. "Okay, but only if you promise."

He made a cross sign over his heart. "You have my word."

"Then I'll stay."

She snuggled back against him.

This whole sex-with-no-strings thing? Not too bad a deal.

As long as she kept her heart out of the equation.

FOURTEEN

GRAY LOVED DAYTONA, AND NOT JUST FOR THE RACING, though this was one of his favorite tracks. He loved the beach, loved the long stretches of highway where he could take one of his cars and head out on a drive. Which was why he'd bought a house out there and stored several of his cars.

He was happy to be home, happy to get out of the trailer and stretch out at his beach house for a while. Before they'd left Kentucky, he'd had a brief meeting with his team to go over the previous race and talk about the upcoming one. They'd reconvene down here after the Fourth of July holiday. He'd told them to be ready to get down to work, because the schedule for this race week would be short and intense. But for the next few days, everyone would have some time off to enjoy their families.

For now, he was content to let his team take care of his race car. He'd rolled in late last night and the first thing he'd done was fall face-first into his bed and pass out. Evelyn had told him she'd be flying down in the morning, so he took the opportunity to catch up on some much-needed sleep.

He'd hesitated in asking her to make the drive down with him, though he didn't know why. Maybe because that was time for Ian and him to catch up and strategize on race stuff. And maybe part of it was his and Evelyn's relationship—or non-relationship, since that's what they'd both agreed it was—was still new, and he didn't want the whole damn team knowing about it. Because once the team knew, it would only be a matter of time before everyone knew. And that meant media involvement, which he'd prefer to keep to a minimum.

But for the next few days, he wanted Evelyn at his house, and in his bed, so he got up and took a quick shower, then dressed and went to the garage, deciding on his '67 GTO, since it had been a long time since he'd pulled her out for a spin. He folded back the cover, smiling as he smoothed his hand over the sleek black finish. His staff did a great job taking care of his cars while he was on the road, knowing as soon as he came home he'd want to take one—or more—for a ride.

He grabbed the keys and slid into the leather seats, inhaling the sweet smell of eras gone by. When he fired her up, the rumbling engine roared to life, exciting him at the thought of taking the GTO out on the roads for a little action.

Too bad the U.S. had speed limits. With a grin, he slipped on his sunglasses and pulled out onto the street, then hit the highway, letting out the clutch as he gave it some gas.

It was still early, so the sun hadn't risen high enough to heat him up. Not that he minded, since nothing could be as hot as when he was in his race car. Plus, in the convertible, the wind blew through his hair and his mind went blank. He gripped the steering wheel as he and the GTO became one.

There was nothing that made him happier than being behind the wheel of a car, whether it was competitively or just out for a joyride.

He knew for a fact that driving—racing—was what he was supposed to be doing with his life. Evelyn's question about law school had made him pause, but only for a second. He was most comfortable, most himself, most at home, behind the wheel. That's where he belonged, and that's where he was going to spend the rest of his life. The whole law school thing had been born out of guilt because he hadn't done what his parents—what his father—had wanted him to do.

Funny how that guilt still nagged at him, even after all these years. And he didn't buy that his father was a changed man. Men like Mitchell Preston didn't change. They played at changing, so the public would vote for them.

He knew his father better than anyone, knew he was one of the best actors out there. He knew what his dad was capable of—and what he wasn't capable of.

Shaking off dark thoughts that had him tensing on the wheel, he blew out a breath and took the exit leading to Evelyn's hotel.

The valet whistled as he came around to Gray's side.

"GTO? That is one sweet ride."

Gray pulled a hundred dollar bill out of his pocket and waved it at the wide-eyed valet whose name tag read *Oscar*.

"Oscar, park it like you own it and this'll be yours when I pick her up. Understood?"

"Yes, sir," Oscar said. "She'll be in bubble wrap until you're ready for her."

"Thanks. I won't be long."

He pulled his phone out of his pocket and dialed Evelyn, who gave him her room number. It didn't take him long to figure out she'd scored a bungalow down on the beachfront.

Smart woman. He headed down the front steps of the hotel and toward the left. She was waiting for him at the fountain.

"Afraid of taking me to your room?"

She smiled at him. "I'm enjoying the beach way too much to spend much time in my room."

She looked beautiful, dressed in a pair of shorts and a tank top. He slid his hand in hers. "Then let's go to the beach."

She looked down at his jeans and tennis shoes. "You're hardly dressed for a beach walk."

"I have stuff in my car."

"Where are we going?"

"Lots of places. You have a swimsuit?"

"Yes. Let me grab my bag."

She started to turn away, but he grasped her wrist. "You might want to grab some clothes for tomorrow, too. Just in case you don't make it back tonight."

Her brows raised. "Are you intending to kidnap me?"

"The thought occurred to me."

"All right then. I'll pack the bag accordingly. You can come with me to my room if you'd like."

"It's okay. I'll just watch the ocean here and wait for you." If he went to her room, they likely wouldn't get anything done on his agenda today, and he had a lot of plans.

She gave him a knowing smile. "I'll be right back then."

One thing he liked about Evelyn was her efficiency. She was back in about five minutes, a small bag slung over her shoulders. He took the bag from her.

"Nice view."

"I splurged on my budget a little. Okay, a lot. Normally, I wouldn't care what kind of hotel room I stayed in, because after a while they all look the same to me. But here? I love the idea of taking an early morning walk on the beach. So while we're in Florida, I decided . . . screw it. I'm going to take advantage of every spare second I have to indulge my love of the ocean."

He laughed as they headed up the stairs toward the front lobby. "I didn't know you were an ocean lover."

"Almost all of the places we moved to when I was a kid were landlocked, so any chance I have to be near the water is a thrill for me. I can't get enough of the beach and the ocean."

He signaled for Oscar, who nodded and went on the run to retrieve his car. "I actually have a house here."

She turned to face him. "You do not."

"I do. I love it here."

"I'm so jealous."

"Since we race here twice a year, I've grown accustomed to the beach and ocean myself. I'm a big fan."

"I'll bet you have a house on the beach, too."

His lips curved. "I'll take you to my house later."

"God, I'm so going to hate you if you have a house on the beach."

He grinned at her, then heard the rumble of the GTO. Oscar, smart boy that he was, didn't abuse the privilege of driving it, so it was a tame rumble as he drove it up to the front of the parking area.

"Oh, my God," Evelyn said. "This is your car?"

"One of them," Gray said as he held the door for her.

Gray paid Oscar, who grinned and pocketed the money. "Man, it was fun just to drive it and park it. Thanks."

"My pleasure. Thanks for taking care of her for me."

He slid in, pulled down his sunglasses, and turned to Evelyn, who was running her fingers over the seats. "I love muscle cars. I might not be as in the know about racing, but I do love muscle cars." She ran her fingers over the GTO symbol on the dash. "God, Gray. This car is so sexy."

He grinned, put it in first, and headed out.

She pulled her sunglasses out of her purse, not seeming to care when he hit third gear and pulled onto the highway, her hair blowing in the breeze. She grabbed a ponytail holder and wound her hair up into it. "Where are we going?"

"Just for a ride along the ocean highway right now. I figured I'd give you a little tour, and give me a chance to blow the dust out of her carburetors."

She dragged her gaze away from the view of the ocean and to him. "One of the cars. So this isn't your only one."

"No."

"How many do you have?"

"Right now I have six."

"Good lord. I've got to see them."

He loved a woman who got excited over a muscle car. "You will. But first, we'll hit the water."

She looked out the windshield with a grin on her face. "Fantastic."

As they drove, he stole glances at Evelyn. She never once complained about her hair blowing or the hot sun beating down on her. She tilted her head back, laid her arm on the door, and watched the ocean go by.

He was in one of his favorite cars, with a beautiful woman occupying the seat next to him. What more could he ask for?

They drove for about forty-five minutes, then he pulled into a marina, parked the car in a corner slot far away from the traffic. He gave a wave to the parking attendant, Walter, who he knew would give an eagle eye to his baby, making sure no one would park next to her. He grabbed their bags and left his keys at the desk. Walter nodded from his spot on the high perch of the lot.

"I thought we were going to hit the beach," Evelyn said.

He slipped his hand into hers as they headed down the wooden deck. "We will. Be patient."

He led her to the boat that was parked toward the end of the slip.

"Seriously? You have a yacht?" she asked as he helped her on board.

"It's a boat."

"It's a yacht. I know the difference."

"Whatever." He handed her the bags. "You want to store these down in the galley while I get us ready to take off?"

She took the bags from him. "I suppose this is your . . . boat."

"Yeah."

She rolled her eyes, then headed down to the galley. He got them untied and pushed off, then started the engine, easing through as they headed out. Evelyn came up and stood next to him while he pushed past the warning zone, then gave it some gas.

"You might want to take a seat."

She grabbed the chair next to his and he cranked the speed up, the bow rising as he churned through the waves. He was damn happy to be on the sea again. During the racing season he didn't get many days off, and very rarely got to come home and play with his toys. He was glad for Evelyn's company, for an excuse to take the boat out today.

He found the isolated cove and, after carefully checking where he was, dropped the anchor.

Evelyn had gone downstairs and changed into a sinful, skimpy red bikini he couldn't wait to get her out of. They climbed out of the boat and waded to shore, tossing their bags on the beach.

"Feel like snorkeling?"

"I'd love to."

He grabbed the gear out of his bag and they hit the water.

Normally when he came to town for this break in his schedule, he'd bring the boat out, kick back, and do some fishing, or just idle and clear his head. If there was an available woman, he might drag her along, but usually he preferred the time alone to rest and regroup.

As they swam along the surface of the cove, Evelyn grasped his hand and drew him to look at something several times, whether it was one of the many colorful fish that inhabited this area, or the coral that lived around the cove. He could tell from the wide smile on her face and the way she excitedly tugged him along that she was pleased.

When they came back to shore, she threw her arms around him.

"It's beautiful down there, Gray. Thank you."

He slipped an arm around her wet body and drew her against him. "You're welcome. It's one of my favorite spots."

She grabbed towels and set them down to sit on, then grabbed his hands and he sat next to her.

"I can see why. The colors of the coral are amazing. Did you know coral are an endangered species? Overfishing and environmental pollution of our waters have had a severe detrimental effect on more than sixty percent of the world's coral reefs. This could be disastrous to our entire ecosystem."

He cocked a brow. "Something you're passionate about, obviously?"

"Yes. I've told you I love the beach and the water, and I wasn't kidding. I've lobbied for laws to be passed to limit overfishing and to post sanctions on those companies that leave behind nets and equipment that can harm the coral."

He swept his hand over her hair. "Maybe it's something you can talk to my father about sponsoring." He wanted to laugh at that thought, but he could see she was serious about it and didn't want to puncture her balloon of hope.

She cocked her head to the side. "Gray, your father chairs a committee on environmental pollution. It's one of his primary causes."

"Seriously."

"Yes. He and I have lobbied hard for legislation to protect coral reefs, as well as other key environmental legislation. He's written groundbreaking papers on the effects of global warming, overfishing, and the pollution of our waters. I'm surprised you didn't know that."

He didn't know that, and it didn't sound at all like something his father would be the slightest bit interested in. "Mitchell Preston cares about the environment? Since when?"

She sighed. "I told you. He's changed. Maybe you should check out the other issues he's passionate about."

Gray still found it hard to believe his father cared about anything other than what would serve his interests or line his pockets. "Yeah. Maybe."

"Anyway, this area here is a slice of paradise."

"It's also a protected area. Fishing isn't allowed, nor is recreation."

"Really? To protect the coral?"

"Yes."

She looked around. "So . . . we shouldn't be here, either."

"It's all right. I'm the one who worked to get new coral planted in this area. It had been damaged by those very things you talked about—fishing and environmental pollution."

"You put money into restoration of this area."

"Not by myself. Me and a group of investors."

She reached for his hands. "Maybe you and your father share more common interests than you're aware of."

He looked out over the water.

"Several years ago, I came out here to do some snorkeling. It had been a while since I'd been here, and I hated what I saw when I went down."

She squeezed his hand. "Bleaching of the coral?"

"Yeah. This was a heavy fishing area, and over-recreated. They were destroying the coral and the aquatic life that depended on it. I vowed then to do something to change it. So along with several friends with big bank accounts, we arranged for transplantation of healthy coral, and lobbied and won the rights to secure this area from fishing and recreation."

"You did a good thing."

He smiled. "I feel like I own a part of this area now." He turned to her. "Not as my personal playground, but because I had the right to give it back to the sea life and to the coral. That's who it really belongs to."

She climbed onto his lap and framed his face with her hands. "You continually surprise me, Gray Preston."

He clutched her hips. "Yeah? In what way?"

"As soon as I think I know who you are, you surprise the living daylights out of me. Here I think you're some rich guy whose job it is to burn thousands of gallons of fossil fuels a year, and it turns out you're a closet environmentalist."

"Hey, I'm just a guy who happens to have a lot of money, so I can toss it at causes like this."

"Oh, don't go trying to downplay this. Lots of people have a lot of money. This was personal to you and you did something about it."

He smiled. "I got to spend some time watching them transplant the coral. It was amazing. Kind of like watching babies grow. Stupid, I know."

"Not stupid at all. I would have given anything to see it. Your father would be so proud of you to know you're a part of something like this." At his blank stare, she added, "Thank you for bringing me here today and letting me see it. It's such an important cause for me. And for your father."

Yeah. His father. Still hard to believe he and his dad saw eye to eye on anything, especially an environmental issue. Evelyn kept telling him that his father had changed. He still found that hard to believe.

But maybe . . .

He didn't want to think about his father. Not when a wet, barely clad Evelyn sat on his lap and stroked his shoulders. "Let's get back to the boat and rinse off some of this sand."

He stood with her in his arms and they went back to the boat.

They rinsed off in the shower and Gray pulled out some drinks and sandwiches he'd had delivered to the boat before they arrived.

"What? No champagne and lobster?"

He frowned, until she laughed.

"I'm kidding. Considering you have this ridiculous yacht, I thought I'd nudge you."

"Oh."

She rolled her eyes. "Really, Gray. You need to lighten up and get my sense of humor."

"I guess so. Sorry."

"Iced tea and turkey sandwiches is perfect. I'm starving."

They sat on the back of the boat and ate, and he explained in greater detail about the coral project that he'd spearheaded. He could tell by the way she nodded that she was making mental notes.

"You're going to do some social media connection thing between this and me and my father, aren't you?"

She lifted her gaze to his. "I'd love to. With your prior approval, of course. It is an amazing cause, showcases you in a good light, and brings the plight of the sea and the coral to a greater audience. That can't be a bad thing."

"I guess not." He polished off his second sandwich, then bagged up their trash and pulled out another iced tea for both of them. When he saw her nose getting red, he brought out the sunscreen and spread some across her nose and cheeks.

"Thanks," she said, rubbing it in. "Darn freckles."

He kissed the tip of her nose. "Those freckles are sexy."

She stretched out in the shade. "They weren't when I was gangly and flat chested at fourteen. My hair was a darker red then. I looked like Little Orphan Annie."

"I would have thought you were hot."

She laughed. "No, you would not have. You would have pointed and laughed like the other boys did."

"Hey, Little Orphan Annie totally trips all my hot buttons."

She snorted, then flipped over onto her belly. Her bikini bottoms were doing him in today. They covered her ass, but gave him tempting glimpses of the underside of her cheeks. And those legs of hers made him hard.

Too bad they didn't have enough privacy here. He could take her below, but he had other plans for Evelyn today.

Then again, he could give her a little tease.

He went over with the sunscreen in his hand. "Your back is getting red."

She lifted. "Is it? I can't get any sunscreen on there."

"I'll take care of it." He put some of the cream in his hand and rubbed it over her shoulders and back, loving the feel of her smooth skin under his hands. Her eyes were closed, her head resting on her arms as he massaged her.

And when she moaned, his cock hardened. It would be so easy to spread her legs and spear her with his cock, to ride her hard and fast until they both got off.

Instead, he rubbed more lotion over her legs, inching his way up to her thighs. He listened to the sound of her breathing, then parted her legs to slip between them, teasing her inner thighs with his fingers.

Her breath caught, but she was languid, not tense.

She trusted him.

There were no other boats around since this was a restricted area and he'd gotten permission to be here today, so he didn't expect company. As long as no planes flew over, they'd have some privacy.

He wouldn't need long; he was already learning her body.

He untied the side of her bikini.

"Gray."

Her voice was barely a whisper.

"Yeah."

"What are you doing?"

"I'm going to make you come. Relax and let me."

No objection, just a slight lift of her butt as he slipped his hand underneath her.

She was already wet, hot, and pulsing as he slid his finger inside her.

"Oh," she said, her pussy gripping his finger. He slipped another finger inside her.

He sat next to her and used his other hand to find her clit, petting her, circling the nub until she arched against him, her pussy tightening around his fingers. He pulled out, then began to fuck her faster as he circled her clit.

"I want to fuck you like this. With me behind you, pumping inside you hard and fast until we both come."

"Yes," she said, arching her hips and slamming them down, meeting every thrust of his fingers with cries of abandon. Whatever reservations or hang-ups she'd had before she'd met him had been obliterated, because when she came, she dug her nails into the cushion and let him know in a very loud voice that made his dick twitch.

"Oh, God, yes, I'm coming."

"That's it. Let me have it all, babe."

She cried out and undulated against his fingers until she was out of breath, her hips collapsing against the cushions. He stroked her pussy, taking her up again, and this time, he grabbed a condom, climbed behind her, and dropped his trunks, sliding effortlessly into her.

"Oh, please, fuck me, Gray," she said, her pussy a tight sheath as he filled her.

He'd wanted to wait, but he couldn't. He needed to be inside her, needed to feel her gripping him, tightening around him as he gripped her hips and slammed his cock home.

"Fuck. Yeah," he said as he powered in deep, then retreated, only to thrust harder, go faster, reaching underneath to stroke her clit and bring her right to the brink again. And when she let go, he went with her, releasing that desire he'd held in check all day, erupting inside her with a loud groan while she cried out and reached for him, bucking back toward him.

He rolled to the side and dragged Evelyn against him, their bodies slick with sweat.

"I think I'm stuck to you," she finally said.

He smiled. "Sunscreen and sweat."

"Nice combo."

"How about another shower, this time without the swimsuits on?"

She turned over to face him. "You mean . . . naked? Out here on the ocean?"

"Yup."

"That could lead to sex, you know."

He arched a brow.

"Can we both fit?"

"Or die trying."

She laughed. They dashed into the shower, where they realized in a hurry that Gray was way too big and it wasn't going to be possible for both of them to fit in that tiny shower. He waited while Evelyn rinsed off, then he hopped in. By the time he got out, she'd put on her clothes and was standing at the mirror in the small sleeping area combing the tangles out of her hair.

Their gazes met in the mirror and she smiled at him, a knowing, I-just-had-sex-with-you-and-it-was-great kind of smile.

He liked this woman. Too much, probably, all things considered.

Deciding he didn't want to ponder the ramifications of that, he headed upstairs to pull anchor and head back to shore.

FIFTEEN

SEX AND A DAY OF RELAXATION WAS A GREAT WAY TO unwind from all the tension that had been hovering around her for far too long. Evelyn decided she should maybe ponder taking a day off now and then. And maybe start having sex more often.

She hadn't been this relaxed in a very long time. She had Gray to thank for that.

After they docked the boat—yacht, no matter how much he wanted to argue that it was just a "boat"—they headed back to Gray's most awesome GTO, and took the beach road toward Daytona.

She expected him to take her back to her hotel, so she was surprised when he turned off the highway and into a driveway right off the beach.

"Where are we going?" she asked.

"My place."

His place. When they reached the end of the driveway and she saw the ocean, she sighed. He had a beautiful, huge home that sat right on the beach.

"This is your place."

"Yeah."

He pulled into the garage—which was also incredible, since it looked like six garages all lumped into one. One of the doors opened and he drove the GTO in and parked it.

The other part of the garage was dark, so when he got out of the car and he hit the light switch, she couldn't help the look of awe that crossed her face.

There were five other cars sitting there, all covered up with tarps. It was like anticipating Christmas.

She lingered after he picked up their bags, staring at the covered cars.

He grinned and grabbed her hand. "I'll show them to you. Some other time."

"You're really going to make me wait?"

"Yup. The beach is there for us to explore. I thought you might want to take a walk."

She did. But she really did want to see those other cars.

Reluctantly, she let him lead her inside the house, which was magnificent, with views of the beach and ocean from nearly every room. There was an enormous kitchen with amazing appliances, a center island for cooking, and the most beautiful dark marble countertops she'd ever seen. She ran her fingertips over the smooth surface as they made their way past the dining room and a gorgeous black table that could easily seat a dozen people.

The living room was sunken and filled with leather and chrome furniture. It was all homey feeling though, and not cold and masculine. The white floors certainly helped brighten everything up, as did the myriad of floor-to-ceiling windows that showcased the incredible views.

She turned to him. "This is amazing. I don't know how you ever leave this place."

He smiled. "It's hard sometimes, but I love my job, so that makes it easier."

"I imagine so." Her gaze flitted to the winding staircase. "Bedrooms upstairs?"

"Yeah." His lips lifted in a smile. "We'll get to those later. How about a walk?"

"Definitely."

They headed out back onto the deck and down the stairs toward the beach. It was secluded, the nearest house rather far away.

"You must own a lot of land," she said as they made their way south along the shore.

"A bit. I like my privacy."

"For all those wild parties you throw when you're here?"

"I've been known to have a few during the off-season. But I wouldn't say they're wild. I just don't want my nearest neighbor to be able to peek into my bedroom."

She held her hand up to shield her face from the sun, trying to guess how far away the nearest house was. "I don't think your nearest neighbor could see into your bedroom with a high-powered telescope."

He laughed. "Just the way I like it."

The waves churned to shore, casting frothy water over her feet and ankles. The cool water felt good as they walked their way down the beach.

Evelyn wondered what it would be like to have a house like Gray had, to be able to sit on his deck and watch the waves roll in and out.

Not that she'd want to make this her permanent home. But a vacation home? A place to bring the kids? And the dog—she'd definitely want a dog or two. Maybe a Labrador, who'd want to take a leap into the ocean to fetch a ball or a Frisbee.

She laughed. It was always fun to plan out her imaginary family. The one she'd likely never have.

"What are you giggling about over there?"

She lifted her gaze to him, could imagine a dark-haired son with Gray's stubborn chin, or a little girl with his eyes.

Whoa. Shaking off those thoughts immediately, she smiled at him. "Just playing the what-if game while we walked."

"Yeah? Tell me."

"Oh, it was nothing, really."

He squeezed her hand and pulled her to a stop. "Evelyn. Tell me."

"I was just daydreaming about your big house with its stunning ocean view, thinking what it might be like to live in a place like that. Then I decided I wouldn't necessarily want to spend the rest of my life here, but it might be nice to have it as a vacation home, where I'd bring my imaginary children along with my imaginary dogs here for vacations. I even had my imaginary dogs fetching Frisbees from the water."

His lips curved, and she wanted to trace that smile with her fingertips.

"Yeah? That sounds like a pretty good plan. You should add that to your things-to-do-someday list."

"I don't think I have a list like that."

They resumed walking. "You should. Everyone should have a list like that."

"Do you?"

"Uh . . . no."

She shoved into him and laughed. "Then why tell me I should have one?"

"Because it's a good idea, you planning to become President of the United States and all. You should get started on all those goals. Like getting married and having kids and a dog. You're not going to get elected president being single."

"I'm too busy getting someone else elected right now. I'll worry about myself later."

He stopped again and pulled her against him. "You should put yourself first more often."

She'd thought much the same thing this morning when she realized how much being with Gray had helped her unwind. "I've thought about that."

"Have you?"

"Yes. I'm very relaxed right now. And thanks to you, I've decided I should take more downtime."

He skimmed his fingers along her back, making her wish she still wore her bikini instead of a tank top and shorts. She had loved the feel of his hands on her bare skin when they were on the boat. And what he'd done to her, the way he'd shattered her. She wasn't sure any man had ever learned her body so quickly, or if any man would ever make her come the way Gray could. A dangerous thought, because she didn't want to become emotionally attached to him.

It was just sex—mind-blowing, really awesome sex, but that's all it was, so making more out of it than what it was would only make her miserable when it was over.

And that was the hard truth she had to face.

She wanted more than just sex, and it was high time she started doing something about it.

But she wasn't going to be doing something about it with Gray Preston. He wasn't the forever and ever and two kids and the big yard and settling down and being supportive while she hustled through her political career kind of guy. He was racing cars and being on the road ten months out of the year kind of man. And that didn't fit with her lifestyle, any more than hers fit with his.

This was a fling. A great fling, but when it was over they'd go their separate ways, and then she'd see about getting that house with the big yard and the tire swing.

He tipped her chin up with his fingers and her gaze met his, her body melting under the warmth of his whiskey eyes.

"Did I lose you?"

Not yet. But eventually, she'd lose him, his great hands, his incredible body, and the way he made her feel when he touched her.

"No. I'm right here." Which was where she'd stay. In the moment, not waxing romantically about what could be, somewhere down the road in her future.

Somewhere far down the road.

He brushed his lips across hers and she melted into him, and when he explored her mouth with his tongue, she opened for him. He wrapped his arms around her and tugged her close. Here, out on the beach, with cool ocean water swimming over her feet, he could still heat her body to boiling.

He pulled his mouth from hers, his gaze heavy lidded and filled with the hunger that made her pulse beat erratically.

"Let's go back to the house."

She nodded and he grasped her hand. This time, their walk was faster as his thumb drew lazy circles over the top of her hand, driving her crazy. Her skin felt on fire, tuned in to his touch. By the time they climbed the back stairs and went through the doorway, she was ready to tear his clothes off with her teeth.

Apparently he felt the same way, because they kicked off their shoes right inside the door and he yanked her up the stairs, both of them out of breath from their near run down the beach. There was no tour of the bedrooms. He shoved open the master bedroom door and she got the barest glimpse of filtered light and windows and an amazing balcony before Gray picked her up and threw her onto one very large, soft bed. She fell into a mass of blankets and laughed as Gray climbed on top of her.

He framed her face and kissed her, his erection rubbing against her, dampening her, preparing her for him. She pulled off her top, and when he reached for her shorts, she lifted her hips, anxious to get clothes out of the way. He stood and she smiled as he tore his shirt off and tossed it aside. Content to just watch, he dropped his shorts, his cock hard as it sprang up. She reached for it, stroking him from base to tip.

"God, I like your hands on me," he said, tangling his fingers in her hair.

She swallowed, her throat going dry as she looked up at him and saw the desire on his face. He didn't even attempt to mask the hunger he felt for her. So many men played it cool, seemed to want that kind of power over a woman where she was the one in need and he couldn't care less. But Gray's face was etched with need as she moved her hand over him, and she knew just how much he craved her touch. In that, she had all the power, which only heightened her own desire. This true expression of sensuality, of intimacy, was such a revelation.

She drew up on her knees. "Touch me. I need your hands on me, too."

He reached behind her and undid the clasp of her bra, pulling it off and throwing it to the floor. She stood on the bed, holding on to his shoulders as he drew her panties down her legs. She started down to the mattress again, but Gray said, "Stay there."

She held on to him and he cupped the globes of her butt, drawing her toward his mouth. She shuddered when he found her sex, his tongue snaking out to curl around her clit.

She looked down and watched him, this viewpoint so different than anything she'd ever experienced as he held firm to her and drove her crazy with his mouth and tongue, diving in to lick and suck her until she was certain she wouldn't be able to stand. But she did, because she craved the orgasm that drew ever closer as he sucked on her clit and slid a finger into her pussy to fuck her.

"Gray," she whispered, so close her legs trembled.

He mumbled against her, flattening his tongue along her sex until she knew she was going to let go. But still, she held back, wanting to prolong the sweetest pleasure imaginable until she couldn't any longer. And when she came, he dug his fingers into her butt cheeks, holding her while he licked her through a shattering orgasm that made her dizzy.

She fell to the bed and Gray pulled her to the edge, his cock bobbing near her lips.

"Now, suck me and make me come, just like this."

Still panting, her pussy still spasming from the aftereffects of one mind-blowing orgasm, she opened her mouth and he slid his cock inside. She closed her lips over his shaft and let him feed his cock to her. He held the back of her head and slid it in and out.

"Fuck. Yeah, I like that," he said, and she could tell from the way his gaze was riveted to her face that he enjoyed having her at his mercy.

She enjoyed the taste of him, giving him the same kind of pleasure he gave her. She shifted, rolling onto her back and dropping her head down off the bed so he could watch his cock go down her throat.

"Christ, Evelyn." He leaned over her, pumping his cock between her lips while he massaged her breasts. She reached between her legs, so caught up in the moment, her senses heightened by his touch and the way he watched her that she couldn't help but want to get off again.

"You're making me crazy doing that," he said, his voice tight with strain as he slid his cock over her tongue. She clamped tight, closed her mouth, and swallowed as she moved her hand over her clit and pussy, wanting to come when she made him come.

He brushed his fingers over her breasts, teasing her nipples, pulling at them until the pleasure between her legs intensified. She was so close to coming she had to hold up. She wanted him to go with her.

"You ready to come?" he asked. "I'm going to come in your mouth, Evelyn. I want to come hard."

She hummed against his cockhead and slid her fingers in her pussy, rubbing against her clit until she couldn't hold back the rushing orgasm. She moaned as she came.

"Fuck yes," Gray yelled, and erupted into her mouth. She arched against the hard climax while swallowing everything he gave her, wanting to prolong it for him. When he went soft in her mouth, she let go, flicking her tongue at the head.

He fell onto the bed next to her and pulled her against him. It took her a few minutes to regain her bearings, but she finally got a look at the oversized bedroom, the wraparound balcony, and the amazing maple furniture that looked like it had been hand crafted.

"Nice room," she finally said.

He laughed, then dragged her out of bed. "Wait 'til you see the bathroom."

He was right. A window overlooking the ocean caught her attention right away, but the shower was decadent, with its multiple showerheads and a whirlpool tub with so many massaging jets she was determined to take a soak in it before she left.

They showered, dressed, then went downstairs.

"Hungry?" he asked.

"Yes. All that sex drives my appetite."

"Hopefully it drives your appetite for more sex."

She arched a brow. "Right now it's driving my appetite for food."

He opened the refrigerator. "Chicken?"

"How do you have food in your fridge?"

"My staff knows my schedule. They make sure the house is well stocked when I'm going to be home."

How utterly convenient. "Fantastic." She came up beside him. "I'll make a salad. And we can grill some vegetables."

He frowned. "No baked potato?"

After grabbing what she wanted out of there, she closed the fridge door. "A little healthy won't kill you. Besides, you need the extra vitamins, what with all this sex we're having."

"I need the extra carbs to cope with all this sex we're having."

She couldn't resist the grin. "Go grill the chicken. I'll prep the vegetables and make the salad."

He prepared the chicken on a plate, then grumbled, "I still think a baked potato would be better."

"Whiner. Go."

After dinner, they took a long walk on the beach. The sun had set and the ocean was silver and spectacular in the moonlight.

"I could get used to this," she said, holding Gray's hand as they took a slow stroll. "I might become clingy like one of your groupies and leave my career in politics and decide to squat on your property here."

He paused, studied her in silence. She hoped he knew she was just kidding.

"Do you do windows? Because it's hard to find good housekeepers here."

She snorted out a laugh. "Sadly, I suck at cleaning."

He sighed. "Then I'm afraid it's a no."

"Damn. I was already mentally packing. But only if you leave the keys to all those cars you have parked in the garage."

"Yeah, that's not gonna happen."

Now she paused, tugging on his hand to stop them. "You wouldn't trust me with your precious classics?"

"Not on your life. I'm the only one who drives those babies."

"What happens when you get married someday and your wife wants to tool around in that GTO? Are you going to tell her the same thing?"

"Hell yes. I don't want some woman, fresh from her manicure, getting pink nail polish on one of my cars."

She rolled her eyes. "It's a good thing I brought that up. You'll have to be sure to have the no-driving-the-muscle-cars entered into the prenup."

He went quiet. She wondered if the whole marriage and prenup thing was a sore spot for him in some way.

"Uh oh. I hit a sore spot, obviously. Have you ever been serious enough to get close to marriage?" she asked.

He grinned. "No sore spot at all. I'm just making a mental note about no-driving-the-cars in the prenup. And no, I've never gotten remotely close to marriage yet. Have you?"

"No. But believe me, I've got my prenup already planned out."

He turned to her. "You do?"

"Hell yes. I have to protect all those assets in my nine-hundred-square-foot apartment. No way is some guy going to get his greedy hands on my George Washington Chia pet."

He laughed, then grabbed her around the waist. "Smart-ass."

She squealed as he picked her up and held her above the water, threatening to drop her into the waves. But then he put her down in the sand, and looked at her.

"What would you like to do now?"

She gave him a grin. "How about a tour of those cars in your garage?"

SIXTEEN

ONE BY ONE, GRAY LIFTED THE COVERS OFF HIS MUS-
cle cars. First the '69 Mustang, followed by the '70 Firebird, the '67
Chevelle, the '69 Charger Hemi, and finally the '68 Shelby GT.
With each reveal, Evelyn gasped with delight.

He had to admit, secondary to racing, these cars were what fu-
eled him. He didn't take much pride in possessions, frankly could
give a shit if he lived in a multimillion-dollar house on the beach or
a one-bedroom apartment somewhere. Material things didn't matter
to him. But these cars did, because they represented the one thing
he enjoyed the most—fast cars.

"Can I get close?" she asked.

"You can touch. Don't worry about it."

She ran her fingers across the hood of the Chevelle, almost rever-
ently. She turned to him. "When I was in college, there was this one
guy in my government class who had a car similar to this one. He'd
drive it to class every day and when I was walking along, I'd hear the

roar of the engine. It never failed to make the hairs on the back of my neck stand up. I had to cross the parking lot to get to the building, so I found myself lingering outside and waiting for him to show up just so I could see him pull that car into the lot."

He leaned against one of the cars. "So, you had a thing for him, huh?"

She laughed. "No, I had a thing for his car."

"Did you go out with him?"

"No. I was very . . . bookish back then, very much into focusing on school and not so much on guys. But oh, he had a hot car."

"That's what I keep telling you. You missed out on having some guy take you riding at high speeds in a muscle car."

She threw a gaze over her shoulder at the Chevelle. "You could rectify that now, you know."

He loved that she shared his passion for these cars, even if she wasn't yet aware of it. "Sure. Choose one."

She didn't even hesitate. She pointed to the Chevelle "This one. Definitely."

"You got it." He walked over and pulled the keys off the rack. "Slide on in."

Her cheeks pink with excitement, she slid into the passenger seat while Gray hit the garage door button. Lap belt fastened, he put the car into gear and backed out, then drove onto the highway, knowing exactly what stretch of deserted road he could take her to. When he pulled off, the road was pitch black.

"Where are we going?"

"Nowhere special," he said, then downshifted, let out the clutch, and hit the gas, cranking up the speed, conscious of his surroundings. No one was ever on this road. He'd tested the cars on it before, so he knew he had smooth sailing for the next several miles.

He got it up over a hundred and twenty, pretty slow by his standards, but by the time he slowed it down to under sixty, he took a glance over at Evelyn. She had a death grip on the seat and the arm-rest and her cheeks were dark pink. He pulled to a stop.

"Okay?" he asked.

She slowly turned her head to face him. "Oh. My. God."

He didn't know if that was a good thing or a bad thing, at least until she broke into a wide grin and asked, "Can we do that again?"

He laughed. "Sure. I'll turn around and we'll hit it on the way back."

He downshifted again, then cranked the speed up, this time going a little faster. Sure, he was showing off for her, but he also knew the capabilities of this car and wouldn't do anything to over-stress the engine. By the time he slowed it down, she had her hand on his thigh and was clutching tight.

"You okay?" he asked with a short laugh as he pulled to the side of the road.

"Honestly? It made me wet."

Which made his dick instantly hard. "How wet?"

She gave him the kind of direct look a man definitely paid atten-tion to. "You have a condom on you and I'll show you how wet."

Thank God he had shoved one into the pocket of his jeans be-fore they went out tonight—just in case something like this might come up. And something was definitely up. He turned off the en-gine, jammed his foot on the emergency brake, and shoved his hand into his pocket, retrieving the condom. "It just so happens . . ."

She slid off her sandals and unbuttoned her shorts. "How alone are we out here?"

He unzipped his jeans. "Alone enough. Get those shorts off and get over here."

It was a flurry of activity as he shifted the seat back as far as it would go while Evelyn shimmied out of her shorts and panties. She grabbed the condom packet from his hands and tore the wrapper open while he pulled his cock out and shrugged his jeans and boxer briefs down far enough to pull out his cock.

She got the condom on him, giggling as she did. "I feel like a teenager, only I never did any of this when I was a teenager."

He grabbed her and kissed her until his balls throbbed, then licked her bottom lip. "Babe, you missed out."

She braced her hands on his shoulders. "Time to start rectifying that."

She straddled him and he grasped her hips, holding on to her while she slid down on his aching cock.

"Oh, yeah," he said, watching his shaft disappear between her sweet pussy lips. "You feel good."

She tilted her head back, her ponytail bobbing in the moonlight. He slid his hand under her shirt and pulled the cups of her bra down so he could get to her breasts while she rocked back and forth on his dick.

When she met his gaze, she leaned forward and kissed him, the kiss so blistering hot he could blow his load right now. But he held, wanting her to come. The look on her face was so beautiful as she rode him, dragging her clit over his flesh, her lips open as she breathed heavily.

She grabbed his hand and put it on her clit. "Touch me," she whispered. "Make me come."

God, he loved that she was so open, so expressive and eager to explore new things. He shifted back so he could have better access and rubbed her clit, giving her the friction she needed by arching his hips upward. The sounds she made told him she was close, which was a damn good thing because it was killing him not to come.

And when she tightened around him and let out a hoarse cry, he let go, gripping her hip with one hand while he continued to rub her clit with the other, releasing and jerking as he came with her. She dug her nails into his shoulder and rode out her own orgasm until she collapsed against him, her lips pressed against his neck.

It took her a while to raise her head. Her hair was mussed, her ponytail had come undone, her lips were swollen from his kisses, and one bra strap peeked out of her tank top. She'd never looked sexier.

"Your poor, pristine car," she said, smoothing her hand over the back of the seat.

"The car is fine," he said, pulling her forward for a long, lingering kiss that made his cock spring to life again. When he released her, she arched a brow.

"Much as I would love round two, my hips are cramping from being in this position."

He laughed and she crawled over to the passenger seat. They fixed their clothes and she found her ponytail holder on the floor of his side of the car.

"I probably look like I've been out drinking all night," she said, taking a glance at herself in the rearview mirror.

He grabbed her hand. "You look well and truly fucked, which to me makes you look sexy as hell—and gorgeous."

She grinned. "Good enough."

They put their seat belts on and he started up the car. It growled to life and he put it in first, heading back toward the house.

It was late, and he knew tomorrow—the Fourth of July—would be a big day.

Tomorrow, he'd have to face his father again.

Fun time was over.

They climbed into bed and he pulled Evelyn against him.

"I had a wonderful time today," she said as she laid her head on his chest. "Thank you."

"You're welcome. Thanks for spending the day with me."

He lay there silently while he looked outside and listened to the ocean waves. The one thing he loved the most about being here was the ocean, how it could always obliterate whatever thoughts plagued him and lull him to sleep.

Not tonight, though.

"You're not sleeping," Evelyn said, smoothing her hand over his chest.

He looked down at her. "If you're noticing me not sleeping, then neither are you."

She smiled up at him. "Something on your mind? Tomorrow, maybe?"

"Maybe."

She sat up. "Do you want to talk about it?"

He didn't even want to think about it. He pulled her down and smoothed his hand over her hair, content to remember the day he'd had with this remarkable woman. He refused to let thoughts of his father ruin what had been such a special day. A relaxing day. A day he'd needed, one that had really surprised the hell out of him. Evelyn continually surprised him.

"No. There's nothing to talk about. It's just one day."

"Yes, it is."

Running his hand down the silky strands of her hair had a calming effect on him. He closed his eyes and let sleep claim him.

SEVENTEEN

GRAY HADN'T COUNTED ON HIS FATHER'S PRIVATE JET picking them up at the airport and whisking them to Oklahoma, but it shouldn't have surprised him. He figured Evelyn had booked them a commercial flight, but she said it was easier for them to use the senator's plane.

Gray had long ago stopped making use of Preston money for anything, other than the money his grandfather had left specifically for his use. Otherwise, he'd made it on his own by working hard and earning his own money.

He hadn't flown in the Preston jet in years. Then again, he hadn't been to the ranch in a long time, either, so as one of his father's cars took them from the airport to the ranch, he wondered how much, if anything, had changed.

He and his mother usually met on neutral ground, which didn't sit well with her, but it was what it was and that's how things had to be these days. He didn't come home for holidays anymore because he knew his father would be there. His younger sister, Carolina, didn't appreciate that, either, but she'd always been Daddy's girl. She worshipped their father, and Gray would never get in the way of their relationship. He missed his sister, but there were other ways of seeing her, too, though she was busy with her own life. At least she'd show up at a few of his races every year and the two of them would catch up on each other's lives.

"Do you know my sister?" he asked Evelyn as they rode in the backseat of the private car.

Evelyn smiled. "Yes. I see Carolina a lot when she visits your father in Washington. We've become friends. I can't wait to see her today and catch up."

There was an interesting dynamic. Evelyn and his sister— friends. He hadn't expected that. "I'd appreciate it if you'd keep what's going on between us, just between us."

She cocked her head to the side. "Of course, Gray. I'm very discreet." She gave a quick glance to the private screen between them and the driver before shifting her gaze back to his. "I'd also appreciate your discretion. Though you don't think much of your father's politics, my job is very important to me. If your father senses any impropriety, or thinks I'm not giving this campaign my all, it could put my position with him in jeopardy."

He'd never thought about it from her position, only how everything having to do with his father—with his family—affected him. Sometimes he really was an insensitive ass. He picked up her hand and pressed a kiss to the back of it. "Despite how hard it's going to be to keep my hands off you today, Miss Hill, I'll do my best to pretend we're just working together. I'll even let my father know how much I resent your interference in my everyday life."

She beamed a smile. "That would be perfect. And speaking of my interference in your life—" She pulled out her laptop. "This is the agenda for today, including media opportunities and what I plan to post to your social media accounts. I'd like your approval before you get too busy with family things."

He looked it over. True to her word, she kept it all pretty benign, the information she'd put together saying only that he'd be spending the holiday with his family, including his father, the senator, and his mother. No campaign stuff, at least not yet, though she had mentioned they'd be taking photos throughout the day. They could go over those later.

"This looks fine," he said, swiping his knuckles across her cheek. "Thanks for checking with me."

"You're welcome. Thanks for letting me post something about today."

"You're welcome."

Her gaze lingered on his. It was going to be difficult not touching her today. Yesterday had been great, because he'd been free to be with her, to spend time with her, and to put his hands on her whenever he felt like it.

Today they'd go back to being professional strangers again.

"Have you been to the ranch before?"

She shook her head. "No. I'm excited to see it. Your father talks about it a lot, and your mother loves this place. She tells me she can't wait for your father to retire so they can spend more time here."

He couldn't imagine his father ever retiring from politics. "Which could be a while, especially if he gets the VP nomination and they win."

"That's true."

The car pulled down a dirt road. Gray had to admit he was looking forward to visiting the ranch, and when they pulled up to the main gates and he saw Preston Ranch scrolled in iron, he took a deep breath.

His issues with his father aside, this was home. Thousands and thousands of acres of home.

"Wow," Evelyn said, leaning closer to the window to look out as they drove past a herd of cattle. She dragged her gaze away from the window. "I've read the books about your father and studied his bio extensively, so I know the ranch has been in your family for generations, but seeing it in person is a sight to behold."

He smiled. "Yeah, it was a privilege to grow up here. I learned a lot from my grandfather."

They drove the mile or so to the ranch house. The car stopped and Gray got out and held his hand out for Evelyn.

She stepped out and he wanted to pull her against him and kiss her. She looked so fresh and cute in her white pants and navy striped top. She'd pulled her hair up today since it was hotter than a blazing forest fire out here. That was the one thing he remembered about the family Fourth of July barbecues. You could always count on them being blistering hot. Then again, there was the pool to cool things down.

Maybe Evelyn would don her bikini today. He had that thought to look forward to.

"You ready for this?" she asked.

He cocked her a grin. "Are you? There are lots of family members here. Plus, I might have invited some of my friends."

Her brows rose. "You did?"

"Yeah. A few of my college buddies are in town for a charity golf tournament. They asked me to join in, but I wanted some downtime at my place in Florida so I turned them down."

"Oh, that's too bad, but I'm looking forward to meeting your friends."

He laughed. "Wait 'til you meet them before you say that."

He led her through the front door of the house, a blast of cold air instantly cooling him down.

"Oh, this is lovely," Evelyn said. "It has your mother's mark on it."

"Yeah," he said, smiling as he saw the simplicity that was the earmark of his mom. He'd always loved the two-story house. When he was a kid it had seemed like a mansion. Hell, even now it was oversized and his mother complained that she was waiting for him and Carolina to fill it with grandkids. He sure as hell wasn't ready for that, and Carolina was busy becoming the next great fashion designer, so he doubted she'd be popping out babies anytime soon.

Speaking of his mother—ever the eagle-eyed hostess, she spotted them in the crowd and moved in a hurry to greet them. She enveloped Gray in a hug.

"Thank you for coming," she said, and after he hugged her back, she pulled away, but didn't let go of his hands. "I wasn't sure you'd show up."

"With my bodyguard here? You think I had a chance to say no?"

His mother glanced over at Evelyn and grinned. "So, she's doing a good job?"

"She's a pain in my ass."

"Grayson. Watch your language." His mother let go of him and hugged Evelyn. "I'm so happy to see you. Is my son being mean to you?"

Evelyn gave Gray a once-over. "Nothing I can't handle. Don't forget I swim with sharks every day."

His mom patted Evelyn on the shoulder. "That's so true. But don't take any guff from him. He can be . . . difficult to manage at times."

"Hey. I'm standing right here, Mom."

She winked at him, then looped her arm in Evelyn's. "Let's go find you two something to drink. Come along, Grayson."

And just like that, he was eight years old again, tagging along behind his mother. He rolled his eyes and followed them out to the back patio. There were kids in the pool and at least a hundred people spilled out over the back lawn. Shade tents had been set up all over the property, beer and whiskey were plentiful, and the smell of barbecue permeated the whole area. It was controlled chaos, and there were plenty of staffers present to make sure everyone was catered to.

Typical Preston holiday party.

His mother had disappeared somewhere with Evelyn while he'd been gaping, so he grabbed a beer and settled in against the wall, greeting a few cousins and aunts and uncles and doing his best to ignore the obvious political types he could spot ten miles away. Despite everyone being in casual dress, he knew who was here to enjoy the holiday and who was here to gain political favor with his father.

Speaking of, he spotted his dad surrounded by a circle of men, no doubt talking the state of the country and how their political opponent couldn't possibly solve those issues. His dad appeared to be reveling in being the center of attention as the men hung on his every word.

Yeah, some things never changed.

"I can't believe you showed up."

At the nudge in his back, he swung around and grabbed his sister in a hug. "I can't believe you showed up." He kissed her cheek, then set her down. "Aren't you afraid to be gone from New York for more than fifteen minutes? What if a fashion trend changes and you miss it?"

"You are such a smart-ass."

"And you cut your hair. I like it."

She swept her now chin-length brown hair behind her ears. "It was long, and always in my way. This is easier. And thanks. Look at you, being all complimentary. You've hardly even noticed me before."

"I've noticed you plenty," he said, slinging an arm over her shoulder. "I've noticed you being a pain in my ass my entire life."

She laid her head against his shoulder. "You've always said the sweetest things to me."

"Yeah, well, I do like your hair, but you're too skinny. You need to eat."

She laughed. "Dork. I am not. I'm perfectly healthy. I've just discovered yoga and good eating and finally lost the weight I needed to lose. That and the stress of work."

"You were never overweight." Though he had to admit she looked great in her skinny jeans and some kind of silky tank top. Still, she was his sister, who he'd once nicknamed Pudge, which was cruel as hell, but that's what brothers did.

"Okay, then, you look awesome."

She patted his chest. "There might be hope for your species yet."

"Thanks."

"Don't get excited. I didn't say there was hope for you."

"See, this is what I enjoy about homecomings. All the family love."

"Yeah, me, too," she said, grabbing a carrot stick from the food tray.

"Have you seen Mom?"

She straightened. "Yeah. Why?"

"She ran off somewhere with Evelyn."

"Oooh, Evelyn. What's going on with you and Evelyn?"

He rolled his eyes. "Nothing. I need to talk to her about the plan for today."

"Oooh. You and Evelyn have plans for today?"

"Jesus, Care. Are you twelve?"

She laughed. "Sometimes. When it's convenient or when it pisses you off. So what is going on with you and Evelyn?"

He'd have to be careful what he said in front of his nosy sister. He led her over to one of the many picnic tables spread out on the lawn, choosing one in a shady spot. They took a seat next to each other. "Nothing's going on with Evelyn. Dad assigned her to do some so-

cial media shit with me for his campaign. I want to get it over with
so I can actually enjoy being here today."

"Yeah. Right. You and Dad in the same hemisphere? You won't
enjoy today."

"You have a point."

"And you need to get over it. He's not the same person he used
to be."

"So everyone keeps telling me. He looks the same to me. Though
he's lost a lot of weight, no doubt to be more camera-ready for this
big election."

Carolina grasped his upper arm, focusing his attention on her.
"Seriously, Gray. When was the last time you sat down with Dad and
had an honest conversation with him?"

His senior year of high school, when he'd told his father he
wouldn't be going to Harvard. "I don't need to have a conversation
with him. I know who he is. And what he's capable of."

"Give it another try. He's changed in the—what—twelve years
since the two of you had that blowup?"

Gray shrugged. "It's not worth rehashing. We both said everything that needed to be said back then."

"You know, if you agreed to work on Dad's campaign, at some
point the two of you are going to have to talk."

He looked at her and smiled. "Hey, I can talk. I'm good at talking."

"I mean a real talk."

"Not going to happen. But I can toe the party line as good as any
of them. You've seen my media interviews, right?" He shot her a
golden boy grin. "I'm a star, baby."

"Oh, for God's sake. I give up."

"What do you give up on?"

"Hi, Evelyn," Carolina said, smiling up as Evelyn stood on the
other side of the table.

"Am I interrupting a private talk?"

Carolina laughed. "My brother and I do not have private talks. Sit and tell me what's been going on?"

"Did Gray tell you I'm working with him?"

"He did. How . . . tragic for you."

Evelyn smiled. "He's not too bad. Though he wasn't happy at the beginning."

Gray folded his hands on the table. "I love how people talk about me like I'm not even here."

"Well, you weren't happy about it, were you? As I recall, you threw me out the first night."

Carolina looked from Evelyn to Gray. "You did not."

"He did," Evelyn said. "Politely, but he did."

Gray had to nod and play this game. He knew what Evelyn was doing. "Yeah. I did. And then Mom showed up the next day."

Carolina looked horrified. "She did not."

"She did," Gray said, then shifted his gaze to Evelyn. "Because *someone* called her." He still remembered how pissed off he was about that. But he gave props to Evelyn for not taking no for an answer. Her passion was one of the things he admired so much about her. Their gazes met for a few seconds, the attraction between them hotter than the air around then. It was Evelyn who forcibly pulled her gaze away.

Carolina put her hands to her mouth, stifling a laugh. "You did not."

Evelyn didn't even try to hide her smug smile. "I have an assignment. I had to pull out the big guns. I always get what I want," she said, directing her attention to Gray.

If she kept looking at him like that he was going to get hard, and then he'd end up stuck with his hands folded in his lap.

"Oh, my God, Evelyn," Carolina said. "You so rock."

Forcing in a deep breath, Gray said, "She doesn't rock. She's a pain in the ass. She follows me around like . . . I don't know, it's like I have an extra appendage."

Evelyn rolled her eyes, looking to Carolina. "It's not that bad. For him, anyway. For me, that's a different matter."

Carolina grabbed Evelyn's hand and laughed. "Oh, Evelyn. You have my deepest sympathies. I spent sixteen years living with him. I know what it's like."

"Whatever, brat. I gave you rides to school. I made you popular."

"I think I had the popularity thing sewn up just fine without your help, dickwad."

"Whatever, Pudge."

Carolina narrowed her gaze. "Now that was a low blow, Zit Face."

Evelyn enjoyed the hell out of watching brother and sister argue. Being an only child, she had never had siblings to fight with, so this was unfamiliar to her. But oh so amusing as they hurled insults at each other like they were both kids again. Still, it seemed like good-natured fun, both of them laughing as each of them tried to one-up the other in the zinger department.

She was almost sad to see it end when Gray stood. "I need another beer. And to empty the contents of the one I already had."

"Way too much information," Carolina said.

He laughed. "Can I bring you back something to drink?"

"I'd love an iced tea, if you don't mind," Evelyn said, her gaze lingering on him. She tried not to watch him, not to wish they were alone together. She hoped she didn't give too much away.

"Tea. Got it," he said, and she couldn't help but notice the smile he gave her.

"Thanks."

"I'll have tea, too," Carolina said.

After Gray walked away, Carolina asked, "So how did you get roped into working with my brother?"

"Actually, it was my idea. I suggested it to your father."

"Seriously?"

"Yes. Gray has a potential voter block we could make use of."

"Oh. Of course. Him being so popular and all. I forget about that. To me he's just my annoying, pain-in-the-ass brother that I love more than life itself. I don't think of him as some hotshot race car driver that has millions of fans."

Evelyn laughed. "No, I imagine you don't see him that way."

"So, how's it going?"

"We're still in the getting-started phase, but so far, so good."

"And how long have you two been sleeping together?"

Her stomach knotted. She put on her best blank face. "I don't know what you're talking about."

"Evelyn. Please. The sparks shooting off between the two of you were like an early fireworks show. I almost had to excuse myself to go inside and cool off."

She could lie her way out of it, but this was Carolina. She might be Gray's sister, and she might be the senator's daughter, but she was also Evelyn's friend. She trusted Carolina, so she laid her head in her hands. "Oh, God. Is it that obvious?"

"To me it is. But Gray's my brother. And you're one of my best friends."

She lifted her head. "It's nothing really. A fling."

"Obviously it's something. I've never seen you like this about a guy." Carolina wrinkled her nose. "My brother? Really? Are you in love with him?"

"Of course not!" Then, realizing she'd denied that a little too vehemently, she said, "Not that he isn't totally loveable."

Carolina laughed. "Please. You don't need to defend his honor. He can be a real asshole. I just meant, is it serious between you two?"

"No. It wasn't supposed to happen at all. But now that it has, we're keeping it . . . simple."

"Okay. Well, good luck with that. Things that are supposed to be simple usually end up being anything but."

"You aren't going to say anything to your father, are you?"

Carolina grabbed her hand. "Look. I will always be honest with my dad if I think something can harm him. But what's going on between you and Gray doesn't have anything to do with him. You're my friend, and in matters of romance, I'm loyal to you. I know this is your job and you want to protect it, so don't worry about me saying anything. First and foremost, though, I worry about your heart."

She squeezed Carolina's hand. "My heart is fine. I know what I'm doing."

Carolina let out a short laugh. "I wonder how many women have uttered those words right before getting their hearts broken?"

"Too many, probably. But enough about me. Tell me about your enviable career in fashion design."

Carolina took a deep breath, then sighed. "It's been a dream come true. I love what I do and I'm so lucky. And I love New York so much."

"And the clothing line? How's that coming along?"

"Slowly. I don't want to make any missteps. I'm still a baby in this industry, so working for David sustains me right now."

"But you still want to launch your own line someday."

"Of course. What designer doesn't?" Carolina smiled. "But if you launch too soon, before you're ready, you blow your one and only chance of success. So I'm taking those baby steps right now and working on a line I believe will work."

Evelyn grabbed Carolina's hands "I'm so excited for you. I can't wait to see what you come up with."

"It's nerve-racking, trying to design your own line while working for another designer."

"Does David know what you're doing?"

"Of course not. No designer wants to believe he has competition from within his ranks. Plus, he's such a paranoid diva. He'd fire me on the spot."

Evelyn laughed. "I can't imagine how difficult that must be. So you work at home on your own designs?"

"Yes. And as hard as David works me, it keeps me busy at night and on— Oh, hell, no. What are you doing here?"

Evelyn turned around as a shadow spilled over the picnic table. A tall, mouthwateringly gorgeous man came forward, a wide grin showing off straight white teeth and a devilish smile.

"Nice to see you too, Lina."

"It's *Carolina*, you idiot."

The gorgeous guy grinned. "Where's your brother?"

"It's not my day to watch him, but you should definitely leave and find him."

Tall, tanned, and sexy took a seat next to Carolina. Wow. He was stunning, with shaggy raven black hair and the most unusual gray eyes. And the body. Oh, the body.

He half stood and leaned over the table, extending his hand. "Since Carolina has decided to be rude, I'm Drew Hogan, a friend of Carolina's brother."

"Evelyn Hill. I work for Senator Preston."

"Nice to meet you, Evelyn."

"Guard your panties, Evelyn, or Drew will try to get in them within the next five minutes."

"Ouch, Lina," Drew said, before he turned his attention back to Evelyn. "She lies. I'm a lot smoother than that, and a gentleman. I'd give it at least a half hour and buy you a drink first before I tried to get your clothes off."

Evelyn laughed. "Thanks for the warning."

She shifted her gaze to Carolina, who was staring daggers at Drew.

Interesting.

"And again, Drew. What are you doing here?" Carolina asked.

"Gray invited me."

Carolina rolled her eyes. "Whatever for?"

Drew shrugged. "No idea. For some reason, the bastard likes me."

"Fortunately for you, someone does."

Carolina's insults seemed to roll off Drew's back. He looked at Evelyn. "She's mean to me. You feel sorry for me, don't you, Evelyn?"

"Not in the least. I would imagine you could hold your own, even with a prickly female."

"Well, Lina has her share of thorns." He picked up Carolina's hand, and despite her tugging to release it, held it firm. He pressed a kiss to the tips of her fingers. "But I know for a fact there's a sweet rose underneath."

"You are such a dick, Drew." Carolina jerked her hand away and shoved it in her lap. "Why don't you go find Gray and leave me—us—alone?"

"No need to look for me. I'm right here."

Evelyn looked up as Gray took a seat beside her. He handed the women their iced teas.

Gray shook Drew's hand. "I'm glad you came."

"Me, too," Drew said with a grin. "Though your sister's not."

Gray shifted his gaze to Carolina and quirked a smile. "Still pissed at him, huh?"

Carolina lifted her chin. "I'm not pissed at Drew. I don't feel anything for him at all." She stood, walked around the table, and pressed a kiss to Evelyn's cheek. "We'll chat later."

"Okay." Evelyn definitely wanted to know about Carolina's past history with Drew. But in the meantime, she focused her attention on the two incredible-looking men sitting at her table.

"I can't believe *you're* here," Drew said to Gray.

"Yeah," Gray said with a half smile. "Me, either."

"Is this your doing?" Drew gave Evelyn a brows-raised questioning look.

"You could say that. My job is to work with Gray on helping his father's campaign."

"No shit." Drew shifted his gaze to Gray. "So you're working with your dad now?"

"Indirectly," Gray said. "Something about introducing my fans to my dad through social media."

"Ah." Drew nodded. "More voters. Gray has a big fan base."

"Exactly," Evelyn said. "And what do you do, Drew?"

Drew grinned. "I play hockey."

"Oh, I love hockey. Who do you play for?"

"New York."

"Wow, that's a very successful team. And you went to college with Gray?"

"Yeah. We go way back." Drew focused his attention on Gray. "Speaking of, missed you at the golf tournament."

"Yeah, sorry man. The schedule just didn't work out for that. How did it go?"

"Great. Trevor came in third. I was fifth. Garrett was tenth."

Gray nodded. "Pretty good showing. Bet Garrett hated you both beating him."

"He did," Drew said with a laugh. "Lost a thou on a bet we made, too. That one stung."

"That's what he gets for betting on golf with you guys." Gray looked around. "Where are Garrett and Trevor?"

"Garrett and Alicia had to leave right away, so he sent his regrets and told me to tell you he'd call you later this week. He said they're going to try and make your race in Kansas City. Trevor's around here somewhere."

"Probably hitting on some poor woman."

"Likely."

"There are more of you?" Evelyn asked, astounded by two of these gorgeous men. That there were four? It wasn't possible.

"Yeah," Gray said, turning to her with that smile that always gave her stomach butterflies. "Trevor, Drew, Garrett, and I roomed together in college."

"Here," Drew said, pulling out his phone. "Here's a picture from our last get-together at the lodge."

Evelyn took his phone and inspected the photo. Good lord. That much gorgeous man flesh in one place should be illegal. She swallowed and gave him the phone back. "Great picture."

"Thanks." Drew turned back to Gray. "Hey, I heard Briscoe was sick."

Gray frowned. "How sick?"

"Pretty bad. They think it might be cancer."

Evelyn laid a hand on Gray's arm. "Who's Briscoe?"

Gray turned to her. "Bill Briscoe and his wife, Ginger, were our dorm parents in college. They were like parents to all of us when we were there. We got close to them. Nice people. Really nice people." He shifted his gaze to Drew. "Have you been by to see them?"

"Not yet. I was going to go tomorrow. You want to come?"

He nodded. "I need to get back to the track, but we could go in the morning."

"Trevor wants to go, too," Drew said.

"Good. Have you talked to Haven yet?"

"Yeah. She's up from Dallas to be with her folks."

"Haven is Bill and Ginger's daughter," Gray explained to her.

Evelyn nodded. She could tell this upset Gray, that he was obviously close to Bill Briscoe. How sad for the family to be going through something so troubling. She hoped he'd be all right. It was hard to care about someone, to know they were hurting and not be able to be there for them. She squeezed his arm and he laid his hand over hers.

"Whoa. What's going on here?"

She looked up to see one of the men from the picture Drew showed her. This must be Trevor, just as devastatingly gorgeous as Gray and Drew. He was tall and well built, with dark hair that fell across his forehead. A woman would itch to brush that hair away from his mesmerizing eyes, just so she could get a better look. And his mouth—oh, he had amazing lips.

Wow.

Gray pulled away from her, stood, and shook Trevor's hand.

"Trevor, this is Evelyn Hill."

She stood, too, and shook his hand. "Very nice to meet you, Trevor."

"You too, Evelyn. It's good to see Gray's taste in women is improving."

Evelyn laughed. "I work for his father."

Trevor cocked a brow and flashed those amazing green eyes at her. "So you're not his girlfriend?"

"No."

"Too bad. The bleached blondes with short skirts and big boobs he tends to drag around are pretty low class. You, honey, are dynamite in a very classy package."

She couldn't help but smile at the compliment. "Well, thank you for that, Trevor."

"Knock it off, Trev. I've got dibs on her," Drew said.

Trevor shot a look at Drew. "My guess is she wouldn't give you the time of day."

"You can both knock if off," Gray said. "She's with me."

"Which means what, exactly?" Drew asked.

"It means she's with me." Gray gave them both a look and Drew shrugged.

"Too bad," Drew said. "Once you get bored with him, Evelyn, let me know. I'm way more fun."

Evelyn found this conversation absolutely fascinating. The two of them had agreed to be hands-off today, and yet Gray had more or less inferred that they were . . . together. At least to his friends. Maybe he was trying to keep them from hitting on her. She had no idea.

She excused herself and went in search of Carolina. She found her sitting on the patio talking to Loretta, so she sat with them and visited for a while, until Loretta hopped up to see to a few of the guests' needs, leaving her and Carolina alone again.

"So?" Evelyn asked.

Carolina sipped her drink. "So what?"

"So are you going to tell me about you and Drew?"

"Oh. That. It's nothing."

"It didn't look like nothing to me."

"He's a jerk."

"He's a pretty hot jerk."

"Yes, he's hot. And he knows it, too. He's always known it."

Evelyn sat back and took a sip of tea, studying Carolina, who was searching the crowd. When Carolina's gaze settled over Drew and lingered there, she knew something was up.

"Okay, spill. What went down with you and Drew?"

Carolina sighed and pulled her attention away from Drew, who was currently standing in a group with Gray and Trevor. Admittedly, Evelyn understood the attraction. Drew was incredibly handsome, with a strong jaw and killer smile. And there was no denying he had an amazing body, showcased oh so well in those jeans and that tight T-shirt. If her libido wasn't already focused on Gray, Evelyn would be very attracted to him.

But the thing was, she wasn't attracted to Drew. Or Trevor, despite them both being gorgeous and obviously available.

She was, however, extremely attracted to Gray, who kept shooting looks her way and smiling at her. Which was very inappropriate considering they were surrounded by a lot of the people she worked with. And despite her being on her best behavior today, she couldn't help but look back. He was like a giant sex magnet.

Damn him.

"Are you sure you want to talk about me and Drew, considering you're having hot sex fantasies about my brother right now?"

She jerked her attention back to Carolina. "What? I am not."

Carolina laughed. "Yes, you were. Your tongue was practically hanging out. And you might want to wipe the drool from the side of your mouth."

She reached up to touch her lips, then gave Carolina a glare. "You are not funny. And you're changing the subject so you don't have to talk about Drew."

"Caught you, though." Carolina took another swallow of lemonade. "There's not much to tell. I had a stupid schoolgirl crush on him that went very badly."

"How badly?"

"I followed him around the college campus. I was two years behind Drew and Gray and the others, so once I hit campus, I thought I could meet all the hot guys through Gray. My big brother, of course, wanted nothing to do with his dorky little sister. And Drew teased me incessantly. I was a late bloomer, too, so it wasn't until I hit twenty or so that I learned all about makeup and fashion—"

At Evelyn's shocked look, Carolina nodded. "I know, I know. You'd think since fashion is my life, I would have wrapped myself in designer clothing from age twelve. Not so. I was a big, dumb moron who didn't know how to dress or make myself look decent until I took some classes."

"I find that so hard to believe."

Carolina laughed. "Sometimes I look back and I'm appalled at my younger self. And you know those cartoons where the cartoon character has a big lightbulb go off over their heads? That was me. It was like I had this sudden awareness of fashion and what clothes fit my body type and looked good on me. I styled my hair and learned all about makeup, and suddenly guys noticed me."

Evelyn's lips curved. "Bet that was fun."

"Oh, it was. By the beginning of my sophomore year of college, I was partying like there was no tomorrow. I gained a lot of knowledge that year."

"I'll just bet you did."

"I felt very worldly and experienced, when in reality I had no clue what men were about. So when Gray graduated, I decided to hit up my smoldering crush with my newfound expertise about men."

"Your smoldering crush being Drew."

She nodded. "Yes. And he, having a penis, didn't turn me down. We had one blistering-hot night of no-holds-barred sex. I thought I had seduced him and he would fall head over heels in love with me, now that he'd seen the transformed Carolina."

Evelyn could sense where this was going. "But that didn't happen."

Carolina let out a short laugh. "No. He left me in bed the next morning, packed up, left school, and I never heard from him again."

"Ouch. I'm sorry."

She shrugged. "It's ancient history. I was heartbroken at the time, of course, all those youthful dreams being shattered."

"I'm sure you were. Young men can be so insensitive."

"Well, in retrospect I realize now it wasn't entirely his fault. He'd made no promises to me of forever or love. But at the time I had stars in my eyes because I was convinced I was in love with him. And he used my feelings for him to get me in the sack. At the time I was crushed. And he could have handled letting me down a little better."

"Yes, he could have. But men can be such assholes."

"Yes, they can. The problem is, because he's stayed friends with Gray, I've run into him over the years here and there. So I can't forget that hideously bad decision I made."

"So you still have feelings for him."

Carolina frowned. "No. Not at all. I'd just like Drew Hogan to go away and not come back so I never have to think about that stupid mistake I made."

It was obvious Carolina still had feelings for Drew. Denial was a powerful protector. "I'm sorry."

"Don't be," Carolina said with a slight laugh. "It's in the past. Too bad Drew can't stay there."

EIGHTEEN

GRAY FIGURED IF HE MANEUVERED HIS WAY THROUGH the crowd often enough, he could avoid his father the entire day.

Having Trevor and Drew here had helped. He'd spent most of the day hanging out with them. It was always great to see his friends from college. With all their busy schedules and their respective sports keeping them occupied, it was hard to find time to get together, so he was grateful they'd made the trip out here today.

Plus, it helped him steer clear of his father. If he could, he'd avoid him the entire trip. It was doable, except for one major obstacle—make that two—Evelyn and his mother. He could avoid one person just fine, even two people. But three? Impossible. Evelyn approached from one direction, his mother from the other, and it would look obvious if he turned tail and ran.

"I've been looking for you," his mother said as she grasped his hand. "Did you eat?"

His fill of barbecued ribs, and then some. "Yes, Mom. I ate. Did you?"

She laughed. "I nibble."

"And that's why you and Carolina stay so thin."

"Carolina does look fantastic, doesn't she? She's talked me into taking yoga classes. She claims the flexibility will be good for me. I'm going to sign up next week."

"Good for you." He kissed the top of her head and watched Evelyn approach.

"It's nearing time for Mitchell's speech," Evelyn said. "Gray, would you like to talk to your father before?"

Not particularly. He'd like to get through the day not having spent any time with his father at all. But his mother was right here and she'd tan his hide if he avoided his dad. "Uh, sure."

"Great. If you'll excuse us, Loretta, we'll get that started."

"Of course."

He moved in beside Evelyn as they made their way through the crowd.

"You've been avoiding me," she said.

"No, I haven't. I was just catching up with my friends."

"I think you've been doing your best to avoid your father."

"That, too. You know I don't want to be here." He stopped, turned to face her. "Check that. I love being home again. I just don't want to talk to him."

She brushed fingers with him, and the contact was electric. "I know you don't, but it's a part of what you agreed to."

He gave a short nod. "Let's just get this over with."

Gray had seen his father on television. He'd even texted him and talked to him on occasion over the past few years. He'd used the lodge last year for the get-together with the guys from school, so he'd had to talk to his dad about that. His dad had been generous and hadn't put up a fuss about wanting to see him or asking for anything in return—surprisingly.

But he hadn't seen him in person in years. Now, they approached where his father was sitting with some of his—what? Friends? Political associates? Hell, he had no idea who these people were.

His stomach tightened. He raised his chin and prepared himself for anything.

Mitchell Preston had lost a considerable amount of weight. He had always been on the hefty side. A lot of liquor and extravagant living would do that to a person. Now, he looked fit and healthier than Gray could ever remember seeing him. He still had a full head of thick hair, though it was mostly silver now, with a few strands of black threaded through it.

He stood, turned to his table of friends. "Gentlemen, I'd like to introduce you to my son, Grayson. Gray is one of the finest auto racers on the circuit these days."

As he made the introductions, Gray was shocked. That was the first time Gray could ever remember his father even acknowledging what he did for a living.

"If you'll excuse me, gentlemen, I need to talk to my son."

Evelyn gave his dad a smile. "Senator, I hope things have gone well for you today."

He shook Evelyn's hand. Didn't hug her or tug her close or even leer at her. "They did, Evelyn. Thank you for all you're doing to help out."

"It's my pleasure. I'll get an email out to you at the end of the week to update you."

"I'd appreciate it."

"How does it look for the nomination?"

He smiled, a genuine smile filled with hope. "It looks promising. The Cameron campaign has been in touch. It looks like the vetting process is in full swing."

She laid her hand on his arm. "I couldn't be more thrilled for you, Senator. I think they're choosing the right man."

"Well, let's not get our hopes up, but my fingers are crossed. In the meantime, we still have a lot to do. And what you're doing with Gray is a good start."

"So tell me what else is being done and what I can do," she said.

As they walked along, Gray listened. It was all purely professional as his father filled Evelyn in on the goings-on for his chances at becoming the vice presidential nominee. And Evelyn talked to him about social media and campaign strategy and some numbers for the candidate on the other side.

Pretty interesting stuff. Evelyn knew a lot off the top of her head, which led him to believe she was very knowledgeable about her job. And his dad didn't once look at her boobs, her legs, or her ass, but instead kept eye contact, which of course could have been because Gray was right behind them. But he'd also watched his father during the day today, and hadn't once noticed him looking at any other woman—except his mother. His dad had caught his mother's gaze several times throughout the day today, and smiled at her. She'd smiled back. Hell, the two of them had looked more in love with each other than at any time Gray could remember.

Campaign strategy? Something put on for the public? Who the hell knew? He dragged his fingers through his hair, more confused than ever.

They stopped at a table just off the main stage where the band had been playing.

"Gray," his father said. "I want to tell you how much I appreciate your being here. How much I appreciate your agreeing to do all of this, especially since I know you didn't want to."

"I'm doing it because Mom asked me to," he said before thinking.

His father lifted his chin, then nodded. "Well, for whatever reason, thank you. I know we've had our differences in the past. I hope we can come to an understanding in the future."

"An understanding about what, Dad?"

"You know. The past. I want to move forward, not look behind."

"Yeah. That would be easier for you, wouldn't it?"

His father laid his hand on his arm. "Gray, let's not do this today."

Or, ever? That would be the Mitchell Preston way. Sweep it all under the rug, never talk about it. There were so many things he wanted to say, so many things that had been left unsaid in the past. So many things he wished his father would voice right now. He waited, but nothing was forthcoming.

He didn't believe the pain he saw in his father's eyes, didn't care to see it. How could his father be in pain? Gray had never done anything to him. Gray hadn't cast him aside and told him to get the hell out of his house, out of his life, and go fend for himself because he hadn't lived up to expectations, because he refused to be molded according to someone else's whims and ideals.

Screw his father and his fake pain.

"Gray." Evelyn's voice penetrated the haze of anger that shrouded him.

He shot his gaze to hers. "What?"

She blinked. "Are you ready?"

Fuck that. "No."

Her eyes widened. "What?"

"I said no." He started to walk away, but she grabbed his hand.

"Don't do this. Don't walk away."

He pulled his hand away from hers. "Don't fucking tell me what to do."

Anger, old hurts, and just plain fury blazed the path in front of him. He didn't even see the people around him as he made his way toward the house. The only thing he knew was he needed to get away from his old man before he suffocated, before the old memories choked him.

Evelyn followed him, all the way into the house, up the stairs, and into one of the bedrooms. He needed an escape, away from this place, from the memories of all the disappointments, the times when, according to his father, he'd failed to measure up.

Would one goddamned apology have cost him so much?

He paced the room while Evelyn sat on the bed and watched.

Finally, she asked, "What's gotten you so pissed off?"

"I don't want to talk about this."

"You have to talk about it with someone. Holding it inside isn't going to solve anything."

"There's nothing to talk about."

"Obviously there is."

He stopped, looked down at her. "Get out, Evelyn."

She didn't budge. "I'm not leaving you like this."

"I said get out. This is my house and I want you out of here. I need some time alone."

"That's the last thing you need right now. You're upset and you need someone to talk to."

He let out a laugh. "Trust me, the last thing I need right now is to talk."

She stood, came over, and grasped his arms. "Then tell me what you need. Let me help you."

He needed to not think about his father, about his past and all the hurts that he'd buried for so long. One visit home, one short conversation, and the memories were all here, choking him, making it hard for him to breathe.

His salvation stood right in front of him, the concern on her face tearing right through him.

"You know what I need? I need you. I don't want to talk, Evelyn. I need to put my mouth on you and sink inside you and just not fucking think for a while."

She lifted up and swept her hand around his neck, placing her trembling lips against his.

"Then take what you need, Gray."

It was all he needed to hear. He wound his arm around her waist, picked her up, and moved a foot toward the door. He pressed the lock button, then carried her to the bed. He laid her on it and followed her down, his mouth on hers in a frenzy of passion and need. Her tongue wound around his, her whispered moans a balm to his aching psyche.

He lifted her shirt and found the silken softness of her skin, not realizing how much he'd missed touching her until that very moment. He raised her top and unclasped her bra, cupping a breast in his hand, soaking up her cries with his mouth as he teased her nipple. Each sound she uttered made his dick harder. He rocked his hard-on between her legs, the driving force of his need.

He raised up and slid between her thighs, teasing her. She licked her lips and raised her legs, locking them around his hips.

"Please," she whispered.

He needed to make her come, wanted to hear her cries as she came apart for him.

He drew down her pants and underwear and buried his face in her pussy. She smelled and tasted like sweet heaven, soothing his soul as she grasped a handful of his hair to hold him in place as he licked and sucked her clit, holding on to her as she writhed in pleasure beneath him.

"Gray," she said. "I'm going to come. Oh, yes, I'm going to come." He lapped at her pussy, then latched onto her clit and took her there. She grabbed the nearest pillow and screamed into it as she let go. He held on to her hips and licked her until she was moaning again, and then he unzipped his pants and sank into her while she was still quivering.

Her eyes widened with shock as he grasped her hands and lifted them above her head.

"I want you to scream again for me," he said, pulling back only to thrust harder and bury himself deep.

She reached underneath his shirt and scraped her nails down his back. "Yes. Just like that. Harder."

He loved that she matched him, that she arched against him, squeezing his hand as he powered inside her, faster and faster, grinding against her until she tightened around him.

He kissed her, his tongue sucking hers inside until she whimpered and bucked against him. He wanted her to come again, wanted to feel her pussy grab his dick in a tight vise and squeeze the come right out of him. And when he felt the tremors, he rubbed against her, rocking his pelvis over her sensitive flesh until she cried out against his lips. He raised her knee and buried himself deep, lifting her butt with his hand and powering up into her as he came with a harsh groan, emptying himself into her.

Out of breath and sweating, he rested his lips against her neck, loving the feel of her soft fingertips stroking his back.

When he came to his senses, he realized what he'd done.

He'd taken her, fast and furious—and without a condom.

He'd used her. He'd satisfied his own needs and taken, without thought for her needs or what she wanted.

He was no better than his father.

NINETEEN

EVELYN FLOATED BACK DOWN TO REALITY, NOT EVEN caring they were at his parents' house, that someone might have heard. What they'd shared was passionate and wild and like nothing she could have ever imagined.

But she could tell the moment everything had changed. One minute she and Gray were locked together. He was kissing her neck, lazily stroking her leg. The next, he tensed, and his head shot up, panic written all over his face.

"Oh, shit. Evelyn, I'm so sorry."

She frowned. "For what? For this? I'm not. I know it's a little unorthodox, being at your parents', but honestly—"

"No." He jumped off the bed and she realized they were both still half clothed, which made what had just happened between them so much—sexier.

She sat up. "What's wrong?" He'd been so upset earlier, and she had no idea why, though she suspected it had something to do with his father. She wished he would open up to her, talk to her about what bothered him.

He grabbed his pants, slid them on, and zipped them up. "I didn't use a condom. I am never—and I mean never—irresponsible like that. I can't apologize enough."

"Oh. I'm on the pill, Gray. You don't have to worry about me becoming pregnant. I assume you're always careful about protection, as am I."

He sat on the bed next to her and picked up her hand. "I am always careful. I've never been with a woman without protection before. I hope you believe that. I'll get tests. I get tested frequently. Jesus, I am so sorry."

She felt so bad for him, for this day he was having. She stroked up and down his arm. "Quit beating yourself up over this. I loved sharing this moment with you today. Didn't you?"

"I used you to make myself feel better."

"You made me come—twice. I hardly feel used."

His lips curved in a hint of a smile. "That's good. But I still feel shitty."

"Well, if you're going to continue to self-flagellate, I suppose you could buy me some diamonds."

He snorted out a laugh. "You don't seem like the diamonds-as-apology type of woman."

"That's quite possibly the nicest thing anyone's ever said to me."

She got up and went into the attached bathroom to clean up. Lord, her hair was a mess, her lips were puffy, and she had to do some definite damage control. She smoothed her hair and corrected her clothing, but there was nothing she could do about the flush on her face. Hopefully people would think it was the heat.

Gray came in and wound his arms around her, then kissed her temple. "I love making love with you. But I was wrapped up in my own head—" He pointed to his forehead. "This one. And not thinking about covering up the other one. I'm sorry for not thinking about your protection."

She turned in his arms, then lifted up to kiss him. "Thank you. But I got caught up in the heat of the moment, too. Remember, it takes two people. We're fine, okay?"

"Okay." He kissed her. "And I'm sorry about that shit with my dad. He screws with my head even without trying. I ruined your day."

"You didn't ruin my day at all."

"Let's go do the speech and photos thing."

"Don't do that on my account, Gray."

"I am doing it for you. And for my mom. But most important, I'm doing it for me. I made a commitment and I'm going to stick with it. The old man isn't going to run me off anymore."

She slid her fingers up his arms. He was relaxed, no tension in his muscles. "If you're certain that's what you want, let's go."

"I'm sure."

They found the senator outside with Loretta. He looked concerned when they met up, not upset or angry.

"Everything okay?" he asked.

Gray gave a curt nod. "Fine. Sorry for the delay. Are you ready to get started?"

Evelyn squeezed his arm. "I'll get the media in place, then we can begin."

She got everyone assembled, then went up to the podium and introduced Gray.

He was perfect as he spoke about the holiday, what it meant to him, and thanked those in service for fighting for his country. And though he didn't highlight his father's accomplishments as senator, you couldn't tell there was friction between them or what Gray personally felt about his dad as he introduced him. He was polite and courteous as he made the introduction. Then the senator stepped up and they hugged briefly before the senator took the podium to make his remarks.

All in all, a great few moments, and she'd have good quotes, photos, and sound bites for social media.

"Did I do all right?" Gray asked when the senator finished speaking and the crowds began to disperse.

"You did great. Thank you. I know that wasn't easy for you."

He shrugged. "It was over fast. That part was good."

She laughed. They grabbed more food and drink, and Gray crowded around with Trevor and Drew, laughing while they told him about the golf tournament. She was glad he was relaxed now. She worried for him after that tense exchange with his father. Though not many words had been said, there were undertones of history between them, things from Gray's past she obviously didn't know about that ran deep and upset him.

She wished he would talk to her about them, but he obviously didn't trust her enough yet to open up. And she wouldn't force it. Maybe someday.

At dark, there were fireworks, a spectacular forty-five-minute display that left Evelyn in awe. After, the guests began to leave. Evelyn made sure to thank the media who'd come for the speech and to make arrangements to receive copies of the sound bites and photos. She'd already grabbed some photos and quotes and put them up on the senator's social media accounts since it was important to be in real time for the senator, but she'd do more in the coming days.

They had already made arrangements to spend the night on the ranch. Evelyn was glad they didn't have to drive to the airport and fly out tonight. It had been a long, exhausting day and she was ready for bed.

Though it would have been nice to go to bed with Gray, they had separate bedrooms. And since this was his parents' home, sneaking into his room would not be a good idea.

So he walked her up to her room and said good night. Since his mother had also walked up with them, his good night was very short and curt.

"See you in the morning," he said, his gaze lingering.

She looked over his shoulder at his mother, who stood at the top of the stairs, obviously wanting a word with her son. So she smiled. "Good night, Gray."

She closed the door, washed up, and put on a tank top, then climbed into the bed in the guest room she'd been assigned. She worked on her laptop, posted some photos to Facebook and tweeted, caught up on her email, then set her laptop aside and turned out the lights. She stared up at the whirring ceiling fan while she mentally rehashed the day in her head.

There was a lot in her head, from her conversations with Carolina to the questions surrounding Gray's relationship with his father to the heat-inducing sex she'd had with Gray in this very room earlier today. She smoothed her hands over the cool sheets, recalling the desperate way he'd taken her, the way it had felt when he was inside her, the way he'd made her come. He knew her body, knew what it took to bring her right to the brink, then make her fall.

Her body swelled with arousal. She softly sank her teeth into her bottom lip and slid her hand into her panties, her mind filled with visuals of Gray sinking into her today.

Then her phone rang.

"Crap." She turned and looked at the display.

Was he psychic? She grabbed her phone and clicked it on.

"Gray."

"You sound out of breath. What are you doing?"

"Uh . . . nothing."

"Where are you?"

"In my room."

"What are you doing?"

"I was restless."

He was silent for a moment, and she could imagine him smiling. "And just what are you doing alone in your room, Evelyn?"

"Thinking about you and hating that I'm not in your room."

She heard shuffling. "Oh, yeah? Is that why you're out of breath?"

"You could say that."

"Were you touching yourself while you were thinking of me?"

He made it so easy. She settled back against the pillows and cradled the phone against her ear. "Yes."

"Do it again."

"What are you doing?"

"Now that you've made my cock hard, I'm stroking it."

She took a deep breath. "I feel like a teenager."

"Did you ever have phone sex when you were a teenager?"

She stifled a laugh. "No. I've never had phone sex at all."

"Then you're about to have a first. What are you wearing?"

She laughed. "A tank top and panties."

"Did you slide your hand inside your panties and stroke your pussy?"

The man had to be psychic. "That's what I was doing when you called."

She heard his low hum of approval. "Then I'm glad I interrupted you before you got to the really good part."

The sounds he made as he shifted in bed were driving her crazy. She had to use her imagination to visualize what he might be doing.

"We could . . . video chat, you know." She knew what kind of phone he had, and he did have that feature.

"Hmm, we could, couldn't we?"

She pressed the button, and within thirty seconds his face was on the screen. He gave her a lopsided grin. "You look sexy."

"It's dark in your room."

"I like it this way. That way you can see me, but not really see me."

All she could see was his face and upper body, but she saw his shoulder move. "What are you doing, Gray?"

"Rubbing my cock. When you answered the phone, you made that out-of-breath sound you make when I'm fucking you."

She sucked in a breath and shifted down, then spread her legs, sliding her hand over her sex. "I didn't know I made a certain sound."

"Oh, I've memorized all the sounds you make. Your breath catches when I rub your clit or suck your pussy. And your moans—I really like those."

She slipped her hand in her panties, and released the sound he liked, grateful that his parents slept downstairs. "This is a little wicked, doing this in your parents' house."

"That's what makes it fun. If my mother wasn't such a light sleeper and didn't get up several times a night, I'd be in your room taking your clothes off right now."

"I'd like that. I really wanted to go to your room with you to-night."

"Pull your straps down, Evelyn. Let me see your breasts."

It was hard to maneuver the phone with one hand and direct the camera in the right place, but she dropped the straps on her tank top, revealing her breasts.

"Nice. I wish I was there to suck them."

Her pussy tightened with arousal. She brought the camera back so she could see him. "When you say that, I get wet."

"That's good. Touch yourself for me, tell me how wet you are."

"Hang on." Anxious to be rid of her panties, she pulled them down and left them at the foot of the bed, then picked up the phone and spread her legs, patting her sex, teasing her clit, letting him watch her face as she tucked two fingers into her pussy. "Oh, that's so good."

"I like watching you, Evelyn. Will you do that for me in person sometime?"

"Yes. Only if you'll touch your cock for me at the same time."

He rolled to his side and she watched his arm. "I'd love to jack off for you."

She found her clit and caressed it, using the heel of her hand to apply the right amount of pressure as she kept her fingers busy inside her pussy. "I wish you were here, that you were inside me."

"I'd like that. My balls are tight and my cock's so hard it's ready to burst."

"Show me how you do it, Gray."

He moved the camera and she watched his hand gripping the base of his shaft, the way he squeezed as he pumped his fist over his cock, then eased up at the tip, rolling his thumb over it, then used a steady rhythm to pump up and down.

It was the most exciting thing she'd ever seen. She rolled her hand over her pussy as she watched, mesmerized.

"I'm ready to come, Evelyn," he said, and she looked at him, watching the strain on his face as the movements of his arm grew faster and more frantic.

"Me, too. Talk to me, Gray. Make me come for you."

"Rub your pussy faster. I want to hear you scream for me."

"Oh, God. I can't scream. Your parents will hear."

"Then roll over and scream into the pillow. I just want to know you're coming. And I'll come with you."

"No. I want to watch you come. I'll hold back, but the next time you make love to me, I'll scream loud for you."

His hand was working hard over his cock now. Sweat beaded down the side of his face. "Now, Evelyn. I want you to come now."

"I'm so close." Her nipples tightened and she felt the stirrings of orgasm. "I'm going to come, Gray. I'm going to come."

With his guttural groan, he rolled over onto his back, holding the camera out so she could see the streams of come spurting onto his belly.

"Oh, God, yes," she said, fighting back the scream as her climax slammed into her. He turned his face to the camera, his cock held tightly in his fist as he lifted his hips and she buried her fingers in her pussy while she shuddered through a wild, crazy orgasm that left her shaking and sweaty.

When it was over, she dropped the phone onto the mattress and had to catch her breath.

"Hey," he finally said. "I need a few minutes. I'll be right back."

"Me too," she said, staring up at the ceiling fan, still trying to breathe normally. She rolled off the bed and went into the bathroom. When she came back, Gray's face was smiling at her on the phone. He was stretched out on his side as he lay on the bed.

"Thanks for that," he said. "That took away the last of the day's tension."

She grinned at him. "Mine, too. I think I might even be able to sleep tonight."

"Good. I'd still like it better if you were in my bed."

Her stomach fluttered. "I'd like it better, too."

"Tomorrow night, you will be."

"Good night, Gray."

"'Night, Evelyn."

She clicked off, rolled over, and closed her eyes, unable to remove the smile from her face.

TWENTY

GRAY HAD EVELYN CHANGE THEIR FLIGHT. NOW THAT HE knew Bill was sick, it was important that he at least stop by and see him. They were flying out later that afternoon, which would still give him plenty of time to meet up with his crew and prepare for practice and qualifying.

"Tell me about Bill Briscoe," Evelyn said as they drove to the university.

Gray smiled as the memories flooded him. "He and his wife Ginger were dorm parents the entire four years I was at the university. And from day one, Bill was the father figure I needed—hell, the father figure all of us guys needed. He gave me advice and discipline and warmth and compassion, especially during those critical college years when I floundered, when I felt lost and alone after . . ."

He paused, realizing he was going on and on about stuff he normally didn't talk about—with anyone.

"You can tell me, Gray. It's not like this is going to end up in social media. This is personal and I understand that."

"After my father and I had a falling out when I decided not to go to Harvard and took the baseball scholarship to Oklahoma. Things were rough after that."

"Because your father thought your schooling and career should go one way, and you wanted to go in another direction."

"Yes. He wanted me to go into law, and eventually follow him into politics. That was never my passion."

She nodded. "Because sports had always been what you loved."

Funny how easily she understood that, and his father never had. "Yeah. The old man was pissed when I turned down Harvard."

"Understandable. It's always a parent's dream that a child will follow in their footsteps. I'm sure he was disappointed."

"Oh, he was more than disappointed. He railed about it, called me a failure, and told me I was wasting my life. And then he cut me off financially from the family money. He told me if I was going to insist on making this mistake, I'd be doing it on my own."

"Oh, God." She laid her hand on his leg. "I'm so sorry, Gray."

He shrugged, keeping his gaze firmly on the road. "I was so used to him always having to have his own way, by the time he'd made that decision I'd already figured that's probably what he was going to do."

"Didn't your mother run interference for you?"

"She tried, but once Mitchell Preston makes a decision, no one can change his mind. There wasn't much she could do. The family money is all his. But I had the scholarship to Oklahoma, so I didn't need his money. I worked my ass off at school, worked part-time to cover whatever the scholarship didn't. I managed just fine. Even got an offer from a major league team."

He glanced over at her. She was frowning.

"But you didn't pursue baseball."

"Yeah, I know. It was enough to know I could have succeeded. I liked playing ball, but my love was always in racing. After I graduated college I pursued it professionally, made it my full-time career."

"You've done very well for yourself. You should be proud. And all without Preston money."

Hearing the words from Evelyn sank deep into his chest. "Thanks. I got lucky and raced with someone who showed me the ropes and allowed me to hone my instincts. He gave me a car and let me show what I could do. After I won a championship, the money from sponsors started rolling in, enough to sustain me until I turned twenty-five. That's when I received the inheritance my grandfather left for me, something my father couldn't control.

"I took that money and started Preston Racing, went out on my own and built a successful race team, won another championship."

When she didn't say anything, he shifted his gaze to hers. "What?"

Her lips curved. "There's such a spark when you talk about racing. I can't imagine you ever having that kind of fire in you in law or politics."

He let out a laugh. "I'd have hated it. I'd have been miserable."

"Not many people get to do what they love."

He took the exit that would lead to the main road and the college. When he stopped at the light, he turned to her. "You are."

"That's true. I guess both of us are very lucky."

"I guess we are. And I have Bill Briscoe to thank for that. He kept me focused, made me pull my head out of my ass. I arrived with a huge chip on my shoulder and a lot to prove. He knocked that off and told me to stop thinking about my dad, stop being mad at him and start focusing on myself."

He turned left at the light and made his way down the road. "He helped shape who I am today. I owe him a lot. I just hope he's okay."

Evelyn leaned over and squeezed his leg. "Me, too."

Bill and Ginger's house was on campus, just down the street from the dorms. Gray parked in front and got out.

"Drew and Trevor aren't here yet, but there's a car I don't recognize in the driveway. It might be Haven," he said as he held the door for Evelyn.

"Haven being their daughter?"

"Yeah. She was around a lot when we were in school. Even attended the college. She's the same age as Carolina. She tutored Trevor for a while." Gray smiled. "God, he hated that."

The house looked the same, though it could have used a new coat of paint. The white trim was flaked in spots, and a few of the porch steps looked like they could use some reinforcing—or maybe replacing. Otherwise, the one-story ranch-style house still had hanging geraniums, the same two white rocking chairs on the porch, and the front door was open as always.

Gray knocked on the screen door. "Anyone home?"

"Someone's always home," Ginger Briscoe said. "Come on in."

Gray shook his head and turned to Evelyn. "Ginger and Bill don't believe in strangers. You knock, you're always welcome to come in."

Evelyn looked a little wide eyed with disbelief over that one. So had Gray, the first time Bill had told him that, but that's the kind of people they were.

He held the door open for Evelyn and they stepped in. Something was cooking. Smelled like chicken.

Ginger came down the long hallway, her face beaming in a wide smile as she spotted him.

"Grayson Preston. I can't believe you're here." She opened her arms and he picked her up in a hug.

"Miss Ginger. It's been too long."

She squeezed him, patted him on the back, and when he set her down, her smile was still as wide as the entire state.

"What are you doing here? Shouldn't you be out somewhere breaking speed limits?"

He laughed. "I was at the ranch for the Fourth, so thought I'd drop by. Miss Ginger, this is my friend Evelyn Hill. Evelyn, this is Ginger Briscoe, best cook in all of Oklahoma and the most gorgeous woman in the state."

"Oh, you're still a sweet talker, I see." Ginger turned to Evelyn and, though Evelyn had started to extend her hand, she folded her into a hug. "If you're with Gray, you get a hug from me. Nice to meet you, Evelyn."

Evelyn blinked and looked surprised. "Nice to meet you too, Ginger . . . Mrs. . . . Miss Ginger."

"There you go. Now you two must be thirsty. How about some sweet tea? I just made a fresh batch."

Gray nodded. "That'd be great. Where's Bill?"

"He's in the kitchen bothering me while I'm trying to cook. Come on back. He'll be pleased as punch to see you."

Gray took Evelyn's hand and led her down the hall. Yeah, still the same yellow and blue striped wallpaper, still the same dark hardwood floors throughout the house, the same white tile in the kitchen. And everything polished and clean and smelling like lemon oil. It reminded him of home, way more than the ranch ever had.

Ginger looked the same, maybe a little older and a little heftier than the last time he'd seen her. But still sharp and filled with energy.

When they walked into the kitchen, though, his heart sank.

Bill, on the other hand, had changed. He'd lost a considerable amount of weight, his hair was thinner, his skin sallow.

"Well, look who decided to drop by. I thought you forgot our address." With a wide grin, Bill stood, though not without some effort.

Gray went over and put his arms around him, trying not to tear up at the sight of the man who'd been more of a father to him than his own father. He fought back the tears and forced a smile as the two of them parted.

"Yeah, I know. I've been bad about coming to visit, but I'm here now, aren't I?"

Bill offered up a smile. "Yeah, I guess you are."

Gray introduced Bill to Evelyn.

"Isn't she just the prettiest thing I've ever seen—aside from my Ginger, of course," Bill said, then turned to Gray. "Prettier than most of those floozies I've seen you with on TV. This one has class, Gray. You should marry her."

Evelyn coughed and Gray's lips curved into a smile. "She's definitely pretty, and classy."

"Sit and rest," Ginger said, putting out two glasses of tea.

"Thank you, Miss Ginger," Evelyn said.

"And she's polite, too," Ginger said.

"So tell me what you're doing coming all the way out here," Bill said.

"I had some extra time, and I know it's been a while since I've been back. Besides, I wanted to show Evelyn the campus."

"Ohhh," Bill said, winking at Evelyn. "Trying to impress you, is he?"

"Apparently." Evelyn smiled at Gray. She knew he was making it up as he went along, and he appreciated her follow-through. "Though I am very impressed. This is a beautiful school."

"Where did you go to school, Evelyn?" Ginger asked.

"Georgetown."

"Also a lovely place. Bill and I had occasion to take a trip to Washington, D.C., a few years back. Toured a few of the colleges there. Georgetown is quite the place."

"Thank you. I enjoyed attending school there."

There was another knock on the door. "Lordy, but this is a busy place today," Ginger said. "Come on in," she hollered.

"I smell roasted chicken. Is it lunchtime yet?"

"Oh, good heavens. Is that Trevor?"

"Yes, ma'am," Trevor said. "And I dragged Drew with me."

Bill blinked, then frowned and looked at Gray. "Did you know they were coming?"

Gray smiled. "We talked about it yesterday. They were at the ranch with me. We got all nostalgic about times at the dorms, and talking about you and Miss Ginger. They said they might come by today."

"I can't believe it." He got up, moved around the table—slowly, Gray noticed—and made his way down the hall. He was enveloped by both Trevor and Drew.

"Man, you're gettin' old," Trevor said. "I might be taller than you now, or you're shrinkin'."

Bill laughed. "I can still whup your butt, young 'un."

"I don't doubt that," Trevor said. "I was always just a little bit afraid of you."

"That was my master plan to keep you all in line."

After the guys hugged Ginger, she set more tea at the massive table. "Sit, boys," she said.

"Yeah, well, you had to be intimidating to handle all of us, didn't you, Bill?" Gray asked.

"Oh, I don't know," Ginger said. "You were all such good boys."

Bill snorted. "That's just what I told her. She didn't know the real you. All a pain in my butt, sneaking out past curfew, smoking in the dorm rooms—"

"Who smoked in the dorm rooms?" Evelyn asked.

"That was Garrett," Drew said.

"No it wasn't. It was you," Trevor said. "You got drunk one night and decided to smoke an entire pack of cigarettes. And that was after all that Jack Daniel's."

"Oh. I remember that," Gray said with a snicker.

"So do I," Bill said, giving the evil eye to Drew. "Who do you think sat up with your sick ass all night long while you puked your guts up."

"Funny," Drew said. "I don't have much recollection of that night."

"Yeah, I'm sure it wasn't the last time you did it, either," Bill said.

Gray listened as they reminisced, his heart aching as he looked over at Bill. It was obvious Bill wasn't in good shape, but he wouldn't let on that he wasn't feeling well.

When Bill took Trevor and Drew into another room to go find old photo albums, Gray took Ginger by the arm.

"How bad is it, Miss Ginger?"

Tears sprang to her eyes. "It's bad, Grayson. It's in his liver. Doctors say there isn't much they can do."

Gray took a deep breath. "Is there anything I can do to help? If you need money, if he needs to go somewhere else for treatment . . ."

She squeezed his arms. "Darlin', if I thought throwin' money at this would help him, I'd have been on the phone callin' in favors from every kid who'd ever passed through our doors." She shook her head. "Money can't help him now. It's in God's hands."

He bent his head and closed his eyes. Ginger put her arms around him and he hugged her close. When he opened his eyes and looked across the kitchen, Evelyn had tears streaming down her face.

EVELYN'S HEART ACHED FOR GRAY. IT WAS CLEAR HE loved Bill and Ginger Briscoe, that the four years he'd spent at the school and in the dorms were some of the best of his life, and that

Bill had helped shape the man he'd become. The Briscoes were kind people with good senses of humor and a belief system that would help Ginger get through the rough times ahead.

She also had a strong support system, an entire school apparently, because it was clear a lot of people loved them both. Gray, Trevor, and Drew all worshipped Bill. She listened to story after story about what a hero he was to them, how he'd saved their butts when they'd almost gotten into trouble, or how he'd disciplined them when they'd crossed the line. But it was all said with such respect that it left Evelyn with a sense of awe about the man.

He'd be leaving an amazing legacy behind. It was a shame he'd be leaving at all.

Ginger was preparing roasted chicken and said there was plenty for everyone. Evelyn had convinced her she could be useful in the kitchen, despite Ginger's protests that company didn't help out. So she'd sliced carrots and peeled potatoes and had made a huge salad, not used to feeding a bunch of hungry men. But it was nice to stand side by side with Ginger and do something quietly for a while.

"You dating that boy?" Ginger asked.

Evelyn didn't quite know how to answer that, so she started with the truth. "Actually, I work for his father."

"The senator?" Ginger took a side step back. "What do you do for him?"

Evelyn explained her job and what she was doing with Gray.

"Now that's interesting work. You must be very smart."

Evelyn laughed. "I think I do okay."

"I'm glad to hear that. It's important to always hold your own, Evelyn. Never rely on a man to be your everything in life."

"Oh, I never intend for that to happen."

"Good. Haven—that's our daughter—she's the same way. Maybe to a fault. That girl has an independent streak as wide as the Rio Grande. Always thinking of her career first, no time for a man in her life. I'm beginning to fear she's never going to give me grand-children."

Evelyn laughed. "Does your daughter live here?"

"Oh, no. She couldn't wait to get off this campus. As soon as she graduated college, she moved to Dallas. But she comes home regu-larly to visit, more so now that Bill has been sick. She's here today—that's her car in the driveway. She wandered off to visit some friends, so she should be back soon."

"That's nice that she has her independence but she's not so far away that she doesn't come home to see you."

"What the hell are all these cars doing here? Is there some party I didn't know about?"

"Oh, that'll be Haven now," Ginger said, wiping her hands on a dish towel.

The screen door banged open.

"Hi, honey," Ginger said, hugging her daughter.

"Hey, Mom."

A gorgeous girl with short raven hair and big blue eyes entered the room. She wore tattered capris and a double tank top that hugged her slender body, but nothing could hide those spectacular breasts. Wow, was she ever stunning.

Haven smiled when she saw Evelyn. "Oh, hi. I'm Haven Briscoe."

"Evelyn Hill. Nice to meet you."

"Same here. Did you go to school here, Evelyn?"

"No. I'm here with Gray Preston."

"Ohhh." She turned to her mother. "Gray's here?"

"He's out back with your dad. Drew Hogan and Trevor Shay are here, too."

"Oh. Well. Trevor's here, huh?" Haven sucked in her lower lip. "I'll be upstairs for a minute."

"Don't you want to go outside and greet the guys first?" Ginger asked.

But Haven was already halfway down the hall. "In a minute, Mom."

Evelyn arched a brow. That was interesting. Her entire demeanor changed when Trevor's name was mentioned.

The guys all came back inside.

"Did I hear Haven come back?" Bill asked.

"Yes," Ginger said. "She ran upstairs. She'll be back in a minute."

"Haven's here, huh," Trevor asked as he washed his hands at the kitchen sink.

Also interesting, as Trevor took a long glance down the hallway where Haven had disappeared.

Evelyn wondered what that story was about. She'd have to ask Gray.

"That lawn mower is done for," Gray said, muscling Trevor out of the way as soon as he'd washed his hands. "I'll hit the hardware store and get you a new one."

"You'll do no such thing," Ginger said, putting the carrots in a bowl and setting them on the table. "We can buy a new mower."

"I saw a sign down the road as we were coming into town," Drew said, taking his turn next at the sink. "Several of the students from one of the local fraternities have started up a mowing business. I guess they're staying in town for the summer and need the cash."

"You got all that from reading a road sign as you were passing by?" Ginger asked, folding her arms.

Drew shrugged. "I might have jotted the number down, and I might have called while we were out back."

"It would take some stress off Bill having to mow," Gray offered. "Especially now that we've determined the mower isn't repairable."

"It's a temporary fix, at best," Bill said. "But until we can get a new mower, it would give those boys some income."

Ginger held out her hand. "Give me their number. I'll look into it."

Drew pulled the number up on his phone and wrote it down on a piece of paper, then handed it to Ginger. She smiled as she put it in her jeans pocket.

"Now sit. All of you. It's time for lunch."

Haven walked in. "Hey, y'all."

"Hey, baby girl," Bill said, pulling her into his arms. "Did you have a nice visit with your friends? I'm sorry I was asleep last night when you got in."

"Hey, Dad. Thanks, I did." She squeezed her eyes shut as she hugged her dad. "And I got in pretty late, so don't worry about it."

Evelyn's heart ached for Haven as she swiped a tear away before she pulled back. She took a long look at him. "You look like you might have put some weight on. Eating those Oreo cookies again when Mom isn't looking?"

Bill grinned. "Maybe a few."

"I can hear, you know," Ginger said. "Now y'all sit."

Everyone took a seat. Gray sat next to Evelyn. Obviously Ginger and Bill had seats next to each other. Drew and Trevor scrambled for chairs, which left one open for Haven—right next to Trevor.

Haven hesitated.

"Well, go on and sit, honey," Ginger said. "He isn't gonna bite you."

"I might." Trevor looked up at Haven and grinned. Haven glared, but settled into the chair.

Lunch was delicious, and the conversation was lively. There was a lot of reminiscing about the guys' college days, including teasing of Haven.

"If he hadn't passed that math class, we weren't sure Trevor was ever going to get sprung from the dorm," Gray said with a grin.

"It was like prison," Trevor said. "I felt like Rapunzel in the tower. Without all the hair, of course," he said, winking at Evelyn. "If it hadn't been for Haven, I might still be stuck in my room."

Haven scooped peas onto her fork, refusing to meet Trevor's gaze.

"Oh, I remember how reluctant you were when we asked you to tutor Trevor," Ginger said to Haven. "You would have thought we'd asked the worst thing in the world of her. She dragged her feet and said she didn't want to. You remember that, honey? Lord, you were so difficult."

Haven lifted her head up at that remark. "As I recall, I wasn't the difficult one."

Trevor cocked a brow. "She means me."

"Well, you were a pain in the—" Drew glanced over at Bill and Ginger. "Butt."

"I was not. I was cooperative as he—heck. I wanted out of that room."

Haven snorted. "You were a pain in the ass. Uncooperative. Thought you knew everything—except math, science, and history. And when the going got tough and you were forced to actually knuckle down and do the work, you tried to bribe me into taking the math test for you."

"Haven," Ginger said. "Trevor wouldn't do such a thing."

She met her mother's gaze straight on. "Of course not. He's an athlete, therefore he can do no wrong."

Trevor remained silent, but he cast a curious glance at Haven. Now Evelyn really wondered what the background was on these two. Was there animosity over the tutoring? It seemed like so much more than that. A lot of tension sizzled between them.

"Anyway, it all worked out. Trevor passed all his classes," Ginger said with a wide smile. "We were so proud."

"Excuse me," Haven said, taking her plate to the sink.

Trevor's gaze followed her as she left the room.

After lunch they sat out on the porch and sipped tea. Even Haven got over whatever had upset her and joined them, though she sat as far away from Trevor as possible. Evelyn noticed Trevor throwing looks her way, but Haven wouldn't meet his gaze.

When Evelyn went inside to refill her tea, Haven came in, too.

"Can I pour some for you?" Evelyn asked.

"Sure. Thanks." Haven leaned against the kitchen counter to drink her tea, so Evelyn took a seat.

"You live in Dallas?"

"Yes. For now."

"What do you do there?"

"I'm in broadcasting."

Evelyn smiled. "What a fun career."

"Sometimes it can be. Other times it's a nightmare. Depends on the day and what I'm covering."

"You do the news?"

"Sports," Haven said with a grin, the pride evident on her face.

"Wow. Tough field for a woman."

"It can be. Right now I've got a line on a national gig, so keep your fingers crossed for me."

"Congratulations. I hope it works out for you."

"Thank you. I'm really excited about it."

"I'm learning a lot about auto racing, and sports in general, from being around Gray."

Haven's gaze tracked outside. "Gray's a fantastic guy. He was always so nice to my parents, and to me." She returned her gaze to Evelyn. "And you work with Gray's father, the senator?"

"Yes."

"I'm surprised Gray has anything to do with you. He wasn't too fond of his dad back in his college days. I guess that's changed."

She appreciated Haven's blunt honesty. "I think they're still working on it. Sometimes it takes a while."

Haven sipped her tea. "I guess it does."

Speaking of things that took a while to process . . . she sensed

Haven needed someone to talk to. Maybe that's why she was lingering in the kitchen with Evelyn. Something she couldn't unload on
her mother, maybe?

"I might be speaking out of turn, and please tell me to mind my
own business, Haven, but I sensed some friction between you and
Trevor?"

Haven looked down at her worn canvas shoes for a few seconds
before dragging her gaze back to Evelyn. "Oh. That. Yeah. He and
I had a few go-rounds in college."

Evelyn arched a brow, but didn't say anything. If Haven didn't
want to talk about it, she wouldn't ask again.

"He was so . . . prickly," Haven finally continued. "So supremely,
arrogantly confident. And I had the worst crush on him. I was gangly and shy and I wore glasses. And these—" She pointed to her
breasts. "I hid them. I was awkward enough without having boobs to
deal with. I had no idea what to do with a boy. And Trevor was this
hot and sexy athlete, and God, I was so tongue-tied around him."

"A first crush kind of thing?"

Haven sighed. "In the worst way. Trevor, being the hot stud that
he is, he knew it. And he played me, using his sweet talk and batting
those long dark lashes at me to get me to do anything he wanted."

Warily, Evelyn asked, "And just what did he want?"

With a laugh, Haven said, "Tutoring. He needed to pass all his
classes, so what better way than to get the brainy girl to help him."

"You didn't want to?"

"It was exactly the opposite. I'd have done anything for him if he
crooked a finger in my direction. He didn't have to play me. I studied
with him and cajoled him into working harder than he ever wanted
to work. The problem was, he didn't want to do the work. What he
really wanted was to find a way to cheat the tests."

Evelyn leaned back in the chair and took a sip of tea. "No shit."

"No shit. Life always came easy for Trevor. Sports? Piece of cake.

Getting a girl into bed? Please. All he had to do was give them that wicked smile of his and panties came off faster than a dress on prom night. Academics, though? Not so much. That he had to work at, and when he struggled, he tried to figure out an angle."

"There is no angle with academics. It's pass or fail."

"Exactly. I tried to tell him that, while he whispered sweet talk in my ear about how easy it would be for me to do his homework for him and cheat the tests. I refused, so he tried to get me into bed. I know he figured he was doing the poor dorky girl a favor."

Evelyn crossed her arms, irritated on Haven's behalf. "And?"

"I might have been gawky and had an Oklahoma-sized crush on the boy, but I wasn't stupid. I had my own academic career to think of. No way was I going to risk it. I said no."

"Good for you."

"I made him learn. And oh, was he ever upset with me. Girls didn't turn him down much, you know. If ever. I told him he was going to have to learn using his head." She pointed to her temple and laughed. "This one, not the one in his pants."

Evelyn laughed. "Good for you. So what happened?"

"He finally realized he was going to have to open a book. He struggled with it, but he did it."

"So you pushed him, he passed his classes, and then what?"

"Then he went on his way, of course," Haven said with a laugh. "I was glad to get rid of him. He was an annoyance I could do without."

Somehow Evelyn didn't think Haven had gotten over Trevor that easily. She sensed some heartbreak in there and the tension between them was obviously still present.

But before she could ask, Ginger came in. "Hey, are you two going to hide out in here?"

Haven pushed off the counter and grabbed her tea. With a smile, she slid an arm around Ginger's waist. "Just some girl talk, Mom."

"Everyone has moved into the living room. We're going through pictures."

"I hope you didn't drag out old pictures of me."

Ginger squeezed Haven's arm. "You were the prettiest little thing."

Haven rolled her eyes. "Yeah, sure I was."

As they walked down the hall, Evelyn realized how much she missed her own mother. It was time for a phone call.

They stayed for another hour, long enough to go through old photos. Evelyn loved seeing Gray in his college days, so handsome and looking like he was having the time of his life. And in a baseball uniform, he looked so different.

"We thought for sure he'd end up on a major league team," Bill said as they closed the book on one of the photo albums. "Then again, he loved to sneak out to the track with his friends and race those cars."

"I always knew he had racing in his blood," Trevor said, leaning back on one of the recliners. "Baseball couldn't hold a candle to his love for fast cars."

Gray smiled. "I liked playing ball. But I loved racing. There was no comparison."

Ginger patted his knee. "As long as you're doing something you love with your life, honey. It's all that counts."

They talked for a while longer, but then Gray said they needed to head to the airport. Trevor and Drew were going to stay for the rest of the day, which made Evelyn feel better. At least they weren't making a mass exodus.

"Thank you so much for lunch," she said to Ginger. "It was such a pleasure to meet you."

She and Ginger hugged, and then she hugged Bill. "I wish only the best things for you."

He smiled down at her. "What will be will be, sweetheart. You take care of our boy."

"I'll do the best I can." She took his hands in hers. "Please don't give up. As long as you're here—standing here—there's still hope."

He gave a short nod and kissed her cheek.

Before the tears filled her eyes, she stepped off the porch and let Gray say his good-byes to everyone. They climbed in the car and drove off.

Gray was silent on the trip out of town toward the airport.

She wished she could offer words of comfort, but she knew there was nothing she could say that would make him feel better, so she slid her hand across and laid it on his leg. They returned the car at the airport and boarded the senator's plane.

When they took off, Gray closed his eyes and laid his seat back. She was sure he had a lot to think about, so she left him to his thoughts, once again wishing she could remove his pain.

"I hate this," he finally said, his eyes still closed.

She'd been working on her laptop when he spoke. She shut it and set it aside. "I know you do. I'm sorry for your friend Bill. He and Ginger seem like the nicest people."

He opened his eyes and swiveled the chair to face her. "They are. He is. I don't know what she's going to do without him."

"There's nothing that can be done for him medically?"

"According to Ginger, no. She said he's terminal."

She reached over and squeezed his hand. "I'm so sorry, Gray. I wish there was something I could say or do that would help."

"Come here."

She unbuckled her lap belt and he pulled her onto his lap. She laid her head on his shoulder and he caressed her back, though she felt like he was the one who needed comfort.

"What about contacting one of the premier cancer treatment

centers to see what they can do?" she asked. "They're making great strides in treatment for cancer these days. Surely Ginger and Bill haven't explored every option. They might just not know what's open to them."

He nodded. "I pulled Trevor and Drew aside and talked to them about that, and we got Garrett on text. We're going to make some calls. I don't plan to give up and I don't want Bill to, either."

"Good. I know you don't want your father's help, but he could assist. He has very strong connections at some of the finest hospitals in Washington."

"If it comes to that, I'll get down on my knees and beg for my father's help. I'll let you know."

"Good. I'll be happy to do anything I can."

He smoothed his hand over her hair and met her gaze. "Having you with me helps. I don't know why, but it's nice to not be alone."

Her heart squeezed. She was getting in deeper with him every day. This visit to his ranch, meeting his friends and the people that meant something to him had only served to show her a side of him she hadn't seen before. If she thought she was going to remain emotionally distant, it wasn't working. He was showing himself to be a kind, compassionate man, a man with depth and intricacies she hadn't known about.

It made her want to delve deeper, to know him at a level that scared her.

Because she knew that falling in love with him would break her heart in the end.

TWENTY-ONE

QUALIFYING WENT WELL, THOUGH GRAY FELT LIKE HE was rushing to catch up after being gone. Still, he could race in his sleep.

Pushing aside the dark thoughts of what went down at Bill and Ginger's, he focused on the race, on his car, and what the next race meant for his team. Everything else had to be put on the back burner, though fortunately, Evelyn had taken the ball and run with it as far as Bill was concerned. She was on the phone with Drew and Trevor, and even though she hadn't met Garrett, she'd made contact with him, too. She was coordinating everything on his behalf.

He didn't know what he'd do without her, something that gave him a huge sense of relief and a knot in the pit of his stomach at the same time. Because eventually he would have to do without her.

Something he refused to think about as he took turn two at a hundred and ninety-six miles an hour.

Focus on the race. Don't wreck. This track was treacherous, he was in third place right now on the number sixteen's bumper and Donny was on his. Having his team member bump drafting him meant they had a shot to win this thing. His race team was in position to have a one-two finish today if he didn't screw this up. He had to scrub his mind of everything else and think only of racing—of winning. The remainder of the season was ahead of him, and if he won this race, he could lock himself into position to make the finals. That's what was important today. It was all that mattered.

They all pitted with forty-two laps to go. It went smoothly and Donny took up position on his tail again, but Gray knew the end of this race was going to be anything but easy. Racers always tended to lay back until the end, and soon enough they'd be jockeying for position and making a push on the outside to charge up front.

He was ready. He and Donny had a strategy. They were going to make the same push to get out front and sail through the finish line.

A wreck with twenty laps to go put him on the inside lane, right behind the leader, with Donny on the outside lane above him.

It was go time, twelve laps left, now or never. He knew what needed to be done, so when the pace car pulled off and the checkered flag waved, he pushed the number forty-seven, who had a fast car all day. Donny jumped down behind him and as soon as they cleared the car on the outer lane, Gray pulled up, Donny right with him.

They sailed past the forty-seven, momentum carrying them. The forty-seven, without his drafting partner, was left in the back. Gray and Donny shot forward and took the bottom lane, picking up speed. He knew Donny was going to start heating up, but there were seven laps to go now, and no holding back. He just had to hope their engines would keep going, because without Donny pushing him, he was screwed.

His heart pounded as they held the lead. McClusky pulled to the outside lane, his teammate Darren Lavelle pushing him, but the outside lane was tougher, and Gray and Donny were still holding the lead with three laps to go.

"Come on, baby," he said, tightening his grip on the wheel as they rounded the curve to take the white flag.

One lap to go.

Adrenaline pumping, he hoped to God Donny didn't do something stupid like try to pass him for the win. His time would come later, and he wasn't in the points race. His job today was to push Gray to a win.

As Gray took the checkered flag, he yelled out and pumped his fist, then downshifted, giving Donny a big fucking thumbs-up. He thanked his crew on the radio, then did the burnout of all burnouts for the screaming fans.

Damn, that was a good race. And it put him in solid position in the points.

In the winner's circle, he climbed out and sprayed soda all over his crew. Donny came up and gave him a big hug. When he pulled back, he slapped Donny on the back.

"You did a damn fine job out there today, kid."

Donny grinned. "Second-place finish is all right by me, boss. I'll take it."

"We'll get you in the winner's circle yet. Really aggressive driving. I'm so proud of you."

After that it was interviews and photos with the sponsors. Today, Gray didn't care. He coveted this win and his team needed it badly. Now they were virtually a lock to make the finals, so he handled every interview, and at the end of the day, headed back to his house on the beach.

This morning he'd given Evelyn a key to his house so she wouldn't have to wait to go back to her hotel. She was already there, and had grabbed them some food. She was wearing a sinfully sexy sundress, her feet bare as she lounged on his sofa, her laptop in her lap.

She put it aside when he walked in and threw her arms around him, planting a seriously hot kiss on his lips.

Now this was much better than coming home to an empty house. He wound his arms around her and tugged her even closer, then carried her upstairs to his bedroom. He needed her touch, craved her sweet scent, and since he'd been nonstop busy since they'd returned to the racetrack, they'd had no time together, because she'd been scarce, too, catching up on her own work.

He laid her on the bed and climbed on, laying his hand on her breast. She moaned against his lips and rubbed his already hard cock.

He liked that no words needed to be spoken between them, that she needed him as much as he needed her.

He drew the straps down on her sexy little dress and bared her breasts. "I could use a shower, and I likely smell like sweat and gasoline. I know I need a shave," he said as he finally pulled his lips from hers.

She dragged the palm of her hand across the scruff on his face. "Don't you dare leave what we've started here. You smell good and I like this stuff on your face. Now make love to me before I die."

With a low growl, he bent and took a nipple between his lips, sucking it deeply into his mouth. Evelyn's low moan of approval made his dick twitch. He rocked against her hip as he cupped her breast and fed more of it into his mouth. When he rubbed his face over her tender flesh, she whimpered.

"God, I really do like that scratchy beard. I wonder what it would feel like between my legs."

Now that was an invitation if he ever heard one. He stood and dragged her legs over the edge of the bed, then lifted her dress to reveal pink silk panties, barely held together by thin straps at her hips.

He carefully grasped those flimsy strips and dragged her underwear down her hips and legs, parting her legs to kiss her inner thighs.

"Please, Gray."

He murmured against her inner thigh. "Please what, baby?"

He could feel her entire body shudder. "Please lick my pussy and make me come."

"I like it when you beg." He snaked his tongue out and slid it across her sex, rewarded with her primal moan that drove him crazy. He cupped her butt and raised her hips, then put his mouth on her and laid his tongue over her clit.

She lifted her head and met his gaze. "You're going to make me come. Fast. It's been too long."

He rocked his tongue back and forth over her clit, then slid it inside her.

"Gray. Yes. Do that again."

He did as she asked.

"Faster. Go back and forth like that faster. Oh my God, that feels so good."

He did exactly as she wanted, watching her expression as her mouth opened and her breaths came in short bursts. She gripped the covers, arched her hips toward him, and let out a wail as she came, shoving her pussy in his face as if to tell him she wanted a lot more of what he was giving her.

Oh, man, he liked making her come, loved the way she trembled as she let go. He loved her taste, the way she gave him everything when she climaxed.

He grabbed a condom and unzipped his pants, pulled out his cock, and sheathed himself. He pulled her butt to the edge of the bed and sank into Evelyn while she was still throbbing from her release.

She raised up and grabbed his arms, pulling herself onto his cock, burying him deeper in her.

"Fuck." He held on to her as she impaled herself on his aching dick. He leaned over and covered her body, then lifted and thrust again, pressing against her tender flesh. His hands roamed over the sweet softness of her hip and leg as he rolled her knee back so he could drive in deeper.

She swept her hand over his hair, his face, her thumb brushing his lower lip before cupping the back of his neck to bring him down for a deep, shattering kiss that nearly undid him. He closed his eyes and lost himself in her scent, the taste of her, the feel of her wrapped around him, squeezing him until he couldn't hold back and all he could do was power into her over and over until her whimpering moans turned to harsh cries.

She raked her nails down his back, demanding, unrelenting. He continued to lever his hips and roll against her clit, needing her to shatter again, wanting her to come with him, to bond her to him in a way that even he couldn't explain.

And when she did, when she cried out, he absorbed the sound with his lips and let himself release, his own groans mixing with her cries as he poured himself into her.

He wasn't sure, but he might have passed out. It had been a long, really hot day. Coupled with the earlier part of the week, he was done for. All he could remember was scooting over onto the bed and cool, soft hands stroking his brow.

"Congratulations, by the way," Evelyn whispered.

"Mmm, thanks," was all he could recall saying before his eyes shuttered closed and his mind went blank.

When he woke sometime later, he was alone in the bed. The lights were out, but his throat was sand dry. He was still half dressed and felt like he had a hangover. And Christ, he needed a shower and some food.

He climbed out of bed and jumped in the shower first, then grabbed a pair of shorts and slid those on.

When he ventured downstairs, Evelyn was in the living room, in the same position she'd been in when he first walked in, when she'd jumped up and kissed him and he'd jerked her into his arms and taken her up to his bedroom and made love to her. And that's all he remembered.

He whisked his fingers through his still-damp hair. "I guess I passed out?"

She looked up and smiled at him. "Not surprising. You were tired." She laid the laptop to the side. "Are you hungry now?"

"Starving."

"I put the food away. Let me heat it up."

"I can do that. Were you working?"

She nodded. "I'm behind and getting caught up."

"Then you stay where you are and I'll heat up the food. Did you eat?"

"Earlier. I was hungry."

"Don't blame you." He fixed himself a plate and warmed it up in the microwave, then grabbed water and took a seat next to her on the sofa.

"Will it bother you if I turn on the TV?"

She looked over at him and pressed a kiss to his lips. "Not at all, but thank you for being considerate and asking."

Damn, she was pretty in that dress. He could take her back to bed right now and go for round two, but his grumbling stomach won over thoughts of sex, so he left her alone. He turned to the race channel and watched interviews and recaps of the race while he shoveled in food. After he was full, he put the empty plate in the dishwasher, grabbed another water, and sat beside her. She looked to be concentrating, though on what he had no idea. Some social media stuff, he could tell, but she kept switching screens to her email, and then another document and a fancy spreadsheet, too. It made him dizzy, so he caught up on sports until she started yawning and put her laptop away.

She laid her head on his shoulder and placed her palm on his chest. "Get enough to eat?"

"Yeah. I feel a lot better now. Sorry about falling asleep on you earlier."

She lifted up to look at him. "Don't apologize for that. You must have been exhausted. It was so hot out there today. I could hardly stand it, and I was in the shade in the pit box. I can only imagine how sweltering it must have been in that car."

"It was like a hot box in there. But nothing I'm not used to."

"Still, it's no wonder you fell asleep. I'm surprised you could even get it up."

"Honey, I can always get it up for you."

She laughed. "Good to know." She stifled a yawn.

"Now I think it's you who needs some sleep."

She yawned again. "No, I'm fine."

"Caught up on your work?"

"For the most part, yes. I posted photos from the Fourth of July party at the ranch, integrated the social media accounts, and I have some sound bites, both photographic and video, that need your approval before I post them."

He nodded. "Send them to me and I'll look them over. After you go to sleep."

"I can stay up with you."

"No. You go to bed. I'm good for another hour. Email me those files."

She grabbed her laptop and addressed an email to him, explaining that she was attaching the files along with a short explanation of where she was going to send them once he approved them.

"Good enough." He stood and took her hand, then pulled her up. "Now, bed for you."

"Wow, you're no fun."

"I was fun earlier," he said as he took her to the bedroom.

She laid her head on his shoulder. "Yes, you definitely were."

Once in the bedroom, he drew the straps of her dress down, and when it dropped to the floor, she stepped out of it.

"Into bed with you."

Without so much as a squeak of a protest, she climbed into bed and turned on her side to face him.

"I don't like sleeping without you."

That admission made his stomach clench. "I'll be back soon." He bent and brushed his lips across hers. She smiled, but her eyes were already closed. He turned off the light and shut the door.

He opened his laptop and retrieved the email from Evelyn, reviewed the photos and videos. She had a good understanding of how innocuous he wanted his association with his father to be. There were photos of him standing in the vicinity of his father, a few family shots of Gray with his mom and dad and Carolina, videos of Gray interacting with his family as a whole during the Fourth of July gathering, along with Gray talking about how happy he was to be back at the family ranch again. Nothing political, nothing of him directly endorsing his father. He shot her a "Good to go" email and closed his laptop, then stared upstairs.

Yeah, he didn't like sleeping without her either, but the day would come when they would each go their separate ways.

Then what?

He didn't want to think about that day.

TWENTY-TWO

THE NOMADIC NATURE OF AUTO RACING REMINDED EV-
elyn of the campaign trail, so it was no hardship to pack up again and
move to yet another city. And the city after that, and the city after
that.

After Daytona Beach, Gray had suggested she stop staying at
hotels, since she spent all her time sleeping in his bed, anyway.

They'd argued that point in every city the past few weeks.

She told him she had an expense account and she had to book a
hotel room in each city, otherwise everyone would wonder where she
was sleeping. Gray said it was no one's business where she was sleeping. She disagreed. She had a reputation that mattered to her, so she
continued to book a room in each city, and not once had she spent a
single night in said hotels.

And as she looked out over the racers from her perch on the pit
box, spotting Gray's car instantly, she was reminded of last night,

when she'd tried to admonish Gray that it was late and he had a race today and he should be asleep.

Instead, he'd kept her up and kept her coming time and time again with his hands and his mouth and his beautiful cock until she couldn't remember how many orgasms she'd had.

She wondered if he was tired, if her staying with him every night at his trailer would affect his concentration on race days. She'd have to monitor his performance today, because she wouldn't want to be the cause of him wrecking or having a poor race result.

She sighed and leaned back, trying to relax but finding it increasingly more difficult to do so.

She was embedded so deep in this relationship with Gray, and she had no idea what she was going to do when it was over.

Walk away with a giant smile on her face and a heart in tatters, she supposed. She'd promised herself she'd guard her heart, and she'd done a lousy job of it, because she kept growing closer and closer to him, which was dangerous not only to her heart, but to her career.

She hadn't come here to fall in love. She'd come here to work, which was heating up and keeping her busy, thankfully. It was becoming clear to her, to the senator, and also to the media, that Senator Preston was the front-runner to be selected to be on the ticket with John Cameron as his vice presidential running mate. It wouldn't be announced officially until the convention in a few weeks, but the time was drawing closer and her time with Gray would soon be coming to a close.

It was an exciting time for her, politically. She couldn't wait to get to Atlanta for the convention. This was the moment she'd dreamed about since she first went to work for the senator. It would be his time in the spotlight, something he'd fought so hard for—something everyone on his team had fought for.

But for some reason the idea of packing up and leaving Gray

brought nothing but a giant knot of anguish in the pit of her stomach.

She shook off thoughts of her impending departure. There was still a lot to do here. Her campaign to gain potential votes for Governor Cameron and for Senator Mitchell still lay with Gray. She'd beefed up his social media accounts, and tied him in with the senator by reminding people that Gray's father was running for political office, and that Gray had endorsed his father's campaign. She listed all of the reasons Gray thought his father and Governor Cameron would make good candidates for vice president and president. He'd been generous in allowing her to post photographs and even these few political sound bites, something he'd sworn he'd never do.

Week by week he'd been bending. She knew it was for her and not for his father. She wished she could mend that relationship somehow. Not for the good of the campaign, but for father and son.

For Gray.

If she could just get the senator to show up here, to come to a race, to show Gray that he was here for him. She knew that would go a long way to show Gray that his father cared.

But she wouldn't interfere, wouldn't dare meddle in their relationship. That was going to have to be something that flowed naturally and on its own.

So instead, she hung out in the pit box, becoming something of a statistician after several races. Ian had been great about teaching her everything there was about all those screens and what they meant. She was too curious to remain ignorant. Now she knew how many laps Gray could go before he ran out of fuel and how his engine was running.

He had come in fifth and seventh the last two races. Respectable, but not what Gray wanted. Of course, he wanted to win every race.

Today, though, was a road race, a totally different animal according to Gray. The track wasn't oval but more like driving a twisting, winding road along the countryside, though at much higher speeds. And instead of going really fast and making a lot of repetitive left turns, it was a harrowing event where drivers blocked other drivers, and restarts were a free-for-all, especially as they neared the end of the race, when it was critical to be up front.

Gray had already told her road courses weren't his forte. He'd explained his talent was speed and the standard track, not constant downshifting, braking, and right turns then left turns.

And it showed. He was twelfth at the restart. Donny, his team-mate, was fifteenth. She bit her lip and leaned forward as they got the green flag. Within four laps, Gray had moved up to tenth, which wasn't bad, but it was so hard to pass on this tight, twisty course, and as the laps counted down and drivers were shoved off the course by other more aggressive drivers, she worried for Gray, especially as Cal McClusky hit him from behind. She squeezed her hands to-gether, certain he was going to spin out. He corrected, though, and barreled forward, maintaining control.

She exhaled, watching him pass one car, then another, leaving Cal two cars behind him. But he couldn't make enough headway in the time left, and he ended up in eighth place at the finish line.

All things considered, not too bad. Donny finished twelfth and neither of them wrecked.

At the end of the day, they met in the trailer. Gray invited Donny and Stacie to join them for pizza. Evelyn and Stacie had already picked it up when Gray called her to tell her their interviews were almost finished.

The guys grabbed water and fell into the booth while Evelyn and Stacie got out the plates and napkins.

"Rough one today?" she asked.

"I hate road courses." Gray grabbed two slices of pizza and put them on his plate.

"Me, too," Donny said. "They're hard to maneuver. It's not even racing, man."

Stacie gripped his arm. "You did good. You got a top fifteen finish on a course that's not your strong suit."

Donny shrugged and bit into his pizza.

"She's right," Gray said. "You suck at road courses, and a top fifteen isn't bad. I'd call that a win."

"And you're still leading in points," Donny said with a wide grin.

"Which is important for our team right now," Gray said. "We've got some tough races ahead. It's only going to get more competitive. I'm only leading by thirty points. McClusky and Stellen are right on my heels. They're both hungry. I have to drive every race like it's the championship."

"I don't know how you do it," Evelyn said. "There must be incredible pressure on you."

Gray shrugged. "You just have to focus on each individual race, not look too far down the road."

"That's what I keep telling Donny," Stacie said. "One race at a time."

"It's a good philosophy," Gray said. "If you start overthinking, you're screwed."

After they ate, the guys parked in front of the television to watch recaps of the race and to dissect their team performances. Evelyn and Stacie hung out in the kitchen.

"So, how are things going between the two of you?" Evelyn asked, keeping her voice low so the guys wouldn't overhear.

Stacie grinned. "Better. I'm going back to school in the fall."

"Are you? That's great." She took a quick glance over to where Gray and Donny were engrossed in the sports station before turning her attention back on Stacie. "And how does Donny feel about that?"

"Actually, he's being very supportive. He told me I can't help him with his career until I finish my education. He wants me in school, and he told me even though he'll miss me, he promises to pull his head out of his ass and become the best driver on the circuit."

"Good for him. And for you."

"I'm excited. I'm going to miss him like crazy, but I'm also so close to being finished with school that I know if I just concentrate my efforts, I'll be done in no time and then the two of us can be together permanently."

"I think you're making the right move."

"I do, too. Plus, he's hinted he wants to get married in the next year or so. I told him we need to take it one step at a time, but this is the first time I've really seen him so focused and committed."

"I'm happy for you, Stacie."

The glow emanating from Stacie was evident in her wide grin. "Thanks. I'm happy for me, too. For a while there it looked like there was no way things were going to work out for us. Now, everything's falling into place. I just had to have faith in him. And he has to learn to trust me. I love him and he has to realize I'm not going to leave him just because I'm not with him every second."

"I have faith in both of you. I know it's going to be fine."

Stacie looked over at Donny, who caught her gaze and winked at her.

"See?" Stacie asked, lifting her shoulders and holding out her hands. "Freakin' perfect."

Evelyn wished she had the same confidence in her relationship with Gray, but there was no way things would work out between them.

There would be no miracles at the end of their relationship. Technically, they weren't even in a relationship. They were working together, and they were bed buddies. And that's as far as it went.

But being with Gray made her crave a relationship. Someone to come home to at night, to discuss the day's events with, to snuggle under the covers with and make love with. She'd gotten used to that with Gray, and despite having spent the majority of her adult years alone—contentedly at that—now she wanted something different.

The idea of some nameless, faceless stranger, though, didn't appeal to her in the least.

But that person wasn't going to be Gray, and she'd just have to deal with that.

After Stacie and Donny left, Evelyn put away the leftover pizza and pulled the trash bag out. She was headed to the front door with it when Gray came out of the bedroom.

"Where are you going with that?"

She stopped and turned. "The Dumpster."

He laughed. "Give me that. I'll take it."

She put a fresh trash bag in the can while he took out the trash. When he came back in, he leaned against the wall near the kitchen while she finished wiping down the counter. She looked up to find him staring at her.

"What?"

"Nothing. Me taking out the trash, you wiping down the kitchen counters. This just seems so domestic and . . . comfortable."

She laughed. "Uh oh. Is that a bad thing?"

He came over and wrapped his arms around her, pulling her back against him. "No. It's a good thing."

He kissed the side of her neck, one of her favorite spots. She tilted her neck to the side to give him better access. And when he began to use his teeth to scrape across the tender spot between her neck and shoulder, she shuddered and let out a low moan.

"Aren't you tired?" she asked as she rested her head against his chest.

"Is that your polite way of saying you're not in the mood for sex?"

She smiled and snaked her arm around his neck. "I'm always in the mood for sex."

"See? This is why we're compatible. And no. I'm never too tired to make love to you."

He cupped her breasts, massaging them through her T-shirt and bra, driving her crazy because she wanted his hands on her naked flesh, while he was content to tease her with caresses. She finally pulled her T-shirt off and flicked the front clasp of her bra, popping it open.

He pulled it off and reached for her breasts, brushing his fingers over her nipples.

"That's what I needed," she said, her voice filled with the desire that never failed to capture her whenever Gray put his hands on her. The wonder of how she fell under his spell in an instant wasn't lost on her. And when he put his arm around her back and bent to take one aching bud between his lips, he made her gasp. She watched as he sucked her nipples until her clit and pussy throbbed.

And then he turned her around and leaned her over the counter. "I want you this way," he said, dragging her shorts and panties off.

She stepped out of them and he kicked her legs apart, unzipped his pants, and left her only long enough to grab a condom. He slipped his hand between her legs.

"You're wet, Evelyn. Are you ready for me?"

"Yes." She was ready for his cock, ready to come as he slid his hand back and forth over her aching sex. And when he found her clit and massaged her, she lifted up on her toes, moving her body in rhythm to his strokes.

She arched against him, so close to orgasm that she rested her head on her hands and concentrated on the delicious sensations his stroking fingers caused.

And when she came, she bucked back against him, crying out. He removed his fingers and slid his cock inside her, increasing the wild ride of her orgasm as his shaft filled her and he began to move inside her.

He tucked an arm around her waist, protecting her body from the countertop as he began to thrust inside her. She was still throbbing from the lightning-like pulses of her orgasm, still hadn't come down from that high before he had her on another as he plunged repeatedly into her. She reached down to caress her clit, wanting to go there yet again, this time with Gray as he grabbed her hip and dug his fingers into her while he propelled himself ever deeper.

And when she came again, he went with her, licking the back of her neck, making her shiver with delight as the two of them connected in the most intimate of ways.

He lay over her back, both of them sweating and breathing heavily. He played with her breasts as they came down easily from the magnificent high he'd taken her on.

"Now I'm tired," he said.

She smiled as he lifted her up and turned her around. He kissed her, a sweet, deep kiss. "How about we go to bed?" she asked.

"Is that your way of telling me you want to have sex again?"

She laughed. "You're killing me, Gray."

"No, I think you might be killing me, Evelyn."

TWENTY-THREE

GRAY YANKED THE COVERS OFF EVELYN EARLY THE
next morning.

"Wake up."

She burrowed under the pillow, grabbing the air in search of the
blanket. "Go away. It's too early." Didn't the man ever sleep?

"We have important things to do today."

She rolled over and half opened her eyes. "What important
things?"

"I thought we'd go spend some time in New York today."

That woke her up in a hurry. "Really?"

"Yeah. Take a day off before we head out of town."

She sat up and hung her legs over the side of the bed. "That
sounds like fun."

"Ever been?"

She shook her head. She'd always wanted to go.

"Then let's get going."

Gray had already showered, so she scrambled back to her hotel, took a quick shower, changed, and packed. Gray had already arranged a private plane to take them there since they'd only have the day. A car met them at the airport and drove them into Manhattan.

Evelyn unashamedly sat at the window like a geeked-out tourist as they entered the city, gawking at the amazing skyline, picking out the Chrysler Building and Empire State building, her heart climbing into her throat as she spotted the Statue of Liberty. She'd always planned to take a week's vacation in New York, and had an agenda of places she wanted to see. There'd just never been time.

"I know. We aren't going to be able to do it all. But I can give you an overview," he said as the car let them out in Times Square.

"What about our bags?" she asked as the car drove away.

"The driver will take care of them."

Trusting Gray, she shrugged, and with no small amount of glee, she did a complete turnaround, gaping at the immense blinking signs, the sheer amount of humanity crowding the sidewalks and clamoring for space amidst the cluster of traffic and honking horns. Tourists walked Times Square, no doubt as shell-shocked as she was.

She turned to Gray. "I've seen this before in movies, but it's nothing like being here."

He grinned and took her hand. "Come on."

They walked along the street and Evelyn took in every sight and smell, the street vendors hawking everything from pretzels and hot dogs to clothing and jewelry. The police were out in force, patrolling on foot and on horseback. It seemed like there was a cop every three feet. In a city with millions of people crowding and shoving into her, she'd never felt safer, surprisingly.

Gray stopped and grabbed them a bus ticket for the tours.

"A bus tour, really?" she asked, surprised he'd want to do something like that. It was totally something she would have done, likely the first thing because she'd be so eager to see everything all at once.

"You'll enjoy this. I've done it before."

She halted and stared at him. "You have. You, the rich guy, took a tourist bus."

"Best way to see Manhattan, in my opinion. You can hop on and off at any stop. We'll take both of them so you can see everything."

"I'm stunned."

He laughed. "Come on. Let's go get in line."

He bought them water and they waited for the big red double-decker buses. When it was their turn, they climbed aboard the top of the bus. She looped her arm around Gray's and leaned against him.

"I'm ridiculously excited about this," she said as the bus took off.

Gray was quiet and she was anything but, commenting on everything she saw on the tours, from Union Square to Chinatown to the Flatiron Building. The architecture of buildings they passed particularly fascinated her, and she grabbed her phone and snapped pictures of building fronts that caught her eye, especially some of the old churches.

She scanned the map. "Oh, the Met is coming up." She looked at Gray. "Do you mind?"

"We can go anywhere you want."

They hopped out at the Metropolitan Museum of Art and went in. Lord, but the place was huge. They grabbed a map and maneuvered their way through several of the exhibits.

"You need an entire day—possibly two or three—just to see everything. There are more than two million works in here," she said, reading the information sheet. It was overwhelming.

"Yes," Gray said. "But it's worth it."

"You've been through here."

He nodded. "More than once."

"What's your favorite thing?"

"Greek and Roman Art." He led her to the section, showed her some of his favorite pieces.

"This is one I could look at for hours," he said, showing her a marble sarcophagus.

The intricacies were awe-inspiring. She took his hand and laid her head on his shoulder, examining it with him, absorbing the detail and appreciating the work that had gone into it. They wandered the section and looked at each piece. She found herself watching Gray as he admired the sculptures, noted the way he cocked his head to the side, how long he would study the pieces.

Who would know this about him if he hadn't taken the time to share his love of art? He was such a complex man and she loved that about him.

When they left the exhibit, he turned to her. "Your turn. Show me what you love."

She gazed up at him and smiled. "Okay."

She looked at the map and led the way, her pulse thrumming at the thought of seeing the paintings.

When they got to the section it took some twists and turns. The rooms were like a maze. She was glad to have Gray with her, because she might have gotten lost without his help. But as soon as she found the Impressionist wing, she went to the paintings and stopped in front of the first Renoir she saw.

Gray came up and put his arm around her. "They're beautiful."

"It's hard to believe I'm actually seeing them up close like this." She wanted to reach out and touch them. Of course she knew she couldn't, but they were so beautiful. She moved along and looked at each one in the gallery, though her favorites were the Renoirs and Monets. She understood now why there were cushioned seating areas in the center of each gallery, why some people sat and just stared for hours.

Art was such an amazing thing. She couldn't draw at all, but she had such an appreciation for the talent of those who could paint beautiful works that spoke to her heart in this way.

She laced her fingers with Gray's as they left the gallery. "I think someday I'll come back to New York and spend every day for a week coming in here to just sit and reflect."

"It's peaceful. Gives you a chance to clear your head."

They left the Met and Gray pulled her half a block down the street. There was a vendor cart and he ordered them two hot dogs and a drink.

"You haven't truly experienced New York until you've had a hot dog from a vendor cart."

She laughed. "Then by all means, we have to have one."

They walked a little farther down the street and stopped at one of the benches under the shade trees, eating while people buzzed by on their way to wherever they were going. The hot dog was good and it was blistering hot outside, so the shade helped. She enjoyed people watching, so Gray suggested they walk to the next tour bus stop, and since they would be walking along Central Park, she didn't mind the walk at all.

They grabbed the bus and made a few more stops. Gray took her to lunch at an amazing bistro where she had the most perfect Greek salad with stuffed grape leaves, kalamata olives, and feta cheese, topped with dressing so delicious she wanted to scoop it up with a spoon. It was an open-air place so while she ate she people watched, and with so many people going by, it was such a pleasurable experience. She and Gray tried to imagine where they were all going, what kind of jobs they had. She got distracted a little by checking out the fantastic shoes the women wore.

Women knew how to dress in this city. She felt extremely underdressed in her capris and canvas shoes, but at least she was comfortable.

They grabbed the bus and ended up back where they started. She loved seeing everything, but it was an exhausting day. Gray hailed a cab. It was a harrowing ride, kind of like a roller coaster in an amusement park with lots of twists, turns, and abrupt stops. But she felt like she'd been truly indoctrinated into New York culture. And she was a little nauseated, too, likely because she was still rubbernecking and playing tourist, craning her neck up to see the tall buildings and people watching as the taxicab performed death-defying acts by barely missing pedestrians and other cars. There was a lot of horn honking going on, and the taxi driver seemed put out by the other cars and the pedestrians getting in his way.

It was insane, really.

"That was interesting," she said after they climbed out and the cab pulled away, shoving itself into the flow of stop-and-go traffic.

Gray laughed. "Yeah. Welcome to New York."

It took her a few seconds to register that they had stopped at The Plaza.

"I am so not dressed to have drinks here," she said.

"We're not having drinks here." They went to the registration desk, where he shocked her by checking them in. The registration clerk told Gray that their suite was ready and their bags had already been taken up to their room.

The hotel was the most beautiful thing she'd ever seen. Very Old World, mixed with every modern convenience. And when she walked into the suite, she could have died from the beauty. It was a town house suite—two floors of utter decadence, with a dining room, a living room, an upstairs bedroom, and a marble-floored bathroom she might never want to leave.

There was a huge terrace that looked out over Central Park.

The first thing she did was step out onto the terrace. Gray followed.

"This is lovely. And the view is amazing." She turned to him. "Thank you for bringing me here."

"You're welcome. I thought you might like to stay here tonight."

"Tonight? I'm thinking of moving in permanently. You'll have to drag me out of here, kicking and screaming."

"I get a bug to get out of that trailer every now and then."

She laughed. "I imagine you do. This is very . . . expansive." And, she imagined, sinfully expensive. As she looked out over the park and the skyscape, she was envious of those who lived in this beautiful city.

"I could live here."

"At the Plaza or in Manhattan?"

She laughed. "Definitely in Manhattan, though it's decadent to think about living in this suite."

"Yeah? You like what you see?"

"What's not to like? I love that you can walk everywhere, that there's awesome transportation. I love the sights of the city, the never-ending choices in food, the atmosphere, the frenetic pace."

"It is nice here. But I still like my place on the beach the best. There's a quiet that I can't get anywhere else."

She leaned against him. "I can appreciate the beauty there, too. The nice thing is you could afford to have homes in a lot of places."

"That's true. And you like the heartbeat of D.C."

"I do, but mainly for work. D.C. lacks the beauty of New York or the quiet peacefulness of the beach in Daytona."

"You should marry a rich guy who can give you houses in all your favorite places. Then, when you're not busy ruling the world, you can vacation there."

She laughed. "Yeah, in a perfect world that'll happen."

He kissed her neck. "Dream big, princess. You never know what might happen."

He turned and walked inside. She watched him go, pondering what he said.

* * *

GRAY WANTED TO MAKE THIS NIGHT PERFECT FOR EVE-
lyn. After they showered, they got dressed. Evelyn looked beautiful
in a cream-colored dress that hugged her curves at the top and had
a sinful slit up the side. And those heels made her legs look spectacular.

"Oh, did you want to stay in tonight?" he asked as he met her at
the foot of the stairs.

She frowned. "I thought we were going out. Is this dress not
the right choice?"

He took her hand and brushed a kiss across her knuckles. "You're
a knockout, but I don't know if I can go out in public with a hard-on."

She laughed. "Thank you. I still have no idea where we're going."

"You'll see." He tucked her hand in his arm and they took the
elevator down to the lobby, where a car was waiting.

"I feel a little decadent," she said as they slid into the back of
the private car.

"Do you? Good. It's nice to get away from the dirty track every
now and then and live like the rich folks do."

She laughed. "Gray, you *are* the rich folks."

He arched a brow. "Am I?"

The driver took them to the restaurant, where a valet opened the
door for them.

"Welcome to Daniel."

"Oh, I've heard of this restaurant. It's one of the finest in Manhattan," Evelyn said as they made their way inside. "But very hard to
get into. How did you get a reservation? I heard you have to make
them a month or so in advance."

"Well," Gray said after he'd given his name and they were shown
to their table. "I have a few connections here and there."

"Is that right? I'm impressed."

They looked over the wine list. "What would you like?" he asked.

"I love wine. All sorts. Something red and smooth?"

He nodded and ordered a bottle after their sommelier made a few suggestions.

"This place is lovely, Gray. Thank you for bringing me here."

"I'm glad you like it."

"You're constantly surprising me."

"Am I? How's that?"

"I don't know. Every time I think I know you, it's like you peel a new layer off that onion."

He cocked a brow. "Yeah? Good. I'd hate to be predictable. Predictable is boring."

"Trust me, Gray. You are anything but boring."

They had dinner and Gray paid the check. The car was waiting for them and took them to the theater district. He watched Evelyn's eyes widen as the car let them out in front of the theater.

"Seriously?"

His lips curved. "I thought you might want to see a show while we're here."

She squeezed his hand after they got out of the car. "I'd love to. And it's a musical. I love musicals. How did you know?"

He shrugged. "A wild guess."

As they took their seats near the front of the theater, Evelyn whispered, "I feel like Cinderella tonight. You're the prince and you're making all my dreams come true." She brushed her lips against his. "Thank you for that."

Gray sucked in a breath at the emotion rolling around his gut. He didn't know what to do about it—what to do about Evelyn and all these feelings that seemed to pummel him whenever he spent time with her. And those feelings were growing, making him wonder how he was going to live his life without her after she was through with her business with him.

Which made him wonder how he could maneuver it—adjust his life—so the two of them could stay together.

The lights went down and the music started. Evelyn grabbed his hand tight and didn't let go through the entire production, which was cute and funny. He loved hearing her laugh and he enjoyed the musical because Evelyn enjoyed it so much. She talked about it nonstop on the ride back to the hotel.

"I know I've been going on and on since we left the theater, but did you like it?" she asked as they rode up the elevator.

"I did. It was fun. I laughed a lot."

She grinned. "I did, too. And the music—oh, the music was amazing. Every song was catchy and fun and the voices of the actors were tremendous. I'm so envious of their talent."

He slid his key in and unlocked the door to their suite, then turned on the lights. He tossed his wallet on the table near the door, then turned to her. "You have many talents, Evelyn."

"Yes, but singing isn't one of them. I was always jealous of the choir and drama students in college. It's something I wanted to do, but I don't have the voice."

He came up to her and put his arms around her. "Maybe you can sing for me sometime—in the shower—and I'll judge you."

She laughed. "Not a chance in hell that's ever going to happen."

"You don't trust me to be unbiased?"

She laid her palms on his chest. "I wouldn't abuse your ears that way."

"Now I think you're too hard on yourself."

"And you obviously haven't heard me sing, in the shower or elsewhere."

He smiled at her and pulled away, then poured a liqueur for both of them from the well-stocked bar. He turned on music, a sultry R&B station that settled smoothly into her bones.

"I thought we'd have a drink on the terrace," he said.

"That sounds nice." She took her drink from him and followed him outside.

The night was perfect, the heat of the day eased by the cloud cover and the light breeze. Evelyn walked to the edge of the terrace and looked out over the city. "It's even more beautiful at night." She turned to him as he came up beside her. "Have I thanked you for bringing me here?"

"Numerous times. And I'm enjoying it as much as you are."

She took a sip of the liqueur. "Oh, this is good. You're spoiling me."

He slid his hand up her back, enjoying the feel of her skin against his hand. "I like spoiling you. Usually it's work all the time, people surrounding us, and then at the end of the day the two of us holing up in the trailer. Now what kind of treat is that for my woman? I have to get you out of there on occasion and show you a good time."

Evelyn took a deep breath. His woman? God, he melted her panties with that statement. As if the whole day hadn't completely taken her breath away, he had to make a comment like that and make her second-guess everything about their relationship.

She took a deep breath, then turned and leaned against the railing. "You've shown me beyond a good time. This has been such a surprise today, Gray. I've enjoyed everything about seeing New York. But the best part has been sharing it all with you."

"I'm glad."

She took his glass from him and laid both their drinks down on the table. Then she moved into him, sliding her palms up the lapels of his jacket, relishing the firm chest underneath her hands. He wrapped an arm around her waist and drew her closer, then cupped her neck, his breath warm against her lips as he surprised her by taking her hand in his and moving around the terrace.

"Are we dancing?"

"We are. You look so gorgeous, you should be dancing."

She tilted her head back, filled with awe and desire for this man who was making all her dreams come true. "You do realize I'm standing on the terrace of a magnificent hotel, dancing with one very hot, handsome man. I don't think my life could get much better."

His lips curved as he twirled her expertly around. "Well, you could be a senator right now. Or maybe the president. Then your life would be perfect."

She laughed. "I'm living a pretty good life right now. I have no complaints."

"Neither do I. Besides, I don't think I'd appreciate the secret service interrupting our private time. I do like having you all to myself." He dipped her, then kissed her, turning her world upside down.

When he righted her again, she smiled at him.

"I like that myself, and I don't think I'm ready just yet to be president. If I were, I'd have to behave myself and I wouldn't be able to take advantage of you." When the song ended, she backed him in to the darkened corner of the terrace.

He cocked a brow. "Take advantage of me in what way?"

With a sly smile she slid her hands down his shirt, over his magnificent abs. "Touching you. Outside, where someone might see us. A president would never be able to get away with doing that."

She cupped him, measured his length with her hand as she pressed her body against his.

"Probably not, but then again, I've heard the secret service can be very discreet."

"And I like my privacy. Maybe I'll be content with the job I have. So I can have rendezvous like this." She squeezed his cock through his pants, loving the rapid intake of his breath as she massaged him.

In a heartbeat, he turned her around so it was her back against the wall, her body shadowed and protected. "I doubt that. You should be able to have whatever you want. In whatever way you want it."

His voice had gone low and deep, a sensual tone that never failed to send ripples of desire through her. "Anything I want?"

"Yes."

She met his gaze and reached for the zipper of his pants. "This is what I want, Gray. You. Now. Like this."

Gray brushed his hands over Evelyn's rib cage, watching the movement of her silk dress, the way it molded to her body. He reached down and slid his hand into the slit of her dress—that teasing slit that had tormented him all night with glimpses of her sexy thigh.

He stopped—looked up at her. "That's a garter belt," he said.

She smiled and loosened his tie. "It might be."

He smoothed his hand over the skin of her thigh, flicking the garter belt. "I need you naked."

She lifted her leg and rested it over his hip. "And I need you inside me. Right here, where I can look at New York while you make love to me."

He sucked in a breath, his dick throbbing and hard. He dropped to his knees and circled her ankles with his fingers, tilted his head back to see Evelyn looking down at him. Everything about her turned him on tonight, from these sexy shoes to the garters and that slit in her dress, to the way she laughed unabashedly at the theater to her bold proposition to him a minute ago.

Hell, she didn't just turn him on tonight, but every night. It didn't matter if she was dressed up and on the town, or whether she was in shorts and a tank top in his trailer. She was so ingrained into his life, so much a part of him, that every touch, every look, sent him into a frenzied state of desire.

He wanted her all the damn time, no matter where they were.

Especially tonight as she leaned against the wall of the terrace, her silk-clad legs smooth and sexy as he slid his hands along her calves. He felt her slight tremble as he inched his fingers under the hem of her dress. He found her panties and drew them down her legs. She held on to his shoulders as she stepped out of them, as he tucked them into his pocket.

"Souvenir?" she asked.

"Maybe."

She took a deep breath and he lifted her foot, positioned her leg over his shoulder, and eased between her legs, raising her skirt as he did, his fingers brushing the straps of her garters.

"This is so damn hot," he said. "I'm going to fuck you in these tonight."

She gave him a wicked smile. "That's the idea."

He leaned in and brushed a kiss across her thighs, then the top of her sex, teasing her until she grabbed his hair.

"Gray. Lick me. Make me come."

He loved that she demanded her pleasure, that whatever issues she'd had when they first met had dissipated and she could come for him anywhere, in any position.

Like here, on a rooftop terrace. He took a deep breath, inhaling her scent, then licked her pussy, rolling his tongue across her clit until she let out a loud moan. No one would hear her. That's why he'd selected this suite, because it gave them complete privacy. He wanted to hear her scream into the New York night.

He laid his tongue against her and slid his fingers inside her. She was hot and oh so wet, her pussy quivering as he finger fucked her while he sucked the hard bud, rolling his tongue over it until she writhed against his face.

"You're going to make me come. I'm going to come so hard, Gray."

He wanted that, wanted her falling apart under his tongue. And when he hummed his approval, she lifted up on her toes and rocked her pelvis against his face, crying out as she came. He held on to her while she shuddered out her pleasure and he licked her up, eager to give her every second of orgasm she could get.

When her legs started to buckle, he rose and pulled her against him, taking her mouth in a kiss that was likely more about his need than hers. He had to touch her, to let his fingers dive into her hair to feel the softness there, to let his tongue tangle with hers and share with her just how damn good she tasted.

She was just as eager as he was, her hands sliding up his arms and over his shoulders, gripping him while she sucked on his tongue. His cock tightened, a stranglehold of pain and pleasure as she moved against him.

He lifted her and she wrapped her legs around him. He took them inside, their mouths still fused as he made his way—half blind, since he didn't want to stop kissing her—upstairs, where he deposited her on the bed.

Hair askew, dress raised over her hips, and those gorgeous legs exposed, she looked wanton and totally fuckable.

He unbuttoned his shirt and undid his tie as he stood over the bed and looked his fill. "You are the most beautiful woman I've ever seen."

Evelyn stared at him with a knowing smile. "And I'm one very lucky woman."

She got up on her knees and turned around. "Unzip me."

He pulled the zipper down, stopping halfway to press a kiss to her back. She let the dress slip from her shoulders, revealing a cream-colored bra that did very little to contain her breasts.

And then there was the garter belt.

After Gray removed his clothes, he smoothed his hands down her legs. Most women were bare legged these days, especially in the hot summer months. In fact, he hadn't even noticed the stockings Evelyn was wearing until he caught sight of the garter belt from the slit in her dress.

Jesus, that was hot, a lost art of seduction. The stockings were silk and under his hands, they made his balls tighten.

He laid her flat on the bed and spread her legs, stroking her thighs. "You're a seductress in these."

She reached for his cock. "Come over here and let me suck you."

His stomach tumbled, and for the first time, he felt like he was being seduced instead of being the seducer. He pulled her to the edge of the bed and her hands slid over him like a silken waterfall. She snaked her tongue over the soft head of his cock before grasping him firmly in her hands.

She looked up at him. "Have I ever told you how much I love your cock, how looking at it and touching it makes me wet?"

He drew in a shaky breath. He wasn't sure he wanted her to know how much her words weakened him. "It makes my cock hard to hear it. Take me in your mouth, Evelyn. I need to watch you suck me."

Her head hung partially off the bed, her hair loose and flowing. He cradled her head in his hand and lifted her, guiding his cock between her parted lips. The first touch of her hot, wet tongue to his sensitive head made him jerk. God, it was so good, and being able to watch her like this, on her back, her body spread out like a wicked angel, was every man's dream.

He fed her his cock inch by inch and she took it willingly, using her mouth and her hands to take him deep, her tongue rolling over his shaft as she explored him. He watched her throat work as he thrust forward, careful not to be too forceful, but unable to control the fierce desire that seemed to take over as her sweet mouth worked him, sucking him in and making his balls ache as he fought the need to come right then.

He swept his fingers over the cups of her bra, teasing the swells of her breasts, pulling the cups down to reveal her nipples. They were taut, tight points.

"Does sucking me make your nipples hard, Evelyn?"

Her gaze met his and she hummed against his dick, making him close his eyes as she tightened her grip on him with her mouth and hands. He played with her nipples, brushing his thumb across them in a teasing caress, cupping the globes and giving the buds a gentle squeeze. If he was in a better position he could suck them—which he would, later. But right now all he could do was hold on, because he couldn't fight the rising tide of his orgasm.

He straightened, holding her head in his hand, and watched as his cock slid between her sweet lips.

"I'm going to come in your mouth," he said, his voice a tight strain as he held on to what little restraint he had left.

Evelyn made eye contact, watching him as he let loose a loud groan and released, his body flooded with adrenaline as he pumped into her willing mouth. She reached up and held on to his thighs while he rocketed against her, shaking with the force of his climax.

Panting, he laid his palms on the mattress while Evelyn licked his shaft and released him. When he had the strength, he turned her around so her legs dangled off the edge of the bed.

He smiled down at her. "You wreck me."

Her lips curved. "That's good. Because you always do the same thing to me."

He bent to kiss her, tasted himself on her mouth, and licked the curve of her lips, then wound an arm around her waist to deepen the kiss. She moaned and wrapped her legs around him. He swept his hand over her stockings and his dick began to harden again, especially when she arched against him.

He fell onto the bed, keeping his weight off her but needing to feel her body close, needing his cock rubbing against her wet, hot pussy. He reached for one of the condoms, put it on in a hurry, and was inside her, taking in her gasp of pleasure with his mouth on hers.

He rose up, wanting to watch her breathe, to watch her breasts rise and fall as they moved in unison. He wanted to touch her, to rub his fingers over her clit as he thrust in and out of her. He wanted to watch her eyes darken as she rushed ever closer to climax.

And when she wrapped her legs around him again, when her pussy tightened around his cock and he knew she was ready to go off, that's when he sank deep, when he fucked her harder, when he rubbed his chest against her breast and levered his hips against hers.

And when she screamed, it was the sweetest music she could ever sing, because it made him come hard, grinding against her and groaning out his own orgasm as he slid a hand under her butt to draw her even tighter against him while they both rode it out until they were spent and panting in each other's ears.

"I don't think I can move ever again," she said a few minutes later.

He smiled and swept her hair out of her face. "Fortunately for you, it's not quite time to check out yet."

She laughed. "Good. I might be stuck like this for many hours."

"Yeah, but I'm hungry."

She rolled over on her side to face him. "What is it with men and sex and the need for food?"

"Protein replacement. When we ejaculate, we have to replenish, you know."

She rolled her eyes. "I think that's just an excuse to have a late-night burger."

"Probably. So what would you like?"

She sat up and slid off the bed. On the way to the bathroom she stopped, turned, and looked at him. "A burger, of course."

TWENTY-FOUR

EVELYN WAS BEYOND EXCITED TO BE IN ATLANTA, NOT only for the race but the upcoming convention. It was going to be an exciting couple weeks.

Gray agreed to go to the convention and be at his father's side. The week of the convention was a bye week for racing, so it couldn't have turned out more perfectly if she'd planned it.

The social media campaign had been going well, and she'd even gotten Gray more involved in that, doing some of his own posts on Facebook and Twitter, which was not only introducing his fans to the senator, it was getting them more involved with Gray on a racing level, which his fans loved. He'd been doing a great job talking about his father and what he was doing on the campaign trail, his father's platform, and what Gray believed his father could do for the country. Gray mixed that in nicely with weekly race information—how he felt about the last race and information about the upcoming race. He kept his followers in the loop, both politically and race-wise.

He was gaining more followers every day, and hopefully he could see the value of being more directly involved in social media. It was a win-win.

She'd been trying to convince him to give a speech at the convention now that the senator was definitely going to be Cameron's running mate. So far, Gray had said no, but she could tell from his voice and his body language it wasn't a firm no. She understood his reluctance. He wasn't a political kind of guy. Just being at the convention with his dad would be enough support. But if he gave a speech it would seal the deal, and Evelyn knew they'd garner a lot of votes.

Patience. She paced the confines of the trailer. She had to be patient, and everything would fall into place. Which was hard to do when all her peers and everyone who'd been with the senator were working so hard right now at the hotel near the convention center, while she was blazing a hole in Gray's carpet in his trailer, stopping every few minutes to chew the last stubs off her fingernails or send an email or check polls or the latest blogs or statistics.

Doing nothing when the campaign was about to go into full swing was making her crazy. She wanted to be on the front lines.

She also wanted to be with Gray. This was a big race. He hadn't done all that well in the Michigan or Bristol races and he'd dropped in the standings. Now in second, Atlanta was important. She needed to be here with him.

Actually, she didn't. Her being here wouldn't make him race any better. She needed to listen to her own advice. She'd told Stacie that Donny didn't need her to be here holding his hand. The same held true for Evelyn.

Still, she *wanted* to be here, supporting him. She chewed on her fingernail and stared at the latest polls coming up on her laptop.

"You really shouldn't be here."

She whirled to find Gray staring at her from the steps, horrified that she'd so lost track of time.

"Tell me I didn't miss practice."

His lips curved as he threw his gear into a chair. "It was practice, Evelyn. Not a race."

Dammit. "I'm so sorry. I just popped in here to check some stats and answer a few emails, which I could have done on my phone. And then I got involved reading some political blogs and a few news capsules. Then I made a few phone calls—"

He jerked her into his arms and kissed her, which always seemed to calm the adrenaline rush work brought out in her. When he pulled away, she was languid and turned on. But still felt guilty.

"I'm still sorry I missed practice."

"And I don't expect you to park your ass out there and watch me every second. You have a job and it's crunch time. You should be at the convention center. You should pack up and go."

She shook her head. "I need to be here with you. You're my job right now."

He tucked her hair behind her ear. "I've already agreed to come to the convention. Your job here is done. Go work for my dad. I think I can race without you."

"You can. But I'm not going to let you. There will be plenty of time for me at the convention after you race this weekend."

He slid his arms around her. "You're a stubborn woman, Evelyn."

"I prefer determined."

QUALIFYING HAD BEEN TOUGH, HOT AS HELL, AND JUST as frustrating as a race. And it hadn't yielded the results Gray had been looking for.

A sixth-place spot wasn't going to put him where he wanted to be. He thought his time had been great. Obviously not great enough. Even worse, Donny had crashed during qualifying, so he'd have to start the race in the back.

After he answered what seemed like a thousand questions about Preston Racing team's backslide over the past few weeks, which to Gray hadn't seemed like a backslide at all, he was hot and tired and in need of Evelyn's sweet face. He looked around the pits for her, shocked as hell to see his father there.

What the hell was Mitchell Preston doing here? As far as Gray knew, his father had never once attended one of his races. How utterly timely for him to show up at qualifying, a week before the convention. Of course he was all smiles as the cameras were in his face. Gray could well imagine what his father was talking about.

Himself. His campaign. Stumping for votes. Telling the American people how important it was that they vote for him. Maybe something tying Gray into his campaign.

All bullshit.

It was the last insult to an already miserable fucking day. He headed over to where his father was surrounded by cameras. Evelyn caught his gaze and smiled, meeting him halfway, looping her arm around his and stopping his forward progress.

"Are you surprised?"

He dragged his gaze away from his dad. "What?"

"That your father's here."

He dragged his head from the fog of confusion. "What are you talking about? Did you arrange this?"

Now it was her turn to look confused. "Me? Of course not. I had no idea he was going to show up. He shocked the hell out of me when he called and said he was here. I scrambled to get him in. Thank God for Ian, who helped us out. He hung out here watching everyone qualify, Gray."

Sure. He had the whole time to work the crowd. "I'm sure he did."

She frowned. "Aren't you happy? He's talking to reporters right now."

"Of course he is. That's what he does. That's why he's here."

It was just like school again, his father only showing up to stump for votes. He was only here for self-serving reasons. Not for Gray.

Not ever for Gray.

He waded into the crowd of photographers and reporters and pulled his father close.

"Gray," his father said, his smile wide. "You did so well today. I had no idea you were so talented. I'm so proud of you."

Of course he had no idea, because he'd never shown up. But he wouldn't do this here. Not in front of all these reporters.

He smiled for the cameras, but turned so only his father could hear.

"I won't let you manipulate me, old man. Get the fuck out of my sport."

He turned and walked away, not bothering to look back to see the expression on his father's face.

Because he didn't care how Mitchell Preston felt.

He should never have agreed to this media circus. He knew from the outset it would be a mistake, a clusterfuck.

Seeing his father at home in the middle of that media storm of reporters and photographers set Gray off. This should have been about racing, not politics, and he knew then he'd been right all along.

He should have said no. No matter what kind of emotional blackmail his mother had tried to use on him, he should have said no.

Because he was suddenly eight years old again, with that gut-punch feeling of hurt because his dad had just let him down.

And no matter how old he got, that feeling was never going to go away.

TWENTY-FIVE

EVELYN LEFT THE SENATOR IN THE HANDS OF HIS AIDES, instructing them to wind down the interviews and get the senator out of there, that there'd be no joint interviews with Gray and Mitchell Preston today. She made up the excuse that Gray had other commitments today, and they'd try for another day.

She knew where to find him—in his trailer, the only place he could be assured of privacy.

Surprisingly, he hadn't locked her out. She shut the door, found him nursing a beer, his fire suit hanging around his hips.

"What was that about?"

He shrugged and ignored her, taking another long swallow of beer.

She moved into the room and stood in front of him, arms crossed. "Your father came here today to watch qualifying, you know."

He smiled around the rim of the bottle. "My father came today to use me to get votes and face time."

"Uh, no. The only thing he said on camera was how proud he was of you, and what an amazing driver you were."

Gray snorted, tossed the beer into the trash and got another out of the fridge, then resumed his seat.

Irritated, she leaned against the arm of the chair across from him. "Why do you find that so hard to believe?"

He didn't even look at her, just past her. "Because he never once saw me play ball when I was a kid. Or in high school or in college. He was always too busy with politics, with his career, which was so much more important than his own kid. Except one time, he showed up at my game. God, I was so excited to see him there, until I realized it was an election year. He wasn't even watching me play. He was glad-handing the parents in the stands, trying to get votes. I could have walked off the field and he wouldn't have known the difference. He didn't even know I was there."

"I'm sorry, Gray. That must have hurt."

He shrugged. "I got over it, and got used to his indifference."

"I can't imagine you could ever get used to that. But that's not the Mitchell Preston I know. The Mitchell Preston I know is warm and caring."

He dragged his gaze to her. "Yeah, he was always warm and caring with beautiful women."

She rolled her eyes. "I told you he's never been like that with me."

"So you've said."

"Don't be insulting to me just because you're pissed at your dad. I think you know me better than that."

"Do I? You seem to defend him a lot."

He was hurt, and lashing out at her because his father wasn't there to take his anger out on. A part of her understood that, even though his words hurt her. "I defend him because of who he is and what he stands for. He isn't the man you describe to me. Believe me,

I know about his past. I wasn't going to work for someone I hadn't fully vetted. But after his heart attack, he changed."

Gray frowned. "What heart attack? My father never had a heart attack."

"Uh, yeah, he did, Gray."

"When?"

"Eight years ago. It nearly killed him, and it sure as hell scared the shit out of him. It changed his life and changed his outlook on everything, from politics to his relationships with his staff, the way he lived his life and his relationship with his wife. He said he reached out to you afterward, but you refused to respond."

Gray shook his head, unable to fathom what Evelyn said was true. Eight years ago he'd been . . . what? Racing. Loving his life, just getting started.

He didn't remember his father contacting him. Then again, they corresponded, but that was right after his grandfather died, too. When Gray inherited the money. He remembered his father calling him, trying to see him. He figured his father was going to try to convince him to reevaluate and go to Harvard. He wanted no part of that, so he resisted the contact with his father.

No. "That can't be true."

"It is true."

He went for his phone, called his mother.

"Where are you?" he asked.

"At the convention hotel."

"I'm coming over. Don't leave."

"All right."

He looked at Evelyn.

"I'll come with you."

He gave a short nod and went into the bedroom to change clothes, came out a few minutes later and grabbed his keys. The

ONE SWEET RIDE 259

drive to the convention hotel was a short one. He didn't say anything on the way and fortunately Evelyn didn't either.

He had nothing to say, all he could do was think back all those years.

His mother opened the door to her suite.

"He's not here," she said as she let them in. "He has meetings."

"Why didn't you tell me about Dad's heart attack?"

His mom looked at Evelyn, then went to sit down on one of the sofas in the suite.

"Your father didn't want you to know. He didn't want you to feel obligated to be by his side simply because he'd fallen ill. He wanted to repair his relationship with you based on mutual respect and understanding, not because of his health."

Gray sucked in a breath. "The media doesn't know."

"No. He'd fully recovered. He changed his entire lifestyle, his diet. No more alcohol and he exercises all the time now. It was a life-changing event for him, Gray, in so many ways."

And Gray had never known about it.

"And he called me?"

"A few times, until you made it clear you wanted no contact. He made Carolina and me promise not to tell you about it, so we didn't. He figured you'd come around eventually."

But he hadn't, because he thought his father was the same man he'd always been.

"You believe he's changed?" he asked his mother.

She smiled at him. "I doubt I'd still be with him if he hadn't." She patted the spot next to her on the sofa and Gray sat next to her.

"I'll go get us something to drink," Evelyn said. "Give you two some time to chat."

"Thank you," Loretta said.

When Evelyn left the room, his mother grasped his hand in hers.

"I know you think I was blind to your father's faults all those years, but I wasn't. I put up with a lot from him, but those days were about to come to an end. We were fighting a lot and I told him I was through.

"After the heart attack, he cried for the first time in years, told me coming that close to death made him realize what an arrogant fool he had been. He told me he had the best life, the best family, and he'd taken it all for granted, that he'd put his career first and he'd just assumed I'd follow him along wherever he went. He apologized to me and asked me for forgiveness. He confessed all his failings to me and I told him I'd stay with him under one condition—that we go to marriage counseling. He agreed instantly."

"That surprises me, considering if that ever came out it could hurt his career."

His mother nodded. "It surprised me, too, since your father's public image was always his priority. But he told me he didn't care. He promised me that I would forever and always come first in his life, and since then he hasn't once backed away from that promise. We're together on his campaign trips, and his phone and his email are an open book to me. It's like we have a second chance at love again. That trust was hard earned, but he has it from me again."

"How did he ever get to the VP position given his past?"

She smiled. "He never cheated on me, Gray. He was a workaholic and a heavy drinker, and often an arrogant ass, but he never cheated. He liked to flirt with young girls. I hated that."

Gray gave her a dubious look. His mother shot one right back at him.

"Do I look like a fool, son?"

"No, ma'am, you don't."

"Trust me, I'd know. He told me he wanted to feel young, and he always gave the ladies the eye, but he would have never cheated on me. And if he had, believe me, when they vet someone for vice president they're very thorough. They've gone through his past with a fine-toothed comb."

"Does Cameron know about the heart attack?"

His mother nodded. "Of course. We held nothing back. Cameron appreciated your father's honesty. I wasn't kidding when I said your father has changed. He's one of the healthiest men in politics now."

That's why his dad looked so different when Gray saw him at the ranch.

"And Cameron believes in him."

His mother nodded. "Yes. He believes in your father's policies, too, and his vision for the future."

"And you don't think it's going to come out during the campaign."

She shrugged. "If it does, we'll deal with it. I don't think it will matter. He is who he is now, not who he once was. Cameron believes in him. So do I. He's an amazing man, Gray. He's warm and compassionate and he loves his family."

Or at least some of them. Gray gave her a confused look. "But there's been this Grand Canyon–wide chasm between him and me and I don't understand why."

His mother smiled. "He's tried, Grayson. You keep shutting him down. If you think about it, he's been accommodating of all your requests—like using the lodge at the country club, or using the plane anytime you want it. He's been trying for years to open a dialogue with you. It's been you stonewalling the reconciliation."

Gray sat back against the sofa. His mother was right, at least partially. He and his father had always had lousy communication skills, and God knew he always had blinders on regarding his dad, always wanted to see the worst where he was concerned. But maybe he just hadn't seen the signs, maybe he refused to see the olive branch his father had been trying to extend all these years.

And when he saw his father with his fans and the media today, he had just assumed the worst, because of the painful memories of his childhood.

He looked at his mother. "So now what?"

She squeezed his hand. "I guess that's up to you."

GRAY FOUND HIS FATHER EXITING A MEETING WITH A few other senators. He paused when he saw Gray, no doubt expecting some sort of confrontation.

Gray approached and his dad excused himself from his colleagues.

"Got a minute?" Gray asked.

"For you, all the time in the world."

Gray took a deep breath. "Let's go talk somewhere quiet."

"Sure." He led them down the hall. One of his aides, a cute brunette in her mid-twenties, stopped him. "Megan, this is my son, Gray. This is Megan Alberts, one of my aides."

Gray shook her hand. "Nice to meet you."

"You, too, Mr. Preston." She turned to the senator. "Senator, the governor called and needs a few minutes of your time as soon as you're available. He says it's important."

He nodded. "Tell him I'm with my son right now and I'll let him know as soon as I'm free. This is a priority."

"Yes, sir."

She gave a quick nod to Gray and hustled off.

"I know you're busy," Gray said.

"I've spent my whole life being busy. I think you and I need to talk." He used his key card and let them into an empty suite. The lights came on.

"Something to drink?" his father asked.

"I'm good right now, thanks."

"Okay. I'm going to grab a glass of water, if you don't mind. All this talking makes me thirsty."

Gray waited while his father put some ice in a glass and poured water from the well-stocked bar. He looked out the window at the convention center and the city ahead.

"You're damn good at what you do, Gray. I'm sorry I missed it until now."

He turned to face his father. "Well, you've been busy."

"I need to be less busy."

Gray's lips lifted. "If you and Cameron win this election, I imagine you'll be more busy."

His father let out a soft laugh. "You're probably right. Hell of a thing, huh?"

"I guess so." He leaned against the windowsill. "I didn't know about your heart attack. I wasn't listening when you reached out. Are you okay?"

"Healthier than I've ever been in my life, thanks to some amazing doctors and your very pushy mother who makes sure I eat all the right things and exercise."

"Good for Mom. And I'm sorry."

"I'm the one who's sorry. I wasn't there for you when you needed a father. And for the times I was, I was a shitty father. I can't make up for that, son. I did everything wrong."

Emotion tightened within him, all these feelings, all the things he wanted to say but had held inside his whole life.

"Go ahead," his father said. "Say what's on your mind."

"I hated you, resented you for picking politics over me. And it hurt to not see you in the stands during my games."

His father nodded. "Like I said, I did it all wrong. I'll never be able to make up for what I missed. You're such a goddamn good athlete. What you can do with a car—Jesus, Gray, it's magnificent watching you drive."

The pride and awe in his voice was real. It was so real it was painful. "Thanks."

"And this is what you should be doing—what you should have always been doing. I didn't understand it then. I do now. I can never take back the things I said or the way I said them. I can only apologize for saying them. You made the right choice. You'd have been a terrible politician, but you're one hell of an auto racer. Life's way too short not to do what you love. Always do what you love."

Gray nodded. "I have been, Dad."

"So you're happy."

"Never been happier."

"And does that happiness include Evelyn?"

Gray cocked a brow. "Evelyn?"

His dad set his glass of water down and stood. "You know, it's my job to be observant. I see the way the two of you lock gazes. Reminds me of me and your mother, the way we were when we first fell in love. And when we fell in love again." His dad smiled. "So . . . you and Evelyn?"

He wasn't prepared to have this kind of conversation with his father. "I . . . don't know. We have two different lifestyles. She wants a career in politics."

"And you'd deny her that?"

Gray frowned. "Hell no. She should have everything she wants."

His father smiled. "Good. I agree. She's amazing and smart and talented and ambitious, but also sweet and loving. Your mother adores her. So does your sister. I could see the two of you together."

This was the most bizarre conversation he'd ever had with his father.

"I don't know how I could make it work."

"You were always a smart boy, Grayson. And you've been able to have everything you've ever wanted. If the two of you are meant to be together, I'm sure you'll figure it out."

TWENTY-SIX

GRAY FOUND EVELYN IN HIS PARENTS' SUITE, SHE AND his mother huddled together on the sofa. She stood to face him.

"Yes, Dad and I talked. We didn't hug or anything, but I think we're going to be okay."

He saw the relief on his mother's face. "I'm glad. For both of you." He hugged his mom. "Me, too."

They visited for a while, then he and Evelyn left to head back to the racetrack. Mentally exhausted, all he wanted to do was go to bed, close his eyes, and clear his head.

Evelyn was great about reading his moods, because she didn't grill him about his conversation with his father, just climbed into bed with him and laid her head against his chest.

Surprisingly, though, he couldn't sleep, couldn't shut off the thousands of thoughts going through his mind. He finally sat up and turned on the light.

Evelyn scooted up against the pillows and drew her knees up to her chest.

"Would you like to talk about it?"

He thought for a few minutes, then said, "I understand so much now, and I get the whole forgiveness thing. But I feel like I have all these years of anger and resentment that I'm supposed to just let go of instantly."

"But you can't. Not just yet."

"No."

"It's going to take time, Gray. I think it's all right to allow yourself some baby steps with your dad. You don't have to have this instantly close relationship with him tomorrow, you know? Isn't it enough to know the truth, to know what happened and that he wants a relationship and forgiveness, and to just take it day by day?"

"I guess so."

"And I think you're still carrying years of resentment inside you. One 'I'm sorry for all that' from him just isn't going to cut it, is it?"

He looked at her. "Thanks for that. I think that's what's bothering me. I feel like him saying 'I'm sorry' should be the end of it, but it doesn't feel like the end of it for me."

"Nor should it. Years of indifference don't just disappear with one apology. He has a lot to make up for."

"For some reason, I thought you'd be on his side."

She laughed. "Hey, I'm Switzerland here."

"A very political statement. Maybe you'll end up being Secretary of State."

She climbed onto his lap. "Not a chance, buddy. It's all the way to the White House or nothing."

He grasped her hips and snaked his way up her rib cage, his fingers playing with the thin tank top she wore. "Ambitious women make me hard."

She rocked back and forth against his erection. "Hmmm, so I've noticed."

He cupped her breasts, swept his thumbs over her nipples, watching them bead through her tank top. "And apparently thinking about becoming the president makes you hard."

"That's from you touching me. Politics doesn't excite me sexually."

"Good to know." He lifted her tank top over her head and took a moment to stare at her breasts, at her perfect nipples. He pulled her toward him, fitting one hard bud between his lips. The sounds she made as he licked and sucked her nipples made his dick twitch and his balls tighten, made him want to be inside her while he licked at her breasts.

With a little maneuvering, she rose up and removed her panties while he shrugged out of his boxers. Evelyn dove into the drawer where he kept the condoms and with deft movements rolled one on. As she eased onto his cock, he sucked in a breath, every time with her like the very first time he'd been inside her. It was always a new experience, and as he lifted her on and off his cock, watching the way she threw her head back and arched while she rode him, he wondered how he was going to make this work. For her and for him.

Because there was no doubt he was in love with her, and once the convention was over, once he'd done his job and she'd done hers, he wanted her in his life.

Her thighs squeezed him just as her pussy wrapped around his cock, owning him like she owned his heart. He wasn't one for deeply emotional shit, but God he had it bad for this woman. He cupped the nape of her neck and brought her in for a kiss, needing that connection with her as he powered into her. And when she whimpered and dug her nails into his shoulders, as she rode to her orgasm and brought him to his, he felt everything pour out of him. He wrapped his arms around her and brought her close as he came, kissing her with everything he had, communicating to her without words how he felt, wondering if somehow she could tell the difference.

She lay splayed out on top of him afterward, drawing circles on his chest.

"I don't know if that solved any of your problems," she said. "But it sure felt good."

He smiled. No, it hadn't solved any of his problems, but making love with her always made him feel better. She was his connection, always made him feel less alone in the world, and had since the first time they'd been together.

He didn't know what he was going to do to keep her in his life, but he'd move heaven and earth to make it happen.

"Evelyn."

She sat up. "Yes?"

"Have you thought much about what's going to happen when the convention is over?"

She gave him a blank look that told him nothing. "Not really. There's always so much that goes on day to day, I always have to stay in the present. I'll likely head back to Washington and start on the presidential campaign. There'll be a lot to do between now and November."

"Yeah, you're probably right."

He detected no emotion on her face, no sadness at the prospect of her leaving him.

Was what he felt one-sided? He thought there was something special between them, but maybe that was just him. Maybe to her what they had was just a fling, and she'd be perfectly satisfied to walk away at the end.

Evelyn had those dreams of the big house with the oversized yard and the tire swing, but she was also a realist. She knew the two of them were as far apart in worlds as two people could be.

Maybe she was the only one thinking clearly about this.

And maybe he was the only one emotionally invested in them.

But he'd also never been a coward. He loved Evelyn and he wasn't going to let her walk away. He just had to figure out how to make this happen so they could both have everything they wanted.

EVELYN PAUSED, WAITING FOR GRAY TO SAY ANYTHING that would lead her to believe he felt something for her.

She was in love with him. Crazy in love with this lean, sexy athlete who was so much more than what he showed on the surface. Underneath, he was tender and romantic and vulnerable, and that he'd showed her all of that, that he'd trusted her with all his emotions, had meant so much to her.

When he'd asked her what was going to happen after the convention, she thought that was going to be the opening, that he'd start a dialogue about the two of them—about their future.

Because she really wanted a future with him. She knew it was an impossible future. He had his racing career, which took him all over the country, and she was going to be firmly planted in D.C. once Governor Cameron and the senator won the election. And they *were* going to win the election. She'd do everything in her power to make that happen.

It wasn't like she'd be able to hop from city to city with him. She'd be so busy with the senator, who'd become the vice president. But Senator Mitchell was also Gray's father. They'd find a way to make this work.

If that's what Gray wanted.

Then again, maybe he'd brought up what would happen after the convention to start easing his way out of this relationship. He might want to let her down easy. After all, he'd never promised her anything. They'd been having a wonderful time, but not once had they talked about a future together. Given their differing lifestyles, anyone with half a brain would realize the two of them, as a couple, made no sense at all.

They both had brains, and she had always been a realist. The idea was ludicrous. They'd never see each other. It would end before it ever got off the ground. The best, kindest thing they could do for one another would be to part as good friends, especially since she intended to be in his life at least for the next eight years. They'd run into each other whenever he saw his father, at least whenever he was in Washington. If their relationship ended badly, that could get ugly, and she'd worked too damn hard to lose her job over a relationship.

No, best to end things on a good note, so they could see each other and be friendly, remember the good times they had, and leave it at that.

After all, her career meant the world to her.

Someday, she'd figure out how to have it all.

But she wasn't going to have everything she wanted with Gray.

"Tired?" he asked her as he smoothed his hand over her hair.

She nodded. "A little."

"You're juggling a lot. You know it's okay if you want to head over to the convention."

"Trying to get rid of me?" she asked with a faint smile, hoping he wouldn't keep pushing her away, even though it was inevitable.

"No. Trying to make this easier on you."

She wanted to ask if the "easier" part was her doing her part at the convention or the end of their relationship. But she couldn't bring herself to say the words. She was brave in so many aspects of her life and her career, but in this, she felt weak. "I don't need easy."

"I'll leave that up to you, then. If you want to stay for the race tomorrow, I'll be happy to have you here. But it won't crush me if you feel the need to get back to your job."

In other words, he was giving her up, giving her the chance to be the first one to walk away.

Damned if she'd do that. "I want to see you race tomorrow."

"Okay." He pulled her back into bed and shut off the light. She lay there, staring into the darkness, trying to figure out how they were going to bridge this gap, this silent dance of the end of their relationship.

It hurt. And she hated it.

TWENTY-SEVEN

RACE DAY DAWNED BRIGHT AND SUNNY AND PROMISED to be miserably hot, just the way Gray liked it.

It was going to be a great day. He and Donny were both going to race well. He could feel it.

Having Evelyn in the pit box meant everything to him. He'd woken her up this morning by making love to her, a silent, smokin'-hot way to start the day. He'd rolled her over and slid inside her before she was fully awake. She'd run her hands all over him, kissing him with a quiet desperation that he couldn't quite fathom.

It had felt an awful lot like good-bye, and he didn't like that feeling at all.

He was still going ahead with his plans, but he really needed to talk to her first, rather than presume. He'd talk to her after the race today. She was going to head to the convention center after the race, and he knew he wouldn't have much time with her after that because she'd be busy with his dad and all things politics for the next week.

It was time he declared how he felt about her, so she'd be clear, and so he wouldn't take any major steps without knowing if she felt the same way about him.

They'd kept their relationship discreet, so he kissed her in his trailer before heading out to do his pre-race media interviews. Evelyn had headed to her hotel to pack up and check out, then she'd come back to the track. As he climbed into his car, he saw her in the pit box smiling down at him. He winked at her and after that it was all business for him as he strapped in and took his position in the line of cars gearing up for the race.

It was going to be a grueling race today.

He couldn't wait to get started.

SITTING IN THE PIT BOX WAS HELL WHEN ALL EVELYN wanted to do was stand and pace. Or maybe get in one of those cars and put it to the floor and see how fast she could drive off some of this excess anxiety that had been plaguing her for the past few days.

The roar of the engines for the past three hundred miles only added to her stress level. She was biting her nails because Gray was in tenth place, and she knew it wasn't where he wanted to be. A pit road miscue and his car not performing the way he wanted to meant he had to be frustrated not to be in the front.

But there was still time for him to make his way to the lead and pull off a desperately needed win. She rocked back and forth in her chair and Ian gave her the side eye again. She was certain her constant mobility drove him crazy, but there wasn't much she could do about it, given her current state. There was just too much going on in her mind—the race, the upcoming convention, what a win for

Senator Preston would mean to her career, and the most important thing—her relationship with Gray.

She was going to miss him so much. She'd never once thought her career would get in the way of how she felt about a man. Career had always been the most important thing in her life, and she thought it always would be, no matter what.

Now she found herself wondering how she could juggle her career and still have the man she loved, and what Gray would say if she presented the option of the two of them figuring out a way to be together.

She dragged her fingers through her hair for the umpteenth time, not knowing what to do. What if she told him how she felt and he didn't feel the same way? She'd never been rejected before. It would hurt so badly.

But what if she didn't tell him how she felt, and the two of them parted and he never knew? They could have an amazing life together. Was she willing to walk away from that because she was afraid of that rejection?

She was stronger than that, and she knew it.

She was going to tell him after the race today that she was in love with him, and if he didn't feel the same way, she'd survive. At least she'd know. At least she'd have laid it all out there.

"Sonofabitch," Ian said, pushing himself to his feet.

She hadn't even seen the crash. All Evelyn saw was smoke. Her heart stuttered as she searched the field of cars for the number fifty-three, hoping and praying he wasn't in the middle of the sudden wreckage and flames from the ugliest crash she'd ever seen.

She held her breath, scanning the cars that had slowed down and passed the carnage. She couldn't even count the cars involved in the smash-up, but it looked like the ones that had been involved were demolished.

As the other cars passed by, she looked at their numbers. She saw Donny's car and breathed a sigh of relief, but there was no number fifty-three.

Oh, God.

She looked at Ian, his mouth set in a grim line. He was talking on his headset, and when he pulled it off and scrambled out the pit box, she knew something had gone terribly, terribly wrong.

She climbed down in a hurry, anxious to get information from someone, but all she heard were mumblings about an ambulance and air flight and that the hospital had been alerted.

She finally grabbed one of the crew members by the arm.

"Is Gray hurt?"

He gave her a short nod.

Her stomach dropped. "How badly?"

"Nobody knows yet. They have to cut him out of the car first, then they'll helicopter him to the local hospital."

She reached for the nearby equipment, dizziness overtaking her.

Cut him out of the car? Oh, dear God. She grabbed her phone out of her pocket to call Gray's parents.

EVELYN HAD WAITED WHILE GRAY HAD BEEN THROUGH X-ray and CT scans and then his parents had spoken with the doctors. Donny and Stacie were there with her along with Ian, so she was glad not to be alone.

They kept the cameras out. The racing organization was great about taking care of feeding the media information.

All Evelyn could do was sit and wait and pray that he was going to be all right. She couldn't handle looking at the television, which was set to the sports station that had been replaying the crash nonstop.

She'd looked once, seeing Gray hit from behind and sliding down the track. He'd been broadsided and had gone airborne before slamming into the wall. There'd been a chain reaction and he'd been hit again. Then again.

It had been a brutal, horrendous crash. He was lucky to be alive and she thanked God for the organization's safety requirements and the vehicle safety standards that the drivers always complained about but were the main reason he was alive right now.

When the senator came downstairs, she stood, her legs shaking. He came over to her and took her hands.

"He has a concussion and a broken leg and probably a couple broken ribs. He's going to be fine, though."

Tears filled her eyes and she hugged the senator. "Thank you for telling us. How's Loretta?"

"Tougher than I thought she'd be. Carolina was packing to head this way. Loretta called her."

"Good." She sniffled and smiled. "Is it all right if I see him?"

"I'll take you up."

She introduced him to Ian. The senator took a few minutes to speak with Ian, then he took her up via the elevator to the ICU.

"He's going to be fine, Evelyn."

"Yes, sir."

"You love him."

She didn't even hesitate. "Yes, sir."

"He loves you too, you know."

She let the tears fall. "I was afraid he was going to die. I don't know what I'd do without him."

He squeezed her hand. "You're not going to be without him. But he's going to be pissed off about this crash."

She laughed through the tears. "I'm sure he will be."

When they got to the entrance of the ICU, she went and hugged Loretta.

"God smiles on the idiots," Loretta said. "Such a dangerous sport."

"But he's so good at what he does, Loretta. You know as soon as he's able, he'll be right back out there."

She sighed and squeezed Evelyn's hands. "I know."

"He's pretty out of it right now, heavily medicated," Mitchell said. "He might not be awake."

"I won't be long. Thank you for letting me see him."

She was buzzed in and went to his room, pausing at the doorway to take a deep breath.

Gray, her strong, indestructible hero, was hooked up to tubes and IVs, and was bruised, bandaged, and looked utterly broken. Pushing back the tears, she walked in.

He was asleep. She sat in the chair next to him and slid her hand under his.

"You have to heal, Gray. And take your time doing it, which I know you're going to hate."

He didn't move, and all she heard was the soft whirr of the machines.

"And maybe think about slowing down for a few minutes?" She smoothed her other hand over the top of his.

"I will if you will."

Her gaze shot to his. His eyes were half open.

"You're awake."

"I have the worst fucking headache."

Relief flooded her. "I'll bet you do. That was some show you put on at the race today."

"Yeah. And a DNF. I hate not finishing a race. That's going to fuck me up in the standings."

It figured he'd think about his position. "That's probably the least of your worries right now."

"I'm screwed for this season, babe. That's not good."

She caressed his hand. "I'm sorry, Gray. I know how close you were, how much this meant to you. But right now you have to focus on recovering. That has to be your priority."

He swallowed, licked his lips. "I'll be back in a car in no time."

"Yes, you will." Though the thought of him racing again terrified her. But it was who he was and what he did. What he loved. And she loved him. Which she was going to tell him. But now wasn't the time.

His eyes drifted closed. "You need to go help my dad become the vice president, you know. No more races to watch now."

His last words were slurred.

"I'll be back to check on you."

"Nah. I'll be fine here. Go do your job, Evelyn. Go become president. I won't stand in your way."

Now he wasn't making sense at all. She got up and pressed a kiss to his forehead and left the room, because she knew his mom would want to come back in.

"He woke up for a few minutes and talked to me. Now he's sleeping," she told his parents when she met them outside the door.

"I'll just head back in then," Loretta told them.

"I'll meet you in there in a minute," Mitchell said. He turned to her. "He really is going to be fine."

"I know that. I'll head over to the convention hotel and handle things on that end so you can stay here tonight."

"Thanks." He took a deep breath. "It wasn't so long ago I would have let Loretta handle this. Politics would have been more important. Not that this isn't an important time for me."

She laid her hand on his arm. "The campaign won't kick into gear for a few more days. This is your time to be a father. Maybe make up for some of those things you lost."

"He told you."

"Yes."

His lips curved. "One of the things I've always appreciated about you is your brutal honesty, Evelyn."

"It's not my job to pass judgment on you, Senator. But you do have some relationship building to do with Gray."

"He still resents me."

"That's not for me to say. But he does need you right now. And that's purely my opinion. It would mean a lot to him that you're here."

"I'm worried about him. There's no place I'd rather be right now than here."

"Good. I'll take care of things on the campaign end. I'll call you or text you if anything urgent comes up."

"Thanks."

She took off, but she wanted to be at the hospital.

As she climbed into her car, she stared up at the rooms of the hospital.

She'd always loved her job, and when she was away from it longed to be back at it.

This was the first time she resented her job.

She wanted to be with Gray. And her job was getting in the way of that.

TWENTY-EIGHT

CRUTCHES SUCKED.

So did having bodyguards and a fucking entourage of people who treated him like he might collapse any second. But those were his doctor's orders—and his parents', and the only way he was going to be allowed to attend the convention.

At first he'd argued with his father, who told him it was absolutely unnecessary for him to be there, that it was more important for him to focus on his recovery.

He'd been surprised as hell to find his father lingering at his bedside for so many days, when the most important political campaign of his career was happening. But his dad had told him that the accident had scared the hell out of him, and he'd wasted enough time on politics and hadn't spent enough time with his son. A son, his father admitted, that he might have lost that day. And he'd already lost enough time with Gray. So the campaign could just go fuck itself.

Gray had laughed at that, though it had hurt like hell to laugh.

Maybe Gray had been blind to his father's overtures all these years, because there was no way in hell the old Mitchell Preston would have allowed anything—not even Gray's accident—to stand in the way of him becoming the vice presidential nominee.

Granted, it wasn't happening right after his accident, but face time with the media and with the delegates was so important.

Still, his father wouldn't budge, not even after Gray had been discharged from the hospital two days later and had been comfortably put up at a suite at the conference hotel. Being the prospective vice presidential nominee had its privileges, including getting an extra suite at a hotel that had been sold out a year in advance.

His father had hired him a private doctor and nursing staff to oversee his care, which was totally unnecessary. He had a residual headache from the concussion, his leg had been set in a cast, and the ribs would eventually heal, though the ribs were what hurt the most.

That and his pride. Losing out on this year's championship utterly sucked. He hated letting his team down. But Ian had been to the hospital and had come up to the suite and told him the crew were just relieved he hadn't died in that crash, a crash that had come about because of the circumstances of racing and nothing more. Cars got too close and bumped and sometimes the younger racers weren't paying attention. Hell, he couldn't even blame Cal McCluskey, who hadn't even been in his vicinity at the time of the crash, though he'd been wrecked, too.

Though apparently the crash had had a sobering effect on Cal, who'd hit the wall six cars back. He said his reaction time had been bad, that he could have avoided it if he hadn't been drinking the night before. Cal admitted to being an alcoholic and had ended his race season early, deciding to enter rehab.

It was a good choice—the right choice. Gray hoped Cal cleaned up and came back to racing the next season. He was a good, hard competitor and Gray wanted to see him come back clean.

As for Gray, he'd just been in the wrong place at the wrong time, and he'd been the one to take the hit. A really bad hit that had cost his team the championship. Fortunately, he already had another driver lined up to drive the number fifty-three the rest of the season, because he sure as hell wouldn't be doing any driving. The thought made him itchy and restless, but there was nothing he could do about it. And they were fortunate to have a week off so Ian could get Alex Reed ready and give him some practice time in Gray's car.

He was damn lucky to get Alex, who didn't have a full-time ride this year. Alex would do a great job driving for him the rest of the season.

Next year, though, Gray would be ready to climb back into his own car and kick some serious ass.

In the meantime, he was free to soak up the convention.

Pretty impressive stuff. Lots of speeches, which weren't really his thing, but since he was holed up in the hotel, he got to watch Evelyn in action. He hadn't told her he was at the hotel, and hadn't spoken to her since he was discharged from the hospital.

She was busy doing her job and he didn't want to get in her way, so he had his mother tell her that he was headed home to Daytona, that he was tired, and they'd touch base after the convention.

His thought was to surprise her, that maybe she'd get a few free minutes and he could hold her, kiss her, and finally have that conversation he'd wanted to have with her after the race on Sunday.

Except the race hadn't turned out like he'd expected, and they'd never had a chance to talk. He also knew her schedule here at the convention, since she was right by his father's side. She was running constantly, meeting with delegates and press and working on that whole social media thing she did so well. So he sat back and did his recovery thing and kept tabs on her while also working on a few surprises for her that he'd maybe spring on her after this was all over with.

His dad stopped by several times a day to see how he was doing, a fact that still shocked the hell out of him. He wouldn't say they were close as a father and son should be yet, but his dad had gone out of his way to make Gray a priority, and that meant a lot to him, especially since his father had zero expectations of Gray making an appearance on the convention room floor. In fact, his dad had expressly forbidden it, which made Gray laugh since he was well past the age where his dad could forbid him to do anything he had a mind to do.

And he had a couple things in mind.

Starting tonight.

EVELYN WAS RUNNING FROM ONE END OF THE CONVENtion floor to the other, her head filled with so many things on her to-do list she was grateful for the calendar on her phone, because her brain was utterly fried.

She was exhilarated, and exhausted, thrilled and terrified, and so excited for Senator Mitchell. This was his moment, what they'd worked so hard for all these years.

She'd listened avidly to every speech this week, excitement building each night for the upcoming Cameron/Preston ticket. She stood front and center, prepared to listen to more great speeches tonight, so proud of everything they'd accomplished.

As one of Atlanta's representatives spoke, Evelyn responded to a few emails that had gone unanswered while she'd been busy today. And maybe she'd been purposely throwing herself into every activity possible so she could focus on work and not on Gray.

God, she missed him so much and wished she could be in Daytona with him, taking care of him. She was certain he had plenty of people watching over him. Loretta and Carolina both assured her he was being well cared for and she didn't have to worry about him, but she couldn't help herself. She felt both guilty and a little hurt that she hadn't been able to see him since that night in the hospital, but that was the nature of her job. And also his choice.

He hadn't called her. She tried not to take that personally, or as a sign of things to come in their relationship. He had a bad injury, and was likely concentrating all his efforts on resting and recuperating, not on thinking about her.

But her heart still hurt so badly, which was why she spent every moment of every day throwing herself into work.

Besides, this was the way things were going to be. Her time with him was over. He had his life, and she had hers, and her job was about to go on overdrive for the next few months. She had no time for a relationship, no time to work on whatever it was she and Gray had together.

It was time to sever the ties.

"And now, I'm so proud to introduce, fresh off one very frightening injury at our local racetrack this past weekend, Senator Mitchell Preston's son, Grayson Preston."

Her head shot up. Gray was here?

He hobbled across the stage on crutches and her first thought was to rush up there to help him. But he smiled at the representative and made his way, albeit slowly, to the podium, to the raucous cheers of the crowd on the convention floor.

He was in pain. She could tell from the sweat that beaded on his upper lip as she made her way closer.

When the applause died down, Gray looked out over the crowd.

"I've never been much of a public speaker. I've always let my driving do the talking for me." He looked down at the crutches. "Sometimes my driving outlines my mistakes for me, too."

The crowd laughed.

"But the one thing I know for certain is what Governor Cameron and my father, Mitchell Preston, can do for our country."

His speech was eloquent, impassioned, family oriented, and politically perfect. It was clear he spoke from the heart and his speech wasn't practiced, nor had it been written for him. If it had been, she would have been the one to write it.

And she hadn't even known he was coming.

"So I'm very proud to introduce you to my father, Senator Mitchell Preston."

The applause was thunderous, the people in the convention center already one hundred percent behind Gray's father. Evelyn took it all in as Mitchell came out and gave his son a handshake, then a very gentle hug. The looks they gave each other were filled with genuine warmth.

It was a perfect moment, and the media caught it all. But it was more than that, because Evelyn saw the bonding between father and son, and that meant more than anything.

She stood and listened to Mitchell's speech, one she'd helped him prepare. But her gaze followed Gray off stage. She wanted to go to him, to talk to him, but her job was to be there for the senator, so she stayed put while he spoke of the country's needs and his ideas on how to fulfill them. She was so proud of him, and when he finished, the convention floor thundered its approval.

It was a shining moment, one she was fully caught up in.

It wasn't until hours later, when all the interviews for the day were finished, that she was able to ask the senator about Gray's appearance tonight.

"I had no idea he was going to appear. I told him not to," the senator said.

"I thought he was in Daytona."

The senator smiled. "I put him up in a suite here at the hotel."

Her eyes widened. "He's been here the whole time?"

"Yes. He didn't want you to know."

Hurt clenched her stomach. "Why is that?"

"He wanted you focused on what you needed to do here, not on him. He said your job is your priority."

"I see." How nice of him to make that decision for her, or to think she couldn't juggle both. A familiar refrain, and one she'd heard before. "Is he still here?"

"Of course." The senator gave her Gray's room number and, once she was certain the senator didn't need her anymore that night, she headed up there.

It was unfair to fight with a man who was physically down. But then again, he'd looked capable standing at the podium tonight, hadn't he?

She knocked at the door and a very attractive woman answered. She wore a pantsuit and looked official. And gorgeous, with her dark hair pulled back in a ponytail and her exotic eyes all sexy.

Dammit.

Evelyn cocked a brow.

"May I help you?" the woman asked.

"I'm here to see Gray."

"He's not receiving visitors."

"Oh, he'll see me." She brushed past. The woman objected, but Evelyn didn't care.

"I tried to stop her, Gray," the woman said.

Gray was sprawled on the sofa, his casted foot resting on an ottoman.

"Hey," he said, smiling at her. "It's okay, Cathy. This is Evelyn, my dad's aide. And Evelyn's a good friend of mine. Evelyn, Cathy's my nurse."

His dad's aide? That's how he introduced her? And yeah, this Cathy chick totally looked like a nurse.

Not.

Evelyn gave her a clipped nod.

"Cathy, why don't you take off for the night? I'm good here."

"Are you sure?"

"Yup. I'll call you if I need anything."

"All right. Good night." Cathy picked up her bag and left the suite.

"Come sit down. You want something to drink?"

"No. I want to know why you didn't tell me you were here."

He grabbed the remote and turned off the television, then gave her a smile that heated her all the way to her toes. She ordered her body to ignore that physical response to him.

"Because I didn't want you worrying about me or fussing over me. I knew you had a big job to do this week. I knew how much you'd been looking forward to it. And that's what you needed to focus on. Not on me."

She folded her arms over each other. "I see. And you think I'm too stupid to multitask?"

"Uh, I didn't say that." He studied her. "Are you pissed at me?"

"You're damn right, I'm pissed at you. Do you have any idea how worried I was about you? My God, Gray. That accident was horrific. I've thought about you all week, worried about you, wondered how you were doing."

"Exactly. And this was your week to shine. The last thing you needed was to think about me."

She rolled her eyes. "Don't treat me like I'm a simpleton. I could have handled your father's appearance at the convention along with caring about you. And don't presume to make decisions for me and my life. I thought you were better than that, better than those people who told me I couldn't be the kind of woman who could have a career and a man in my life, who couldn't have everything I wanted."

"So what are you saying?"

"Right now I'm saying I'm damn angry with you for pulling yourself out of my life when you were hurt because you thought I couldn't handle it and my career, too. I thought better of you. I guess I was wrong."

"Now hang on." He struggled to get up, and he winced, reached for his side.

It gave her the advantage. His crutches were across the room. "Just stay where you are."

"I want to talk to you—face-to-face."

"We don't have anything to say to each other that requires you standing up."

Out of breath from the attempt to get up, he leaned back against the sofa. "Now who's the one presuming?"

Pain lanced her as she realized she was arguing with him about nothing. "This is pointless anyway. We already knew our relationship was going nowhere, that once the campaign finished, so were we."

His expression went icy cold. "Oh, is that what *we* knew? Or did you just make that decision for us?"

She lifted her chin. "Be realistic, Gray. How would we make it work? I'm going to be in D.C. That's my home base. That's where I want to be and where my future lies. And you're"—she waved her hand—"everywhere else."

"So you've decided that you and I can never work. And there you go presuming again."

She refused to let him bait her. "It just doesn't make sense and we'll both get hurt in the long run."

"Yeah, might as well cut our losses while we can, right? A good campaign strategist knows when to get out of a race before an impending loss."

"Yes. That's it exactly."

He reached for the remote. "Then I guess we're done here, Evelyn."

She stared down at him, already missing him, aching to lie down beside him and put her arms around him one last time.

But he was right. It was time to cut their losses.

"I guess we are, Gray."

She turned around and headed toward the door, pausing to take one last look. "You should call your . . . nurse to help you off the sofa."

She closed the door to the suite behind her and made it all the way to her room before the tears started to track down her cheeks.

She left the light off as she entered her hotel room, closed the door, and fell onto the bed, staring up at the ceiling.

It was over between them.

It should be a relief. Now she could concentrate on the presidential campaign with nothing else on her mind, no emotional entanglements.

Just work. Just the way she'd always liked it.

She smiled into the darkness, realizing the idiocy of that statement.

She'd just walked away from the man she loved. And she'd never told him she loved him.

Despite the fact it was "for the best," as she'd told him, it wasn't the best.

Not for her, anyway.

She rolled over on her side and closed her eyes, needing to shut it all out, just for a few minutes.

Maybe tomorrow she'd be back to her old self again.

And then again, maybe she'd never be her old self again, because being with Gray had changed everything.

The floodgates burst and she let out a soft sob, then anguished cries as pain wrapped itself around her, squeezing her until she couldn't breathe.

She'd lost him. She loved him, hadn't wanted to leave him, and she'd let everything go anyway.

There was no winner at all in this race.

* * *

GRAY THREW THE REMOTE ACROSS THE ROOM.

Dammit. Shit. Fuck.

That's not the way this should have gone down.

He dragged his fingers through his hair, so damn frustrated. He wanted to jump off the sofa and go after Evelyn, to pull her into his arms and kiss her until the frustration and misunderstandings were obliterated.

Seeing her tonight had made him so happy.

Why hadn't she been happy, too?

He'd wanted to surprise her, not piss her off.

Had he presumed? He hated being one of those guys. He leaned his head back against the sofa and stared at the white ceiling fan blades, their soft whirring sound the only noise in the otherwise quiet suite.

He was a guy, and guys weren't all emotional and shit. Women liked to think they could do all that multitasking. And God knew Evelyn was a master at it.

He blinked. She was right. He'd made decisions for her instead of telling her where he was. He would have loved to have seen her this week, even if only for a few minutes here and there. She'd have given him comfort when he was feeling like shit, which was mostly every goddamned day since he'd done the flying car bit.

So why hadn't he let her? Because he thought he knew what was best for her?

Since when? She was an independent woman more than capable of juggling her job and their relationship.

But maybe the accident and subsequent end of his season had altered his mood more than a little, and he'd backed off his relationship with Evelyn because of it. What better way of altering a relationship than calling all the shots, right? It was the one thing he'd been able to control in this whole out-of-control week.

Only he hadn't been in control of the relationship with Evelyn any more than he'd been in control of the number fifty-three during that hellish wreck. So he'd gained nothing, and lost everything.

Now what was he going to do about it? Because Evelyn had just walked out on him, out on them, and effectively ended things between them.

How was he going to fix this now? Or could he even fix it?

He grabbed his phone and made a call. He needed help.

TWENTY-NINE

"WOW. YOU REALLY KNOW HOW TO FUCK UP A RELATION-ship, don't you?"

A week after the convention, Gray was resting on the back deck of his place in Daytona. At least he had company. His best friend Garrett had a day off and was playing Tampa Bay next, so he and his fiancée, Alicia, were spending the day with him.

"This is not the pep talk I'm looking for, buddy."

Garrett laughed. "Hey, if you want a pep talk, call someone else. All you're gonna get from me is honesty. You fucked it up. Am I right, Alicia?"

Alicia winced. "I was hoping I wouldn't get dragged into this one, but yes. He's kind of right, Gray. There's nothing worse than telling a woman she can't do it all. And you hid from her. While you were injured. You know a woman who cares about you would want to check on you and be sure you were okay. What were you thinking?"

Gray sighed. "I was trying to help. But I made the wrong choice. I get that now."

"Well, that's a first step—admitting you were an asshole," Garrett said, lifting the beer to his lips. "Now what?"

"I have no idea. She's back in Washington and busy as hell with the presidential campaign."

"So?" Alicia asked. "If you want her, go after her."

Gray rapped on his cast with his knuckles. "I'm a little slowed down here."

"Oh, the poor millionaire," Garrett said. "You mean there's something you can't do? Gimme a break. You've always been the man with a plan. There's nothing you can't do, cast and broken ribs or not. So what's got you flummoxed?"

He looked out over the water. "I don't want to hurt her again."

"Man, love really screws with your head, doesn't it?"

"Hey," Alicia said, giving Garrett a mock glare.

"I didn't say it screwed me up. Just Gray."

Alicia laughed and turned to face Gray. "So, do you have a plan? And hopefully that plan doesn't include manipulating her again?"

"I thought I had one, but it might make her angry if I did something without her knowledge again. Ours is a complicated relationship, and getting to that place where the two of us could be together isn't easy."

Alicia leaned over and laid her hand on his. "Gray. It doesn't matter who you are or what your circumstances are. Love is never easy. But if she's worth it, you'll find a way to make it work."

He missed Evelyn. He'd always enjoyed kicking back and relaxing here at his beach house. Right now he was frustrated because he couldn't even be at the track until he was more mobile, but he was thinking more about Evelyn than racing, and for him, having a woman take precedence over his career was a first. That meant something.

It meant she was worth fighting for.

He would make this work.

"I have an idea or two. I want to run it by you both and you can tell me if you think it sucks or not."

Alicia grinned. "You know I'd love to help. I want you to be happy."

"I don't care if you're happy or not," Garrett said. "But I do like the view here, man, so if it means we get to stay a little longer, I'm all ears."

"Garrett," Alicia warned.

Gray laughed, knowing Garrett would bend over backward to help him out. "I knew I could count on you, Alicia. Garrett, you're on beer duty."

"Done. Beer for me and Alicia, lemonade and a pain pill for you."

"You're so funny."

"Okay, seriously," Garrett said. "I'm happy to lend an ear or do whatever I can to see true love prevail." Garrett sent a look over at Alicia that had her smiling in return.

Yeah, this love stuff? Well worth the struggle if it meant Evelyn would look at him the way Alicia looked at Garrett.

"I like the two of you together," Gray said. "He was cranky the last time I saw him."

"He's still cranky," Alicia said. "But he has his moments."

"She loves me, so she's blind to my faults."

"I'm not that blind, buddy," Alicia said. "Remember, I've seen you at your worst."

"True that. That's how I knew you were a keeper."

Gray laughed. "Yeah, anyone who could put up with Garrett at his worst and loves him anyway? You should get a medal, Alicia."

Alicia grinned and cast a look at Garrett. "I don't need a medal. I got the guy."

Garrett grasped her hand and pressed a kiss to her knuckles. "I love you too, babe."

"Jesus," Gray said. "Any more of this and I'm going to have to find my crutches and give you two some alone time. Can we get back to me and Evelyn now?"

"Sure," Garrett said. "Let's get you and Evelyn that happily ever after."

THIRTY

EVELYN DIDN'T EVEN HAVE TIME TO BREATHE.

After the convention, they'd gone back to Washington. She'd unpacked, sent everything to the dry cleaners, and barely had time to renew her acquaintance with her apartment before they were on the campaign trail.

Not that travel was unusual for her. But this was a presidential campaign, and it was the big time—everything she'd hoped and dreamed for.

Mitchell was fabulous, and working with Governor Cameron's team was syncing up beautifully. They had high hopes that, come November, the governor would be the new president. The polls were strong because the Cameron/Mitchell team was in high favor.

They were due in Florida for a campaign stop, and as they hit Fort Lauderdale, Evelyn pondered the proximity to Daytona Beach, her thoughts gravitating to Gray.

Not that her thoughts didn't center on him every single day anyway.

She'd assumed once the campaign started it would be easy to forget about him, that she'd be way too busy to think about him, and she'd get over the hurt.

That wasn't happening.

She missed him. Her body craved his touch. She missed sleeping with him at night and sharing her thoughts and ideas with him. She missed the sound of his voice, missed arguing with him about every topic under the sun. She missed the way he laughed, the way his smile made her entire body tingle.

She missed racing and found herself scanning the sports outlets for news about how Preston Racing's team was doing.

Alex Reed, who was currently driving the number fifty-three, had placed fifteenth in the last race. Pretty darn good considering he was new in the car. And Donny had placed fifth. Great for Gray's team. She was happy for him and he must be frustrated as hell not to be there, not to be racing or even be at the track.

She missed seeing him in his fire suit. God, he looked good zipped up in that thing, and even better out of it.

Her body reacted instantly and she pushed the visuals aside.

It was time for her to get a grip. She and Gray were over. Some day she'd run for office herself and match up with some representative or senator or lawyer and they'd have similar careers in Washington and it would make so much more sense for her future.

How utterly . . . boring.

She shuddered out a sigh and buried herself in work at the local campaign stop.

When her phone rang, she smiled as Carolina's name popped up. "Hey."

"Hey yourself," Carolina said. "Fort Lauderdale, right?"

"Yup. Where are you?"

"In D.C., actually. You're flying back in tonight?"

"Yes. This is the last of our Florida stops."

"Can we have lunch when you get back?"

"Hang on. Let me check my schedule." She did a quick check. If she adjusted a few things . . . "Yes, I can definitely do that."

"Awesome. How about one o'clock?"

"Perfect." They made plans to meet.

It would be nice to spend a lunch hour with Carolina. She needed some downtime, even if it was only an hour or two.

And maybe Carolina would fill her in on how Gray was doing. Evelyn and the senator were busy on the campaign, and she refused to constantly ask him about Gray. They were over and done with, so it was best to cut those ties.

THE NEXT DAY HER MORNING WAS FULL GETTING caught up at the main office, so she had to hustle to the restaurant to meet Carolina, who as usual looked fresh and well put together in a bright sheath dress with a beautiful scarf.

"You look gorgeous," Evelyn said, kissing Carolina's cheek.

"You look like you could use a nap."

They sat at the table at the outdoor café in Georgetown and sipped tea and had salads. Carolina filled her in on what was going on with her fashion line, but they mainly talked about the senator and the election.

"You're busy," Carolina said in between bites of chicken salad.

"Understatement. I haven't slept."

"But this is what you wanted."

"It is. I have no complaints."

"And have you seen Gray?"

She took a deep breath. "No. Unfortunately, that's over."

"Is it? Why?"

She shrugged. "We're just worlds apart."

Carolina laughed. "Oh, that excuse. Did you even try, or did you get cold feet?"

"It's a little more complicated than that. And hey, why did you assume the breakup was my fault?"

"Because I know you. You'd look for any excuse to not make it work. 'Oh, he's a lawyer, it would never work between us.' 'Oh, he's not a lawyer, it would never work between us.' 'Oh, we're from two different worlds, it would never work between us.'" She laid the back of her hand against her forehead for dramatic emphasis.

"I am not like that at all." She paused, then cocked her head to the side. "Am I?"

"I think you look for reasons not to be in love because you're afraid it'll threaten your lifelong career goals, and if you do fall in love, God forbid you might have to compromise."

Evelyn set her fork down. "I do not do that. Do I?"

Carolina shrugged. "I'm biased in this regard because Gray is my brother and he's a giant pain in the ass, but I love him. And I think you do, too. So what did he do that was so terrible?"

"You knew he was at the suite the week of the convention, didn't you?"

"Yes. But he didn't tell you because he didn't want you worrying about him being hurt when that was your big week." Carolina's eyes widened. "That was it? That's why you broke up with him?"

Hearing it from Carolina made her sound petty and selfish. "I could have handled it, you know."

"You'd have been a basket case. Hell, you were a basket case even without dealing with Gray and his injuries. So he was being thoughtful and you kicked him to the curb."

Evelyn twirled the glass of iced tea around with both hands. "You make me sound like such a heartless bitch."

Carolina laughed. "Not at all. Honey, I'm sorry. It's just that I think you're so afraid of love and commitment and what it might mean for your future goals. Come on, take a chance. My brother's not a bad guy, you know."

Her head shot up. "Of course he isn't, Carolina. God, do you have any idea how much I love him?"

"Well, no, I don't. The question is, does he have any idea how much you love him?"

Tears pricked her eyes. "Oh, you bitch. Now look what you're doing to me." She fished in her purse for a tissue.

Carolina's lips curved. "Oh, you're melting, you're melting. What a cruel, cruel world . . ."

"So not funny."

"Give it up, Evelyn. You're in love. Throw your lot in with my big bad brother and see how it goes."

She sighed. "You're right. I have to throw in the towel. In the midst of this utter chaos, where I'm surprised I can even remember to put my underwear on the right way every day, I still can't get him out of my head. Or my heart."

"Dammit. Now I'm going to get all weepy." Carolina held out her hand, and Evelyn passed her a tissue.

Carolina was right, though. She had purposely evaded the one person she loved, had put that road block up so she wouldn't have to deal with being in love with him, when there was no avoiding it.

And now she had to face it—face him—and finally do something about it.

THIRTY-ONE

FINDING A WOMAN ATTACHED TO A SENATOR IN THE midst of a presidential campaign was a lot like finding a lost contact lens in the middle of the Atlantic Ocean.

They were like moving targets, rarely in one place for long before picking up stakes and heading into new territory.

Fortunately, Gray had a pretty good "in" with the vice presidential candidate, so he called his dad and found out they were in D.C. for the day, but they'd be heading out the next afternoon for Colorado.

Travel sucked, but at least he was off the crutches now and in a walking cast, and his ribs had healed enough that he could more or less breathe again without feeling like ten swords were simultaneously stabbing him.

His dad told him that Evelyn was either at the campaign headquarters or at her apartment where she sometimes worked when she needed quiet time. Gray wanted to surprise her, so he tried the campaign headquarters first. Since it was late afternoon, he figured he'd find her there, but one of the staffers told him she was working at home today. So he climbed back into the private car he'd hired and gave them the address to her apartment.

Taking a deep breath—or as deep as he could take with his fucked-up ribs—he rang the bell to her apartment.

"Yes?" she answered at the speaker.

"Hey."

"Gray?"

"Yeah."

"Oh, my God. Come in. Do you need help?"

"Just buzz me in, Evelyn." Though he was really happy she was on the first level and not the third.

She buzzed and he moved to open the door. She was already there, opening the door for him.

"What are you doing here?"

She was in her suit, though she'd removed the jacket, leaving her in a pencil skirt and silk blouse, very similar to the first time he'd met her. Her hair was pulled up and she looked professional—and gorgeous.

"Thought I'd drop by. If that's okay."

"It's very okay. Come in and sit down."

She shut the door and he made his way to the most comfortable-looking chair in her living room.

"No crutches?"

"No. I hated those damn things," he said as he put his leg up in the reclining chair. "I harassed the doctors into getting me off of them as soon as possible."

"I'm glad. Can I get you something to drink?"

"Water would be good."

She hurried into the kitchen—she seemed nervous, which kind of made him happy since he was nervous as hell.

She brought him the water, which he downed in about three gulps. God, his throat was dry. This was like his first date all over again. He set the glass on the table next to the chair.

She took a seat on the small sofa and clasped her hands together.

"Been busy?" he asked.

"Very. You?"

"Not at all."

She gave him a small smile. "I'm sorry. I know how frustrating that must be for you."

He shrugged. "I'm dealing with it. Alex is a good driver, though. He'll finish out the season for the number fifty-three decently enough, and I'll be back in the car in time for Daytona in February."

"Are you healing well?"

"Doctors all say I'm doing fine, but I'm restless. It's hard for me to just sit and . . . heal."

"But it's important that you don't push yourself."

He let out a laugh. "Pushing myself is what I do best. I'm not much of a sitter. I did spend some time at the beach house."

"I'm sure that was relaxing."

"It would have been more relaxing if you'd been there with me."

She frowned. "Obviously, that wasn't possible."

"No. You have a job to do." He pushed up and stood. So did Evelyn.

"You're leaving?"

"Actually, I'd like you to take a ride with me, if you can spare a few minutes."

"A ride where?"

He gave her a direct look. "Just trust me?"

She studied him. "All right. Let me grab my purse."

He led her outside where his car was waiting. She climbed in and he shut the door behind them. "You have the address, Tom."

"Yes, sir."

She looked over at him. "I admit to being more than a little curious."

"It's not far."

He hoped to God this worked, that she wasn't angry when he showed her, that she understood his intention.

When they pulled up the drive, she looked over at him. "I don't understand."

"You will when I explain. Let's get out."

Evelyn got out and looked over the stunning home. She'd seen the For Sale sign when they pulled into the long driveway, could only imagine the price since the property itself must cost a fortune, considering its location in Georgetown.

"All these trees, and is that a pool back there?"

"Yeah. Tennis court, too. Let's go inside and take a look."

A woman stood by, nodding and smiling as she opened the door for them.

Inside was even more breathtaking. Rustic and homey, with hardwood floors and exposed wood beams, it was open and expansive, with high ceilings and wide windows, curving staircases, and the most amazing bathrooms and kitchen Evelyn had ever seen. Obviously a restored farmhouse, it boasted huge rooms and a playroom, and she lost count of the number of bedrooms.

There was even an enclosed porch, and acres of green lawn and mature trees. After being back in her cramped apartment, Evelyn was in love with the place.

"Wow," was all she said after the tour. "That was fun. Whose place is this?"

Gray nodded at the Realtor, who left them alone in the kitchen.

"It could be ours."

Her heart stuttered. "Excuse me?"

"Ours. Yours and mine." He hobbled over to her and took her hands in his. "I want us to be together, Evelyn, which I know won't be easy, but nothing worth having ever comes easy. I learned that a long time ago. If there's something you want, you have to work hard to have it. And I want you."

She took a deep breath. "Gray."

"I love you, Evelyn. I might have handled some things badly, and for that I'm sorry. I know you're capable of juggling the entire world on your shoulders, but you don't have to do it alone. Do it with me. Marry me."

She couldn't hold back the tears. "Gray. I love you, too, and I let my own fears get in the way of telling you that. And for that I'm the one who's sorry. You were only trying to help me, to clear the way for me to be able to do my job, and instead of being grateful, I jumped all over you and walked away from you. Please forgive me for that because I've been so miserable without you."

She walked into his arms and his lips came down on hers. She relished his anguished groan of need as he kissed her. Suddenly, everything that had been wrong was suddenly right again, and her world was dizzy because of it. She held on to him like she never wanted to let go of him again.

She would never let go of him again.

When she broke the kiss, she swept her fingers over his cheekbones, his lips, and his strong jaw. "You bought this house?"

"I put a deposit down on it. If you don't like it, we'll keep looking. But I saw the trees and thought several of them were strong enough for a tire swing."

"Oh. God. Yes. I love this house, Gray. It's perfect for you and me and our children." She brushed her lips across his, unable to believe he remembered the tire swing. "But what about your house in Daytona? Please don't sell it."

"Congress recesses, Evelyn. I'm not selling the house in Daytona. I thought we might also want a town house in New York. You liked it there, too."

She took a deep breath and let it out. "You're too good to me."

"I don't know about that. You've been pretty good to me, too. I'd say we're good for each other."

He let the Realtor know he'd sign the paperwork on the house tomorrow, then he and Evelyn left.

"I know this isn't going to be easy," he said. "We have very diverse careers and there are going to be times we won't see each other. But people who love each other make time for each other. And I have days off after each race. And I promise you, when I'm not racing cars I'll be racing home to you. And to our children."

She scooted closer to him, to lean against him. "I want to marry you and have babies with you as soon as humanly possible."

He grinned. "I can arrange that."

"I know you can."

The driver let them out at Evelyn's apartment. They made their way inside, and once he closed the door, Gray pushed Evelyn against it. "I think we should consummate our engagement."

"Definitely." She started to kiss him. "Are you . . . uh . . . up for that?"

He took her hand and laid it over him, where he was already hard. "Babe, I'm definitely up for it. I've been aching for you."

"Then let's get you comfortable and get me naked so we can get you inside me in a hurry."

She led him over to the oversized chair he'd been sitting in earlier. He eased into it and she leaned over him to undo his belt buckle. The searing look of desire he gave her turned her liquid. She dragged her fingernails over the denim of his jeans, down his erection as she teased him.

"Hurry," he rasped, lifting against her hand as she dragged the zipper down, then eased his jeans open and freed his cock. He was hot and heavy in her hands and she stroked him, her nipples tingling as he groaned.

She kicked off her shoes and unzipped her skirt, letting it fall to the floor, then very deftly undid each button on her blouse, watching his gaze go dark as she pulled it off to reveal her pink bra and matching panties.

"You are so goddamn sexy, Evelyn," he said, his fingers gripping the sides of the chair.

She reached behind her and undid the bra, then shimmied out of her panties and straddled him, her body pulsing with need. He cupped her breasts as she took his mouth in a searing kiss that left her breathless and throbbing.

She gripped his cock and eased down over him, sliding him into her. With each inch, she was reminded of how well they fit together, and when he was buried inside her, she stilled, meeting his gaze.

"I love you," she whispered, then began to rock against him while his shaft swelled inside her, making her quiver.

He pulled the clip from her hair and tangled his fingers in the strands. "I love you, too." He drew her forward and kissed her, a kiss that she felt all the way to her toes, so filled with passion and emotion that she knew without a doubt she would love this man until the day she died.

He took her hands in his and then arched up into her, rolling his hips toward her. She met his thrust by grinding against him, her body filled with him, her heart filled with his love, deepening their connection until she was so close she was crying out with the need to come.

"I'm there, Gray. Come with me."

"I'll go when you go. I'm going to come in you, Evelyn."

Just hearing the words set her off, and she splintered like a burst of fireworks, her orgasm exploding from within. She arched her back and dug down deep against him while he powered up into her and released with a shout, holding on to her hips.

It was intense and a moment she wouldn't soon forget as Gray pulled her toward him for a blistering kiss that sealed the two of them as one. And when they both came down from that epic high, he held her, stroked her back, and whispered his love again to her.

It was perfect, and it would be forever.

"I think you're late for work," he murmured some time later.

"I think I'm probably hurting your ribs," she said, not giving a shit about work right now.

"My ribs went numb like an hour ago."

She laughed and climbed off, then helped him up. They went into the bathroom to clean up, then climbed into bed together.

"Seriously, Evelyn, shouldn't you be working?"

"Yes. But I'm taking the afternoon off."

"Okay." He pulled her next to him and they settled like that.

"I need to get you a ring. We'll have to go shopping. My mother will be appalled if we announce our engagement and you don't have a ring."

"Mmm," was all she said as she drew imaginary circles over his chest.

"What are you doing for dinner tonight?"

She lifted her head. "Nothing. Why?"

"I'll have some rings brought in and you can pick out one you like."

She blinked. "Just like that?"

"Well, yeah. I want to tell people we're engaged as soon as possible. Can't have some slick politician swooping in and trying to take you away from me while I'm in a weakened state."

She rolled her eyes. "I don't need your ring on me to tell everyone that I'm in love with you and we're going to be together forever."

"I like the sound of that. But still, I need to make a phone call. By tonight, there'll be a ring on your finger."

The one thing she knew about Gray Preston was, when he was

determined to make something happen, it happened. "Okay. Ring on my finger tonight. Got it."

He leaned back and pulled her against him again. "See? There's nothing we can't accomplish together. Just wait 'til we start making babies."

She grinned. She couldn't wait for that part, either.

Dear Reader:

I hope you enjoyed Gray and Evelyn's love story in *One Sweet Ride*. There will be more stories to come in the Play-by-Play series, when Carolina and Drew's story, *Melting the Ice*, releases in February 2014.

In the meantime, I'd like to introduce you to Emma Burnett and Luke McCormack, the first couple in my new Hope contemporary romance series. *Hope Flames* is the first book in this series, and will follow the lives of people who live in Hope, Oklahoma, a small town in northeast Oklahoma. I've wanted to write a small-town contemporary romance series for a while now, and fortunately, Berkley has given me the chance to do that.

Emma has returned to Hope after a long absence, and has set up a veterinary medicine practice. She's come to town carrying scars from her past, hoping to clean the slate and start fresh. The last thing she wants is to get involved with anyone, as her last relationship left bitter memories that can't be easily forgotten. But when she meets police officer Luke McCormack, he reminds her how long it has been since she's opened her heart. Luke has scars of his own from a bad marriage, so he steers clear of relationships, but there's something about Emma that draws him in. Can the two of them heal their damaged pasts and find a love that will give them hope for the future? I hope you'll pick up *Hope Flames* when it releases in September 2013, and enjoy this first chapter excerpt that follows.

As always, thank you for your support. I love hearing from you!

Jaci

HOPE FLAMES

WHO KNEW GOING HUNDREDS OF THOUSANDS OF DOL-
lars in debt could be so exhilarating?

Emma Burnett could barely contain her excitement as she looked over every aspect of her just-about-to-open new veterinary practice with a heavy dose of pride and more than a little trepidation.

It was six fifteen in the morning. Her staff would be arriving soon. She grinned at the thought. She had a staff now.

"We're here, Daisy. We made it."

Daisy, her yellow Labrador retriever, thumped her tail and looked up at her, dark eyes filled with adoration. You had to love a dog because no matter what happened, they'd always love you back. You could have an awful day, be grouchy and in the worst mood, and your dog would still sit at your feet and be there for you.

Emma rubbed Daisy's head and locked up her bag in her office, then closed the door, moving into the lobby. Daisy followed along, sniffing every square inch of gleaming tile Emma had spent the weekend polishing to perfection.

Sure, she could have had a cleaning service do that, but this place was hers and she wanted to do it herself.

This place was hers. She still couldn't quite believe it.

She swept her hand over the reception desk, tapped her finger on the desktop computer that was hopefully filled with appointments for the day, then moved on through the double doors leading to the back room where the sparkling instruments awaited her first touch.

Cages were ready, and so were the exam rooms. The OR was prepped. Everything was spotless and sterilized.

She was in debt up to her eyeballs, but come hell or rising water from the creek down the road, this place was all hers now. It had taken years and more than a few major detours, but Hope Small Animal Hospital was now owned and operated by Dr. Emma Burnett, DVM.

She inhaled and blew it out, letting the dual feelings of satisfaction and utter terror wash over her. At least this time it was a healthy dose of terror. Not like before.

It would never be like before again. She'd lost five years of her life on that mistake and now, at thirty-two, she was making a late start. But after going back to school and working with a veterinary group in South Carolina, she was finally home and on her own with a practice that was all hers.

A knock on the front door made her startle. She curled her fingers into her palms.

"Calm, Emma. This is your big day." She hurried to the door, grabbing her keys out of her lab coat pocket.

It was Rachel, her receptionist, along with Leanne, her tech. Her two assistants were the gas in the engine that drove this clinic. She smiled and unlocked the door. "Good morning."

"Mornin', Dr. Emma," Rachel said with a grin, her arms laden with donuts and coffee. "Thought you could use these."

"It's so good to be back here again," Leanne said, her long blonde hair braided into two pigtails, her purple scrubs plastered with tiny paw prints.

Totally adorable.

"You're my lifesavers. Both of you. Thank you."

They sat in the tiny break room together and ate donuts, drank coffee, and went over the appointments for the day.

"You have a full day, Dr. Emma," Rachel said.

"Really? That's great." She wanted to leap up and pump her fist in the air, but that would be so unprofessional.

"Doc Weston always had a full waiting room." Leanne licked donut icing off her fingers. "Everyone was disappointed when he had to close so suddenly. So were we."

"No kidding," Rachel said. "Leanne and I were lucky to hook up with the Barkley clinic on the north side of town after Doc Weston closed, but Barkley sucks."

"Understatement," Leanne said. "The doctors there are dicks."

Emma would not smile about that. Really, she wouldn't.

Leanne nodded. "I've been spreading the word about the reopening. It's like Field of Dreams, honey. People will come."

Emma let out a hopeful sigh. "That's so good to hear." She wanted to be busy. She needed to fill this place up with clients.

Since Dr. Weston had retired six months ago, the clinic had been closed and Hope residents had to go to the other clinic for animal care. Bruce Weston had been a wonderful veterinarian. He'd taken care of Emma's terrier Soupy and her collie Max when she'd been a kid and she'd loved him, had always been eager to come here and look at all the pictures of animal breeds on the walls of the exam rooms, check out the charts and the models of the insides of dogs and cats. She'd been curious and he'd always been willing to answer her questions. Besides her utter love of animals, Dr. Weston had been one of the primary reasons she wanted to become a veterinarian. He was kind, patient, and had taken just as much care of the owners as he had of the animals.

She'd been sad to hear about his heart surgery and subsequent retirement, but happy for him now that he and his wife Denise were moving closer to their grandchildren in Colorado. She'd been ecstatic that he'd been amenable to her buying out his practice. It had taken a whirlwind trip from South Carolina back here so she could meet face-to-face with him to iron out the particulars once she'd found out his practice was for sale. He'd been generous in his price and had helped her work out the loan details so she could get it done.

Maybe her luck was finally changing.

At six forty-five they cleared out the remnants of donut nirvana and Rachel, ever efficient, booted up the computer, while Emma and Leanne set up the rooms and instruments, ready for the first patients to start rolling in.

And did they ever. The first clients started coming in as soon as they opened the doors at seven. The clinic offered drop-off service for people on their way to work in Tulsa. Since they were on the main road leading to the highway, it was convenient. People could drop off their animals, Emma would diagnose and treat them throughout the course of the day, and their owners would pick them up on their way home from work. She charged a minimum boarding fee to house them for the day.

By eight o'clock, the appointment customers started piling in and Emma reacquainted herself with the people in her town. She'd been so busy renovating the clinic, updating inventory, and working with her staff since she'd come home that she'd had no time to visit with anyone. She wished she'd had a chance to see her sister, but Molly didn't come home. Ever. Period. If she wanted to see her little sister, she had to first track her down, since Molly was as mobile as they came, and then fly or drive to whatever location Molly called home that particular month.

They talked on the phone at least once a week, and that would have to be good enough for now.

At the moment she had her hands full with a hundred and forty pounds of very exuberant Newfoundland, who was happily slobbering on her neck as she performed an exam.

"He's very healthy, Mrs. Lang," she said, as she and Leanne wrangled King, who was determined to play with them. He stuck out his tongue and slurped her face.

Good thing she appreciated dog drool.

"He's eating my pear tree. Bits of bark at a time." Mrs. Lang did not look happy.

"Do you take him out for walks? How big is your backyard? Do you have other dogs for him to play with?"

"King is our only dog, and the yard is small. And, well, he's kind of a lot to handle. It was my husband Roger's idea to get him." Mrs. Lang looked mournfully at King. "He was such a cute little puppy."

Many people thought puppies were so cute. The problem was, cute puppies often grew into giant dogs. Like King. "He needs exercise and stimulation. There's a great park over on Fifth. Does he walk on a leash?"

"Yes. Very well. I made Roger take him to those classes."

"Excellent. If you walk him twice a day and take him to the park, it will help work off all this energy he has. Also, I highly recommend neutering him. You don't want him to get out and father a bunch of unwanted pups, do you? And it will help settle him."

"Oh, of course. Let's do that." She smirked. "Roger won't like that. Men and their . . . equipment, you know. They take it so personally. I'll tell him it was your suggestion and he'll do it. And I'll make sure we walk him." She patted her stomach. "We could all use the exercise."

The morning flew by in a blur of shots, exams, worming, and one tiny and filthy pit bull puppy someone had found in a ditch. She was a mass of flea-bitten adorable, a brown and white baby who'd either been abandoned or lost. The person dropping her off said she couldn't keep her because she had two Rottweilers at home and couldn't possibly handle one more dog, but she couldn't leave her shivering in the morning cold, either. Though it was spring and the days were warming, the nights were still cool.

Emma assured the woman they'd clean her up and find her a good home. She examined the pup, and other than needing a serious flea bath and a good meal, she was healthy, thankfully. She gave the pup to Leanne, who took her away to give her the flea bath and her first round of puppy shots.

She only had time for a quick bite of the peanut butter and jelly sandwich she'd packed for lunch when the second round of afternoon clients came in. Daisy wound her way around the clinic, checking in on Rachel and Leanne as they did their work, too. Emma was so thankful to be this busy, she had no complaints. They were jammed all afternoon until the last pickup at closing, when her staff finally left.

It was quiet. She swiped her hair out of her eyes and breathed a sigh of utter contentment as she walked around the clinic.

It had been a good first day. This was what she'd wanted, what she'd worked so hard for. She'd lost sight of it for a while and thought she'd never have it.

"Hello? Is anyone here?"

Daisy's ears perked up and she bounded out of the office at the sound of the deep, booming voice in the lobby.

Emma had thought she'd locked the door.

She hurried out to see a man holding a German shepherd by the leash who sat regally while Daisy tried to play with it.

"Daisy, come here."

Daisy came over and sat dutifully next to her, her tail whipping against Emma's lab coat.

"Can I help you?"

"Yeah. I saw your lights were still on and was hoping you'd still be open. My dog hurt his leg."

He came toward her, and she took a wary step back, until he walked under the overhead lights and she saw he was wearing a cop uniform. She breathed a sigh of relief.

"You scared me there for a second."

"I'm really sorry. Luke McCormack. I'm local police here. This is my dog, Boomer."

McCormack. Last name sounded familiar but she couldn't remember. She'd definitely remember a guy who looked like him. Tall, broad shouldered, wearing a uniform that fit him—very well. Dark brown pants, lighter brown shirt. Gun strapped to his hip. Very dark hair, cut short, full lips. Serious expression, which only made him look . . .

Hot. Sexy. Though she didn't think about men being sexy these days.

As he approached, she noticed the dog was only using three of his legs to walk on. "Oh. What happened?"

"We were chasing a perp—uh, a suspect. Boomer must have twisted his leg in a hole or something because he yelped and came up limping. I was headed toward the Barkley's vet clinic and saw Doc Weston's office was open again, so figured I'd stop here first. If you're closed, I can—"

"Of course, I'll look at him. Bring him on back." He walked side by side with her and she noticed how very tall and broad he was.

Daisy wound between them, licking the officer's hand and staring up at him adoringly.

Yeah, some watchdog you are, Daisy. Daisy wasn't exactly what one could consider a personal bodyguard, unless excessive licking and an overabundance of affection counted as weaponry.

Emma led the officer into the exam room and flipped on the lights, then turned around and knelt down, trying to calm her stupid, raging heartbeat. She smiled at the dog. "Okay, Boomer. Let's take a look."

"Boomer. Sit," the officer said.

The dog sat and she examined his leg. He whimpered as she pressed on it. After finishing the exam, she lifted her gaze to the police officer. "Officer McCormack, I'd like to get an X-ray of this leg. I don't think anything's broken, but I want to be sure."

He nodded. "Okay."

"You can come back with me. It'll calm him to have you there."

She brought them back to the X-ray room and he helped her get Boomer on the table while she got his leg in place for the X-ray.

"So, you bought Dr. Weston's practice?" he asked

Again, that voice of his. Deep and seriously sexy. It was doing something to her nerve endings she found decidedly . . .

Uncomfortable wasn't the word. She just noticed his voice. And so did her body. "Yes. I bought it right after he retired."

"I'm sorry, but I don't think I got your name."

She looked up at him and frowned, then realized she'd been a complete moron and hadn't bothered to introduce herself. "I'm so sorry, Officer. I'm Emma Burnett."

"Nice to meet you, Emma. Are you new in town?"

"Actually, I grew up here. My parents live over on Willow."

He nodded. "Did you go to Oakdale High?"

"No. I went to Hope High."

"Oh. I went to Oakdale."

That's why she didn't recognize him right off. He'd gone to the high school nearer to the county line. "Your name sounds familiar. Did you play football for Oakdale?"

"Yeah. Wide receiver."

She remembered reading about him in the newspaper. He'd been good.

"So this is your clinic now?" he asked.

"Yes, sir."

She grabbed the film and slid it in.

"Luke."

She looked up. "Excuse me?"

"Call me Luke. Not 'officer,' and definitely not 'sir.' Too formal."

He'd cracked a smile. He had a quirky, kind of off-kilter smile, and greenish blue eyes that went really well with his dark hair. He had a rugged face, a square jaw, and again, that really sexy mouth.

Not that she was looking at him in *that* way, because she didn't do that anymore. She and men were definitely off-limits. She'd learned her lesson the hard way.

But that didn't mean she couldn't be nice to her clients. "Okay, then, Luke. Let's get this X-ray going. I need you to position his leg here for me, then if possible, ask him not to move."

"No problem. Boomer—stay."

Boomer lay perfectly still as they went behind the screen so she could take the shot.

"Good boy," Luke said to Boomer after the X-ray was taken. He swept his hand over the dog's back and neck, showing care and affection.

She liked seeing that in a dog's owner.

"Just one more film and that should do it. I need to turn him this way."

Luke helped her, and she couldn't help noticing his hands. Strong. Big. Masculine, with a fine sprinkling of dark hair on his forearms.

He hadn't worn a coat inside, and had some serious muscle peeking out from the hem of his uniform shirt.

But she wasn't looking, and she definitely wasn't interested, despite the pinging in her nerve endings that thought otherwise.

Chemistry couldn't be denied. But that was biology. She had a choice, and she already knew what her choices were these days regarding men.

She took Luke behind the screen and captured the second X-ray.

But he did smell really good, though it wasn't cologne. Shampoo, maybe? Or soap? Did they make scented soap for men? She had no idea.

But she wasn't interested, so it didn't matter what kind of soap he used.

"Are we done?"

She looked at him. "Yes. Yes, we are." She turned one way and he went the other, so they bumped into each other. He reached out for her arms to steady her, and she found herself staring up into those amazing eyes of his.

"Sorry," he said, with a deep laugh that Emma felt deep in her belly.

"No. It's my fault." He took a step back and she moved around him.

He had her acting like a teenager, all filled with raging hormones. Ugh.

"Just wait here a second with Boomer so I can make sure we don't need to retake any shots."

She hurried out of the room, and took a deep breath when she got into the reading room.

What was wrong with her? She'd had male customers all day long. Some had been really good-looking, too, yet none of them had affected her like Luke was doing now.

Likely because she hadn't been alone all day. That had to be it.

She never put herself in a position to be alone with a guy. And though Luke was a police officer, owned a dog, and seemed all nice and trustworthy, she knew better than to trust any man.

She'd been naïve and trusting once, and it had cost her dearly. She was never going to be that stupid again, no matter how gorgeous a man was, or how nice he seemed.

Or how good he smelled.

Besides, this was the year of her career and nothing else. And so far, day one had been spectacular.

Wanaque Public Library
616 Ringwood Ave.
Wanaque, NJ 07465

WANAQUE PUBLIC LIBRARY

3 6044 00089 5405

WANAQUE PUBLIC LIBRARY
616 Ringwood Ave.
Wanaque, NJ 07465
(973) 839-4434

SEP - - 2013